STRANGE AFFAIR

PETER ROBINSON

STRANGE AFFAIR

AN INSPECTOR BANKS MYSTERY

MACMILLAN

First published 2005 by Macmillan
an imprint of Pan Macmillan, a division of Macmillan Publishers Limited
Pan Macmillan, 20 New Wharf Road, London N1 9RR
Basingstoke and Oxford
Associated companies throughout the world
www.panmacmillan.com

ISBN 978-0-330-53639-4

1 3 5 7 9 8 6 4 2

A CIP catalogue record for this book is available from
the British Library.

Typeset by IntypeLibra London Ltd
Printed and bound in the UK by
CPI Mackays, Chatham ME5 8TD

For Sheila

'Though our brother is upon the rack, as long as we ourselves are at our ease, our senses will never inform us of what he suffers. They never did, and never can, carry us beyond our own person, and it is by the imagination only that we can form any conception of what are his sensations.'

Adam Smith, *Theory of Moral Sentiments*

'A friend loveth at all times, and a brother is born for adversity.'

Proverbs, 17:17.

1

Was she being followed? It was hard to tell at that time of night on the motorway. There was plenty of traffic, lorries for the most part, and people driving home from the pub just a little too carefully, red BMWs coasting up the fast lane, doing a hundred or more, businessmen in a hurry to get home from late meetings. She was beyond Newport Pagnell now, and the muggy night air blurred the red tail lights of the cars ahead and the oncoming headlights across the road. She began to feel nervous as she checked her rear-view mirror and saw that the car was still behind her.

She pulled over to the nearside lane and slowed down. The car, a dark Mondeo, overtook her. It was too dark to glimpse faces, but she thought there was just one person in the front and another in the back. It didn't have a taxi light on top, so she guessed it was probably a private hire car and stopped worrying. Some rich git being ferried to a nightclub in Leeds, most likely. She overtook the Mondeo a little further up the motorway and didn't give it a second glance. The late-night radio was playing Ol' Blue Eyes singing 'Summer Wind'. Her kind of music, no matter how old fashioned people told her it was. Talent and good music never went out of style as far as she was concerned.

When she got to Watford Gap services, she realized she felt tired and hungry, and she still had a long way to go, so she decided to stop for a short break. She didn't even notice the Mondeo pull in two cars behind her. A few seedy-looking people hung around the entrance; a couple of kids who didn't look old enough to drive stood smoking and playing the machines, giving her the eye as she walked past, staring at her breasts.

She went first to the ladies', then to the cafe, where she bought a ham and tomato sandwich and sat alone to eat, washing it down with a Diet Coke. At the table opposite, a man with a long face and dandruff on the collar of his dark suit jacket ogled her over the top of his glasses, pretending to read his newspaper and eat a sausage roll.

Was he just a common-or-garden variety perv, or was there something more sinister in his interest, she wondered. In the end, she decided he was just a perv. Sometimes it seemed as if the world was full of them, that she could hardly walk down the street or go for a drink on her own without some sad pillock who thought he was God's gift eyeing her up, like the kids hanging around the entrance, or coming over and laying a line of chat on her. Still, she told herself, what else could you expect at this time of night in a motorway service station? A couple of other men came in and went to the counter for coffee to go, but they didn't give her a second glance.

She finished half the sandwich, dumped the rest and got her travel mug filled with coffee. When she walked back to her car she made sure that there were people around – a family with two young kids up way past their bedtime, noisy and hyperactive – and that no one was following her.

The tank was only a quarter full, so she filled it up at the petrol station, using her credit card right there, at the pump. The perv from the cafe pulled up at the pump opposite and stared at her as he put the nozzle in the tank. She ignored him. She could see the night manager in his office, watching through the window, and that made her feel more secure.

Tank full, she turned down the slip road and eased in between two articulated lorries. It was hot in the car, so she opened both windows and enjoyed the play of breeze they created. It helped keep her awake, along with the hot black coffee. The clock on the dashboard read 12.35 a.m. Only about two or three hours to go, then she would be safe.

•

Penny Cartwright was singing Richard Thompson's 'Strange Affair' when Banks walked into the Dog and Gun, her low, husky voice milking the song's stark melancholy for all it was worth. Banks stood by the door, transfixed. *Penny Cartwright.* He hadn't seen her in over ten years, though he had thought of her often, even seen her name in *Mojo* and *Uncut* from time to time. The years had been kind. Her figure still looked good in blue jeans and a tight white T-shirt tucked in at the waist. The long raven's-wing hair he remembered looked just as glossy as ever in the stage lights, and the few threads of grey here and there made her look even more attractive. She seemed a little more gaunt than before, a little more sad around the eyes, perhaps, but it suited her, and Banks liked the contrast between her pale skin and dark hair.

When the song ended, Banks took advantage of the applause to walk over to the bar, order a pint and light a cigarette. He wasn't happy with himself for having started smoking again after six months or more on the wagon, but there it was. He tried to avoid smoking in the flat, and he would stop again as soon as he'd got himself back together. For the moment, it was a crutch, an old friend come back to visit during a time of need.

There wasn't a seat left in the entire lounge. Banks could feel the sweat prickling on his temples and at the back of his neck. He leaned against the bar and let Penny's voice transport him as she launched into 'Blackwater Side'. She had two accompanists, one on guitar and the other on stand-up bass, and they wove a dense tapestry of sound against which her lyric lines soared.

The next round of applause marked the end of the set, and Penny walked through the crowd, which parted like the Red Sea for her, smiling and nodding hello as she went, and stood next to Banks at the bar. She lit a cigarette, inhaled, made a circle of her mouth and blew out a smoke ring towards the optics.

'That was an excellent set,' Banks said.

'Thanks.' She didn't turn to face him. 'Gin and tonic, please, Kath,' she said to the barmaid. 'Make it a large one.'

Banks could tell by her clipped tone that she thought he was just another fan, maybe even a weirdo or a stalker, and she'd move away as soon as she got her drink. 'You don't remember me, do you?' he asked.

She sighed and turned to look at him, ready to deliver the final put-down. Then he saw recognition slowly dawn on her. She seemed flustered, embarrassed and unsure what to say. 'Oh . . . Yes. It's Detective Chief Inspector Burke, isn't it?' she managed finally. 'Or have you been promoted?'

'Afraid not,' he said. 'And it's Banks, but Alan will do. It's been a long time.'

'Yes.' Penny got her gin and tonic and raised it to Banks, who clinked it gently with his pint glass.

'Slainte.'

'Slainte,' said Banks. 'I didn't know you were back in Helm-thorpe.'

'Well, nobody put on a major advertising campaign.'

Banks looked around the dim lounge. 'I don't know. You seem to have a devoted following.'

'Word of mouth, mostly. Anyway, yes, I'm back in the old cottage. What brought you here?'

'I heard the music as I was passing,' Banks said. 'Recognized your voice. What have you been up to lately?'

A hint of mischief came into her eyes. 'Now that would be a very long story indeed, and I'm not sure it would be any of your business.'

'Maybe you could tell me over dinner some evening?'

Penny faced him and frowned, her brows knit together, searching him with those sharp blue eyes, and before she spoke, she gave a little shake of her head. 'I can't possibly do that,' she whispered.

'Why not? It's only a dinner invitation.'

She was backing away from him as she spoke. 'I just can't, that's all. How can you even ask me?'

'Look, if you're worried about being seen with a married man, that ended a couple of years back. I'm divorced now.'

Penny looked at him as if he'd missed the point by a hundred miles, shook her head and melted back into the crowd. Banks felt perplexed. He couldn't interpret the signals, decode the look of absolute horror he'd seen on her face at the idea of dinner with him. He wasn't that repulsive. A simple dinner invitation. What the hell was wrong with her?

Banks gulped down the rest of his pint and headed for the door as Penny took the stage again, and he caught her eyes briefly across the crowded room. Her expression was puzzled and confused. She had clearly been unsettled by his request. Well, he thought, as he turned his back and left, face burning, at least she didn't still look so horrified.

The night was dark, the sky moonless but filled with stars, and Helmthorpe High Street was deserted, street lights smudgy in the haze. Banks heard Penny start up again back inside the Dog and Gun. Another Richard Thompson song: 'Never Again'. The haunting melody and desolate lyrics drifted after him across the street, fading slowly as he walked up the cobbled snicket past the old bookshop, through the graveyard and on to the footpath that would take him home, or to what passed for home these days.

The air smelled of manure and warm hay. To his right was a drystone wall beside the graveyard, and to his left a slope, terraced with lynchets, led down step by step to Gratly Beck, which he could hear roaring below him. The narrow path was unlit, but Banks knew every inch by heart. The worst that could happen was that he might step into a pile of sheep shit. Close by he could hear the high-pitched whining of winged insects.

As he walked, he continued to think about Penny Cartwright's strange reaction to his dinner invitation. She always had been an odd one, he remembered, always a bit sharp with her tongue and too ready with the sarcasm. But this had been different, not sarcasm, not sharp, but shock, repulsion. Was it because of their age difference? He was in his early fifties, after all, and Penny was at least ten years younger. But even that didn't explain the intensity of her reaction. She could have just smiled and said she was washing her hair. Banks liked to think he would have got the message.

The path ended at a double-barrelled stile about halfway up Gratly Hill. Banks slipped through sideways and walked past the new houses to the cluster of old cottages over the bridge. Since his own house was still at the mercy of the builders, he had been renting a flat in one of the holiday properties on the lane to the left.

The locals had been good to him, as it turned out, and he'd got a fairly spacious one-bedroom flat, upper floor, with private entrance, for a very decent rent. The irony was, he realized, that it used to be the Steadman house, long ago converted into holiday flats, and it was during the Steadman case that he had first met Penny Cartwright.

Banks's living-room window had a magnificent view over the dale, north past Helmthorpe, folded in the valley bottom, up to the rich green fields, dotted with sheep, and the sere, pale grass of the higher pastures, then the bare limestone outcrop of Crow Scar and the wild moors beyond. But his bedroom window looked out to the west over a small disused Sandemanian graveyard and its tiny chapel. Some of the tombstones, so old that you could scarcely read the names any more, leaned against the wall of the house.

The Sandemanian sect, Banks had read somewhere, had been founded in the eighteenth century, separating itself from the Scottish Presbyterian Church. Its members took holy communion, embraced communal property ownership, practised vegetarianism and engaged in 'love feasts', which Banks thought made them sound rather like eighteenth-century hippies.

Banks was a little pissed, he realized as he fiddled with his key in the downstairs lock. The Dog and Gun hadn't been his first port of call that evening. He'd eaten dinner alone in the Hare and Hounds, then had a couple of pints in the Bridge. Still, what the hell, he was on holiday for another week, and he wasn't driving. Maybe he'd even have a glass of wine or two. He was still off the whisky, especially Laphroaig. Its distinctive taste was the only thing he could remember about the night his life nearly ended, and even at a distance the smell made him feel sick.

Could the drinking have been what put Penny off, he wondered? Had she thought he was drunk when he asked her to dinner? But he doubted it. He didn't slur his words or wobble when he walked. There was nothing in his manner that suggested he'd had too much. No, it had to be something else.

He finally opened the door, walked up the stairs and unlocked the inside door, then switched on the hall light. The place felt hot and stuffy, so he went into the living room and opened the window. It didn't help much. After he had poured himself a healthy glass of Australian Shiraz, he walked over to the telephone. A red light was flashing, indicating messages on the answerphone.

As it turned out, there was only one message, and a surprising one at that: his brother Roy. Banks wasn't even aware that Roy knew his telephone number, and he was also certain that the card and flowers he had received from Roy in hospital had come, in fact, from his mother.

'Alan . . . shit . . . you're not there and I don't have your mobile number. If you've got one, that is. You never were much of a one for technology, I remember. Anyway, look, this is important. Believe it or not, you're the only one who can help me now. There's something . . . I can't really talk about this to your answerphone. It could be a matter of life and death.' He laughed harshly. 'Maybe even mine. Anyway, I'll try again later, but can you ring me back as soon as possible? I really need to talk to you. Urgently. Please.' Banks heard a buzzing noise in the background. 'Someone's at the door. I'll have to go now. Please call. I'll give you my mobile number, too.' Roy left his phone numbers, and that was that.

Puzzled, Banks listened to the message again. He was going to listen a third time, but he realized there was no point. He hated it when people in movies kept playing the same message over and over again and always seemed to get the tape in exactly the right spot every time. Instead, he replaced the receiver and took a sip of wine. He'd heard all he needed. Roy sounded worried, and more than a little scared. The call was timed by his answerphone at 9.29 p.m., about an hour and a half ago, when Banks had been drinking in the Bridge.

Roy's phone rang several times before an answering machine picked up: Roy's voice in a curt, no-nonsense invitation to leave a message. Banks did so, said he'd try again later, and hung up. He tried the mobile number but got no response there, either. There was nothing else he could do right now. Maybe Roy would ring back later, as he had said he would.

Often, Banks would spend an hour or so perched on the window seat in his bedroom looking down on the graveyard, especially on moonlit nights. He didn't know what he was looking for – a ghost, perhaps – but the utter stillness of the tombstones and the wind soughing through the long grass seemed to give him some sort of feeling of tranquillity. Not tonight: no moon, no breeze.

The baby downstairs started crying, the way she did every night around this time. Banks turned on the TV. There wasn't much to choose from: films, a chat show or news. He picked *The Spy Who Came in from the Cold*, which had started half an hour ago. That didn't matter; he'd seen it many times before, and he knew the plot by heart. But he couldn't concentrate. As he watched Richard Burton's edgy, intense performance and tried to pick up the threads, he found his mind wandering back to Roy's phone call, felt himself waiting for the phone to ring, *willing* it.

There was nothing he could do about it right now, but the urgency and fear in Roy's voice disturbed him. He would try again in the morning, in case Roy had simply gone out for the night, but if he couldn't get in touch then, he would head for London himself and find out just what the hell was going on.

•

Why did people have to be so bloody inconsiderate as to find bodies so early on a Saturday morning? wondered Detective Inspector Annie Cabbot. Especially when Banks was on holiday and she was on call. It wasn't only that she was losing her week-end – and detective inspectors don't get paid overtime – but that those first crucial hours of an investigation were made all the more difficult by people being, for the large part, unavailable, making information harder to ferret out. And this was a particularly beautiful Saturday morning; offices would be empty, services reduced as everyone loaded a picnic basket in the car along with the kids and headed for the nearest stretch of grass or sand.

She pulled to a halt behind the blue Peugeot 106 on a quiet stretch of country road halfway between Eastvale and the A1. It had been just after half-past seven when the station desk sergeant rang and woke her from an uneasy dream she forgot, and after a quick shower and a cup of instant coffee, she was on the road.

The morning was still and hazy, with the drone of insects in the air. It was going to be just the kind of day for a picnic by the river, dragonflies and the scent of wild garlic, perhaps a bottle of Chablis cooling in the water, maybe her sketchpad and a few sticks of charcoal. After a few nibbles of Wensleydale cheese – the type with cranberries was her favourite – and a couple of glasses of wine, it would be time for a nap on the riverbank, maybe a pleasant dream. Enough of that, she thought, walking over to the car; life had other plans for her today.

Annie could see that the car's left wing had made contact with the drystone wall, so much so that the wing had buckled and scratched and the impact had brought down a section of the wall. There were no traces of skid marks, no tyre tracks at all on the dry tarmac surface.

There was already activity around the Peugeot. The road had been closed to all non-police traffic, and the immediate area around the car had been taped off. That would cause a few problems when the tourists started to dribble in, Annie thought, but it couldn't be helped; the integrity of the scene had to be preserved.

Peter Darby had finished photographing the body and the car and had busied himself videotaping the area. Detective Sergeant Jim Hatchley and DC Winsome Jackman, who both lived closer to the scene, were already there when Annie arrived, Hatchley standing by the roadside and Winsome sitting half in and half out of the unmarked police car.

'What have we got?' Annie asked Hatchley, who, as usual, looked as if he'd been dragged through a hedge backwards. The little piece of tissue paper he had stuck to a shaving cut on his chin didn't help much.

'A young woman dead behind the wheel of her car,' said Hatchley.

'I can see that for myself,' snapped Annie, glancing towards the open driver's side window.

'Bit prickly this morning, aren't we, ma'am,' said Hatchley. 'What's up? Get out of the wrong side of bed?'

Annie ignored him. She was used to Hatchley's taunts, which had only grown more frequent since she had been made inspector and he remained a sergeant. 'Cause of death?' she asked.

'Don't know yet. Nothing apparent. No obvious marks, no bruising. And officially she's not even dead yet. Not until the doc says she is.'

Annie refrained from pointing out that she knew that perfectly well. 'But you've examined her?' she pressed on.

'I had a quick look, that's all. Didn't touch anything. Winsome checked for a pulse and found none. We're still waiting for Doc Burns.'

'So she could have died of a heart attack, for all we know?'

'I suppose so,' said Hatchley. 'But like I said, she's very young. It smells a bit fishy to me.'

'Any idea who she is?'

'There's no handbag, no driving licence, nowt. At least not as you can see looking through the windows.'

'I checked the number plate on the computer, Guv,' said Winsome, walking over from her car. 'The car's registered to a

Jennifer Clewes. Lives in London. Kennington. Twenty-seven years old.'

'We don't know for certain it's her yet,' Annie said, 'so find out all you can.'

'Right, Guv.' Winsome paused.

'Yes?'

'Wasn't there another one?'

'Another what?' asked Annie.

'Another murder. Like this one. Young woman found dead near a motorway. The M1 not the A1, but even so . . .'

'Yes,' said Annie. 'I remember reading about it in the papers. I can't remember the details. Look into, will you?'

'Yes, Guv.' Winsome walked back to her car.

Annie looked at Hatchley again. 'Has Detective Superintendent Gristhorpe been informed?'

'Yes, ma'am. Says to keep him up to date.'

That made sense, Annie thought. No point having the super come running down here if the woman had pulled over into the lay-by and died of a heart attack, brain aneurysm, or any of the other random failures of the flesh that cause sudden death in otherwise healthy young people. 'Who was first officer on the scene?'

'PC Farrier over there.'

Hatchley pointed to a uniformed police constable leaning against a patrol car. Pete Farrier. Annie knew him; he worked out of Western Area Headquarters, the same as she did. Had done for years, according to all accounts, and was a reliable, sensible bobby. Annie walked over to him. 'What happened, Pete?' she asked. 'Who called it in?'

'Couple over there, ma'am.' Farrier pointed to a man and a woman some yards away from the scene. They were sitting on the grass by the side of the road, and the man had his arm around the woman, whose head was buried in his chest.

Annie thanked Farrier and walked back to her car, took her latex gloves from the murder kit in the boot and slipped them on.

Then she walked over to the Peugeot. She needed to have a closer look at the scene, gather some first impressions before Dr Burns arrived and started his examination. Already a number of flies had settled on the woman's pale face. Annie shooed them away. They buzzed around her head, waiting for the chance to get back.

The woman sat in the driver's seat, slumped slightly forward and listing to the left; her right hand grasped the steering wheel, and her left held the gearstick. Her seat belt was fastened firmly in place, holding her up, and both front windows were open. The key was still in the ignition, Annie noticed, and a travel mug sat in its holder.

The victim wasn't a big woman, but her breasts were quite large, and the seat belt ran between them, separating them and causing them to appear even more prominent. She looked to be mid- to late twenties, which matched Jennifer Clewes's age, and she was very attractive. Her skin was pale, and probably had been even before her death, her long hair was dark red – dyed, Annie guessed – and she was wearing a pale blue cotton blouse and black denim jeans. There were no apparent marks on her body, as Hatchley had noted, and no sign of blood. Her eyes were open, a dull vacant green. Annie had seen that look before, felt that stillness.

Hatchley was right, though; there was something very fishy about the whole set-up, fishy enough at least to warrant a thorough preliminary investigation before deciding upon the scale of the inquiry. As Annie examined the scene, she made mental notes of what she observed and thought for later use.

When Annie had finished, she walked over to the couple who had found the body. They were very young, she noticed as she got closer. The man was ashen and the woman he was holding still had her face buried in his shoulder, though she didn't appear to be heaving with sobs. The man looked up and Annie squatted beside them.

'I'm Detective Inspector Cabbot from Western Area Head-quarters,' she said. 'I understand you found the car?'

The woman turned her face away from the protection of the man's shoulder and looked at Annie. She had been crying, that was clear enough, but now she just seemed shocked and hurt.

'Can you tell me what happened?' Annie asked the man.

'We already told the policeman in the uniform. He was the first to get here.'

'I know,' said Annie, 'and I'm sorry to make you go through it again, but it'll help if you tell me.'

'There's nothing to tell, really, is there, love?' he said to the woman, who shook her head.

'First off, why don't you tell me your names?'

'This is Sam, Samantha,' he said, 'and I'm Adrian, Adrian Sinclair.'

'OK, Adrian. Where do you live?'

'Sunderland.' Annie thought she'd noticed a hint of Geordie burr in his voice, though it was faint. 'We're on holiday.' Adrian paused and stroked Samantha's hair. 'On our honeymoon, in fact.'

Well, they'd certainly remember it for as long as they lived, Annie thought, and not for the right reasons. 'Where are you staying?'

Adrian pointed up the hillside. 'We're renting a cottage. Greystone. Just up there.'

Annie knew it. She made a note. 'And what were you doing down here by the road?'

'Just walking,' Adrian said. 'It was such a beautiful morning, and the birds woke us so early.'

They were dressed for walking, Annie noticed. Not professional ramblers with the plastic-covered Ordnance Survey maps around their necks, ashplants, boots and expensive Gore-Tex gear, but simple, sturdy shoes, light clothing and a rucksack.

'What time did you arrive here?'

'It must have been a bit before seven,' Adrian said.

'What did you find?'

'The car stopped in the lay-by, just like it is now.'

'Did you touch it?'

'No, I don't think so.'

Annie looked at Samantha. 'Neither of you?'

'No,' Samantha said. 'But you might have touched the roof, Adrian, when you bent to look inside.'

'It's possible,' Adrian said. 'I don't remember. At first I thought maybe she was looking at a road map, or asleep, even. I went over to see if she needed any help. Then I saw her, with her eyes open like that and . . .We might never have gone over unless . . .'

'Unless what?'

'Well, it was me, really,' Sam said. 'I mean, like he said, Adrian just thought it was someone pulled over to rest or look at a road-map.'

'But you didn't. Why not?'

'I don't know, really,' Sam said. 'It's just that it was so early in the morning, and she was a woman, alone. I thought we should make sure she was all right, that's all. She might have been attacked or upset or something. Maybe it was none of our business, but you can't just leave, can you, walk on by?' A little colour came to her cheeks as she spoke. 'Anyway, when we got closer we could see she wasn't moving, just staring down like that, and it looked like she'd hit the wall. I said we should go over and see what was wrong with her.'

'Did you know she was dead when you looked through the window?'

'Well,' said Adrian, 'I've never seen a dead person before, but you can sort of tell, can't you?'

Yes, Annie thought, having seen far too many, you can tell. *Nobody home.*

Samantha gave a little shudder and seemed to melt deeper into Adrian's embrace. 'And the flies,' she said.

'What flies?' Annie asked.

'On her face and her arms. Flies. She wasn't moving. She

wasn't even trying to swat them away. I thought how much they must be tickling her.'

Annie swallowed. 'Were the windows open?'

'Yes,' said Samantha. 'Just like they are now. We really didn't disturb anything. I mean, we've seen Morse and Frost on television.'

'I'm sure you have. I just have to make certain. I don't suppose you saw anyone, heard any other cars or anything?'

'No.'

'What did you do when you found her?'

'Rang the police.' Adrian pulled a mobile from his pocket. He wouldn't have had much luck with it around these parts a few months ago, Annie reflected, but coverage had been improved a lot recently.

'And there's nothing else you can tell me?'

'No. Look, we're just so . . . devastated. Can we go home now? I think Sam needs a lie down, and I could do with a strong cup of tea.'

'How long are you staying at Greystone?' Annie asked.

'We've got another week.'

'Stick around,' said Annie. 'We might want to talk to you again.'

Annie went back to rejoin Hatchley and saw Dr Burns's grey Audi arrive. She greeted him and they walked over to the Peugeot. This would be a difficult examination for Dr Burns, Annie knew, because the body was sitting upright in an enclosed space, and he could hardly move it before Dr Glendenning, the Home Office pathologist, arrived. She also knew that Dr Burns was aware the Scenes-of-Crime Officers would be eager to give the car a thorough going-over, so he was being extra careful not to touch any surfaces and damage any possible prints, even though he was wearing disposable gloves. It was the police surgeon's job only to determine and pronounce that the girl was dead – the rest was up to the pathologist – but Annie knew that Dr Burns would like to give her some idea of time and cause, if at all possible.

After feeling for a pulse and examining the woman's eyes, then listening for a heartbeat through his stethoscope, Dr Burns confirmed that she was, indeed, dead.

'The corneas haven't clouded yet,' he said, 'which means she's probably been dead less than eight hours. I'm sure the flies have laid their eggs already, which you'd expect to happen quite soon in summer with the windows open, but there's no sign of advanced insect activity, another indication we're dealing with a relatively recent death.'

Dr Burns slipped off a glove and slid his hand inside the woman's blouse, under her arm. 'Best I can do as far as temperature is concerned,' he said, noticing Annie's curious glance. 'It does help give an approximation. She's still warm, which confirms that death occurred only a few hours ago.'

'It was a warm night,' said Annie. 'How long?'

'Can't say exactly, but I'd guess about five or six hours at the most.' He felt the woman's jaw and neck. 'Rigor's present where you'd expect it to be, and as the heat probably speeded that up, we're still working within much the same parameters.'

Annie looked at her watch. 'Between two and four in the morning, then?'

'I wouldn't swear to it, of course,' said Dr Burns, with a smile, 'but that sounds about right. And don't tell Dr Glendenning I've been making wild guesses. You know what he's like about that sort of thing.'

'Any thoughts on cause of death?'

'That's a bit more difficult,' said Dr Burns, turning to the body again. 'There are no visible signs of strangulation, either ligature or manual, and no petechial haemorrhaging, which you'd expect with strangulation. Also no signs of a stab wound, no blood that I can see, at any rate. It'll have to wait until Dr Glendenning gets her on the table.'

'Could it have been a heart attack, or something like that?'

'It could have been. Heart attacks aren't so common in healthy young women, but if she had some sort of genetic disorder or pre-existing condition . . . Let's say it's within the realm of the possible, but unlikely.'

Dr Burns turned back to the body and probed gently here and there. He tried to loosen the woman's hand from the steering wheel but couldn't. 'That's interesting,' he said. 'Rigor hasn't progressed as far as the hands yet, so it looks as if we're dealing with cadaveric spasm.'

'What does it mean in this case?'

Dr Burns stood up and faced Annie. 'It means she was holding the wheel when she died. And the gearstick.'

Annie thought about the implications of that. Either the woman had just managed to pull into the lay-by when she died, or she was trying to drive away from something – or someone.

Annie stuck her head through the car window, uncomfortably aware of the closeness of the corpse, and looked down. One foot on the clutch, the other on the accelerator, gearstick in reverse and ignition turned on. She reached out and touched the travel mug. It felt cool.

As she moved back, Annie smelled just a hint of something vaguely sweet and metallic. She told Dr Burns. He frowned and leaned forward, apologizing that he didn't have a sense of smell. Gently, he touched the woman's hair and pulled it back to expose her ear. Then he gasped.

'Good Lord,' he said. 'Look at this.'

Annie bent over and looked. Just above the woman's right ear was a tiny star-shaped hole, around which the skin was burned and blackened with a soot-like residue. There wasn't much blood, and what there was had been hidden by her long red hair. Annie was no expert, but it didn't take an expert to realize that this was a gunshot wound fired from fairly close quarters. And if there was no gun in sight, and the woman had one hand on the steering wheel and the other on the gearstick, then it could hardly have been a self-inflicted gunshot wound.

Dr Burns leaned through the window in front of the woman, feeling the other side of her skull for signs of blood and an exit wound. 'Nothing,' he said. 'No wonder we couldn't see anything. The bullet must be still inside her skull.' He stepped away from the car, as if washing his hands of the whole affair. 'OK,' he said, 'that's all I can do for now. The rest is up to Dr Glendenning.'

Annie looked at him and sighed, then she called Hatchley over. 'Inform Superintendent Gristhorpe that we've got what looks very much like a murder on our hands. And we'd better get Dr Glendenning and the SOCOs down here as soon as possible.'

Hatchley's face dropped. Annie knew why, and she sympathized. It was the weekend, but all leave would be cancelled. Sergeant Hatchley probably had plans to go and watch the local cricket team and have a booze up with the lads afterwards. But not now. She wouldn't even be surprised if Banks was called back, depending on the scale of the investigation.

She looked down the road and her heart sank as she saw the first media vans arriving. How quickly bad news travels, she thought.

2

Unaware of the excitement just a few miles down the road, Banks was up and around before eight o'clock that morning, filter coffee and newspaper on the table in front of him, mild hangover held at bay by paracetamol. He hadn't slept at all well, mostly because he had been waiting for the phone to ring. And he hadn't been able to get that song Penny Cartwright had been singing out of his mind: 'Strange Affair'. The melody haunted him and the lyrics, with their images of death and fear, troubled him.

His window framed a view of blue sky above the rising northern daleside, and the grey flagstone roofs of Helmthorpe about half a mile away at the valley bottom, dominated by its church tower with the odd turret on one corner. It was similar to his view from the wall by his old cottage, just a slightly different angle. But it failed to move him. He could see that it was beautiful, but he couldn't *feel* it. There seemed to be something missing, some connection, or perhaps there was a sort of invisible shield or thick fog between him and the rest of the world, and it dimmed the power of all he had held dear to move him in any way. Music, landscape, words on a page all seemed inert and impotent, distant and unimportant.

Since the fire had consumed his home and possessions four months ago, Banks had become withdrawn and taciturn; he knew it, but there was nothing he could do about it. He was suffering from depression, but knowing that was one thing, changing it quite another.

It had started the day he left hospital and went to look at the ruins of his cottage. He hadn't been prepared for the scale of the damage: roof gone, windows burned out, inside a shambles of charred debris, nothing salvageable, hardly anything even recognizable. And it didn't help that the man who had done this had got away.

After a few days convalescing at Gristhorpe's Lyndgarth farmhouse, he had found the flat and moved in. Some mornings he didn't want to get out of bed. Most nights he spent watching television, any old rubbish, and drinking. He wasn't drinking too much, but he was drinking steadily, mostly wine, and smoking again.

His withdrawal had driven the wedge even deeper between him and Annie Cabbot, who desperately seemed to need something from him. He thought he knew what it was, but he couldn't give it to her. Not yet. It had also cooled his relationship with Michelle Hart, a detective inspector who had recently transferred to Sex Crimes and Child Protection in Bristol, much too far away to maintain a reasonable long-distance relationship. Michelle had her own problems, too, Banks realized. Whatever it was that haunted her was always there, always in the way, even when they were laughing or making love. They'd been good for one another for a while, no doubt about it, but now they were down to the 'just good friends' stage that usually comes before the end.

It seemed as if the fire and subsequent spell in hospital had put his life on pause, and he couldn't find the play button. Even work, when he'd got back to it, had been boring, consisting mostly of paperwork and interminable meetings that never settled anything. Only an occasional pint with Gristhorpe or Jim Hatchley, a chat about football or the previous evening's television, had relieved the tedium. His daughter Tracy had visited as often as she could, but she had been studying hard for her finals. Brian had dropped by a few times, too, and now he was in a recording studio in Dublin with his band working on a new CD. Their first as the Blue Lamps had done OK, but the second was slated for much bigger and better things.

More than once Banks had thought of counselling, only to

reject the idea. He had even considered that Dr Jenny Fuller, a consultant psychologist he had worked with on a number of cases, might be able to help, but she was on one of her extended teaching gigs – Australia this time – and when he thought more about it, the idea of Jenny delving into the murky depths of his subconscious didn't hold a lot of appeal. Maybe whatever was there was best left there.

When it came down to it, he didn't need any interfering shrink poking around in his mind and telling him what was wrong. He knew what was wrong, knew he spent too much time sitting around the flat and brooding. He also knew that the healing process – the mental and emotional process, not merely the physical – would take time, and that it was something he had to do alone, make his way step by weary step back to the land of the living. No doubt about it, the fire had burned much deeper than his skin.

It wasn't so much the pain he'd endured – that hadn't lasted long, and he couldn't even remember most of it – but the loss of all his worldly goods that hit him the hardest. He felt like a man adrift, unanchored, a helium balloon let float off into the sky by a careless child. What was worse was that he thought he ought to be feeling a great sense of release, of freedom from materialism, the sort of thing gurus and sages spoke about, but he just felt jittery and insecure. He hadn't learned the virtue of simplicity from his loss, had learned only that he missed his material possessions more than he ever dreamed he would, though he hadn't yet been able to muster up the energy and interest to start replacing those items that *could* be replaced: his CD collection, his books and DVDs. He felt too weary to start again. He had bought clothes, of course – comfortable, functional clothes – but that was all.

Still, he reflected, munching on a slice of toast and marmalade as he scanned the reviews section of the newspaper, things were definitely improving a little each day. It was becoming easier to get out of bed, and he had got into the habit of occasionally taking a walk up the daleside opposite his flat on fine mornings, finding the freshness and exercise invigorating. He had also enjoyed what he heard of Penny Cartwright's singing the previous night and was beginning to miss his CD collection. A month or so ago, he wouldn't even have bothered reading the reviews in the paper.

And now brother Roy, who hadn't even rung or visited him in hospital, had left a mysterious urgent message and had not called back. For the third time since he got up that morning, Banks tried Roy's numbers. He got the answering machine again, the recorded voice telling him to leave a message, and the mobile was switched off.

Unable to concentrate on the newspaper any longer, Banks checked his watch and decided to ring his parents. They should be up by now. There was just a chance that Roy was there, or that they knew what was going on. He certainly seemed to keep in touch with them more than with Banks.

His mother answered and sounded nervous to be getting a call so early in the day. In her world, Banks knew, early morning phone calls never meant good news. 'Alan? What is it? Is there something wrong?'

'No, Mum,' Banks said, trying to put her at ease. 'Everything's fine.'

'You're all right, are you? Still recovering?'

'Still recovering,' said Banks. 'Look, Mum, I was wondering if our Roy was there.'

'Roy? Why would he be here? The last time we saw Roy was our anniversary last October. You must remember. You were here, too.'

'I remember,' said Banks. 'It's just that I've been trying to ring him . . .'

His mother's voice brightened. 'So you two are making it up at last. That's good to hear.'

'Yes,' said Banks, not wishing to disabuse his mother of that little scrap of comfort. 'It's just that I keep getting his answering machine.'

'Well, he's probably at work. You know how hard-working our Roy is. Always got something or other on the go.'

'Yes,' Banks agreed. Usually something about two shades away from being criminal. White-collar, though, which didn't seem to count as crime to some people. When Banks thought about it, he realized he really hadn't a clue what Roy actually did to make his money. Only that he made a lot of it. 'So you haven't heard from him recently?'

'I didn't say that. As a matter of fact he rang about two weeks ago, just to see how your dad and I are doing, like.'

The implied rebuke wasn't lost on Banks; he hadn't rung his parents for a month. 'Did he have anything else to say?'

'Not much. Except he's keeping busy. He might be away, you know. Have you thought about that? He did say something about an important business trip coming up. New York again, I think. He's always going there. I can't remember when he said he was going, though.'

'OK, Mum,' said Banks. 'That's probably where he is. Thanks very much. I'll wait a few days and call him when he gets back home.'

'You make sure you do, Alan. He's a good lad, is Roy. I don't know why you two haven't been getting on better all these years.'

'We get along fine, Mum. We just move in different circles, that's all. How's Dad?'

'Same as ever.' Banks heard the rustle of a newspaper – the *Daily Mail* his father read just so he could complain about the Conservatives – and a muffled voice in the background. 'He says to say hello.'

'Right,' said Banks. 'Say hello back . . . Well, take care of yourselves. I'll call again soon.'

'Mind you do,' said Banks's mother.

Banks rang off then tried both of Roy's numbers again, but still no Roy. There was no way he was going to wait a few days, or even hours. From what he knew of Roy, under normal circumstances if he had buggered off somewhere and not bothered to ring back, Banks would have assumed Roy was sunning himself in California or the Caribbean with a shapely young woman by his side. That would be typical of him and his me-first attitude. As far as Roy was concerned, there was nothing in life you couldn't get through with a smile and a wad of cash. But this was different. This time Banks had heard the fear in his brother's voice.

He deleted the messages from his answerphone, threw a few clothes along with his toothbrush and razor into an overnight bag, checked that the lights were out, unplugged all the electrical items and locked the flat behind him. He knew he wouldn't get any rest until he got to the bottom of Roy's odd silence, so he might as well drive down to London and find out what was happening himself.

•

Detective Superintendent Gristhorpe called the meeting in the boardroom of Western Area Headquarters after lunch, and DI Annie Cabbot, DS Hatchley and crime-scene coordinator DS Stefan Nowak, along with DCs Winsome Jackman, Kev Templeton and Gavin Rickerd, sat in the high, stiff-backed chairs under the gaze of ancient wool barons with roast-beef complexions and tight collars. Their notes and files were set in neat piles on the dark polished table beside styrofoam cups of tea or coffee. Pinned to cork boards on the wall by the door were Peter Darby's Polaroids of the scene. It was already hot and stuffy in the room and the small fan Gristhorpe had turned on didn't do much good.

Soon, when the investigation got seriously underway, more manpower would be allocated, but these seven would remain the core team: Gristhorpe as senior investigative officer and Annie, who would do most of the field work, as his deputy and administrative officer. Rickerd would be office manager, responsible for setting up and staffing the murder room; Hatchley would act as receiver, there to weigh the value of every piece of information and pass it on for computer entry. Winsome and Hatchley would be the foot soldiers, tracking down information and conducting interviews. Others would be appointed later – statement-readers, action allocators, researchers, and the rest – but for now it was of prime importance to get the system into place and into action. It was no longer merely a suspicious death. Jennifer Clewes – if that was really the name of the victim – had been murdered.

Gristhorpe cleared his throat, shuffled his papers and began by asking Annie for a summary of the facts, which she gave as succinctly as possible. Then he turned to DS Stefan Nowak.

'Any forensics yet?'

'It's still early days,' said Stefan, 'so I'm afraid all I can give you at the moment is what we *don't* have.'

'Go on.'

'Well, the road surface was dry and there are no discernible tyre tracks from any other vehicle. Also, we haven't turned up any physical evidence – discarded cigarette ends, spent matches, that sort of thing. There are plenty of prints on the outside of the car, so that will take Vic Manson a while to sort out, but they could be anyone's.'

'What about *inside* the car?' Gristhorpe asked.

'It's in the police garage right now, sir. We should know something later today. There is one thing.'

'Yes?'

'It looks as if she was definitely forced off the road. The left wing hit the drystone wall.'

'But there was no damage to the right wing, at least not that I could see,' Annie said.

'That's right,' Stefan agreed. 'The car that forced her over didn't make physical contact. Pity. We might have got some nice paint samples.'

'Keep looking,' said Gristhorpe.

'Anyway,' Stefan went on, 'whoever it was must have got in front of her and veered to the left rather than come at her directly from the side.'

'Well,' said Gristhorpe, 'what do you do if you're a woman alone and a car comes up fast behind you on a deserted country road at night?'

'I'd say either you take off like a bat out of hell or you slow down and let him get by and put as much distance as possible between the two of you,' said Annie.

'Exactly. Only in this case he forced her over to the side of the road.'

'The gearstick,' Annie said.

'What?' Gristhorpe asked.

'The gearstick. She was trying to get away. She was trying to reverse.'

'That's the way it looks,' said Stefan.

'But she wasn't fast enough,' said Annie.

'No. And she stalled.'

'Do you think,' Annie went on, 'that there might have been two of them?'

'Why?' asked Gristhorpe.

Stefan looked at Annie and answered. It was uncanny, she thought, how often their thoughts followed the same pathways. 'I think DI Cabbot means,' he said, 'that if the driver had to put on the brake, unfasten his seat belt and pull out his gun before getting out, those few seconds might have made all the difference.'

'Yes,' said Annie. 'Though why we should assume a murderer would be so law-abiding as to wear a seat belt is stretching it a bit. And he may have already had his gun out and not bothered to turn off the ignition. But if someone was there to leap out, say someone in the back, with his gun ready and no seat belt to unfasten, then she wouldn't have had time to recover from the shock and get away in time. Remember, she'd probably be panicking.'

'Hmm,' said Gristhorpe. 'Interesting. And possible. Let's keep an open mind for the time being. Anything else?'

'Not really,' said Stefan. 'The victim's been taken to the mortuary and Dr Glendenning said he should be able to get around to the post-mortem sometime this afternoon. In the meantime, it still looks very much as if death was due to a single gunshot wound above the right ear.'

'Any ideas about the sort of weapon used?'

'We've found no trace of a cartridge, so either our killer was smart and picked up after himself, or he used a revolver. At a rough estimate, I'd say it's probably a .22 calibre. Anything bigger would most likely have left an exit wound.' Stefan paused. 'We might not have had a lot of practice with gunshot wounds around these parts,' he said, 'but our ballistics specialist Kim Grainger knows her stuff. That's about it, sir. Sorry we can't be a bit more helpful right now.'

'Early days, yet,' said Gristhorpe. 'Keep at it, Stefan.' He turned to the rest of the group. 'Has anyone verified the woman's identity yet?' he asked.

'Not yet,' said Annie. 'I got in touch with Lambeth North. It turns out their DI at Kennington nick is an old friend of mine, Dave Brooke, and he sent a couple of DCs to her address. Nobody home. They're keeping a watching brief.'

'And there are no reports of her car being stolen?'

'No, sir.'

'So it's still more than within the realm of possibility that the registered keeper of the vehicle is the person found dead in it?'

'Yes. Unless she lent her car to a friend or hasn't noticed it's gone missing yet.'

'Do we even know for certain that she was alone in the car?' Gristhorpe asked.

'No.' Annie looked at Stefan. 'I'm assuming that's something they'll be able to help us determine down at the garage.'

Stefan nodded. 'Perhaps.'

'Anyone run her name through our system?'

'I did, sir,' said Winsome. 'Name, prints, description. Nothing. If she ever committed a criminal act, we didn't catch her.'

'It wouldn't be the first time,' Gristhorpe said. 'All right, first priority, find out who she is and what she was doing on that road. In the meantime, I assume we're already making door-to-door enquiries in the general area of the incident?'

'Yes, sir,' said Annie. 'Problem is, there's not much *in* the general area. As you know, it happened on a deserted stretch of road between the A1 and Eastvale in the early hours of the morning. We've got people going from house to house, but there's nothing except a few holiday cottages and the occasional farmhouse within a mile each way of the car. Nothing's turned up so far.'

'Nobody heard the shot?'

'Not so far.'

'An ideal place for a murder, then,' Gristhorpe commented. He scratched his chin. Annie could see by the stubble that he hadn't shaved that morning. Hadn't combed his unruly hair by the looks of it, either. Still, personal grooming sometimes took backstage when it came to the urgency of a murder investigation. At least as far as the men were concerned. Kev Templeton was far too vain, of course, to look anything but his gelled, athletic and trendy best, not to mention cool as Antarctica, but Jim Hatchley had definitely taken a leaf out of Gristhorpe's book. Gavin looked like a trainspotter, right down to the National Health specs held together over his nose by a plaster. Winsome was immaculate in pinstripe navy trousers and matching waistcoat over a white scallop-neck blouse, and Annie felt rather conservative in her plain pastel frock and linen jacket. She also felt unpleasantly sweaty and hoped it didn't show.

Finding herself doodling a cartoon of Kev Templeton in full seventies gear, complete with the Afro and tight gold lamé shirt, Annie dragged herself away from her sartorial musings, admonishing herself once again for having difficulty concentrating these days, and got back to the matter in hand: Jennifer Clewes. Gristhorpe was asking her a question, and Annie realized she had missed it.

'Sorry, sir?'

Gristhorpe frowned at her. 'I said do we have any idea where the victim was driving from?'

'No, sir,' said Annie.

'Then perhaps we should set about canvassing all-night garages, shops open late, that sort of thing?'

'If the victim really is Jennifer Clewes,' Annie said, hoping to make up for her lapse in concentration, 'then the odds are that she came from London. As the road she was found on leads to and from the A1, which connects with the M1, that makes it even more likely.'

'Motorway service stations, then?' Kevin Templeton suggested.

'Good idea, DC Templeton,' said Gristhorpe. 'I'll leave that to you, shall I?'

'Wouldn't it be better to get the local forces on it, sir?'

'That'll take too much time and coordination. We need results fast. Better if you do it yourself. Tonight.'

'Just what I always fancied,' Templeton grumbled. 'Driving up and down the M1 sampling the local cuisine.'

Gristhorpe smiled. 'Well, it *was* your idea. And I hear they do a very decent bacon panini at Woodall. Anything else?'

'DC Jackman mentioned that there had been a similar crime some months ago,' Annie said.

Gristhorpe looked at Winsome Jackman, eyebrows raised. 'Oh?'

'Yes, sir,' said Winsome. 'I checked the details. It's not quite as similar as it appears on first glance.'

'Even so,' said Gristhorpe. 'I think we'd like to hear about it.'

'It was near the end of April, the 23rd. The young woman's name was Claire Potter, aged twenty-three, lived in North London. She set off at about eight o'clock on a Friday evening to go and spend the weekend with friends in Castleton. She never got there. Her car was found in a ditch by the side of a quiet road north of Chesterfield by a passing motorist the following morning and her body was found nearby – raped and stabbed. The way it looks is that her car was forced into a ditch by her assailant. The pathologist also found traces of chloroform and characteristic burning around her mouth.'

'Where was she last seen?'

'Trowell services.'

'Nothing on the service station's closed-circuit TV?' asked Gristhorpe.

'Apparently not, sir. I had a brief chat with DI Gifford at Derbyshire CID, and the impression I got was that they've reached a dead end. No witnesses from the cafeteria or garage. Nothing.'

'The MO is different, too,' Annie pointed out.

'Yes,' said Gristhorpe. 'Jennifer Clewes was shot, not stabbed, and she wasn't sexually interfered with, at least not as far as we know. But you think there could be some connection, DC Jackman?'

'Well, sir,' mused Winsome, 'there are some similarities: stopping at the services, being forced off the road, a young woman. There could be any number of reasons why he didn't assault her this time, and he could certainly have acquired a gun since his last murder. Maybe he didn't enjoy stabbing. Maybe it was just a bit too up close and personal for him.'

'OK,' said Gristhorpe. 'Good work. We'll keep an open mind. Last thing we want is to let a serial killer slip through our hands because we don't see the connection. I take it you'll be activating HOLMES?'

'Yes, sir,' said Winsome. The Home Office Large Major Enquiry System was an essential tool in any major investigation. Every scrap of information was entered into the computer and connections were made in ways even a trained officer might easily miss.

'Good.' Gristhorpe stood up. 'OK. Any—'

There was a knock at the door and Gristhorpe called out, 'Come in.'

Dr Wendy Gauge, Dr Glendenning's new and enigmatic assistant, stood there, looking as composed as ever, that mysterious, self-contained smile lingering around her lips the way it always did, even when she was bent over a corpse on the table. Rumour had it that Dr Gauge was being groomed as Glendenning's successor when the old man retired, and Annie had to admit that she was good.

'Yes?' said Gristhorpe.

Wendy Gauge moved forward. 'I've just come from the mortuary,' she said. 'We were removing the victim's clothing and I found this in her back pocket.' She handed over a slip of lined paper, clearly torn from a notebook of some sort, which she had thoughtfully placed in a transparent plastic folder. 'Her killer must have taken everything else from the car,' Dr Gauge went on, 'but . . . well . . . her jeans were very tight and she was . . . you know . . . sitting on it.'

Annie could have sworn Dr Gauge blushed.

Gristhorpe examined the slip of paper first, then frowned and slid it down the table for the others to see.

Annie could hardly believe her eyes, but there, scrawled in blue ink and followed by directions from the A1(M) and a crude map of Helmthorpe, was a name and address:

Alan Banks
Newhope Cottage
Beckside Lane
Gratly, near Helmthorpe
North Yorkshire.

•

By the time his colleagues back in Eastvale were speculating as to what his name and address were doing in a murder victim's back pocket, Banks was in London, making his way through the early Saturday afternoon traffic past the posh restaurants and Maserati showrooms towards his brother Roy's South Kensington house, just east of the Gloucester Road. It was years since he had driven in London, and the roads seemed more crowded than ever.

He had never seen where Roy lived before, he realized, as he drove under the narrow brick arch and parked in the broad cobbled mews. He got out and looked at the whitewashed brick exterior of the house with its integral garage next to the front door and a mullioned bay window above. It didn't look big, but that didn't matter these days. A house like this, in this location, would probably fetch eight hundred k or more in today's market, Banks reckoned, maybe even a million, and a hundred k of that you'd be paying for the privilege of having the word 'mews' in your address.

All the houses stood cheek by jowl, but each was different in some detail – height, facade, style of windows, garage doors, wrought-iron balconies – and the overall effect was of quiet, almost rural charm, a nook hidden away from the hurly-burly that was literally just around the corner. There were houses on all three sides of the cul-de-sac, and the red-brick archway, only wide enough for one car, led to the main road, helping to isolate the mews from the world outside. Beyond the houses at the far end a tower block and a row of distant cranes, angled like alien birds of prey, marred the view of a clear sky.

There were hardly any other cars parked in the mews, as most of the houses had private garages. The few cars that were on display were BMWs, Jaguars and Mercedes, and Banks's shabby little Renault looked like a poor relation. Not for the first time the thought crossed his mind that he needed a new car. It was a hot morning for June, hotter here than up north, and he took off his jacket and slung it over his shoulder.

First he checked the number against his address book. It was the right house. Next he pressed the doorbell and waited. Nobody came. Perhaps, Banks thought, the bell didn't work, or couldn't be heard upstairs, but he remembered hearing it buzz on Roy's phone message. He knocked on the door. Still no answer. He knocked again.

Occasionally, a car would pass by the archway, on the Old Brompton Road, but otherwise the area was quiet. After knocking one last time, Banks tried the door. To his surprise, it opened. Banks could hardly believe it. From what he remembered, Roy had always been security conscious, fiercely protective of his possessions, had probably been born that way. One of the first things he had done, as soon as he was old enough, was save up his pocket money to buy a padlock for his toy box, and woe betide anyone caught touching his bike or his scooter.

Banks examined the lock and saw that it was the deadbolt kind, which you had to use a key both to open *and* to close. Behind the door was a copy of that morning's *Times* and a few letters, bills or junk. He noticed the keypad of a burglar-alarm system just inside the hall, but it hadn't been activated.

To the left was a small sitting room, rather like a doctor's waiting room, with a beige three-piece suite and a low glass-topped coffee-table, on which lay a neat pile of magazines. Banks flipped through them. Mostly business and hi-tech. Between the sitting room and the kitchen, at the back of the house, ran a narrow passage, with a door on the right, near the front, leading to the garage. Banks peeked in and saw that Roy's Porsche 911 was parked there. The car was locked, the bonnet cold.

Back in the house, Banks opened the door that led to a narrow flight of stairs and called Roy's name. No reply. The house was silent except for the myriad daily sounds we usually tune out: distant traffic, the hum of a refrigerator, the ticking of a clock, a tap dripping somewhere, old wood creaking. Banks shuddered. Someone had just walked over his grave, as his mother would say. He couldn't put his finger on what it was, but he felt a distinct tingling up his spine. Fear. There was no one in the house; he was reasonably sure of that. But perhaps someone was watching the place? Banks had learned to trust his instincts over the years, even if he hadn't always acted on them, and he sensed that he would have to move carefully.

He walked into the kitchen, which looked as if it had never been used for anything but making tea and toast. The whole downstairs – sitting room, passage and kitchen – was painted in shades of blue and grey. The paint smelled fresh. A couple of framed photographs in high-contrast black and white hung in the passage. One was a female nude curled on a bed, the other a hill of terraced brick houses leading down to a factory, its chimneys smoking, cobbles and slate roofs gleaming after rain. Banks was surprised. He hadn't known that Roy was interested in photography, or in art of any kind. But then there was so much he didn't know about his estranged brother.

In the kitchen stood a small rustic wooden table with two matching chairs, surrounded by the usual array of counter-tops, toaster, storage cupboards, fridge, oven and microwave. The table was clear apart from an opened bottle of Amarone with the cork stuck back in, and, half hidden behind the bottle, a mobile phone. Banks picked up the phone. It was off, so he turned it on. It was an expensive model, the kind that sends and receives digital images, and there was plenty of battery power left. He tried the voicemail and text functions, but the only messages were the ones he had left. Was Roy the kind of person who would forget to take his mobile with him when he went out under normal circumstances, especially as he had given Banks the number? Banks doubted it, the same way he doubted that Roy would deliberately leave his front door unlocked or forget to turn on his burglar alarm unless he was really rattled by something.

A wine-rack stood on one of the counters, and even Banks could tell that the wines there were very high-end clarets, Chiantis and burgundies. Above the rack hung a ring of keys on a hook. One of them looked like a car key. Banks put them in his pocket. He checked the fridge. It was empty except for some margarine, a carton of milk and a piece of mouldy Cheddar. That confirmed it. Roy was no gourmet cook. He could afford to eat out, and there were plenty of good restaurants on Old Brompton Road. The back door was locked, and the window looked out on a small backyard and an alley beyond.

Before going upstairs, Banks went back to the garage to see if the car key on the ring fit the Porsche. As he had suspected, it did. Banks opened the driver's door and got in.

He had never sat in such a car before, and the luxurious leather upholstery embraced him like a lover. He felt like putting the key in the ignition and driving off somewhere, anywhere. But that wasn't why he was here. The car's interior smelled clean and fresh, with that expensive hint of leather. From what Banks could see, there were no empty crisp packets or pop cans on the back seat or cellophane wrappers on the floor. Nor was there one of those fancy GPS gadgets that would tell Banks what Roy's last destination was. In the side pocket was a small AA road atlas open to the page with Reading in the bottom right and Stratford-upon-Avon at top left. There was nothing else except the car's manual and a few CDs, mostly classical. Banks got out and checked the boot. Empty.

Next, Banks ventured upstairs, a much larger living space than downstairs because it extended over the garage. At the top of the stairs, he found himself on a small landing with five doors leading off. The first led to the toilet, the second to a modern bathroom, complete with power shower and whirlpool bath. There were the usual shaving and dental-care implements, paracetamol and Rennies, and rather more varieties of shampoo, conditioner and body lotion than Banks imagined Roy would need. He also wouldn't need the pink plastic disposable razor that sat next to the gel for sensitive skin, not unless he shaved his legs.

At the back was a bedroom, simple and bright, with flower-patterned wallpaper: double bed, duvet, dressing-table, drawers and a small wardrobe full of clothes and shoes, everything immaculate. Roy's clothing ran the gamut from expensive casual to expensive business, Banks noticed – looking at the labels: Armani, Hugo Boss, Paul Smith – and there were also a few items of women's clothing, including a summer dress, a black evening gown, Levi's, an assortment of short-sleeved tops and several pairs of shoes and sandals.

The drawers revealed a few items of jewellery, condoms, tampons and a mix of men's and women's underwear. Banks didn't know whether Roy was into cross-dressing, but he assumed the female items belonged to his girlfriend of the moment. And as there was nowhere near enough women's paraphernalia to indicate that a woman actually *lived* there, she probably just kept a few clothes, along with the items in the bathroom, for when she stayed over.

Banks remembered the young girl who had been with Roy the last time they met. She had looked about twenty, shy, with short, shaggy black hair streaked with blonde, a pale, pretty face, with beautiful eyes the colour and gleam of chestnuts in October. She also had a silver stud just below her lower lip. She had been wearing jeans and a short woolly jumper, exposing a couple of inches of bare, flat midriff and a navel with a ring in it. They were engaged, Banks remembered. He tried to remember her name. It was Colleen or Connie, something like that. She might know where Roy had gone. Banks could probably trace her from Roy's mobile's phone book. Of course, there was no guarantee that she was still Roy's fiancée, or that the clothes and toiletry items were hers.

Next to the bedroom, and quite a bit larger, was what appeared to be Roy's office, furnished with filing cabinets, a computer monitor, fax machine, printer and photocopier. Again, everything was shipshape, no untidy piles of paper or yellow post-it notes stuck on every surface, like Banks's office. The desk surface was clear apart from an unused writing tablet and an empty glass of red wine, the dregs hardening to crystal. In a bookcase just above the desk were the standard reference books – atlas, dictionary, Dunn and Bradstreet, *Who's Who*.

Roy certainly kept his life in order, and Banks remembered that he had been a tidy child, too. After playing, he had always put his toys carefully away in their box and locked it. His room, even when he was a teenager, was a model of cleanliness and tidiness. He could have been in the army. Banks's room, on the other hand, had been the same sort of mess he'd seen in most teens' bedrooms on missing-persons cases. He'd known where everything was – his books were in alphabetical order, for example – but he had never fussed much about making his bed or tidying the pile of discarded clothes left on the floor. Another reason his mother had always favoured Roy.

Banks wondered if Roy's computer would tell him anything. The flat-panel monitor sat on the desk, but Banks was damned if he could find the computer itself. It wasn't on or under the desk, or on the shelf behind. There was a keyboard and a mouse, but keyboard, mouse and monitor were no use without the computer. Even a novice like Banks knew that.

Given Roy's interest in electronic gadgets, Banks would have expected a laptop, too, but he could find no signs of one. Nor a handheld. He remembered Roy showing off a flashy new Palm – one of those gadgets that do everything but fry your eggs in the morning – at the party last year.

Needless to say, there was nothing remotely so useful as a Filofax. Roy would keep all that information on his computer and his Palm, and it seemed that they were both gone. Still, Banks had the mobile, and that ought to prove a fruitful source of contact numbers.

There was a Nikon Coolpix 4300 digital camera in one of the pigeonholes behind the computer desk. Banks knew a little about digital cameras, though his cheap Canon was well below Roy's range. He at least managed to switch it on and figure out how to look at the images on the LCD screen, but there was no memory card in it, no images to see. He searched around the adjoining pigeonholes for some sort of image-storage device but found nothing. That was another puzzle, he realized. All the things you expect to find around a computer – Zip drive, tape backups or CDs – were conspicuous in their absence. There was nothing left but the monitor, mouse and keyboard, and an empty digital camera.

One other gadget remained: a 40GB iPod, another little electronic toy Banks had thought of buying. He dipped in at random, hearing snatches of arias here and a bit of an overture there. Banks had always thought his brother a bit of a philistine, didn't know he was an opera buff, that they might have something in common. From what he could remember, when he had been into Dylan, The Who and the Stones, Roy had been a Herman's Hermits fan.

One of the songs Banks stumbled across was 'Dido's Lament' from Purcell's *Dido and Aeneas,* and he found himself listening for just a little longer than he needed, feeling a lump in his throat and that burning sensation at the back of his eyes he always felt when he heard 'When I am laid in earth'. The upsurge of emotion surprised him. Another good sign. He had felt little or nothing since the fire and thought that was because he had nothing left to feel with. It was encouraging to have at least a hint that there was life in the old boy yet. He browsed through the iPod's contents and found a lot of good stuff: Bach, Beethoven, Verdi, Puccini, Rossini. There was a complete *Ring Cycle,* but nobody's perfect, he thought. Least of all Roy. Still, the extent of his good taste was a surprise.

The telephone was like a mini-computer system in itself. Banks managed to dial 1471 and find out that the last incoming call was the one he had made himself that morning before setting off for London. Unfortunately, Roy hadn't subscribed to the extra service that gave the numbers of the last five callers. Banks realized it didn't matter, as he had called at least five times himself. The phone was hooked up to a digital answering machine, and after a bit of dodgy business with the buttons Banks discovered three messages, all from him. The other times he'd called he hadn't bothered leaving one.

Banks thought he heard a sound from somewhere inside the house. He sat completely still and waited. What if Roy came back and found Banks going through his personal things and business records? How would he talk his way out of that one? On the other hand, Banks would be relieved to see Roy, and surely Roy would understand how his phone call had set off alarms in the mind of his policeman brother? Nevertheless, it would be embarrassing all around. A minute or two passed and he heard nothing more, so he put it down to one of the many sounds an old house makes.

Banks opened the desk drawers. The two bottom ones held folders full of bills and tax records, none of which seemed in any way unusual at a casual glance, and the top ones were filled with the usual stuff of offices: Sellotape, rubber bands, paperclips, scissors, scratchpads, staplers and printer cartridges.

The shallow central drawer contained pens and pencils of all shapes and sizes. Banks stirred them around with his hand, and one struck his eye. It was thicker and shorter than most of the other pens, squat and rectangular, rather than round. Thinking it might be some kind of marker, he picked it up and unclipped the top. It wasn't a pen. Where the nib should have been, instead he found a small rectangle of metal that looked as if it plugged into something. But what? Banks put the top back on and clipped the pen in the top pocket of his shirt.

The last door led to a large living room above the garage. It was the front room with the bay window Banks had noticed from the street. The colour scheme here was different, reds and earth colours, a desert theme. There were more framed black-and-white photographs on the walls, too, and Banks found himself wondering if Roy had taken them himself. He didn't know whether you could take black-and-white photos of that quality with a digital camera, but maybe you could. He could still dredge up no memory of his brother's interest in photography; as far as Banks knew, Roy hadn't even belonged to the camera club at school, and most kids did that at some time in the vain hope that whoever ran it would sneak in a nude model one day.

This room, like the rest of the house, was clean and tidy. Not a speck of dust or an abandoned mug anywhere. Banks doubted Roy did it himself; more likely he employed a cleaning lady. Even the entertainment magazines on the table were stacked parallel to the edge, Hercule Poirot style. A luxurious sofa-bed sat under the window facing the other wall, where a 42-inch widescreen plasma TV hung, wired up to a satellite dish and a DVD player. On looking more closely, Banks noticed that the player also recorded DVDs. Under the screen stood a sub-woofer and a front centre speaker, and four smaller speakers were strategically placed around the room. It was an expensive set-up, one which Banks himself had often wished he could afford.

Banks walked to the fitted wall cabinets and cast his eye over the selection of DVDs and CDs. What he saw there puzzled him. Not for Roy the latest James Bond or Terminator movie, not schoolgirl porn or Jenna Jameson, but Fellini's *8½*, Kurasawa's *Ran* and *Throne of Blood*, Herzog's *Fitzcarraldo*, Bergman's *The Seventh Seal* and Truffaut's *The 400 Blows*. There were some films that Banks could see himself watching – *The Godfather*, *The Third Man* and *A Clockwork Orange* – but most of them were foreign-language art films, classics of the cinema. There were a few rows of books, too, mostly non-fiction, on subjects ranging from music and cinema to philosophy, religion and politics. Another surprise. In a small recess stood one framed family photograph.

Banks studied Roy's large collection of operas on both DVD and CD: *The Magic Flute*, *Tosca*, *Otello*, *Lucia de Lammermoor* and others. A complete Bayreuth *Ring* cycle, the same as the one on the iPod. There was a little fifties jazz and a few Hollywood musicals – *Oklahoma*, *South Pacific*, *Seven Brides for Seven Brothers* – but no pop at all except for the Blue Lamps' debut. Banks was pleased to see that Roy had bought Brian's CD, even though he probably hadn't listened to it. He slid it out and opened the case, wondering what it would sound like on Roy's expensive stereo system. Instead of the familiar blue image on the CD, he saw the words 'CD – ReWritable' and that the disk held 650MB, or 74 minutes of playing time.

Banks stuck the CD in his jacket pocket and went over to sit on the sofa. Several remote-control devices rested on the arm, and when he had worked out which was which, he switched on the TV and amp just to see what the set-up looked and sounded like. It was a European football game, and the picture quality was stunning, the sound of the commentary loud enough to wake the dead. He turned it off.

He went back into the office and took the writing tablet from the desk and a pen from the drawer and carried them down to the kitchen with him. At the kitchen table, he sat down and wrote a note explaining that he'd been to the house and would be back, in case Roy returned while he was out, and asked him to get in touch as soon as possible.

He wished now that he had thought to bring his mobile so he could leave a number, but it was too late; he had left it on his living-room table next to his unused portable CD player, having got out of the habit of using it over the past few months. Then he realized he could take Roy's. He wanted to check through the entries in the phone book, anyway, so he might as well have the use of it in case Roy needed to get in touch with him. He added this as a PS to the note, then he put the mobile in his pocket. On his way out, he tried the most likely looking key and found it fitted the front door.

3

'**What do you** make of it, Annie?' Gristhorpe asked.

They were sitting in the superintendent's large carpeted office, just the two of them, and the sheet of paper lay between them on Gristhorpe's desk. It wasn't Banks's writing, Annie was certain. But beyond that, the whole thing was a puzzle. She had certainly never seen the dead woman before, nor had she ever heard Banks mention anyone called Jennifer Clewes. That in itself meant nothing, of course, she realized. In the first place, it might not be her real name, and in the second, Banks might well have been keeping many aspects of his life from her, including a new girlfriend. But if she was his girlfriend, why did she need directions and his address? Perhaps she had never visited him in Gratly before.

Was she new on the scene? Annie doubted it. The way Banks had been behaving lately, withdrawn, moody and uncommunicative, was hardly conducive to pulling a new girlfriend. Who would take him on, the shape he was in? And this woman was young enough to be his daughter. Not that age had ever stopped a man, but . . . Perhaps even more important was that she had ended up with a bullet in her head. Knowing Banks had its dangers, as Annie well knew, but it was not usually fatal.

'I don't know, sir. I'd say the most likely explanation is that it's her own writing. Maybe she copied it down over the phone. We'll be able to find out for sure when we get a sample of Jennifer Clewes's writing.'

'Have you been able to get in touch with DCI Banks?'

'He's not at home and his mobile's turned off. I've left messages.'

'Well, let's just hope he gets one of them and rings back. I'd really like to know why a young woman who was driving up from London to see him in the middle of the night ended up with a bullet in her head.'

'He could be anywhere,' Annie said. 'He is on holiday, after all.'

'He didn't tell you where he was going?'

'He doesn't tell me much these days, sir.'

Gristhorpe frowned and scratched his chin, then he leaned back in his big, padded chair and linked his hands behind his head. 'How's he doing?' he asked.

'I'm the last person to ask, sir. We haven't really talked much since the fire.'

'I thought you two were friends.'

'I like to think we are. But you know Alan. He's hardly the type to open up when he doesn't want to. I think perhaps he still blames me for what happened, the fire and all. After all, Phil Keane was my boyfriend. Whatever the reason, he's been very quiet lately. To be honest, I think it's partly depression as well.'

'I can't say I'm surprised. It happens sometimes after illness or an accident. About all you can do is wait till the fog disperses. What about you?'

'Me? I'm fine, sir. Coping.' Annie was aware how tight and unconvincing her voice sounded, but she could do nothing about it. Anyway, she *was* coping, after a fashion. She certainly wasn't depressed, just hurt and angry, and perhaps a little distracted.

Gristhorpe held her gaze for just long enough to make her feel uncomfortable, then he went on, 'We need to find out why the victim had Alan's address in her back pocket,' he said. 'And we can't ask her.'

'There's a flatmate, sir,' said Annie. 'The lads from Lambeth North got bored with hanging around outside and went in for a look. Jennifer Clewes was sharing with a woman called Kate Nesbit. At least there were letters there addressed to a Kate Nesbit *and* a Jennifer Clewes.'

'Have they talked to this flatmate?'

'She's not at home.'

'Work?'

'On a Saturday? Maybe. Or she might have gone away for the weekend.'

Gristhorpe looked at his watch. 'Better get down there, Annie,' he said. 'Let your old pal at Kennington know you're on your way. Find the flatmate and talk to her.'

'Yes, sir.' Annie stood up. 'There is one other thing.'

'Yes?'

Annie gestured towards the scrap of paper. 'This address. I mean, it *is* Alan's address, but it's not where he's living now.'

'I noticed that,' said Gristhorpe. 'You think it might be significant?'

'Well, sir,' Annie said, hand on the doorknob, 'he's been living at that flat in the old Steadman house for four months now. You'd think everyone who knew him – knew him at all well, at any rate – would know that. I mean, if it was a new girlfriend or something, why give her his old address?'

'You've got a point.' Gristhorpe scratched the side of his nose. 'What action do you think we should take?'

'About DCI Banks?'

'Yes.'

Gristhorpe paused. 'You say he's not answering his phones?'

'That's right, neither his home phone nor his mobile.'

'We need to find him, as soon as we can, but I don't want to make it official yet. I'll get Winsome to ring around his family and friends, see if anyone knows where he is.'

'I was thinking of dropping by his place – both of them – just to have a look around . . . you know . . . make sure nothing's been disturbed.'

'Good idea,' said Gristhorpe. 'Are you sure you're all right on this?'

Annie looked over her shoulder. 'Of course I am, sir,' she said. 'Why shouldn't I be?'

•

Out in the street, Banks tried knocking on a couple of neighbours' doors, but only one answered, an elderly man who lived in the house opposite.

'I saw you going into Roy's,' the man said. 'I was wondering if I should ring the police.'

Banks took out his warrant card. 'I'm Roy's brother,' he said, 'and I am the police.'

The man seemed satisfied and stuck out his hand. 'Malcolm Farrow,' he said as they shook hands. 'Pleased to meet you. Come inside.'

'I don't want to intrude on your time, but—'

'Think nothing of it. Now I'm retired every day's the same to me. Come in, we'll have a snifter.'

Banks followed him into a living room heavy with dark wood and antiques. Farrow offered brandy but Banks took only soda. Much too early in the afternoon for spirits.

'What can I do for you, Mr Banks?' Farrow asked.

'Alan, please. It's about Roy.'

'What about him? Lovely fellow, that brother of yours, by the way. Couldn't wish for a better neighbour, you know. Cheerful, considerate. Capital fellow.'

'That's good to know,' said Banks, judging by the slight slur in his voice and the network of purplish veins around his bulbous nose that Malcolm Farrow had already had a snifter or two. 'I was just wondering if you had any idea where he's gone?'

'You mean he's not back yet?'

'Apparently not. Did you see him leave?'

'Yes. It was about half-past nine last night. I was putting the cat out when I saw him going out.'

Just after the phone call, Banks realized. 'Was he alone?'

'No. There was another man with him. I said hello and Roy returned my greeting. Like I said, you couldn't wish for a more friendly neighbour.'

'This other man,' said Banks. 'Did you get a good look at him?'

'Afraid not. It was getting dark by then, you see, and the street lighting's not very bright. Besides, to be perfectly honest, I can't say my eyesight's quite what it used to be.'

Probably pissed to the gills, too, Banks thought, if today was anything to go by. 'Anything at all you can remember,' he said.

'Well, he was a burly sort of fellow, with curly hair. Fair or grey. I'm sorry, I didn't notice any more than that. I only noticed because he was facing me at first for a moment, while Roy had his back turned.'

'Why did Roy have his back turned?'

'He was locking the door. Very security-conscious, Roy is. You have to be these days, don't you?'

'I suppose so,' said Banks, wondering how the door had come to be unlocked and the burglar alarm unarmed when he got there. 'Where did they go?'

'Got in a car and drove off. It was parked outside Roy's house.'

'What kind of car?'

'I'm not very good with cars. Haven't driven in years, so I haven't taken much of an interest. It was light in colour, I can tell you that much. And quite big. Looked expensive.'

'And they just drove off?'

'Yes.'

'Had you see the man before?'

'I might have, if it was the same one.'

'Was he a frequent visitor?'

'I wouldn't say frequent, but I'd seen him a couple of times. Usually after dark, so I'm afraid I can't do any better with the description.'

'Was either of them carrying anything?'

'Like what?'

'Anything. Suitcase. Cardboard box.'

'Not that I could see.'

That meant that Roy's computer equipment must have been taken later, by someone with a key. 'You didn't see or hear anyone else call after that, did you?'

'Sorry. My bedroom's at the back of the house and I still manage to sleep quite soundly, despite my age.'

'I'm glad to hear it,' said Banks.

'Look, is there something going on? You say Roy's not come home.'

'It's probably nothing,' Banks said, not wanting to worry Farrow. He put his tumbler of soda down and stood up. 'You know, I'll bet they went off to some pub or other, had a bit too much. They're more than likely back at the other bloke's place right now, still sleeping it off. It is Saturday, after all.' He started moving towards the door.

'I suppose you're right,' said Farrow, following, 'but it's not like him. Especially as he'd only just got in.'

'Pardon?' said Banks, pausing in the doorway.

'Well, he'd just come back in, oh, not more than ten or fifteen minutes earlier, about quarter past nine. I saw his car, watched him park it in the garage. I must say, he seemed in a bit of a hurry.'

The phone call to Banks had been timed at 9.29 p.m., which meant that Roy had rung him shortly after he had arrived home. Where had he been? What was it he couldn't talk about over the telephone? While he was on the phone, someone had come to his door, and a few minutes later he had gone out again, most likely with the man who had rung his doorbell. Where had they gone?

'Thank you for your time, Mr Farrow,' said Banks. 'I won't trouble you any longer.'

'No trouble. You will let me know, won't you, if you hear anything?'

'Of course,' said Banks.

•

And why shouldn't I be all right with it? Annie thought as she parked at the top of the hill and walked towards the old Steadman house. Any romantic involvement she'd had with Banks was ancient history, so what did it matter whether he was seeing this

Jennifer Clewes? Except that she was dead and Banks had disappeared.

Annie paused a moment on the bridge. It was one of those early summer days when the world seemed dipped in sunshine and life should be simple. Yet, for Annie, it was not without a tinge of melancholy, like the first sight of brown on the edges of the leaves, and she found her thoughts turning to the unresolved problems that haunted her.

There was a time, she remembered, when Banks had just come out of hospital, that there was so much she wanted to say to him, to explain, to apologize for being such a fool, but he wouldn't let her get close, so she gave up. In the end, they simply carried on working together as if nothing of any consequence had happened between them.

But something *had* happened. Phil Keane, Annie's boyfriend, had tried to kill Banks, had drugged him and set fire to his cottage. Annie and Winsome had dragged him out in time to save his life, and Phil had disappeared.

Officially, it wasn't Annie's fault. No blame. How could she have known? But she *should* have known, she kept telling herself. She should have recognized the signs. Banks had even hinted, but she had put it down to jealousy. She had never been so wrong about anything or anyone before. She'd screwed up relationships, but that sort of thing happened to everyone. Nothing like this. Complete and utter humiliation. And it made her angry. She was a detective, for Christ's sake; she was supposed to have an instinct for people like Phil Keane; she should have sussed him out herself.

In some ways what had happened to her was worse than the rape she had endured over three years ago. This was total emotional rape, and it stained her soul. Because she had loved Phil Keane, though she loathed to admit it to herself, now the very thought of him running his hands over her body, pleasuring her, penetrating her, made her feel sick. How could she have seen no deeper than the charm, the good looks, the keen intelligence, that all-embracing energy and enthusiasm for life that made her – and everyone else in his presence – feel special, singled out for grace?

Well, she knew now that beneath the charm was an immeasurable and impenetrable darkness – the lack of conscience of a psychopath fused with the motivating greed of a common thief. And a love of the game, an enjoyment of deceit and humiliation for their own sakes. But was his charm merely on the surface? The more Annie thought about it, the more she came to believe that Phil's charm was not simply a matter of surface veneer, that it was deeply rooted in the rest of his being, a tumour inseparable from the evil at his core. You couldn't just scratch the surface and see the terrible truth beneath; the surface was as true as anything else about him.

Such speculation shouldn't be allowed on a fine day like this, Annie told herself, battening down the anger that rose like bile in her throat whenever she thought about Phil and what had happened last winter. But ever since then, she had been searching for a hint as to where he might have gone. She read all the boring police circulars and memos she used to ignore, pored over newspapers and watched TV news, looking for a clue – an unexplained fire somewhere, a businessman conned out of his fortune, a woman used and abandoned – anything that fitted the profile she had compiled in her mind. But after over four months all she had was one false lead, a fire in Devizes that turned out to have been caused by careless smoking. She knew he was around somewhere, though, and when he made his move, as he surely would, then she would have him.

A young boy in short trousers, shirt hanging out, sat on the bank of Gratly Beck fishing. He'd be lucky to catch anything in such fast-flowing water, Annie thought. He waved when he saw her watching him. Annie waved back and hurried on to the Steadman house.

After checking out Banks's house, she would have to hurry to Darlington to catch a train to London. The three twenty-five would get her into King's Cross just after six, all being well. It would be quicker than driving, and she didn't fancy negotiating her way through the central London traffic all the way south of the river to Kennington. She would leave her car at Darlington station.

Annie passed the tiny Sandemanian chapel and overgrown graveyard and walked down the path to the holiday flats. Two houses had been knocked into one, the insides re-finished, to make four spacious, self-contained flats, two up, two down. She knew Banks had the one that looked out on the graveyard, because he had mentioned how apt that seemed, but she hadn't been inside. He hadn't invited her.

Though she knew it was futile, Annie rang Banks's doorbell. A tired-looking young woman holding a baby to her breast opened the door to the downstairs flat, having no doubt noticed Annie walking up the garden path.

'It's no use,' she said. 'He's out.'

'When did he leave?' Annie asked.

'Who wants to know?'

Annie pulled her warrant card from her handbag. 'I'm a colleague of his,' she explained. 'There's something important I need to talk to him about.'

The woman looked at her card, but she obviously wasn't impressed. 'Well, he's out,' she said again.

'When did he leave?' Annie repeated.

'About eight o'clock this morning. Just drove off.'

'Did he say where he was going?'

'Not to me. And I wouldn't expect him to.'

'Do you own these flats?'

'Me and my husband. We live in this one and rent out the others. Why?'

'I was wondering if I might have a look around. I assume you have a spare key?'

'You can't do that. It's private.' The baby stirred, made a few tentative burps. She rubbed its back and it fell silent again.

'Look,' said Annie, 'this really is important. I don't want to keep you here. I can see you have the baby to deal with, but I'd really appreciate it if you'd let me have a quick look in DCI Banks's flat. It would be so much less trouble than if I had to go and get a search warrant.'

'Search warrant? Can you do that?'

'Yes, I can.'

'Oh, all right, I suppose,' she said. 'It's no skin off my nose, is it? Just a minute.'

She went inside and returned with two keys, which she handed to Annie. 'I'll be wanting them back, mind,' she said.

'Of course,' said Annie. 'I won't be long.'

She felt the woman's eyes boring into her back as she opened Banks's door and walked up the staircase to the upper flat. At the top, she opened the second door and found herself in a small hallway with pegs for jackets and raincoats and a small cupboard for shoes and heavier clothing. A few bills and circulars sat on the table under the gilt-edged mirror.

The first door she opened led to the bedroom. Annie felt strange poking around Banks's flat with him not there, especially his bedroom, but she told herself it couldn't be helped. Somehow or other, he had become instrumental in a murder investigation, and he was nowhere to be found. There was nothing in the bedroom anyway, except a double bed, hastily made, a few clothes in the dresser drawers and wardrobe, and a cushioned window seat that looked out over the graveyard. Must be quite a pick-up line, Annie thought, if you fancied sharing your bed with someone. 'Come sleep with me beside the graveyard.' It had a sort of ring to it. Then she took her mind off images of shared beds and went into the living room.

On the low table in front of the sofa sat a mobile phone and a portable CD player with headphones. So wherever Banks had gone, he had left these behind, Annie thought, and wondered why. Banks loved his music, and he liked to keep in touch. At least, he *used* to. Looking around the room, she noticed there were no books and no CDs except the copy of *Don Giovanni*, a gift from the lads, which she had brought him in hospital. The cellophane wrapper was still on it. There wasn't even a stereo, only a small TV set, which probably came with the flat. Annie began to feel inexplicably depressed. She tried Banks's answerphone, but there were no messages.

The kitchen was tiny and narrow, the fridge full of the usual items: milk, eggs, beer, cheese, a selection of vegetables, bacon, tomatoes, a bottle of Sauvignon Blanc and some sliced ham – all of it looking fairly fresh. Well, at least he was still eating. A couple of cardboard boxes under the small dining table were filled with empty wine bottles ready for the bottle bank.

Annie glanced briefly in the toilet and bathroom, a quick look through the cabinets revealing only what she would have expected: razor, shaving cream, toothpaste and toothbrush were missing, so he must have taken them with him. Amidst the usual over-the-counter medication, there was one small bottle of strong prescription painkillers dated three months ago. Wherever Banks had gone, he clearly hadn't thought he needed them any more.

She stood in the centre of the hall, wondering if she could possibly have missed something, then realized there was nothing to miss. This was the flat of a faceless man, a man with no interests, no passions, no friends, no life. There weren't even any family photos. It wasn't Banks's flat, couldn't be. Not the Banks she knew.

Annie remembered Newhope Cottage and its living room with the blue walls and ceiling the colour of melting Brie, remembered the warm shaded orange light and the evenings she had spent there with Banks. In winter, a peat fire had usually burned in the hearth, its tang harmonizing with the Islay malt she sometimes sipped with him. In summer they would often go outside after dark to sit on the parapet above Gratly Beck, looking at the stars and listening to the water. And there would always be music: Bill Evans, Lucinda Williams, Van Morrison, and string quartets she didn't recognize.

Annie felt tears in her eyes and she brushed them away

roughly and headed downstairs. She knocked on the door and handed back the keys without a word and hurried down the path.

•

Banks sat in a pub on the Old Brompton Road playing with Roy's mobile, learning what the functions were and how to use them. He found a call list, which gave him the last thirty incoming, outgoing and missed calls. Some were just first names, some numbers, and quite a few of the incoming calls were 'unknown'. The last call had been made at 3.57 p.m. on Friday afternoon to 'James'. Banks pressed the call button and listened to a phone ring. Finally someone picked it up and uttered a frazzled 'Yeah?' Banks could hear Bowie in the background singing 'Moonage Daydream'.

'Can I speak to James?' he said.

'Speaking.'

'My brother Roy Banks rang you yesterday. I was wondering what it was about.'

'That's right,' said James. 'He was ringing to make an appointment for next Wednesday, I believe. Yeah, here it is, Wednesday at half-past two.'

'Appointment for what?'

'A haircut. I'm Roy's hairdresser. Why? Is everything OK?'

Banks rang off without answering. At least Roy had been certain enough at 3.57 p.m. Friday of being around next Wednesday to make an appointment with his hairdresser. Banks had never done such a thing in his life. He went to the barber's and waited his turn like everyone else, reading old magazines.

Banks washed down the last of his curry of the day with a pint of Pride, lit a cigarette and looked around. It was odd being in London again. He had visited many times since he'd left, mostly in connection with cases he was working on, but with each visit he came to feel increasingly like a stranger, a tourist, though he had once lived there for over fifteen years.

Still, that was quite a while ago, and things changed. Down-at-heel neighbourhoods became desirable residences and once-chic areas went downhill. Villains' pubs became locals for the trendy young crowd and upmarket pubs started to go to seed. He had no idea what was 'in' these days. London was a vast sprawling metropolis, and Banks had never, even when he was living there, been familiar with it beyond Notting Hill and Kennington, where he had lived, and the West End, where he had worked. South Kensington might have been another city as far as he was concerned.

He turned his mind to Roy's disappearance, oblivious to the ebb and flow of conversation around him. He would run through the rest of the call list later, back at the house. He also wanted to check out the data CD. There were plenty of Internet cafes around, and some of them would even allow him to read a CD and print out material, but they were far too public, and anything he did would leave traces. He had violated his brother's privacy, but he felt he had good reason, whereas there was no reason at all to risk making any of Roy's secrets known to strangers.

He realized he didn't know anyone in London who owned a computer. Most of the people he had known there, criminals and coppers, had either moved, retired or died. Except Sandra, his ex-wife, who had moved from Eastvale to Camden Town when she left him. Sandra would probably have a computer. But his last meeting with her had been disastrous, and she had hardly been a constant visitor in his days of need. In fact, she hadn't visited at all, merely sent her condolences through Tracy. Then there was the husband, Sean, and the new baby, Sinéad. No, he didn't think he would be paying any visits to Sandra in the foreseeable future.

He also couldn't go official with what he'd got for the same reason he couldn't use an Internet cafe: in case the disc held something incriminating against Roy. If Roy had been up to something dodgy, Banks wasn't going to shop him, not his own brother. He might give him a damned good bollocking and read him the riot act when he found him, but he wasn't going to help put him in jail.

There was one possible avenue he could explore first, someone who would probably be as interested in protecting Roy's reputation as he was. Banks stubbed out his cigarette and reached into his pocket for the mobile. He scrolled through the list of names and numbers in the phone book until he found Corinne. That was Roy's fiancée's name, he remembered, copying the number down into his notebook. Then he put the mobile back in his pocket, finished his drink and walked out to the street.

London was hot and sticky. Of all the places to be during a heat wave, this was not one he would have chosen. People were wilting on the pavements, and the air was redolent with the smell of exhaust fumes and worse, like rotting meat or cabbage.

Banks didn't want to tie up the mobile again in case Roy got his message back at the house and phoned, so he sought out a public phone box and dug out an old phone card from his wallet. He felt as if he were walking into the tin hut where the Japanese locked Alec Guinness in *The Bridge on the River Kwai*. Sweat trickled down his sides, tickling as it ran, sticking his shirt to his skin. Someone had crushed a bluebottle against the glass, making a long smear of dark blood. He could even smell the warm paper of the telephone directory.

Banks took out his notebook and dialled the number he had copied from Roy's mobile. Just as he was about to hang up, a breathless voice came on the line.

'Hello?'

'Corinne?' Banks asked.

'Yes. Who is it?'

'My name's Alan Banks. Roy's brother. You might remember me. We met at my parents' wedding anniversary party in Peterborough last October.'

'Of course. I remember.'

'Look, I'm down in London and I was wondering if we could get together somewhere and have a chat. Maybe over a drink or something?'

There was a pause, then she said, 'Are you asking me out?'

'No. Sorry. I'm getting this all wrong. Please excuse me. Blame the heat. I mean, that's why I thought a drink might be a good idea. Somewhere cool, if there is such a place.'

'Yes, it *is* hot, isn't it. What do you mean, then? I'm afraid I don't follow.'

'I just need to pick your brains, that's all.'

'I remember. You're a policeman, aren't you?'

'Yes, but that's not why . . . I mean, it's not official.'

'Well, you've certainly got my attention. You could come over to the flat.' She paused. 'I've got an electric fan in the office.'

'Have you got a computer?'

'Yes. Why?'

'Great,' said Banks. 'When would be convenient?'

'Well, I've got a couple of meetings with clients this afternoon – I'm afraid free weekends are never a given if you're an accountant out on your own – but I should be done by early evening. Say five o'clock?'

Banks looked at his watch. It was half-past three. 'All right,' he said.

'Good. Have you got a pen and paper handy? I'll give you my address.'

Banks wrote down the address and listened to Corinne's directions. Just off Earl's Court Road. Not far from Roy's at all, then, though another world entirely. He thanked her again, escaped from the sweat box and headed back to the pub.

•

By the time Annie had walked over the bridge and along the lane to Banks's cottage, she had just about succeeded in regaining her equilibrium. The builders had got as far as restoring the roof. From the outside, the place looked perfectly normal, and one might even think someone lived there if it weren't for the lack of curtains and the overflowing skip. Because it was Saturday there were no workmen around, though given how slow they had been, Annie thought, the least they could do was put in a few extra hours to help get Banks back where he belonged. After all, they'd been on the job close to four months now.

It was the first time Annie had been back there since the night of the fire, and just seeing the place evoked painful memories: the feel of the wet blanket she wrapped around herself; the fire bursting out as she broke the door open; the smoke in her eyes and throat; Banks's dead weight as she dragged him towards the door; Winsome's strength as she helped them over the last few feet, a distance Annie thought she couldn't make alone; lying there on the muddy ground spluttering, looking at Banks's still figure and fearing him dead. And, almost worst of all, remembering Phil Keane's silver BMW disappearing up the hill as Winsome had first turned into Banks's drive.

She took a moment to bring herself back to the present. Jennifer Clewes had Banks's address in her back pocket, but it was *this* address, Annie reminded herself. Why was that? She noticed tyre tracks in the dust, but they could have been anyone's. The builders', for example. And despite the sign that said Beckside Lane was a cul-de-sac *and* a private drive, cars often turned into it by mistake. Even so, she made certain not to disturb the tracks.

Annie walked up to the front door of the cottage. Though the building wasn't finished inside, she guessed that the builders would keep it locked to discourage squatters and because they might sometimes leave their expensive tools there overnight. Which was why the splintering around the lock immediately caught her attention. She leaned closer and saw that it looked fresh. The door was new and not yet painted, and the splintered wood was clean and sharp.

Annie's protective gloves were back in the boot of her car, so she used her foot to nudge the door open gently and kept her hands in her pockets. Inside, the place was a mess, but a builders' mess, not a burglar's, by the looks of it. The rooms were divided and the ceiling beams in place, and most of the plasterboarding had been finished except the wall between the living room and the kitchen. It felt odd to be standing there smelling sawdust and sheared metal rather than peat smoke, Annie thought. The stairs looked finished, solid enough, and after a tentative step she ventured up. The once-familiar bedroom was a mere skeleton, with builders' calculations and blueprints scrawled on the walls in pencil. The second bedroom was similarly bare.

She went back downstairs and out to the lane. As she walked away, she turned once more and looked back. *Someone* had broken into the cottage, and recently. She assumed the builders had locked up when they left on Friday, though she would have to check with them to be certain. It could have been thieves, of course, but that seemed too much of a coincidence. Annie realized that she would have to bring in Stefan Nowak and the SOCOs to see if they could establish any links between Jennifer Clewes's car and Banks's cottage.

If it was the same person who had killed Jennifer Clewes, Annie reasoned, then he must have got hold of Banks's address by some other means, because Jennifer Clewes had it in the back pocket of her jeans. Perhaps he already knew where Banks lived and, when he had guessed where she was going, and when he had got to a desolate, isolated stretch of road, he had shot Jennifer and then carried on to Banks's cottage. To do what? Kill him, too? It would certainly make more sense to handle them one at a time.

But Banks hadn't been there; he'd been about a quarter of a mile away, in his temporary flat. Had Banks any idea of what was going on? Was that why he had taken off so early in the morning? That was the big question, Annie realized, heading back up the hill to her car. How much did Banks know and how safe was he now? And she knew that she probably wouldn't find out the answer to either question until she found the man himself.

•

Corinne lived in the first-floor flat of a four-storey building, over-looking the narrow street, not more than fifty yards away from Earl's Court Road. She looked different from the young girl Banks met at his parents', he thought, as she greeted him at the door and asked him in. Her hair was longer, for a start, almost down to her shoulders, and it was blonde with dark roots. The little stud was gone from below her lip, leaving a small flaw in her clear skin, and she looked closer to thirty than to twenty. She also seemed more self-possessed, more mature than Banks remembered her.

'Come into the back,' she said. 'That's where the office is.' An electric fan stood on the table by the open window, slowly turning through about ninety degrees every few seconds, sending out waves of lukewarm air. It was better than nothing.

'Everyone seems to work at home these days,' Banks said, sitting in a winged armchair. Corinne sat at an angle to him, cross-legged, the way some women seem to prefer, and he guessed that this was the space she used to discuss business when clients called at the flat. A jug of water thick with ice cubes sat on the table between them, along with two tumblers. Corinne managed to stretch her upper body forward and pour them both a glass while remaining cross-legged. Quite a feat, Banks thought, considering he couldn't even sit in that position comfortably in the first place. But Corinne seemed to move with a dancer's grace and economy that spoke of Pilates and yoga.

'They say tea's refreshing in hot weather,' she said, 'but the thought of drinking anything hot doesn't have much appeal at the moment.'

'This is fine,' said Banks. 'Thank you.'

Corinne was wearing a plain orange T-shirt tucked into her jeans, and she wore a Celtic cross on a silver chain around her neck. She was barefoot, Banks noticed, and her toenails were unpainted. Occasionally, as she talked or listened, her heart-shaped face would tilt to one side, she would bite her lower lip and her fingers would stray to the cross. Sunlight gilded the leaves outside the window and their shadows danced pavanes over the pale blue walls, stirred by the lightest of breezes.

'Well,' she said, 'I must say you had me all intrigued on the telephone. I'm sorry if I . . .'

'My fault entirely. I wasn't being clear. I hope you don't take me for the kind of man who goes chasing his brother's fiancée?'

She gave a brief, tight little smile that indicated to Banks that perhaps all was not as it should be in the fiancé department, but he let it go for the time being. She would get to it in her own time, if she wanted.

'Anyway,' he went on, 'it's Roy I want to talk to you about.'

'What about him?'

'Do you have any idea where he is?'

'What do you mean?'

Banks explained about the phone call and Roy's absence. 'I got your number from his mobile,' he said. 'He left it on the kitchen table.'

'That's not like him,' she said, frowning. 'None of it is. I can see why you'd be worried. Anyway, to answer your question, no, I don't know where he is. Do you think you should go to the police? I mean, I know you *are* the police, but . . .'

'I know what you mean,' said Banks. 'No, I don't think so. Not yet, at any rate. I don't think they'd be very interested. There could be a simple explanation. Do you know any of his friends?'

'Not really. There was another couple we used to go out with occasionally, Rupert and Natalie, but I don't think Roy has a lot of close friends.'

Banks didn't miss the 'used to', but he let it go for the moment. There was a Rupert in Roy's mobile phone book. Banks would ring him eventually, along with the rest of the names. 'Do you know a burly man with curly grey or fair hair?' he asked. 'He drives a big light-coloured car, an expensive model?'

Corinne thought for a moment, then she said, 'No. Sorry. Rupert drives a slate-grey Beemer and Natalie's got a little Beetle runaround.' She turned up her nose. 'A yellow one.'

'When did you last see Roy?'

'A week last Thursday.' She fingered the cross. 'Look, I might as well tell you, things haven't being going all that well for us lately.'

'I'm sorry to hear that. Any particular reason?'

'I think he's been seeing someone else.' She gave a little shrug. 'It doesn't matter, really. I mean, it's not as if it was serious. We've only been going out about a year. We're not living together or anything.'

'But I thought you were supposed to be engaged?'

'I think that was part of the problem, really. I mean, I'd brought it up, and Roy's impulsive. Neither of us is ready for marriage yet. We called it off, went back to the way we were. That was when the trouble started, really. I don't suppose you can take a big step back like that and expect a relationship to continue the way it was, can you?'

So the engagement had been postponed, or demoted to going steady, and the relationship had cooled, like Banks' and Michelle's. Little brother up to his usual tricks. At least Corinne was to be spared the indignity of being wife number four. 'Even so,' Banks said, 'it must still hurt. I'm sorry. Have you any idea *who* he's seeing?'

'No. I don't even know if I'm right for sure. It's just a feeling. You know, little things.'

Well, Banks thought, there were a few possible names and numbers in Roy's mobile phone book and call list. 'How recently?' he asked.

'Just this past few weeks.'

'And before that?'

'Things were fine. At least, I thought they were.'

'Was there anything bothering him when you saw him last?'

'Nothing that I could see. He seemed much the same as ever. Except . . .'

'Yes?'

'Well, as I said, little things, things a woman notices. Forgetfulness, distance, distraction. That wasn't like him.'

'But he wasn't depressed or worried about anything?'

'Not that you'd know. I just thought he had someone else on his mind and he'd rather be with her.'

'What about drugs?'

'What about them?'

'Come off it. Don't tell me you and Roy never snorted a line, smoked a spliff.'

'So what if we did?'

'Apart from it being illegal, which we'll ignore for the moment, when you get into the drug world you get to meet some nasty people. Did Roy owe his dealer money, for example?'

'Look, it wasn't much. Just recreational. A gram on the weekends, that sort of thing. Nothing more than he can easily afford.'

'All right,' said Banks. 'How much do you know about his business dealings?'

'Not a lot.'

'But you are his accountant, right?'

'Roy takes care of his own books.'

'Oh. I thought that was how you met?'

'Well, yes,' said Corinne. 'He got audited and a friend recommended me to him.' She twirled her Celtic cross. 'Most of my clients are in the entertainment business – writers, musicians, artists – nobody really big league, but a few decent, steady earners. Roy was a bit different, to say the least, but I needed the money. And before you ask, everything was above board.' She narrowed her eyes. 'Roy once told me he was sure you thought he was a crook.'

'I don't think he's a crook,' Banks said, not being entirely truthful. 'I think maybe he stretches the law a bit, finds the odd loophole, that's all. Plenty of businessmen do. What I'm wondering, though, is whether he had any reason to run off. Was his business in difficulties? Had he lost a lot of money, made some errors of judgement?'

'No. Roy's books were good enough for me and the taxman.'

'Look, I've seen his house,' said Banks. 'The Porsche, the

plasma TV, the gadgets. Roy obviously makes quite a lot of money somehow. You said he makes it legitimately. Have you any idea how?'

'He's a gambler. He still plays the stock market to some extent, but mostly he finances business ventures.'

'What kinds?'

'All kinds. Lately he's been specializing in technology and private healthcare.'

'Here?'

'All over the place. Sometimes he gets involved in French or German operations. He has connections in Brussels, the EU. He also spends a lot of time and energy in America. He loves New York. Roy's no fool. He knows better than to put all his eggs in one basket. That's one reason he's been so successful.' She paused. 'You don't know your brother at all, do you?' Before Banks could answer, she went on, 'He's a remarkable man in many ways, a financier who can quote Kierkegaard or Schopenhauer at dinner. But he never forgets where he came from. The crushing poverty. He dragged himself out of it, made something of himself, and it's what drives him. He never wants to end up like that again.'

What kind of a line had Roy been spinning Corinne? Banks wondered. Their childhood hadn't been that bad. Admittedly, she had only seen the relatively decent council house his parents lived in now, and not the back-to-back terrace behind the brickworks where they had lived until Banks was eleven and Roy six. But even then 'crushing poverty' was pushing it a bit. They had always been fed and clothed and never lacked for love. Banks's father had always been in work until the eighties. What did it matter that the toilet had been outside, down the street, and the whole family had had to share a tin bath tub which they filled with kettles of water boiled on the gas cooker? They were no different from thousands of other working-class families growing up in the fifties and sixties.

'It's true we were never very close,' Banks admitted, slapping a fly from the knee of his trousers. 'What can I say? It just happens that way sometimes. We haven't got that much in common.'

'Oh, I know all about that,' said Corinne. 'I can't stand my younger sister. She's a snob and a misery-guts.'

'I don't hate Roy. I just don't know him, and I'm worried he's in some sort of trouble. Something that's made him run away in a hurry.' Banks remembered the CD he had found in Roy's Blue Lamps jewel-case and slipped it out of his pocket. 'I wonder if you could help me with something?'

'Of course.'

It didn't take Corinne long to put the CD in her computer and bring up the list of contents. The icons were JPEGs: 1,232 of them in all. Some were merely numbered, others had names like Natasha, Kiki and Kayla. Corinne opened her image viewer and set a slideshow going.

Banks was looking over her shoulder, hand resting on the back of the chair, when the images started coming up on the screen. The first showed a naked woman with a man's erect penis in her mouth, semen dribbling down her chin, a stoned look in her eyes; the next showed the same man entering the woman from behind, an obviously feigned look of ecstasy on her face. After that came several photos of an extremely attractive blonde teenager in various stages of undress and revealing positions.

That was enough.

Corinne abruptly ended the slideshow and ejected the disc. 'I suppose that just shows you that Roy isn't much different from most men, when you get right down to it,' she said, moving away from the computer. Banks could see that her face was red. She handed the disc back to Banks. 'Maybe you'd like to keep this?'

'Is that all that's on it?' he asked.

'Short of looking at all 1,232 files to make sure, I'd say that's a pretty good guess. Of course, you're welcome to check them all out, but not here, if you don't mind. I find that sort of thing a bit demeaning. Not to mention insulting.'

Well, Banks thought, it had been worth a try. Though he had nothing at all against images of naked women, either alone or with partners, he had seen enough of the sordid side of the porn business to know how bad it could get, especially if children were involved. From what he had seen, though, Roy's collection looked ordinary, the girls of age, if a little on the young side. In a way, it made him feel a bit closer to Roy to find out that he was only human after all, the dirty devil. If only their mother knew. But then his policeman's mind kicked in. If Roy had taken these images himself, on a digital camera, say, rather than simply downloaded them from the Internet, then he could be involved in a sleazy business.

'Did Roy have anything to do with Internet porn?' he asked Corinne, forgetting that she might not be the best person to ask.

'Always ready to think the worst of him, aren't you?' she said.

'I can't see why you're always so quick to leap to his defence after what he's done to you.'

Corinne flushed with anger.

'Believe it or not, I'm trying to help,' said Banks.

'Well, you've got a funny way of showing it.' She looked towards the CD and made a face. 'Anyway, there's your evidence, for what it's worth.'

Banks took the CD. At some point he would examine it more closely, study each of the 1,232 images, just to make sure. Hotel rooms and outdoor locations had been identified from background features in Internet porn. One victim of child pornography in America had been identified from a blurred-out school logo on her T-shirt. If Roy *had* taken any of these pictures, there was a chance of finding out where he had taken them, and who the models were, should it come to that. But not here, not now.

He had just about run out of questions to ask Corinne, and he could see that she had become edgy, anxious for him to leave. Whether it was the effect of the images on the CD or something else, he definitely felt that he had outstayed his welcome. But as he put his jacket on, he remembered the pen-like object he had found in Roy's office drawer. Maybe Corinne knew what it was. He took it out of his pocket and held it out to her. 'Any idea what this is?'

Corinne took the object from Banks, eyed it closely and removed the cap. 'It's a portable mini-USB drive. 'For storing information.'

'Like that CD?'

'Same idea, but not quite as much space. This one's got 256 megs, not 700. Handy, though. You can clip it in your inside pocket, just like a pen.'

'Can we see what's on it?'

Corinne clearly wasn't comfortable delving into Roy's private affairs, especially after what she had just seen on the CD. Banks had been at his job for so long that he had got used to digging deep into a person's private life. As far as the police were concerned, there are no secrets, especially in a major investigation. He often didn't like what he found, but he'd developed a tolerance for people's little quirks over the years.

Most people, when you get past their facade of normality, have some sort of guilty secret, something they've tried to keep from the rest of the world, and Banks had come across most of them in his time, from the harmless hoarders of newspapers and magazines, whose homes were like labyrinths of tottering columns of print, to the secret cross-dressers and lonely fetishists. Of course, they were all grief- and horror-stricken, humiliated that someone had found out their little secrets, but to Banks it was nothing special.

Corinne's reaction made him realize for the first time in a while that what he did was unnatural and invasive. In the short time he had been with her, he had as good as implied that her ex-fiancé, *his* brother, was involved in drugs, illicit sex and fraud. All in a day's work for him, perhaps, but not for a basically nice person like Corinne. Had the job made him insensitive? Banks thought of Penny Cartwright again, and her violent reaction to his suggestion of dinner last night. Was it something to do with what he did for a living, the way he looked at the world, at people? She was a free spirit, after all, so did that make him the enemy?

Corinne plugged the USB drive into her computer. 'Here we go,' she said, and Banks looked over her shoulder at the monitor.

4

Shortly after half-past six that Saturday evening, Annie walked out of the Oval tube station, where she'd been crammed in an overheated carriage with about five million people on their way home from shopping or visiting friends and relatives, and headed down Camberwell New Road, past the park on the corner. Young lads with shaved heads and bare upper bodies lounged on the grass drinking cans of lager and flexing their tattoos, leering at every attractive woman who passed by. A group of younger kids had set up makeshift goals with their discarded T-shirts and were playing football. Just watching them made Annie sweat.

Then she saw Phil.

He was on the other side of the street, walking a dog, some sort of little terrier on a lead. But it was him, she was sure of it. The same lazy grace in his step, the casual but expensive clothes, chin up, slightly receding hairline. Hardly looking, she dashed into the road, aware of horns blaring around her, and she had almost made it across when his attention was attracted by the noise.

He paused and looked towards her, puzzled. Annie got to the pavement and stopped, oblivious to the cursing of the last driver who had barely missed her. It wasn't Phil. There was a superficial similarity, but that was all. The man bent to pat his dog, then with a curious backward glance, he carried on walking towards the traffic lights. Annie leaned against a lamppost until her heartbeat returned to normal, and cursed. This wasn't the first time she thought she'd seen him; she would have to be more careful in future, less jumpy. If she was going to be realistic about it, she had to realize that bumping into him in a street in London was the last thing that was likely to happen.

She was still wired from the train journey. She would have to calm down. She had just made the three twenty-five and had even managed to find a seat in the quiet car, but no matter how many windows had been open, it had still been too hot. And she had been thinking about Phil, which was probably why her mind had fooled her into thinking she had actually seen him across the street. Throughout most of the journey, she had read the tabloids, scouring the pages for any whiff of Phil, but had found nothing, as usual. She had to get a grip on herself.

Despite the rule of quiet, more than one mobile rang during the journey, and Annie could also hear the overspill from someone's personal headphones. It had made her think of Banks, and again she started wondering where the hell he was and what he had to do with Jennifer Clewes's murder. According to the woman with the baby, Banks had left under his own steam that morning, but none of this explained what the hell was going on.

Annie found the house just off Lothian Road. The two DCs assigned to watch the flat were still sitting in the kitchen, the man with his feet on the table, shirtsleeves rolled up, chewing on a matchstick and reading through a pile of letters, and the woman sipping tea as she flipped through a stack of *Hello!* magazines. Two tipped cigarette butts lay crushed in a Royal Doulton saucer. Somehow, both detectives managed to look like naughty school kids caught in the act, though neither showed any trace of guilt. Annie introduced herself.

'And how are things in the frozen north?' asked the man, whose name was DC Sharpe, keeping his feet firmly on the kitchen table and the matchstick in the corner of his mouth. He looked as if he hadn't shaved in about four days.

'Hot,' said Annie. 'What are you doing?'

Sharpe gestured to the letters. 'Just nosing about a bit. Afraid there's nothing very interesting, just bills, junk mail and bank statements, all pretty much as you'd expect. No really juicy stuff.

People don't write letters the way they used to, do they? It's all e-mail and texting these days, innit?'

Considering that Sharpe looked about twenty-one, it was odd to hear him being so critical of 'these days', as they were probably the only days he knew. But the irony in his tone wasn't lost on Annie, and the callous disregard which both of them seemed to display towards the victim's home angered her. 'OK, thanks for keeping an eye out,' she said. 'You can leave now.'

Sharpe looked at his partner, DC Handy, and raised an eyebrow. The match in the corner of his mouth twitched. 'You're not our guv,' he said.

Annie sighed. 'Fine,' she said. 'If that's the way you want to play it. My patience is already running a bit thin.' She took out her mobile, went into the hallway and phoned DI Brooke at Kennington station. After a few pleasantries and the promise of a drink together that evening, Annie explained the situation briefly, then went back into the kitchen, smiled at Sharpe and handed him the phone.

The moment he put it to his ear, his feet shot off the table and he sat bolt upright in his chair, almost swallowing his matchstick. His partner, who hadn't said a word so far, frowned at him. When the call was over, Sharpe scowled at Annie, his face red, turned to the woman and said, 'Come on, Jackie, we've got to go.' Then he made a show of swaggering as slowly as possible out of the house, and with one mean, backward glance mouthed, 'Bitch,' and stuck his middle finger in the air.

Annie felt inordinately satisfied when that little scene was over, and she sat down and poured herself a cup of tea. It was lukewarm, but she couldn't be bothered to make a fresh pot. One of the DCs had opened a window, but it was no use; there was no breeze to bring relief. An empty strand of flypaper twisted in what little air current there was over the sink.

While she was waiting, Annie took out her mobile and rang Gristhorpe in Eastvale. Dr Glendenning had finished the post-mortem on Jennifer Clewes and had found nothing other than the gunshot wound. Her stomach contents consisted of a partially digested ham and tomato sandwich eaten at least two hours before death, which bore out Templeton's theory that she had driven up from London and probably stopped at a motorway service station on the way. Glendenning wouldn't commit himself to time of death, except to narrow it down to between one and four in the morning. The SOCOs were still working the scene and would get around to examining Banks's cottage as soon as they could.

As it turned out, Annie didn't have long to wait for Jennifer's flatmate. At about a quarter to seven, the front door opened and she heard a woman's voice call out. 'Jenn? Hello, Jenn? Are you back yet?'

When the owner of the voice walked into the kitchen and saw Annie she stopped dead in her tracks, put her hand to her chest and backed away. 'What is it?' she asked. 'Who are you? What are you doing here?'

Annie took out her warrant card and walked over to her. The young woman studied it.

'Yorkshire?' she said. 'I don't understand. You broke into our house. How did you do that? I didn't see any damage to the lock.'

'We've got keys for all occasions,' said Annie.

'What do you want with me?'

'Are you Kate Nesbit, Jennifer Clewes's flatmate?'

'Yes,' she answered.

'Maybe you'd better sit down,' said Annie, pulling out a chair at the table.

Kate was still dazed as she lowered herself into the chair. Her eyes lighted on the saucer and her nostrils twitched. 'Who's been smoking? We don't allow smoking in the flat.'

Annie cursed herself for not getting rid of the butts, though their smell still lingered in the warm air.

'It wasn't me,' she said, putting the saucer on the draining board. She didn't know where the waste bin was.

'You mean someone else has been here?'

Annie lingered by the sink. 'Just two detectives from your local station. I had words with them. I'm sorry they were so rude. It was necessary to get in, believe me.'

'*Necessary*?' Kate shook her head. She was a pretty girl, in a very wholesome, no-nonsense sort of way, with her blonde hair cut short, black-rimmed oval glasses and a healthy pink glow on her cheeks. She looked athletic, Annie thought, and it was easy to visualize her tall, rangy frame on horseback. Even the clothes she wore, white shorts and a green rugby-style shirt, looked sporty. 'What's going on?' she asked. 'It's not good news, is it?'

'I'm afraid not.' Annie sat down opposite her. 'Drink?'

'Not for me. Tell me what it is. It's not Daddy, is it? It can't be. I was just there.'

'You were visiting your parents?'

'In Richmond, yes. I go every Saturday when I'm not working.'

'No,' said Annie. 'It's not your father. Look, this might be a bit of a shock, but I need you to look at it.' She opened her briefcase and slipped out the photograph of Jennifer Clewes that Peter Darby had taken at the morgue. It wasn't a bad one – she looked peaceful enough and there were no signs of violence, no blood – but there was no doubt that it was a photograph of a dead person. 'Is this Jennifer Clewes, your flatmate?'

Kate put her hand to her mouth. 'Oh, my God,' she said, tears in her eyes. 'What happened to her? Did she have an accident?'

'In a way. Look, do you have any idea why she was driving up to Yorkshire late last night?'

'I didn't know that she was.'

'Did you know she'd gone out?'

'Yes. We were home last night. I mean, we don't live in one another's pockets, we have our own rooms, but . . . My God, I don't believe this.' She put her hands to her face. Annie could see that her whole body was shaking.

'What happened, Kate?' Annie said. 'Please, try and focus for me.'

Kate took a deep breath. It seemed to help a little. 'There was nothing we wanted to watch on telly, so we were just watching a DVD. *Bend It Like Beckham*. Jenn's mobile went off and she swore. We were enjoying the film. Anyway, she went into her bedroom to answer it and when she came back she said there was an emergency and she had to go out, to just carry on watching the film without her. She said she wasn't sure when she would be back. Now you're telling me she'll never come back.'

'What time was this?'

'I don't know. I suppose it'd be about half-past ten, a quarter to eleven.'

That was consistent with the timing, Annie thought. It would take about four hours to drive from Kennington to Eastvale, depending on traffic, and Jennifer Clewes had been killed between one and four o'clock in the morning, about three miles short of her destination. 'Did she give you any idea about *where* she might be going?'

'None at all. Just that she had to go. Right then. But that's just like her.'

'Oh?'

'What I mean is she wasn't very forthcoming about what she was doing, where she was going. Even if I needed to know when she'd be back, for meals and such. She could be very inconsiderate.' Kate put her hand to her mouth. 'Oh, listen to me. How terrible.' She started crying.

'It's all right,' said Annie, trying to comfort her. 'Try to stay calm. Did Jennifer seem worried, frightened?'

'No, not exactly frightened. But she was pale, as if she'd had a shock or something.'

'Have you any idea who made the call?'

'No. I'm sorry.'

'What did you do after she left?'

'Watched the rest of the film and went to bed. Look, what's happened? Did she have a car crash? Was that it? It can't have been her fault. She was always a careful driver and she never drank over the limit.'

'It's nothing like that,' said Annie.

'Then what? Please tell me.'

She'd have to find out sooner or later, Annie thought. She got up, took a couple of tumblers from the glass-fronted cupboard and filled them with tap water. She passed one to Kate and sat down again. She could hardly bear Kate's imploring expression, the wide, fearful eyes and furrowed brow, the tumbler shaking in her hands. When Kate heard what Annie had to tell her, her life would never be the same again; it would be forever tainted, forever marked by murder.

'Jennifer was shot,' Annie said in a soft, flat voice. 'I'm really sorry.'

'Shot?' Kate echoed. 'No . . . she . . . But I don't under-stand . . .'

'Neither do we, Kate. That's what we're trying to find out. Do you know of anyone who would want to harm her?'

'Harm Jenn? Of course not.' The words came out in gulps, as if Kate were desperate for air.

Kate put the glass down, but she missed the edge of the table. It fell to the floor and shattered. She stood up and put her hand to her mouth, then, without warning, her eyes turned up, and before Annie could reach her she crumpled in a heap on the kitchen floor.

•

'Look,' said Corinne, 'are you sure we should be doing this? These are Roy's private files, after all.'

'It's a bit late to get squeamish now,' said Banks. 'Besides,' he said, gesturing to the CD, 'maybe it's just more of the same.'

Corinne gave him a dirty look and turned back to the screen. 'Well,' she said, 'at least the drive isn't password-protected.'

'And given Roy's concern with privacy,' said Banks, 'that prob-ably means there's nothing really confidential on it.' Or nothing *incriminating*, he thought.

'So what's the point?'

'Perhaps it's something he wanted me to find and read? He'd know I'd be no good at cracking passwords and such. Besides, I need anything I can get. Business contacts, activities, habits, anything.'

'There's quite a mix of stuff,' said Corinne, scrolling down. 'Some Word documents, Money files, Excel spreadsheets, Power-Point presentations, market-research reports, memos, letters.'

'Can you print it out?'

'Some of it.' Corinne started selecting files and the printer hummed into action. It was fast, Banks noticed.

'Can you also copy the contents to another thingamajig?'

'You mean a removable USB hard drive?'

'Whatever. Can you do it?'

'Of course I can. Or at least I could if I had a spare one. Will a CD do?'

'Fine,' Banks said. 'Just as long as we have a copy. The CD as well.'

'What are you going to do with it?'

'I'm going to post them to myself,' said Banks. 'That way I'll have back-ups.'

'But it might mean nothing at all. Maybe Roy's just run off with his new girlfriend. Have you thought of that?'

Banks had. 'Look,' he said, 'it's true that I don't know Roy very well, and I'll take your word that he's an imaginative and bold businessman rather than a crooked one, but you didn't hear the phone call. He sounded *scared*, Corinne. Is that like him?'

Corinne frowned. 'No. I mean, I'm not saying he's a hero or anything, but he doesn't usually back down from difficult situations. Maybe he's been kidnapped or something?'

'Has he ever mentioned that possibility?'

'No. But you hear about it sometimes, don't you?'

'Not that often. But trust me,' Banks said, 'something's wrong. There are just too many loose ends. The missing computer, for a start. If someone went to the trouble to take Roy's entire computer and all the storage devices they could find, then doesn't that seem suspicious to you? They only missed the USB drive and the CD because both were hidden.' Hidden in plain view, Banks might have added, like Poe's purloined letter. 'According to the neighbour, when Roy got in the car with another man, neither was carrying anything. Someone must have gone back and taken the computer stuff between about half-past nine last night and the time I arrived early this afternoon.'

'Has it occurred to you that he might have come back and taken it himself?' Corinne asked.

'Why should he? Where would he have taken it? Besides, his car's still in the garage. He doesn't own another, does he?'

'No. Just his darling Porsche. You're right, if he went anywhere, he'd have taken the Porsche. He loves that car.'

'I don't suppose he has another house, does he? Somewhere he'd go if he had to make a run for it? A villa on the Algarve, perhaps?'

'Roy's not particularly fond of Portugal. And he doesn't own a place in Tuscany or Provence, or anywhere else, as far as I know. At least, he never took me to one. He loves travel and holidays but he says it's too much hassle owning property abroad. It ties you down to just one place.'

'He's probably right.'

Corinne bit on her lower lip. 'Now you've got me really worried.'

Banks put his hand on her shoulder, then took it away quickly, not wanting her to get the wrong idea. She didn't react. 'I'll find Roy,' he said. 'But let's have a look at some of these files first. They might help us find out where to start looking. You know more about his business affairs than I do.'

'That's not saying much. Anyway, there's nothing here that looks even the remotest bit dodgy.'

'How can you tell?'

Corinne faltered a little. 'Well, I don't suppose I can, really. As I said, the drive isn't protected or encrypted, and Roy's hardly likely to write down references to importing heroin, is he?'

'So there's no way of telling?'

As Corinne spoke, she opened and scanned various files. The printer was still running. 'Not from these files. Everything *looks* above board. I think if he were trying to hide that sort of thing, there'd be *something* to set off alarm bells. It's not that easy. Besides, as I've been trying to tell you, Roy's not like that.'

'What about the Money files?'

'Simple income and expenditure. Company profit and loss sheets. Investment returns. Bank statements. Some offshore banking. His finances are in pretty good shape.'

'Roy did a lot of offshore banking?'

'Anyone working at his level of income has to. It's a matter of keeping tax liabilities as low as possible. It's not illegal. Mostly we're looking at memos and correspondence here. You are, of course, welcome to examine them all at your leisure, especially as you took them in the first place, but I'd say you'd be wasting your time. Roy's on the board of a few hi-tech companies, mostly interested in miniature information-storage devices, like that USB hard drive, flash memory cards, that sort of thing. Given the way the world's going, with mobiles, digital cameras, PDAs, MP3 players, and various combinations, it seems a wise enough area to be in. Smaller is better. As a board member, he's paid dividends.'

'What else is there?'

'Recently Roy's become interested in private healthcare. I remember him talking about it. Look.' She activated a PowerPoint presentation that extolled the virtues, and profits, of investing in a string of cosmetic-surgery clinics. 'He's on the board of a chain of health centres, a pharmaceutical company, a fitness club.'

'It all sounds very dull,' said Banks.

'I told you so. But guess who's the one with the Porsche.'

'No need to rub it in. Is there more?'

'A few market-research reports on health and hi-tech, the kind of reports you buy, the expensive kind.'

'I was hoping for a few names.'

'They're here,' said Corinne. 'Memos and letters between Roy and various directors and companies he was involved with. Julian Harwood, for example.'

'I've heard that name.'

'You might well have done. He's quite big in the private health-care field these days. Directs the chain of clinics Roy's involved with. Anything from cancer to breast enlargement. Actually, Roy and Julian have been mates for years.'

'He's not a doctor, though?'

'No, a businessman.'

'Have you met him?'

'Uh-huh.'

'You don't sound impressed.'

'That's maybe because that's exactly what he sets out to do. Impress people. Frankly, I always found him a bit boorish, but it takes all sorts. It still doesn't make him a crook, though.'

'So you don't think there's anything in there to suggest that Roy was involved in any sort of illegal or dangerous business ventures?'

'You can see for yourself it all looks quite kosher. I don't know about dangerous, though.'

'What do you mean?'

'Well, just because it *looks* clean, that doesn't mean the hi-tech companies he worked with weren't selling illegal weapons-guidance systems to terrorists, or that the clinics weren't involved in genetic manipulation. Maybe the cosmetic surgery clinics gave gangsters new faces.'

Banks laughed. 'Like *Seconds*, you mean?'

Corinne frowned. 'I don't know what you mean.'

'It's a film. Rock Hudson. A man gets a new face, new identity.'

'Oh, I see. Well, I suppose my point is that they're not exactly going to announce things like that in letters six feet high, are they? It's a wide-open world. You should know that. Even the most innocuous-looking enterprise on the surface can turn out to be a whole different matter if you dig a little deeper.'

Banks did know that, and it didn't make him feel a great deal easier about Roy.

Corinne collected the pile of printed paper, put it in a folder and handed it to him. 'Here. Be my guest.'

Banks picked up the folder, put it in his briefcase and stood up. 'Thanks a lot,' he said. 'You've been very generous with your time.'

'Don't worry about it,' said Corinne. 'Just find Roy.'

'I will.'

'When you do, will you let me know?'

'Of course. In the meantime, you take good care of yourself. If you think of anything else, or there's anything you need, well . . . you can ring me on Roy's mobile. He left it on the kitchen table. That's how I got your number.'

Corinne frowned. 'That's not like him,' she said. 'Not like him at all.'

'No,' said Banks, and left.

•

Annie hadn't seen anyone faint since she was about nine, when one of the women at the artists' commune where she had been raised keeled over in the middle of dinner. Even then she over-heard some of the adults talking later, and the general agreement seemed to be that drugs were the cause. In the case of Kate Nesbit, it was most likely shock, and perhaps the heat.

Remembering her first aid, Annie acted quickly and placed Kate's feet on a chair to elevate her legs above heart level to restore the flow of blood to the brain, then turned her head to one side so she didn't swallow her tongue. She leaned close and listened. Kate was breathing without difficulty. Lacking smelling salts – never, in fact, having seen or smelt any – Annie just made sure that Kate hadn't cracked her skull when she fell and then went over to the sink to pour another glass of water. She found a tea towel, dampened it with cold water and brought it over with the glass, then she got another glass of water for herself. Kate was stirring now, her eyes open. Annie mopped her brow then lifted her into a sitting position so she could sip the water. As soon as Kate said she felt well enough, Annie helped her back into her chair, then cleared up the broken glass before continuing the interview.

'I'm so sorry,' Kate said. 'I don't know what came over me.'

'That's all right. I'm just sorry I couldn't find an easier way to break it to you.'

'But *shot*? Jenn? I can hardly believe it. Surely that sort of thing doesn't happen to people like us?'

Annie wished she could say it didn't.

'What was it?' Kate went on. 'Robbery? Not . . . like that other poor girl?'

'Claire Potter?'

'Yes. It was on the news for weeks. They still haven't found the man. You don't think . . . ?'

'We don't know yet. Jennifer wasn't sexually assaulted, though.'

'Thank God for that, at least.'

'Her things are missing,' Annie said. 'Handbag, purse. So it could be robbery. Do you know if she carried much money with her?'

'No, never. She always said she could buy everything she wanted with her credit card or debit card.'

That was true enough these days, Annie knew. The only time people seemed to have a lot of cash on hand was when they had just withdrawn some from a cashpoint. 'Look,' Annie went on, 'you shared the flat with Jennifer. You must have been close. I know you're upset, but I'm relying on you to help me. What was going on in Jennifer's life? Men. Work. Family. Friends. Anything. Think. Tell me about it. There has to be an explanation if this wasn't just some senseless random attack.'

'Maybe it was,' said Kate. 'I mean those things do happen, don't they? People killing people for no real reason.'

'Yes, but not as often as you think,' said Annie. 'Most victims know their killers. That's why I want you to think deep and tell me anything you know.'

Kate sipped some water. 'I don't know,' she said. 'I mean, we weren't that close.'

'Did she have any close friends?'

'There was this girl she used to go to school with, up in Shrewsbury, where she grew up. She came around once or twice.'

'Can you remember her name?'

'Melanie. Melanie Scott.'

Annie definitely got the feeling that Melanie Scott wasn't on Kate's list of favourite people. 'How close were they?'

'They went on holiday together last year. It was before Jenn moved in, but she told me all about it. Sicily. She said it was awesome.'

'Do you have an address for Melanie?'

'I think so. She lives in Hounslow, I remember. Out Heathrow way. I'll be able to dig it out before you go.'

'Fine. What was Jennifer like?'

'Quiet, hard-working. And she really cared about people, you know. Maybe she should have been a social worker.'

In Annie's experience, the world of social work was hardly staffed by caring people. Well-meaning, perhaps, but that was a different thing in her mind. 'What about all those mysterious comings and goings?'

'That's just me being silly, really. I like to know where people are and when they'll be back. Jenn didn't always bother to let me know. But she wasn't a party girl, if that's what you mean, or a clubber. I think she was actually rather shy. But she was bright and ambitious. Like I said, she cared about people. And she was funny. I liked her sense of humour. We used to watch *The Office* on DVD together and we'd both crack up laughing. I mean, we'd both worked somewhere like that. We knew what it was like. I'll miss all that,' Kate added. 'I'll miss Jenn.' She started to cry again and reached for the tissues. 'I'm sorry. I just can't . . .'

'It's all right,' said Annie. 'Is that what you always called her? Jenn, not Jenny?'

Kate sniffled and blew her nose. 'Yes. It's what she liked to be called. She hated Jenny. Mostly people called her Jennifer, though. I don't know. She just wasn't a Jenny. Like I'm not a Katy or a Kathy, I suppose.'

And like I'm not Anne, thought Annie. Funny the way names, contractions especially, tended to stick. She had been Annie all the time growing up in the artists' colony, and only at university had people called her Anne. 'The two of you must have talked,' Annie said. 'What sort of things did she talk about?'

'The usual things.'

Christ, thought Annie, this was like trying to get water out of a stone. 'Did you notice any change in her mood or behaviour recently?' she asked.

'Yes. She seemed very nervous and jumpy lately. It wasn't like her.'

'Nervous? Since when?'

'Just this past week or so.'

'Did she tell you what it was about?'

'No. She was even more quiet than usual.'

'Do you think there's any connection between that and her reaction to last night's phone call, the late drive?'

'I don't know,' said Kate. 'There might have been.'

The problem was, Annie realized, that Jennifer's mobile had been taken along with everything else. Still, the phone-company records might help.

'Do you know which network she used?'

'Orange.'

Annie made a note to follow up, then asked, 'Do you have anything with her handwriting on it?'

'What?'

'A note or something? Letter? Postcard?'

Kate turned to a corkboard on the wall by the door. A number of Far Side cartoons were pinned there, along with a few postcards. Kate went over and unpinned one of them, a view of the Eiffel Tower, and carried it over to Annie. 'Jenn went to Paris for a weekend break in March,' Kate said. 'She sent me this. We had a good laugh because she got back here before it did.'

'Did she go by herself?' Annie asked, taking a photocopy of the note found in Jennifer Clewes's back pocket from her briefcase to compare the handwriting.

'Yes. She said she'd always wanted to go on the Eurostar and they had a special deal. She went around all the art galleries. She loved going to galleries and museums.'

To Annie's untrained eye, the handwriting looked the same, but she would have to get an expert to examine it. 'Can I keep this?' she asked.

'I suppose so.'

Annie put the photocopy and the postcard in her briefcase. 'You said she went alone,' Annie went on, 'but isn't Paris supposed to be the city of romance?'

'Jenn wasn't going out with anyone back then.'

'But she has been more recently?'

'I think so.'

'Just think so?'

'Well, Jenn could be very private. I mean, she didn't kiss and tell, that sort of thing. But she'd been getting a lot of calls on her mobile lately, and making a lot. And she'd stayed out all night on a couple of occasions. She didn't usually do that.'

'Since when?'

'A few weeks.'

'But this started before the odd behaviour?'

'Yes.'

'Did she tell you his name? I assume it was a he?'

'Good Lord, yes, of course. But she didn't mention any names. She didn't even tell me that she *was* seeing someone. It was just a feeling I got from her behaviour. Intuition. I put two and two together.'

'But you said she seemed nervous and jumpy. That's hardly

the way a new relationship is supposed to make you feel, is it? And why was she so secretive? Didn't you ever talk about personal matters, say if one of you split up with a boyfriend or something?'

'We've only been sharing six months,' said Kate. 'And nothing like that's happened to either of us in that time. There's that one bloke keeps pestering her, but that's all.'

'Who?'

'Her ex-boyfriend. His name's Victor, but that's all I know about him. He keeps ringing and hanging around. You don't think . . . ?'

'I don't think anything yet,' said Annie. 'Are you sure you don't know his second name, where he lives?'

'Sorry,' said Kate. 'It was over before we started sharing. Or Jenn *thought* it was.'

'What did she think about it? Was she frightened of him?'

'No. Just annoyed, that's all.'

'How did you two come to be flatmates?'

Kate looked away. 'I'd rather not say. It's private.'

Annie leaned forward. 'Look, Kate,' she said, 'this is a murder investigation. Nothing's private. What was it? An advertisement in the papers? The Internet? What?'

Kate remained silent and Annie became aware of the tap dripping in the sink. She heard water from a hose spraying in a garden beyond the open window and a child squeal with delight.

'Kate?'

'Oh, all right, all right. I thought I was pregnant. I did one of those home tests, you know, but I didn't trust it.'

'How does Jennifer come into this?'

'It was where she worked. She was an administrator at a private women's health centre. They specialize in family planning.'

'Like the British Pregnancy Advisory Service? Marie Stopes?' Annie remembered both of these from her own unexpected brush with pregnancy nearly three years ago, though in the end she had gone NHS.

'It's a new chain. There are only a few of them open yet, as far as I know.'

'What's it called?'

'The Berger-Lennox Centre.'

'And they perform abortions?'

'Not at the centre itself, no, but they have satellite clinics, and they arrange for abortions to be performed. That's not all they do, though. They cover the whole range, really, do reliable pregnancy tests, give advice and counselling, physical exams, arrange for abortions or put you in touch with adoption agencies, social services, whatever. They take care of everything. And they're very discreet. One of my friends at work told me about them. Why, do you think it's important?'

'I don't know,' said Annie. But the one thing she did know was that abortion was a red flag for a number of fringe groups, and that people who worked at such clinics had been killed before. 'Do you have the address?'

'In my room. I'll get it for you when I get Melanie's.'

'Fine,' said Annie. 'So how did the two of you meet? You said Jennifer worked in administration.'

'Yes, she ran the business side of things. We got talking in the office while I was filling out the paperwork, that's all. She was explaining it to me, how the system worked, that sort of thing. We just sort of hit it off. We're about the same age and I think she felt a bit sorry for me. Anyway, it turned out I wasn't pregnant, and she asked me if I fancied a drink to celebrate. When we got talking we found out that neither of us was happy living where we were, so we decided to pool our resources and share. We didn't know each other well, but we got along all right.'

'Where did she live before?'

'I'm not sure exactly, but it was near King's Cross. She said it was a really tiny flat and the area wasn't very nice. She didn't like walking there by herself at night. There are a lot of prostitutes and drug addicts on the street. Can I have another glass of water, please?'

Annie wondered why she was asking, why she just didn't go and get it herself. It was *her* flat, after all. Shock, probably. The poor girl looked as if she was likely to faint again at any moment. Annie went over to the sink and filled the two glasses. A fat blue-bottle had got itself stuck on the flypaper and was pushing frantically with its legs, trying to get away, only succeeding in miring itself deeper in the sticky stuff with each new effort it made. Annie thought she knew what that felt like.

'Where did you live then?' she asked, handing over the water.

'Thank you. In Richmond. With my parents.'

'Why did you leave? Was it because you thought you were pregnant?'

'Oh, no. It wasn't anything to do with that. I never even told them. And the boy . . . well, he's long gone now. Richmond is just too far out. I was spending all my time commuting. I work in Clapham. I'm a librarian. It's only a couple of tube stops, and on a nice day I can walk if I've got enough time.'

'I see,' said Annie. 'Why do you think Jennifer was so secretive about this new boyfriend?'

'If you ask me,' Kate said, lowering her voice, 'I think he's married.'

That made sense, Annie thought. Jennifer probably wouldn't have bragged about a relationship with a married man. The fear of discovery was likely to make her nervous, on edge, and maybe the mobile was the safest way to communicate. No chance of getting his wife on the other end. 'But you have no idea what his name is or where he lives?'

'No. I'm sorry.'

'How did they meet?'

'I don't even know if I'm right about any of it,' said Kate. 'My mother always said I have too much imagination for my own good.'

'Guess. Where *might* Jennifer have met someone? What kind of places did she like to go? Nightclubs?'

'No, I've already told you she wasn't like that. Besides, she was usually too tired when she got back from work. She often worked late at the centre. I mean she'd go for a drink or a meal with friends from work now and then, and maybe the two of us would go to the pictures once in a while. Then there was her friend Melanie.'

'Could it have been someone she met at work?'

'It might have been. That's the most likely place, isn't it?'

Annie nodded. She knew that. Work was where she had met Banks and, in a way, Phil Keane. 'Why wasn't she out with him on Friday? It's the weekend, after all. People usually get together.'

'I don't know,' said Kate. 'She just said she was stopping in. She did say she was expecting a phone call at some time, but she didn't know exactly when.' Her face started twitching again as if she was about to cry. 'Should I have known? Should I have stopped her?'

Annie went over and put a hand on her shoulder. 'Calm down, Kate,' she said. 'There's nothing you could have done, no way you could have known.'

'But I feel so useless. Some friend I've turned out to be.'

'It's not your fault. The best thing you can do is try to answer my questions as clearly and calmly as possible. OK?'

Kate nodded but continued to sniffle and dab at her eyes and nose.

'This phone call came between half-past ten and a quarter to eleven?'

'Yes. I think so.'

'What about Jennifer's family?' Annie asked. 'Where do they live? How did she get along with them?'

'Fine, as far as I know,' said Kate. 'I mean, she didn't visit them that often, but they live in Shrewsbury. You don't when they're so far away, do you?'

'No,' said Annie, whose father lived even further away, in St Ives. 'Can you find their address for me, too? Now that we know it is Jennifer's body we found, someone will have to let them know what's happened.'

'Of course,' said Kate. 'I've got that one in my PDA. You know, in case of emergencies or anything. I never thought I'd need them for something like this.' She dabbed at her eyes again, fetched her shoulder bag and gave Annie the address.

Annie stood up. 'And now,' she said, 'can I have a look at Jennifer's room, while you dig out those other addresses?'

5

Banks left his car parked in Corinne's street, only a short walk from Roy's, took the District line from Earl's Court to Embankment and walked up to the main post office behind Trafalgar Square. There he bought a padded envelope and posted both CD copies – Roy's business files from the USB drive and the sex images – to himself at Western Area Headquarters. It was always a good idea, he thought, to have a back-up, preferably stored in a different location. He kept the original CD of JPEGs and the USB drive in his briefcase along with the papers Corinne had printed out for him.

After he had finished at the post office, he dropped in at the first newsagent's he saw and bought another packet of Silk Cut. While he was paying he noticed one of the headlines in the evening paper and looked closer. A young woman, as yet unidentified, had been found shot dead in a car outside Eastvale, North Yorkshire. No doubt if he'd been on duty he would have caught the case, but as things were, it would be Annie's. He didn't envy her having to deal with the media feeding-frenzy that guns always caused, but perhaps Gristhorpe would take care of the press, the way he usually did.

Banks lit a cigarette and started to walk. He had often done so when he worked on the Met, and sometimes it helped him sort out his feelings or solve a problem. Whether it did or not, he always enjoyed walking around the West End at night, no matter how much it had changed in character since his early days on the beat.

Outside the pubs, knots of people stood clutching pint glasses, laughing and joking. In Leicester Square, jugglers and fire-eaters entertained the crowds of American tourists in shorts and T-shirts who milled around drinking water from plastic bottles.

It was a sultry evening and the square was bustling, long queues for the Odeon, metal barriers up, some premiere or other and everyone hoping to catch a glimpse of a star. Banks remembered doing crowd duty there once as a young PC in the early seventies. One of the Bond films, *The Man With the Golden Gun*, he thought. But that had been a cold night, not far off Christmas, as he recalled, he and his fellow PCs linking arms to keep back the onlookers as flashbulbs popped (and they were flashbulbs back then) and the stars stepped out of their limos. He thought he saw Roger Moore and Britt Ekland, but he could have been wrong; he never was much of a celebrity-spotter.

Banks had loved going to the cinema back then. He and Sandra must have gone twice a week before the kids, if he was on the right shift, and sometimes if he was on evenings or nights they'd go to a matinee. Even after Brian was born they had got a neighbour to baby-sit now and then, until undercover work made it too difficult for him.

These days, he hardly ever went at all. The last few times he'd been to see a film, there'd always seemed to be someone talking, and the place was sickly with the smell of hot buttered popcorn, the floors sticky with spilled Coke. It wasn't so much like going to the cinema any more as it was like hanging out in a cafe where they showed moving pictures on the wall. There was a new multiplex in Eastvale, an extension of the Swainsdale Centre, but he hadn't been yet and probably never would.

Banks made his way into Soho. It was going on for nine now, still daylight, but the sun was low, the light fading, and he was hungry. He hadn't eaten since that wretched curry round the corner from Roy's place. Here the streets were just as crowded, outdoor tables at the restaurants and cafes on Old Compton Street, Greek Street, Dean Street, Frith Street overflowing. A whiff of marijuana drifted on the air, mingling with espresso, roasting garlic, olive oil and Middle Eastern spices. Neons and candlelight took on an unnatural glow in the purple twilight, smudged a little by the faint, lingering heat haze. Boys held hands as they walked down the street, or stood on street corners, leaning in towards one another. Beautiful young women in cool, flimsy clothing walked together laughing or hung on the arms of their dates.

Banks made it to Tottenham Court Road before the electronics shops closed and after little deliberation bought a laptop with a DVD-RW/CD-RW drive. It was light enough to carry easily in a compartment of his briefcase, and it would do everything he needed it to and more. It also didn't break his bank account, still bolstered by the insurance money from the fire. He took out the manual and various extra bits and pieces, put them in his brief-case, too, and left the packaging in the shop. After that, feeling hungry, he headed back to Soho.

On Dean Street, Banks found a restaurant he had eaten at once before, with Annie, and had enjoyed. Like all the others, the out-side tables were crowded and the frontage was fully open to the street. Nevertheless, Banks persevered inside and was rewarded with a tiny table in a corner, away from the street and the noise. It was no doubt the least desirable table in the house as far as most people were concerned, but it suited him perfectly. It was just as hot inside as out, so location made no difference as far as that was concerned, and a waitress came over almost immedi-ately with the menu. She even smiled at him.

Banks mopped his brow with the serviette and studied the options. The print was small and he reached for his cheap non-prescription reading glasses. He had found himself relying on them for reading the papers and doing crosswords more often lately.

It didn't take him long to settle on steak, done medium, chips and a half-bottle of Château Musar. He sipped at his first glass of wine while he was waiting for his meal and the rich, complex flavour was every bit as powerful as he remembered it. Annie had liked it, too.

Annie. What was he going to do about her? Why had he been

behaving like such a bastard after what she had done for him? She was seriously pissed off at him, he knew, but surely if he really tried . . . maybe he could break through the barrier of her anger. Truth be told, things had been shaky between them ever since they'd broken up. He had been jealous of Annie's relationships, and he knew that she was jealous of his. That was partly what had made his curt dismissal of her in the hospital so unforgivable. But the circumstances had been exceptional, he told himself. He had not been in his right mind.

His steak and chips arrived and Banks turned his thoughts back to Roy. With any luck, he would turn up *something* from the computer stuff – why would Roy hide it otherwise? – a name, a company, something that would send him in the right direction. The problem was that he would more likely than not turn up *too* much, and Banks didn't have a slew of DCs to send out on the streets to filter out the red herrings. Perhaps he could go back and enlist more of Corinne's help. She had said she would be willing.

For a moment, a shadow of concern for Corinne passed over him with a chill, and he shivered. Had he brought her danger along with Roy's business secrets? But he was sure he hadn't been followed to her house, nor was there anyone on his tail now. She would be all right, he assured himself. He would ring her first thing in the morning, just to make sure.

He had only once had dinner with Roy, he realized as he bit into the juicy fillet. They saw one another in passing at family gatherings, of course, though there had been few enough of those over the years, and Banks had been at Roy's first wedding, but as far as the two of them sitting down to dinner together, there was only the one occasion, and the invitation had come out of the blue, for no particular reason that Banks could gather.

It was in the mid-eighties, when the financial world was reeling with the shock of insider-trading scandals. Whatever he was now, Roy was a stockbroker then, and in his Armani suit, with his hundred-quid haircut, he looked every inch the successful businessman, apple of his mother's eye. Banks had been a mess, much as he was now, he thought, aware of the irony. Approaching burnout in London, career and marriage held together by threads, he was waiting to hear if his application for a transfer to North Yorkshire had been approved when Roy rang him one day at the office – he wasn't even sure his brother knew where he lived at that time – and asked him if he was free for dinner at the Ivy.

The restaurant was packed with entertainment people and Banks thought he recognized a star or two, but he couldn't put names to faces. They certainly looked and acted as if they were stars. After a half-hour of family chat and polite enquiries into Banks's career and well-being over a very expensive shepherd's pie and an even more expensive bottle of burgundy, Roy steered the conversation towards the recent scandals. Nothing was said overtly, but Banks went away with the impression that Roy had been pumping him. Not that he knew anything, but his brother had expressed interest in the way such investigations were done, how the police gathered information, what they thought of informers, exactly where the law stood on the issue, and so on. It was done very well, and it continued over the frozen berries and white-chocolate sauce he had for dessert, but it was definitely a fishing expedition.

There was another thing, too. Banks couldn't be certain, but he had been around drugs enough to recognize the signs, and he was sure Roy was high. Coke, he suspected. After all, that was the drug of choice back then among successful young men about town. At one point in the evening Roy excused himself to go to the toilet and came back slightly flushed and even more animated, sniffling every now and then.

And that, Banks realized, was probably when he first started thinking of his brother as a possible criminal. Before that he had merely been the annoying little brother, the paragon against which Banks was matched and found wanting. Even now, when Banks looked back on their conversation that evening, he still thought he was right, that Roy had been up to something and wanted to run down the odds on his getting caught. Well, he hadn't got caught, and now it seemed he had moved on to other things. But were they more honest?

Banks poured the last of the Château Musar into his glass. Maybe he should have ordered a whole bottle, he thought. But that was too much, and he wanted to keep a reasonably clear head for tomorrow. From what he could see between the clustered diners in the dim light, the street outside was even busier still. The crowd was mostly young and they'd probably be drinking and clubbing until the early hours.

Over coffee and cognac, Banks remembered that he had nowhere to stay tonight. He had forgotten to book a hotel room. Then he felt the pressure of the keys and the mobile in his pocket and he knew that he had decided where he was staying the minute he had pocketed them and left Roy's house. It was useless trying to get a taxi at this hour in the maze of Soho streets, so he walked up to the Charing Cross Road, where he picked one up in no time and asked the driver to take him to South Kensington.

•

Winsome had been patiently ringing Banks's parents and children on and off for most of the afternoon and early evening without any luck. When it came to Banks's friends, she was at a loss to know who they were. He had left an old address book in his drawer, but there weren't many entries, and some were so old the numbers were no longer in service. It felt odd, searching for her boss, poring over the personal address book of someone she called sir and looked up to, but there was no doubt that he might be able to answer a few questions. Winsome also realized that he might be in danger. After all, a woman apparently on her way to see him had been shot, and his half-renovated cottage had been broken into. Coincidence? She didn't think so.

Consulting the list of family phone numbers, Winsome had first called the daughter, Tracy, in Leeds. When she had finally got through to her around teatime, Tracy said she had no idea where her father was. The son Brian wasn't answering his mobile, so she left a message. When she phoned Banks's parents for the third time, early in the evening, a woman answered.

'Mrs Banks?' Winsome said.

'Yes. Who is this?'

'My name's DC Jackman. I work with your son DCI Banks. I've been trying to get in touch with you all afternoon.'

'Sorry, love, we've been to visit my brother and his wife in Ely. Why? What's wrong? Has something happened to Alan?'

'Nothing's happened, Mrs Banks. As far as we know everything's just fine. He's on holiday this week, but I'm sure you know how it is with this job. I'm afraid we need him for something, and it's rather urgent. He seems to have forgotten to take his mobile. I was wondering if you knew where he was.'

'No, dear,' said Mrs Banks. 'He never tells us where he's going these days.'

'I don't suppose he does,' said Winsome, 'but it was worth a try. Have you spoken with him recently?'

'As a matter of fact he rang early this morning.'

'What about, if you don't mind me asking?'

'Oh, I don't mind, dear. It was a little bit odd. See, he was asking about his brother, about Roy, and . . . well, they've never been very close.'

'So it was unusual for DCI Banks to be asking about him?'

'Yes.'

'What did he want to know?'

'He wanted to know if I knew where Roy was, just like you want to know where Alan is. What's going on? Are you sure there's nothing wrong?'

'Nothing to worry about, Mrs Banks. We just need him to help us out with something, that's all. Could you give me his brother's address and phone number if you've got them?'

'Of course,' said Mrs Banks. 'I know his address by heart but I'm no good with numbers. You'll have to wait a moment while I look it up.'

'That's all right,' said Winsome. 'I'll hold.'

She heard the handset laid gently to rest on a hard surface, then the sound of muffled voices. A few seconds later, Mrs Banks came back on the line and gave her the number. 'He's got one of those mobiles. Do you want that number, too?' she asked.

'Might as well.'

'Silly business, people having to stay in touch all the time,' said Mrs Banks. 'Makes you wonder how we managed without all these newfangled gadgets, but we did, didn't we? Listen to me go on. You're probably too young to remember.'

'I remember,' said Winsome, who had grown up in a shack high in Jamaica's Cockpit Country, open to the elements, without telephone or electricity or any of the other myriad things that seemed so essential to life in twenty-first-century Britain.

Mrs Banks gave her the number and Winsome said goodbye. For a moment she sat thinking, tapping her ballpoint on the pad, then she found DI Cabbot's mobile number and picked up the phone again.

•

'Sorry about Blunt and Useless,' said DI Brooke. 'They're a right couple of prize plonkers, but it's hard to get good help these days, and they just happened to be on duty.'

'Blunt and Useless?'

'Sharpe and Handy. Get it?'

Annie laughed. 'It's all right. We've got a few like that ourselves.'

They were sitting in a noisy pub on Brixton Road drinking pints of Director's bitter. David Brooke was about Banks's age, but he looked older and he was much more well-rounded, with a placid moon-shaped red face that always made Annie think of farmers, and only a few tufts of ginger hair still clinging to his freckled skull. His navy-blue suit had seen better days, as had his teeth, and he had taken off his tie because of the heat, which made him look even more like some yokel up from Somerset for a wedding or a football match.

Annie's search of Jennifer Clewes's room had yielded nothing of immediate interest – except that Jennifer collected porcelain figurines, mostly fairytale characters, liked Frank Sinatra, Tony Bennett and Ella Fitzgerald, and read hardly anything that wasn't to do with business and commerce, apart from the occasional Mills & Boon. If her clothes were not for work, they were mostly casual: jeans, denim skirts and jackets, T-shirts, cotton tops. Nothing lacy or flouncy. She had one good frock and two pairs of black high-heeled shoes. The rest of her footwear consisted of trainers and sandals.

Her computer, at first glance, revealed nothing out of the ordinary. There was no diary and no personal papers, only a calendar, the days marked mostly with birthdays to remember. She had a dentist's visit scheduled for the 13th. If there was anything else, it was for the computer experts to find. Annie did, however, acquire a much better photograph of Jennifer – alive and smiling against an ocean backdrop. Kate Nesbit told her it had been taken in Sicily the previous year, when Jennifer had gone there on holiday with Melanie Scott, her old school friend from Shrewsbury.

When she had finished at the flat, Annie phoned and booked a room for two nights at a hotel by Lambeth Bridge, after first ringing Gristhorpe again and clearing it with him. Tomorrow was Sunday, so the Berger-Lennox Centre would most likely be closed. Annie would pay her visit first thing on Monday morning before heading back up north. On Sunday, she would go and talk to Melanie Scott. The local police would inform Jennifer's parents in Shrewsbury of their daughter's death and drive them to Eastvale to make a formal identification of the body.

'So how are things going, Dave?' Annie said. 'It's been a while.'

'Too long, if you ask me. Things are fine, thanks. Actually, the big news is that I'm up for promotion at last. Chief Inspector.'

'Congratulations, Dave,' said Annie. 'Detective Chief Inspector Brooke. Has a sort of ring to it, doesn't it?'

Brooke chuckled. 'It does. How did the interview with the victim's flatmate go?' he asked.

Annie sipped some beer. 'Fine. I didn't find out much, but at least I'm building up some sort of picture of Jennifer, however vague. You know what it's like in the early stages.'

'I do indeed. A slow business.'

'The poor woman, though,' Annie went on, 'Kate Nesbit, the flatmate. She was really upset. I finally managed to persuade her to let me fetch the woman from upstairs to sit with her until her parents can come over. I phoned them and they said they'd be there as soon as possible. What'll happen after that I don't know.'

'I'll have someone keep an eye on her, if you like. Drop by now and then, see how she's doing.'

'Not Blunt and Useless.'

Brooke smiled. 'No, I wouldn't wish them on the poor lass. We've got some good police community-support officers.'

'All right,' said Annie. 'It sounds like a good idea. Thanks.'

'No problem.'

'I don't like to ask,' she went on, 'but do you think you could also spare a couple of DCs to do a house-to-house? I'd do it myself, but I'd like to go out to Hounslow to visit one of the victim's close friends tomorrow.'

'And what would they be asking about?'

'If anyone has noticed anything unusual, or suspicious, strangers hanging about, that sort of thing.'

'I think we can manage that,' said Brooke. 'Wouldn't want our delicate DI's feet getting sore, would we?'

'You're a sweetheart, Dave.'

Annie's mobile rang. She excused herself and walked outside so she could hear properly. When Winsome gave her Banks's brother's address and phone numbers and told her there was a possibility Banks might be there, she had to go back into the pub, take her notebook out of her briefcase and write the information down. She thanked Winsome and hung up.

'Important news?' Brooke asked.

'We may have a lead on our missing DCI,' Annie said.

'Missing DCI?'

'It's a long story.'

Brooke nodded towards Annie's empty glass. 'Another?'

'Why not,' said Annie. 'I'm not driving.'

'What about a bite to eat? Then you can tell me all about your DCI over dinner.'

'Here?'

Brooke looked around and pulled a face. 'You must be joking. Let's have one more drink here, then we'll find somewhere decent over the river, if you're up for it?'

'That'd be fine,' said Annie. 'How are Joan and the kids?'

'Thriving, thank you.' Brooke paused. 'You're not very subtle, you know, Annie.'

'What do you mean?'

'You want to know if I'm still happily married, whether I represent any sort of threat to you. Well, I am, and I don't. Do you behave like that whenever a man offers to buy you dinner?'

'Oh, you're buying. I didn't know that. That's all right, then.'

'Now you're hiding behind flippancy.'

'You're right,' said Annie, 'I'm sorry. I should know better. I've just had some bad experiences recently, that's all.'

'Want to talk about them?'

Annie shook her head. The last thing she wanted to talk about was Phil Keane. Throttle him, maybe; hang, draw and quarter him, even better; but talk about him, no way. Brooke wasn't the type to make a pass, and under ordinary circumstances she would have realized it. He had been married to Joan all those years ago, when Annie was a fresh-faced young DC in Exeter and Brooke was her DS. They had kept in touch sporadically over the years. Anyway, his offer of a shared meal was exactly that and no more, and it bothered her that she reacted as if she could no longer trust an old friend.

'I'm sorry,' Annie said. 'I just wasn't thinking.'

'That's all right. And I'm secretly flattered that you still think I'm a contender.'

Annie tapped him on the arm. 'I'm sure you are,' she said. 'But I'm bloody starving, so how about we skip that other drink here and have one when we get where we're going? Does your offer still stand?'

'The West End awaits us,' said Brooke.

'Any chance we can go via South Kensington?'

•

It was late Saturday night, Kev Templeton thought gloomily, and he was supposed to be shagging that gorgeous new red-headed clerk in records, the one with the big tits and legs right up to her arse, but instead he was driving up the M1 in rain so heavy that his windscreen wipers could barely keep up with it.

Still, this was the next best thing, he told himself, if not even better. The thrill of the chase. Well, not exactly a chase, but at least he was out of the office, on the road, tracking down a lead, driving through the night. This was the life. This was what he had joined the force for. Water cascaded from the windows, lightning streaked across the sky and he could hear the thunder even over the Chemical Brothers CD he was playing at ear-splitting volume.

He knew they didn't take him seriously back at headquarters, just because he was young and took a bit of pride in his appearance. They all thought he was some sort of club-crazy dandy. Well, he liked clubbing, and he liked to look good, but there was more to him than that. One day, he'd show them all. He'd pass his boards and rise up the ranks like a meteor.

Who did they think they were, anyway? Gristhorpe was due to retire any moment now, and he hadn't done any real detecting in years, if ever. Banks was good, but he wasn't a team player and he seemed to be quickly writing himself out of the script due to personal problems. Annie Cabbot wasn't as hot as she thought she was. Too emotional, Kev thought, like she was always on the rag. The only one that really scared him was Winsome. Awesome, as he called her secretly. She'd go far. He could see her as his sidekick when he made superintendent. Could see shagging her, too. Just the thought of it made him sweat. Those thighs.

He had first driven non-stop to the end of the motorway, then turned around, hitting Toddington and Newport Pagnell service stations on the northbound M1 already, showing Jennifer Clewes's photo around without any success. He hadn't eaten at either of the first two service stations – and now as he approached Watford Gap it was going on for midnight and he was feeling peckish. Needed a piss, too. He might as well stop there at the Road Chef. From what he had learned over the years, motorway cafes were all over-priced, and there wasn't much to choose between them.

All the roadside cafes seemed to have a slightly seedy aura at that time of night, Templeton thought; or maybe Watford Gap services were always like that. It was something to do with the lighting and the clientele. Not many nice middle-class families on the road at that hour. Not many old folks either. Most of them, with the odd exception of a commercial traveller or a businessman on his way home from a late meeting, looked like villains. You probably wouldn't go far wrong, Templeton thought, if you made the occasional swoop on motorway cafes. Bound to net a few faces from the wanted posters, at any rate. Maybe he'd pass on the idea to the brass. Then again, maybe not. They'd only steal the credit themselves.

A man came in to the toilet and stood next to Templeton at the urinal, though there was plenty of free space elsewhere. When he started to open a conversation – the usual line about big knobs hanging out – Templeton zipped up, whipped out his warrant card and shoved it in the man's face so hard he staggered back and lost directional control, pissing all over his shoes and trouser bottoms. 'Fuck off, pervert,' Templeton said. 'And think yourself bloody lucky I can't be bothered to arrest you for soliciting. On your bike. Now!' Templeton clapped once, loudly.

The man turned pale. His hands shook as he zipped himself up and, without even pausing at the basin, ran for the door. Templeton washed his hands with soap under hot water for thirty seconds exactly. He hated poofters, and as far as he was concerned they'd made a bloody big mistake when they made homosexuality legal all those years ago. Opened the floodgates, that did, just like they did with immigration. As far as he was concerned, the government should send all the poofters to jail and all foreigners back home – except Winsome, of course; she could stay.

Up in the restaurant, Templeton ordered a cup of tea and sausage, eggs and beans, figuring you couldn't go wrong with something as basic as that, and carried his tray to the first empty table he saw, trying to ignore the smears of ketchup on the surface. The eggs were overcooked and the tea was stewed, but other than that the meal wasn't too bad. Templeton tucked in with as much enthusiasm as he could muster.

When he had finished, he went up to the counter and spoke to the pimply Asian youth who worked there. His name-tag identified him as Ali.

'Were you working here last night about this time?'

'I was here,' said Ali. 'Sometimes it feels like I'm always bloody here.'

'I'll bet it does,' said Templeton, pulling the photo of Jennifer Clewes from his briefcase. 'By the way, I'm DC Templeton, North Yorkshire Major Crimes. Did you happen to see this woman in here?'

'Bloody hell, is she dead?' Ali asked, paling. 'I've never seen a dead person before.'

'The question is, did you see her?'

'What happened to her?'

Templeton sighed theatrically. 'Look, Ali, we'll get along a lot better if I ask the questions and you answer them, all right?' he said.

'Yeah. All right. Let's have a look, then.' Ali reached out his hand, but Templeton held on to the photograph, keeping it just within Ali's field of vision. He didn't want greasy fingerprints all over it.

Ali screwed up his eyes and looked at the photo longer than

Templeton thought he needed to, then said, 'Yeah, she was in here last night. Sat over there.' He pointed to a table.

'What time?'

'Can't remember. It's all the same when you're on nights.'

'Was she alone?'

'Yeah. I remember thinking what's a good-looking bird like that doing all alone on a Friday night, like.'

'Did she seem upset or frightened in any way?'

'Come again?'

'How did she behave?'

'Just normal, like. She ate her sandwich – well, half of it. I can't say I blame her. Those ham and tomatoes do get a bit soggy when they've been sitting—'

'Did anyone approach her at all?'

'No.'

'Speak to her?'

'No. But the bloke at the table opposite was definitely giving her the eye. Looked like a bit of a pervert to me, too.'

'What do perverts look like?' Templeton asked.

'You know. Creepy, like.'

'Right. How long did she stay?'

'Dunno. Not more than ten, fifteen minutes, I suppose. Look, aren't you going to tell me what happened to her? She was all right when she left here.'

'Anybody follow her?'

'The bloke opposite, the pervert, went out not long after her, but I wouldn't say he was following her. I mean, he'd finished his sausage roll. Why would he want to hang around?'

Templeton gazed over the decor. 'Why, indeed?' he said.

'Most people here, they're usually in a hurry, see. Quick turn-over.'

'And no one else took an interest in the woman?'

'No.'

'She make any phone calls?'

'Not that I saw.'

'This pervert, had you ever seen him before?'

'No.'

'Can you describe him for me?'

'He was wearing a dark grey suit, like a businessman, wore glasses with black rims, and he had a long, jowly sort of face, with a long, thin nose. Light brown hair, and not much of it. Oh, yeah, and he had dandruff. Reminded me of someone, but I can't think who. Not the dandruff, I mean, the face.'

'How old would you say he was?'

'Old. Maybe forty or so.'

'Anything else you can tell me?'

'Don't think so. Is this gonna be on *Crimewatch*?'

'Thanks for your help.' Templeton left Ali dreaming of TV stardom and walked back to his car. The rain had stopped and dark puddles reflected the lights. Before setting off back up the motorway, Templeton walked over to the garage and into the night manager's office. There he found a sleepy young man behind the counter and showed his warrant card. The boy seemed to wake up a bit.

'I'm Geoff,' he said. 'What can I do for you?'

'Were you working here last night?'

'Yeah.'

Templeton took out the photograph again. 'Remember her?'

'She looks . . .' He frowned. 'I don't know.'

'She looks dead,' said Templeton. 'Just as well, because she is. Do you remember her?'

'She was here. You don't forget someone who looks like that.'

'Do you remember what time?'

'I can't say for certain, but her credit-card receipt should tell us.'

'She used plastic?'

'Most people do. Petrol's so bloody expensive and cards are convenient. Nowadays you can just swipe the card right by the pump. You don't even have to come into the office. Not everyone likes to do it that way, mind you. Some still prefer the human touch.'

'I don't suppose you've still got last night's receipts?'

'As a matter of fact,' said Geoff, 'I have. There's no pick-up till Monday morning.'

'What are we waiting for? Her name's Jennifer Clewes.'

Geoff located the credit-card receipts and sucked on his lower lip as he made his way through them. 'Just give me a minute. Here, I think this is it.' He held the receipt up for Templeton to see: 12.35 a.m. Which meant she'd get to the junction with the A1 about two hours and a half hours later. It fitted. Templeton thanked Geoff, and just on the off chance asked him about the 'old' man Ali had described.

'The bloke with the dandruff? Old hatchet-face?'

'That's the one.'

'Yeah, he was here, too. Same time as her, now I come to think of it. I caught him giving her the eye when she was bending over with the pump. Can't say I blame him, mind you. Like something out of *FHM*. Hey, you don't think that—'

'Seen him before?'

'Not that I recall. But we get so much traffic.'

'I don't suppose there's the remotest chance that he paid by plastic, too?'

Geoff grinned, flicking through the stack again. 'I told you. Most of them do. Here you are, right after hers. A Mr Roger Cropley.'

'Do you have CCTV?'

'As a matter of fact, we do,' said Geoff.

Thunder rumbled in the distance. Geoff held up the slip and Templeton read the details. So there is a God, after all, he thought.

•

Back at Roy's, Banks first checked the phone for messages. There was only one, and to his surprise it was from Annie Cabbot. Even more to his surprise, it was clearly intended for Roy because she addressed him as 'Mr Banks'. She'd called around at the house earlier, she said, but he had been out. Would he please get in touch as soon as possible? Of course Annie had no idea that Roy was missing. She sounded rather chilly and official, Banks thought, wondering what she was doing in London. Could it be something to do with the murder she was investigating in Eastvale? It was after half-past eleven now, though, and he didn't fancy getting into a complicated conversation with Annie so late. He'd give her a ring in the morning.

He brought the open bottle of Amarone upstairs and watched *A Clockwork Orange* on the widescreen plasma TV. Even with the surround sound turned low so as not to disturb the neighbours, it still filled the room. After that, he fell asleep on the sofa, the bottle still half full.

Banks didn't hear the thunder, nor did he see the lightning, when the storm passed over the London area in the small hours of the morning. What did awaken him, however, at shortly after three, was the distinct melody of 'La donna è mobile' coming from very close by.

As Banks struggled to consciousness, his first thought was that he didn't remember putting a CD of *Rigoletto* on before he went to sleep. Then he remembered Roy's mobile, which sat on the table beside him.

He picked it up and, sure enough, that was the source of the sound. The room was dark, but with the help of the blue back-lighting, he found the right button to push.

'Hello,' he mumbled. 'Who is it?'

At first he heard nothing at all except a slight background hiss, perhaps some sort of static interference. He thought he could hear someone making choking or gagging sounds, as if they were try-ing to hold back laughter. Then he began to think that perhaps someone had rung by accident, and the sounds came from a tele-vision playing in the background.

Something similar had happened to Banks once when he had

forgotten to lock his mobile. Somehow or other he had activated one of the numbers in his phone book, and Tracy got to listen to the questioning of a murder witness. Fortunately, she couldn't make out the conversation clearly, and she knew enough to switch off when she realized what must have happened. Still, it made Banks paranoid about locking the device after that.

Or maybe this was kids, someone's idea of a joke?

The muffled shouting went on, followed by a thud and the unmistakable sound of someone laughing. Then, as Banks looked at the display, a picture began to form. It wasn't very sharp, but it looked like a photograph of a man slumped in a chair, asleep perhaps, or unconscious, his head to one side. Banks couldn't see whether there were other people around, but given the sounds, it might have been some sort of wild party.

Banks was still half asleep, not thinking at all clearly, and he put the phone back on the table suspecting one of Roy's friends of playing some sort of practical joke on him. Whatever it was, he would be better equipped to deal with it in the morning.

6

The thunderstorm that swept across the southern half of the country during the night drove out the muggy weather, and Sunday dawned clear and sunny, the streets rinsed and sparkling after the rain. The temperature was still in the mid-twenties, but with the humidity all but gone it was a comfortable heat.

Annie woke late after a refreshing sleep, though her hotel room had been too hot and she had had to lie in her underwear on top of the sheets. She had turned the control on the wall to cold, but after nothing happened she concluded it was only for show. Perhaps if you believed it really worked you would start to feel cooler, but she didn't have that much faith.

After a lukewarm shower and a room-service Continental breakfast, again scouring the papers for any traces of Phil Keane's handiwork and finding none, Annie checked her mobile in case she'd missed a message from Roy Banks, but there was nothing. She rang the number again, and again she got the answerphone. This time she left an even terser message. She tried the mobile number, but had no luck there, either. She didn't bother leaving a message.

Next she rang Melanie Scott to make sure she would be at home, then she checked in with Gristhorpe at his home and found out that Jennifer Clewes's parents were being brought to Eastvale that morning to identify their daughter. Then Annie set off for the tube.

First she had to take the Northern Line to Leicester Square, then change to the Piccadilly Line, which ran all the way out to Heathrow. Given the more clement weather and the relative emptiness of the train, her journey out to Hounslow passed pleasantly enough, some of it above ground, and she gazed on the rows of red-brick houses, playing fields, concrete and glass office blocks.

She found Melanie Scott's house with the help of her *A–Z*, only about five minutes' walk away from the Hounslow West tube station. Cars filled every available parking spot on both sides of the street, sun glinting on their windscreens, so she was glad yet again that she wasn't driving.

The woman who answered the door looked to be in her late twenties, the same age as Jennifer Clewes. She was one of those excessively thin yet nicely shaped women, with small breasts, coat-hanger hips and a narrow waist. She was wearing denim shorts, which showed off her long, tapered legs to advantage. Jet-black hair hung straight down to her shoulders and framed a pale oval face with large brown eyes, button nose and full mouth. The red lipstick stood out in contrast against the paleness of her skin. Annie hadn't told her much over the telephone, but she must have suspected something was wrong, and she seemed nervous, anxious to hear the worst.

'You said it's about Jenn,' she said as she pointed Annie towards an armchair in the cramped living room. The front window was open and they could hear snatches of conversation and laughter as people drifted by. Melanie sat on the edge of her chair and clasped her hands between her knees. 'Is something wrong? What is it?'

'I'm afraid Jennifer Clewes is dead, Ms Scott. I'm sorry I can't think of any easier way to put it.'

Melanie just stared into a far corner of the room and her eyes filled with tears. Then she put her fist to her mouth and bit. Annie went over to her, but Melanie waved her away. 'No, I'm all right. Really. It's just the shock.' She rubbed her eyes and smudged mascara over her cheeks, then took a tissue from a box on the mantelpiece. 'You're a policewoman, so there must be something suspicious about it, right? How did it happen?'

No flies on Melanie, thought Annie, sitting down again. 'She was shot,' she said.

'Oh, my God. It's the woman they found in the car in Yorkshire, isn't it? The one in the papers and on TV. You said you were from Yorkshire.'

'North Yorkshire, yes.'

'They wouldn't give her name out on the TV.'

'No,' said Annie. 'We have to be certain. Her parents haven't identified the body yet.' She thought of showing Melanie the photograph, but there was no point in further distressing her. Kate Nesbit had already identified Jennifer, and by now, Jennifer's parents would have confirmed this.

'I can't believe it,' Melanie said. 'Who'd want to kill Jenn? Was it some pervert? Was she . . . ?'

'There was no sexual assault,' Annie said. 'Do you know of anyone who would want to harm her?'

'Me? No, I can't think of anyone.'

'When did you last talk to Jennifer?'

'A few days ago – Wednesday, I think – on the phone. I haven't actually seen her for two or three weeks. Both too busy. We were going to the pictures next weekend. Chick-flick night. I can't believe it.' She dabbed at her eyes again.

'Do you know if there was anything bothering her, anything on her mind?'

'She did seem a bit preoccupied the last time I talked to her. But I must admit, Jenn goes on about work a bit too much sometimes, and I sort of tune it out.'

'She was worried about work?'

'Not specifically. It was just someone she mentioned. One of the late girls, she said. She worked at a family planning centre.'

'I know,' said Annie.

'Late girls? What are they?'

'I've no idea. That's just what she said.'

'A workmate? Late shift?'

'No, I don't think so. I don't think they worked in shifts. It's not a twenty-four-hour centre. But sometimes she has contact with the clients, through paperwork and billing and what have you, or if there's a problem or something. There was some woman . . .'

That was how Jennifer met Kate Nesbit, Annie remembered, through the centre. 'Can you remember her name?'

'I'm trying. Give me a moment. She spoke it very quickly so I can't be absolutely sure, but it was a rather odd name.' Melanie paused and gazed out of the bay window. A white delivery truck passed by, blocking the sun for a moment. 'Carmen, I think.'

'That was her first name?'

'Yes. Carmen. I remember thinking at the time that it sounded like an actress's name, but that's Cameron, isn't it? Cameron Diaz. Hers was Carmen, like the opera. Her surname was Petri, or something like that. I'm sorry.'

'That's all right.' Annie made a note of the name and put a question mark by 'late girl'. 'Did Jennifer say what she was worried about?'

'No. I'm sorry. Just that it was something this Carmen said.'

'Was this Carmen at the centre to arrange for an abortion?'

'I assumed so,' said Melanie, 'but Jenn didn't say. I mean, that's why people go there, or for advice, you know, if they're undecided, they don't know what to do.'

'Did Jennifer have any particular stand on abortion?'

'What do you mean?'

'Do you think she'd advise clients against it, suggest they keep the child and put it up for adoption instead?'

'Oh, I see. No, not really. Jenn believed it was a woman's choice. It's just that some of the women were . . . you know . . . scared, especially if they were young. Some of them just didn't know what to do. But Jenn wasn't an adviser or counsellor. There are other people to take care of that.'

'But she did have contact with the girls?'

'Sometimes. Yes.'

'But you've no idea *why* Jennifer was concerned about this Carmen?'

'Jenn just had a habit of getting involved in other people's problems, that's all. It can be a bit of a drawback in her line of work. Most of the time she doesn't have any contact with the clients, but sometimes . . . like I said. She's got too sympathetic a nature, and she can't always be objective about things. Or people. Mind you, it's one of the qualities that makes her so special. Sorry. Made. My God.'

'Did Jenn ever receive any threats because of her work?'

'You mean because she dealt with abortions?'

'Yes. There are a number of groups actively against it, some of them violent.'

'She never mentioned it to me. I mean, I think there was a small demonstration once, but nothing came of it. Certainly no violence, anyway. Groups like that would tend to avoid the centre itself because abortions aren't actually performed there, and many of the clients go on to have their babies and give them up for adoption, so I don't think that's a very real possibility.'

Annie realized that Jenn's workmates at the centre would probably be better informed on this topic. She moved on. 'It might be a good idea if you gave me a bit of background. I understand you knew Jennifer a long time?'

'Ever since primary school. We only lived two streets away from one another. And we have the same birthday. Her poor mum and dad . . .' Melanie picked up a packet of cigarettes from the arm of her chair and lit one. 'Sorry, you don't mind, do you?' she asked, blowing out the smoke.

'It's your house,' said Annie. And your lungs, she thought to herself. 'What about later? University?'

'We both did our postgraduate degrees at Birmingham. I took international business, and Jenn studied management.'

'What about your undergraduate degrees?'

'Jenn read economics at Kent and I went to Essex. Modern languages.'

'You kept in touch?'

'Of course. We were practically inseparable in the hols.'

'I understand that just last summer the two of you went on holiday together to Sicily?'

'Yes.' Melanie frowned. 'Look, may I ask just what you're getting at? Are you suggesting there was anything . . . unusual . . . about our friendship, because if you are—'

Annie waved her hand. 'No, nothing like that. None of my business, anyway.' Unless it contributed to Jennifer's murder. 'No, it's just that her flatmate Kate didn't seem to know an awful lot about Jennifer's life, didn't really seem to know much about her at all.'

'That's hardly surprising,' said Melanie. 'Jenn's a very private person in a lot of ways. She shared the flat because she had to – London's so expensive – but it didn't mean she had to share her life. Besides . . .'

'What?'

'Well, I got the impression from Jenn that this Kate was a bit of a nosy parker, always asking questions, a busybody, wanting to know where she'd been and who she was with. Jenn said sometimes it was worse than being at home with her parents.'

Annie had had a flatmate like that once in Exeter, a girl called Caroline, who had even gone so far as to question her on what sort of birth control she used, and on what exactly went on those nights Annie didn't return to the flat. And some of Caroline's forays into Annie's sex life smacked of digging for vicarious thrills; she never seemed to have a boyfriend of her own, and Annie guessed that was how she got her jollies. Not that Annie gave much away, or had even been up to anything, most of the time.

'Why didn't she share with you?'

'Hounslow's too far out for her, and I need to be here because of my work. I'd hate to have to drive to Heathrow and back every day from the city.'

'They didn't get along, Kate and Jennifer?'

'I don't mean that. You can get along with someone who's not the same as you, can't you, in general, even if some of their habits annoy you, as long as you keep a bit of distance?'

'True,' said Annie. 'Sometimes it's better that way.'

'That's what they were like. They got along well enough. Kate kept the place clean and tidy, didn't leave food to go rotten in the fridge, remembered to lock the door when she went out, didn't make a lot of noise. That sort of thing. The things that are important when two people are sharing a common living space. They never had rows or anything. It's just that Kate's a bit bossy as well as nosy. Likes things just so. And she's got a bee in her bonnet about smoking. I won't even go to the house. It's her prerogative, of course, but even so, you'd think people could be a bit accommodating once in a while, wouldn't you?'

'I suppose so,' said Annie. 'What about boyfriends?'

'What about them?'

'Any problems there?'

Melanie pushed her hair back. 'I think Kate got sort of put off men. She had a scare a while back. Thought she was pregnant, so Jenn told me. Anyway, I know nothing about her love life, or lack of it.'

'And Jennifer?' Annie remembered what Kate Nesbit had told her about Jennifer's ex-boyfriend, Victor, and she wanted to find out what Melanie knew about him.

Melanie paused, seemed to come to a decision, then went on. 'Jenn's the serious type when it comes to love,' she said. 'Last year, just before we went on holiday, she split up with someone she'd been seeing for three years and it devastated her. I could have told her it would happen, but you can't do that, can you? I mean, Jenn was pushing him towards commitment, living together, maybe marriage, babies, and it was obvious in the end that she'd scare him off.'

'Is that what happened?'

'Yes.' Melanie laughed. 'The holiday was supposed to be a cure. Get him out of her system. Get rat-arsed and shag lots of good-looking blokes.'

'Is that how it worked out?'

'No. Does it ever? Jenn read a lot of books, and I practised my

Italian on the waiters, who were all over fifty. There wasn't one decent-looking bloke in the whole place. Most evenings we spent commiserating with one another over a couple of bottles of cheap Sicilian wine and most mornings we woke up with splitting headaches. Oh, and Jenn got sunburn on the second day. All in all, I'd say it was a bit of a farce.'

'And afterwards?'

'She got over him.'

'And he her?'

'Not quite,' said Melanie with a frown. 'Jenn did mention that he'd pestered her once or twice, said he'd made a big mistake and asked her to give him another chance, that sort of thing. And he kept trying to phone her.'

'At work or home?'

'Both.'

'When you say "pestered" her, do you mean stalked her, threatened her, what?'

'She just said he pestered her.'

'Can you remember his name and address?'

'Not his address, no, but I've got it written down somewhere. Remind me before you go. I do remember he lives out Chalk Farm way. His name is Victor Parsons.'

'Was Jennifer involved with anyone else, after Victor?'

'I think so. Very recently.'

'Past few weeks?'

'Yes. Couple of months at the most. She was moving very cautiously. Anyway, I got the impression that she liked him a lot.'

'Do you know his name?'

'Sorry, she didn't say. I mean she didn't really say very much about it at all; she was being very cagey. It's just that I've known her for so long, you get to sort of recognize the signs, if you know what I mean.'

'Do you think he might be married?'

'Married? Good God, I hope not. I mean, Jenn wouldn't go with a married man, not *knowingly*. I told you. She was serious about love. Believed in meeting Mr Right and settling down together forever. She wasn't casual about that sort of thing.'

Annie wondered if Kate Nesbit's suspicions were at all justified or were simply the result of Jennifer's natural reticence when it came to affairs of the heart. 'Do you know where they met?'

'At work, I should think. She hardly goes anywhere else, except with me.'

'Look, I know this is probably a bit of a cliché,' Annie said, 'but we do have to ask. Is there anyone you can think of who might have wanted to harm Jennifer? Has anyone at all ever made any threats against her?'

Melanie didn't hesitate. 'No,' she said, her eyes filling with tears again. 'Jenn was a *good* soul, one of the truly *good* people.'

'You don't know of any enemies she might have had?'

'She didn't make enemies. If you ask me, this was one of those random attacks you hear about on the news, maybe a serial killer, someone who didn't know her. Like that other girl, in the spring.'

'What about at work? Was everything all right there?'

'You'd have to ask them, but she never said anything to me about any problems. She liked her job.' She started to cry again. 'I'm sorry. I just can't get my head around it.'

Annie could think of no more questions anyway. She consoled Melanie as best she could and suggested she call a friend to come and stay. Melanie didn't want to, said she'd be fine by herself, and despite the tears Annie sensed that she was probably tougher than Kate Nesbit. Besides, her parents still lived in Shrewsbury, so they could hardly get down to London quickly. Annie left her card with her mobile number, telling Melanie she could ring at any time for any reason, and walked back to the tube wondering why someone so sensitive, serious and special as Jennifer Clewes had ended up a murder victim.

•

When Banks woke on Sunday morning to the sound of birdsong, his head was pounding, his mouth was dry, and he had the distinct memory of something very odd having happened during the night.

He stumbled to the bathroom and drank two glasses of water and took three paracetamol tablets, then he returned to the entertainment room, where he had slept on the sofa. He picked up Roy's mobile and found that the image was still there – he had at least had the sense to save it – and it made no more sense in the light of day than it had in the middle of the night. He found the incoming call on the call list. It was listed only as 'unknown'.

Banks examined the photo more closely. The foreground was out of focus, the figure blurred. Behind the slumped figure was what looked like a wall and Banks thought he could see the fuzzy outlines of letters written on it. There were no actual words he could read, but an expert might be able to glean something from it.

Was the man in the chair Roy? He could be, Banks supposed; the features weren't clear, but the hair looked about right. If it was Roy, was this some sort of oblique way of informing Banks that someone had taken – had kidnapped – his brother? Would a ransom demand come soon?

The man in the photo could still be anyone, though, Banks decided in the end. Perhaps Roy himself had sent the photo. It could be a message of some kind, or a warning. On the other hand, it had been sent to *Roy's* mobile, so was it intended for Roy, or did someone know that Banks had the phone? The latter thought didn't do much to quell Banks's fears for his brother. If someone already knew he was staying at Roy's house and had Roy's mobile, then he had better keep his eyes open and his wits about him.

Banks put the mobile aside and went back to the bathroom, where he removed his rumpled clothes and climbed into Roy's luxury power shower, turning it on full. The jets of hot water pummelled his body back into some semblance of humanity.

As he dried himself on a thick, soft towel, Banks realized that he had left his overnight bag in the boot of his car, which was parked outside. He didn't want to dash out and fetch it right now, so he brushed his teeth with Roy's electric toothbrush, which almost ripped his gums to shreds, and borrowed a clean short-sleeved shirt and socks from his brother's wardrobe. He had to wear his own jeans because Roy's were too long for him and too big around the waist.

After he had found Roy's stash of coffee in one of the kitchen cupboards and made himself a decent pot, Banks took it with him upstairs and returned to the entertainment room and the mobile. The phone call and digital image should be traceable, Banks knew, given the police's technical skills. You could also learn an awful lot from a mobile phone's SIM card. Unfortunately, he didn't have the resources at the moment. How important is it? he wondered.

Banks still couldn't let go of the idea that his brother might have been involved in something illegal and that that was why he'd vanished. Things had threatened to catch up with him and he'd had to run away fast and hide out. If that was the case and Banks brought in the local police, then he risked getting Roy into serious trouble. If something terrible came out – drugs or porno-graphy, for example – and Roy went to jail, it could kill their parents.

On the other hand, there wasn't much more he could do alone except work on the leads he already had: the names from Roy's call list and phone book, and from the files Corinne had printed for him. He knew what his duty was, what he would advise any-one else in his position to do, but still he hesitated. At least he had the laptop now, so he could spend a bit more time on the CD and the USB drive, and there was one person he could turn to for help.

First he went into Roy's office. There was another telephone message, he noticed. It must have come in while he was taking his shower. Again it was from Annie Cabbot, and she simply asked Roy to ring her as soon as possible. Banks had forgotten all about last night's message. He still wasn't sure that he wanted Annie involved – she would definitely want him to make Roy's disappearance an official police matter – but he was curious enough to dial her mobile number and find out what she was after. He got no reception. Making a mental note to try again later, he picked up the telephone and rang Corinne, just to make sure. He breathed a sigh of relief when she said she was fine. She sounded sleepy. He apologized for waking her, said he'd be in touch and rang off.

Finally he dialled a number he had committed to memory. As requested he left a message and fifteen minutes later the phone rang. He snatched up the handset.

'Banks here.'

'So what's so urgent you have to disturb a hard-working copper on his only day off?' asked Detective Superintendent Richard 'Dirty Dick' Burgess.

'I need to see you,' said Banks. 'Urgently.'

•

Detective Chief Inspector Alan Banks weighed heavily on Superintendent Gristhorpe's mind, and not only because if Banks was around, Gristhorpe might be able to spend a bit more time on his drystone wall rather than having to drive into Western Area Headquarters so early on a Sunday morning. No doubt there would be a crowd of reporters to deal with, as the issue of guns always touched a nerve. Despite the strictest gun-control laws in the world, enacted in the wake of the Dunblane massacre, the country seemed to be flooded with cheap illegal guns from Ireland and Eastern Europe, as well as with reactivated firearms.

As it was, he still had a little time in hand, so he took his mug of strong tea out to the back garden and rested it on his chair while he studied various stones from the pile to see which one would fit best. The wall went nowhere and fenced nothing in, but for Gristhorpe it had become almost as necessary as breathing. He would never finish it – how could you finish something that went nowhere? – but if he ever did, he would pick it apart and start again. Wall-building was almost a lost art in the modern Dales, and while Gristhorpe had no pretensions to being an expert, of doing the work professionally, it was both his homage and his therapy.

As he weighed his options, Gristhorpe was pleasantly aware of the sun on his face and the light breeze that ruffled through his unruly thatch of hair, delicate as a woman's fingers. He thought of his wife, Mary, and her feather-light touch, and realized it was over twelve years now since the cancer had taken her. He still missed her as he would miss a part of himself, and not a day went by when he didn't think of her, remember some detail of her face, an expression, her gentle voice, her sense of humour, a certain gesture.

The air, he noticed, smelled of wild garlic, with a hint of tar from the hot road surface. Gristhorpe sipped some tea and decided upon a stone. The one he chose fitted perfectly. Then he dragged his thoughts back to the matter in hand: Banks.

Over the years, Banks had been more than just a junior officer to Gristhorpe. He could remember his first impressions of an edgy, nervous chain-smoking detective on the verge of career burnout and wondered if he had made a mistake in approving the transfer. But Banks had made a journey back to some sort of equilibrium, aided in part by the Yorkshire countryside he had now adopted as his home.

In some ways, Gristhorpe knew that he had been a kind of mentor to the new Banks, not so much in terms of doing the job, but in human terms. Banks was a complex sort, and Gristhorpe wondered if he would ever find the peace and harmony he seemed to be looking for. After the divorce from Sandra, which Gristhorpe knew still hurt Banks deeply, and the messy relationship with Annie Cabbot, Banks seemed to have found a measure of happiness in his isolated cottage, but even that had come to an abrupt and violent end. Where next? Gristhorpe hadn't a clue, and he didn't think Banks had, either.

Gristhorpe drank more tea and looked for another stone. He wanted to know what Banks's connection with the dead woman was before word of it leaked out. At the moment, it was simply a matter of trying to track Banks down through his family, but if that didn't work, then the next step would have to be an official one, and that could harm Banks's career. It would mean using the media. They would have to put his photo in the newspapers, request anyone who thought they had seen him to call the police. And every copper in the country would be on the lookout for him, too. It wasn't only that Gristhorpe wanted to know why the dead woman had Banks's address in her back pocket – the wrong address – but that Annie said the cottage had been broken into, and the builders swore they had locked up as usual after their day's work and left no valuable equipment behind.

Gristhorpe finished his tea and put the stone in place. Too big. He chucked it back on the pile and went indoors. Time to go to work.

•

Banks had a couple of hours to kill before his meeting with Burgess. First he called Julian Harwood and was surprised to get an appointment to meet at Starbucks on the Old Brompton Road at two o'clock that afternoon. Harwood sounded like the kind of person who thought giving you the time of day was doing you a big favour, but the mention that Banks was Roy's brother got his interest.

After that, he had made a written note of the names and numbers in Roy's call list and mobile phone book, just in case. Many of the names on the list matched those in the book, and he found Julian, Rupert and Corinne among them. Others were businesses mentioned in the files Corinne had copied, and then there were services, such as hairdresser, tailor, bank manager, dentist and doctor. None of it told him very much. He rang a few of the numbers, including Rupert's, but nobody knew where Roy was – at least, no one admitted to knowing where he was.

A woman called Jenn figured quite prominently in the last thirty calls – at least ten of them were to or from her – and Banks guessed she was Corinne's replacement. He tried ringing the number but it was unavailable. He wondered if there was any other way he could get in touch with her. The odds were that if she had nothing to do with Roy's disappearance, she would ring his mobile before too long.

As Banks glanced through the stack of memos and accounts, looked at all the company logos and names, he felt frustration set in. None of them meant anything to him, and he didn't have the time or the resources to check them all out. He had no access to the Police National Computer, for a start. He could be looking at the names of dozens of criminals and not even know it. Burgess might help, but he would only tell Banks what he wanted him to know.

Banks spent half an hour having another look around the house and found nothing more of interest. Then he started to examine the JPEG files on the CD he had found yesterday. He sat his new laptop computer on the kitchen table, brewed himself some coffee and managed to follow the instructions and get the machine going. He slipped in the CD and found Windows Explorer tucked away at the bottom of the Accessories menu.

His computer automatically displayed the 1,232 JPEG files as thumbnails. Banks scrolled through these, all images of naked women with file names like Maya, Teresa, April, Mia and Kimmie, or of men and women engaged in sex acts. If he rested his cursor on one of them, information about file dimension, type and size would appear in a little box. Most of the JPEG images were between 25 and 75 kilobytes in size.

When he got to the 980th image, however, Banks noticed that it and the next two were different; all three were numbered with the prefix 'DSC' and showed two men sitting together at what looked to be an outdoor cafe. When he let his cursor rest on one of them, he found that, at 650 kilobytes, it was considerably larger than the earlier images, and that it was taken on Tuesday the 8th of June at 3.15 p.m. by a camera identified as E4300. Roy's Nikon was a 4300 model. According to the 'details' view, the other images were all downloaded the next day, so it looked as if Roy had dragged them in from another folder.

Intrigued, Banks double-clicked on the first image of the two men. He didn't recognize either of them. They were leaning towards one another, in earnest conversation. Both wore white open-necked shirts and light, casual trousers. One was bulkier with curly greying hair, the other younger and thinner with spiky black hair, a goatee and a hunted, watchful expression on his face, as if he was worried about being spied upon.

The following two images were of the same scene, taken in rapid succession. Banks scrolled to the end of the folder, but all he found was more Larissas, Natashas, Nadias and Mitzis.

On Tuesday afternoon, then, Roy had taken three candid photographs of two men in conversation at an outdoor cafe, and on Wednesday he had burned them to a CD, hidden among hundreds of erotic images. He had then placed the CD in the Blue Lamps jewel-case, which stood out like a sore thumb in his music collection.

So who were the men and what, if anything, did they have to do with Roy's disappearance? Banks picked up the laptop and took it upstairs. It was time to learn how to use Roy's printer.

•

DC Kevin Templeton thought he'd died and gone to heaven when he reported to Gristhorpe that morning and the boss said to take Winsome with him and pay Mr Roger Cropley an early visit. The credit-card companies were not exactly forthcoming when it came to providing information, even to the police, but the service station's CCTV cameras showed a number plate beginning with YF, which was the Leeds licensing office. The DVLA offices were closed on Sundays, so Templeton had had to resort to the local telephone directories and electoral rolls. As luck would have it, the name eventually yielded a north Eastvale address, which also meant that Mr Cropley would, in all likelihood, have taken the same road from the A1 as Jennifer Clewes.

Templeton let Winsome drive the short distance to Cropley's, sneaking surreptitious glances at the taut black fabric stretched over her thighs whenever she changed gear. Christ, they could kill a man, he thought with wonder. Then he realized he was so randy that morning because he hadn't shagged the red-headed clerk last night, the way he had intended. She had given him a nasty look, too, when he got to work that morning, one of those looks that said you've had your chance, mate, now on your bike. Still, he knew he could break down her resistance again given the opportunity. He was also tired, he realized, not having slept for more than an hour or so, but that he could deal with.

As the empty Sunday morning streets flashed by, he put his head in detective mode and planned out his interview. He liked Cropley for the killing. There were one or two small glitches, but nothing he couldn't reason his way past: no sexual interference, for a start, which was a bit of a puzzle, and no struggle, either. Then there was Banks's address in the victim's pocket. But Templeton was sure Cropley had pulled her over and tried it on and something had gone disastrously wrong.

'How was your Saturday night?' he asked Winsome.

She gave him a sideways glance. 'Fine. And yours?'

'You already know about mine, spent sampling the delights of motorway cuisine. What did you get up to, then?'

'Up to? Nothing special. Club social.'

'Club?'

'Yeah, the potholing club.'

Templeton knew that Winsome liked to climb down holes in the ground and explore underground caverns. He couldn't think of anything more boring, or, for that matter, more terrifying, given that he suffered from claustrophobia. 'Where d'you hold it?' he asked. 'Gaping Gill?'

'Very funny,' said Winsome. 'Actually we met in the Cock and Bull. You should come along sometime.'

Was she asking him out? 'The Cock and Bull?'

'No, idiot. Potholing.'

'No way,' said Templeton. 'You'll not get me down one of those black holes.'

'Coward,' she said. 'Here we are.'

She pulled up in front of a neat Georgian semi, an unremarkable house with mullioned windows and beige stone-cladding. The street was on a low rise and offered a magnificent view out west to lower Swainsdale. There was a small limestone church with a squat Norman tower at the end of the street, and people were already filing in for the morning service.

Templeton jabbed at the doorbell, Winsome beside him. Despite, or perhaps because of, his lack of sleep, Templeton felt pepped up, excited, like the one time he had taken Ecstasy at a club. Winsome seemed cheerful enough in that cool and graceful way of hers, and if she had noticed him glancing at her thighs in the car, she hadn't said anything.

The man who answered the door didn't look particularly like a pervert, as far as Templeton could tell, except that he was wearing sandals with white socks, but he did match the description Ali had given him at Watford Gap. About forty, with thinning sandy hair, slim but with a beer belly sagging over his worn brown corduroy trousers, he had a long face with pouch-like cheeks and a rather hangdog expression. He reminded Templeton a bit of that actor who seemed to be in all the old sitcom repeats on telly with Judi Dench and Penelope Keith.

'Mr Cropley?' said Templeton, showing his warrant card. 'We're police officers. We'd like a word, if we may.'

Cropley looked puzzled the way they all did when the police came calling. 'Oh, yes, of course,' he said, moving aside. 'Please, come in. My wife's just . . .' He let the sentence trail, and Templeton and Winsome followed him into a living room that smelled of cinnamon and apples, where Mrs Cropley was putting the finishing touches to a colourful flower arrangement. She was taller than her husband, and bony, with strong, almost masculine, features. She looked a bit severe to Templeton, and he could well imagine her cracking out the leathers and whip for an evening

S&M session. The thought made him shudder inside. And maybe it drove Mr Cropley to other things.

'It's your husband we want to talk to,' Templeton said, smiling. 'First off, at any rate.'

Mrs Cropley stood there for a moment before the penny dropped. When it did, she gave her husband a look, then turned and left the room without a word.

Templeton tried to read significance into that look. There was something there, no doubt about it. One of Cropley's dirty little secrets had come back to haunt him, and his wife knew what it was, was letting him know that she knew, and he was on his own.

'We were just going to get ready for church,' said Cropley.

'I'm afraid the vicar will have to manage without you this morning,' said Templeton.

'What's it about?'

'I think you know. First of all, were you driving up the M1 and the A1 late on Friday evening?'

'Yes. Why?'

'What make of car do you drive?'

'A Honda.'

'Colour?'

'Dark green.'

'Did you stop at the Watford Gap services?'

'Yes. Look, I—'

'While you were there, did you notice a young woman alone?'

'There were a lot of people there. I . . .'

Templeton caught Winsome flashing him a glance. She knew. Cropley was evading the question, the first sign of guilt.

'I'll ask you again,' Templeton went on. 'Did you see a young woman there in the cafe alone. Nice figure, hennaed hair. She'd be hard to miss.'

'I can't remember.'

Templeton made a show of consulting his notebook. 'Thing is,' he went on, 'the bloke behind the counter remembers you sitting opposite the girl, and the petrol-station attendant remembers you filling up at the same time this young woman was there. That's how we found out your name, from the credit-card slip. So we know you were there. Do you remember seeing a young woman at the garage? She was driving a light blue Peugeot 106. Think about it. Take your time.'

'Why? What—'

'Do you remember her?'

'Perhaps,' said Cropley. 'Vaguely. But I can't say I was paying much attention.'

'That's not what I heard.'

'Then you heard wrong.'

'Come off it,' said Templeton. 'You were leering at her, weren't you? The attendant said you looked as if you wanted to stick your nozzle in her tank. You fancied her, didn't you? Wanted a piece.' He was aware of Winsome looking askance at him, but sometimes a direct shock to the system worked better than any amount of gentle questioning.

Cropley reddened. 'That's not how it happened at all.'

'Not how what happened?'

'Nothing. Nothing happened. The situation, that's all. I might have noticed her, but I wasn't "leering", as you put it. I'm a married man, a God-fearing man.'

'That doesn't always stop people.'

'Besides, since when has leering been against the law?'

'So you *were* leering at her.'

'Don't put words into my mouth.'

'What were you doing on the road so late?'

'Coming home. That's not a crime, either, is it? I work in London. I usually spend the week there.'

'A commuter, then. What do you do?'

'Computers. Software development.'

'Are you usually that late coming home?'

'It varies. As a rule, I try to get away by mid-afternoon on a Friday to beat the traffic, or early evening at the latest.'

'What was different about last Friday?'

'There was a meeting. We had a deadline to meet on an important project.'

'And if I called your company they'd verify this?'

'Of course. Why would I lie?'

'For all I know,' said Templeton, 'you drive up and down the motorway looking for young girls to rape and kill.'

'That's ridiculous.'

'Is it? Do you read the papers? Watch the news?'

'I try to keep abreast of current affairs.'

'Oh, you do, do you? Well, I don't suppose you've been following the story about the young woman murdered on the road from the A1 to Eastvale, have you? The same road you took. You were following her, weren't you? Waiting for your opportunity. A dark country lane. You cut her off. What happened next? Wasn't she your type after all? Did she struggle? Why did you shoot her?'

Cropley got to his feet. 'This is absurd. I don't even own a gun. I'm going to call my solicitor.'

'Where's the gun, Roger? Did you throw it away?'

'I told you. I don't own a gun.'

Templeton looked around the room. 'We can get a search warrant. Make a mess.'

'Then get one.'

'It'll be better if you tell us all about it,' said Winsome, in a soothing voice. 'We know these things happen, people lose control. Please sit down again, sir.'

'Nothing of the sort happened,' said Cropley, straightening his tie and glaring at Templeton. He sat down slowly.

'Come on, Mr Cropley,' said Winsome. 'Get it off your chest. There were two of them, weren't there?'

'Two what?'

'Two girls. Claire Potter and Jennifer Clewes. What were you doing on the 23rd of April?'

'I can't remember that far back.'

'Try,' said Templeton. 'It was a Friday. You'd be on your way back from London. Get away late that day, too, did you?'

'How do you expect me to remember one Friday out of all the rest?'

'Always stop at Watford Gap services, do you? Like the food there? Or do you stop at other places? Newport Pagnell? Leicester Forest? Trowell?'

'I stop when I feel the need.'

'What need?'

'It's a long drive. I usually take a break when I feel like it. Just the one. Use the toilets. Have a cup of tea. Maybe a sausage roll, a chocolate biscuit.'

'And look at the girls?'

'There's no crime in looking.'

'So you admit you do look?'

'You're doing it again. I simply said there's no crime in looking. Don't twist my words.'

'Were you at Trowell services on the 23rd of April?'

'I don't remember. I don't think so. I usually stop before then.'

'But you have been there on occasion?'

'On occasion. Yes.'

'And maybe you were there on the 23rd of April?'

'I've told you. I doubt it very much. I don't recall being there at all so far this year.'

'Very convenient.'

'It happens to be the truth.'

Templeton could feel his frustration level rising. Cropley was a cool one and he seemed to have mastered the art of not giving anything away. Why would he need to do that unless he did have a secret?

'Look, Roger,' said Winsome, 'we know you did it. The rest is just a matter of time. We can do it the easy way, like this, in the comfort of your own home, or we can take you down to the station. It's your choice. And believe me, every choice you make now will come back to haunt you down the line.'

'What would you do?' Cropley said to her. 'If you were innocent and someone was trying to say you'd done something terrible. What would you do?'

'I'd tell the truth.'

'Well, I am telling the bloody truth, but a fat lot of good it's doing me, isn't it?'

'Watch your language,' Templeton cut in. 'There's a lady present.'

'I'm sure she's heard worse than that.'

'And you a God-fearing man.'

'I didn't say I was a saint. Or a pushover.'

'Right, let's get back to that, shall we. Your unsaintly acts. We might not be able to prove you killed Claire Potter, but we've got a damn good chance of proving you killed Jennifer Clewes.'

'Then you don't need anything from me, do you?'

'Don't you understand?' Winsome said. 'It would make things easier for you later on if you told us now.'

'And what would it do for me? Knock a year off my sentence? Two years? Three years? If I survived that long.'

'That's good, Roger,' Templeton said. 'You're talking about doing time, now. Jail. Shows you're moving in the right direction. What it might mean is the difference in the quality of care once you're inside. See, people like you are on about the same level as kiddy-diddlers as far as the general prison population is concerned, and the court has some discretion as to whether you're to be isolated or not.'

'That's bollocks,' said Cropley. 'There are strict prison guidelines and it doesn't matter a damn whether I confess or not. Besides, you're both missing the point completely. Read my lips. I didn't do it. I have never, not once in my life, raped or killed anyone. Is that clear enough for you?'

Templeton glanced at Winsome. 'So be it,' he said. 'Like I told you, we'll be able to make out a good case from evidence and witness statements.'

'Circumstantial. It means nothing.'

'People have been convicted on a lot less.'

Cropley said nothing.

'What time did you start out on Friday?'

'About half ten.'

'What time did you get home?'

'About five.'

Templeton paused. There was something wrong here. 'Come off it. It doesn't take that long to drive from London to Eastvale, even with a stop or two. Unless you couldn't go straight home after you'd killed the girl. What did you do? Drive around until you calmed down, felt able to face your wife?'

'As a matter of fact, my car broke down.'

'Pull the other one.'

'It's true. I had a breakdown just a short distance past Nottingham.'

'That's very convenient.'

'It wasn't convenient at all. I had to wait over a bloody hour for the AA to come. They said it was a busy night.'

'The AA?'

'That's right. I'm a member. Want to see my card?'

Templeton felt his forehead getting hot. He didn't like the direction this conversation was taking. 'Can you prove this, about the breakdown?' he asked.

'Of course I can. Ask the AA. They'll verify what happened. I was stuck on the hard shoulder from about half-past twelve till half-past two. Wait a minute—'

'What was the problem?'

'Fan belt. That's put a spoke in your wheels, hasn't it? You never told me what time this girl was killed. It was while I was waiting for the AA, wasn't it?' Cropley smirked.

Templeton suppressed a sudden urge to break Cropley's nose. He felt himself running out of steam. If Cropley had been stuck on the M1 until well after two o'clock, he could hardly have killed Jennifer Clewes. 'Your mobile phone records will bear this out?'

'Should do. Will that be all?'

'Not quite,' said Templeton, loath to let the bastard gloat for too long. 'Who left the garage first, you or Jennifer Clewes?'

'She did.'

'And you followed her?'

'No. I was just behind her, but another car cut in front of me. Came right out of the shadows. I overtook them both shortly after and I never saw her again. She must have passed me later, when I was stuck by the roadside, but I didn't notice.'

'What about this other car? Why didn't you tell us about it before?'

'Because you were too busy trying to accuse me of rape and murder. You never asked.'

'Well, I'm asking now. What make was it?'

'A Mondeo. Dark colour. Maybe navy blue.'

'How many people in it?'

'Two. One in the front, one in the back.'

'Like a taxi?'

'Yes, but it wasn't a taxi. I mean, it didn't look like one. There was no light on top, for a start.'

'Private hire car, then?'

'Maybe. Look, I hate to tell you how to do your job, especially as you've been doing it so well, but why don't you ask me something useful, like do I remember the number?'

'I was getting to that,' Templeton said. 'Do you?'

'As a matter of fact I do. Well, some of it, anyway. I suppose I noticed because he pulled out a bit sharply and I had to brake.'

'What was it?'

'LA51.'

Templeton couldn't remember offhand what DVLA office and local tag the first two letters represented, but he knew that '51' meant the car had been registered between September 2001 and February 2002. The rest he could look up. It wasn't much to go on, but it was better than nothing.

'What did the occupants look like?'

'I didn't get a good look,' said Cropley. 'But I think they were both men. I really didn't think anything of it at the time, except that I had to brake rather sharply.'

'Try to remember.'

Cropley thought for a moment. 'The one in the back turned and looked at me after they pulled out. I suppose I tooted the horn at them. Just instinct.'

'And?'

'Well, as I said, I didn't get a good look. It was dark and his face was in shadow. But I think he had dark hair, tied back in a ponytail, and I doubt it was a friendly glance he gave me. I remember just feeling rather glad they didn't stop and beat me up. You hear so much about road rage these days.'

'What you get for going around tooting your horn,' said Templeton.

'They cut me off.'

'Popular girl, Ms Clewes,' mused Templeton. 'First you've got your eye on her, then another couple of blokes come cutting in and spoil all your fun. How did that make you feel?'

'What the hell are you talking about?' Cropley said. 'Can you hear yourself speak? You sound like a cheap television psychologist. Look, you already know I didn't do it, and I've had just about enough of this, so why don't you both sod off and check with the AA.'

Templeton reddened and Winsome gave him a sign that they should leave. He paused a moment, locking eyes with Cropley, then did as she suggested.

'Nice one, Kev,' she said, when they got outside. 'You handled that really well.'

He could tell she was still laughing at him when she got in the driver's seat and the anger prickled at his skin from the inside like hot needles.

7

The pub Burgess chose was flanked by a halal butcher and an Indian takeaway on a narrow street between Liverpool Street Station and Spitalfields Market. Banks took the tube and checked constantly to see if he was being followed. He was pretty sure he wasn't. After receiving the image on the mobile, though, he didn't feel like taking any chances.

It was lunchtime and most pubs were offering the traditional roast beef and Yorkshire pud, but at this place the choice was between nachos with sour cream and spicy chicken wings with BBQ dip. Banks didn't fancy either, so he stuck with a pint of Pride and a packet of cheese and onion crisps while Burgess attacked the nachos and washed them down with cheap lager.

There wasn't exactly any sawdust on the floor, but looking at the state of the place, Banks thought perhaps there ought to be. Most of the lunchtime drinkers were older Bangladeshis, Indians and Pakistanis – clearly not devoutly Muslim. A group were watching cricket on the television, a tourist match in which Essex were playing Pakistan, commenting loudly now and then on a particularly good off-spinner or square cut.

Burgess looked much the same as he had when Banks last saw him in January, except today he was informally dressed in jeans and a Hawaiian shirt that dazzled Banks. But the shaved head and slight paunch were still there, and the cynical, world-weary look had returned to his eyes. All that was new was his tan. After many rises and falls in fortune, Burgess had landed on his feet after 9/11, when the service required men who got things done, no questions asked. Banks wasn't sure what outfit he worked for now, but assumed it was something to do with Special Branch.

'Nice place you picked,' said Banks.

'It's anonymous,' Burgess said. 'Everyone here just minds their own business. Besides, most of the buggers can barely understand English.' Outside the window, the sky had darkened and a few splashes of rain ran down the grimy glass. Burgess looked at Banks closely. 'You look like a worried man. Care to tell your Uncle Dicky what's wrong?'

Banks looked around, saw that no one was paying them any attention, then brought up the image on the mobile and slid it over the table. Burgess picked it up, examined it closely and raised his eyebrows. 'It could be anyone,' he said, handing it back to Banks. 'Some drunk asleep at a party.'

'I know that. But what if it's not?'

'Who do you think it is?'

'It might be my brother.'

'Roy?'

'How do you know his name?'

Burgess paused. 'It was a long time ago.'

'When?'

'About five or six years. Last century, at any rate. No reason to bother you with it at the time.'

'So what brought brother Roy under scrutiny?'

'Arms dealing.'

'What?'

'You heard me. Arms dealing. Don't look so surprised. Your brother helped broker a deal between a UK arms manufacturer and some rich Arab sheikh. Greased the wheels, handled the baksheesh, attended galas at the consulate and so on.'

'Roy did that?'

'Roy would do anything to make a bit of extra cash. He has an extraordinary range of contacts and connections and the bugger of it is that he doesn't even know who half them really are.'

'Naive was never a description I'd have used to describe Roy,' said Banks.

'Maybe not,' Burgess argued, 'but he took too many people at face value. Maybe he didn't want to dig any deeper, find out any more. Maybe it was safer that way and easier on his conscience. Pocket the money and turn your back.'

Banks had to admit that sounded like the Roy he knew. More likely than naivety was lack of imagination. When they were kids, Banks remembered, they had had to share a bedroom for a few days for some reason. Banks was ten, Roy about five. Banks had tried to torment his younger brother by telling him gruesome ghost stories at bedtime, about headless corpses and misshapen ogres, hoping to scare him well into the night. But Roy had fallen asleep during Banks's version of *Dracula* and it was Banks himself who was left unable to sleep, jumping at every gust of wind and creak in the woodwork, victim of his own imagination. Perhaps Roy had taken his colleagues and their claims at face value, perhaps he hadn't wanted to dig any deeper, or perhaps he had just lacked the imagination to extrapolate on the bare facts. Banks reached for a Silk Cut.

'Didn't think you'd last long,' said Burgess, lighting one of his own Tom Thumb cigars and offering the flame to Banks, who took it.

'It's only temporary,' Banks said.

'Of course. Another pint?'

'Why not?'

Burgess went to the bar and Banks watched the cricket while he was gone. Nothing exciting happened. A second pint of Pride on the table before him, he asked Burgess exactly what he knew about Roy.

'You've got to understand,' Burgess said, 'that your brother did nothing illegal. People manufacture the damn things and people sell them. Back then you could sell anything to anyone, anywhere: missiles, landmines, submarines, tanks, jet fighters, you name it. The problem is that they had a habit of ending up in the hands of the wrong people, despite all the red tape. Sometimes they got used on the very people who sold them in the first place.'

'So where did these particular shipments go?'

'They were destined for a friendly country in the Middle East but they ended up in the hands of a terrorist splinter-group.'

'And Roy's part?'

'He had no idea. Obviously. He couldn't see the big picture, didn't want to, no more than the arms manufacturers did. All they wanted was a nice fat profit.'

'What happened?'

'It was the bloke who recruited Roy for the job, an old crony of his called Gareth Lambert, who we had our eyes on. He's history now. Left the country.'

Banks didn't recognize the name from Roy's call list or phone book. He could have missed it, as there were so many, or Lambert could be one of the 'unknown' numbers. On the other hand, if, as Burgess said, Gareth Lambert was history, there was no reason for Roy to have his phone number. 'And Roy?' he asked.

'One of our lads had a friendly word in his shell-like.'

'And after that?'

'Not even a blip on our radar,' said Burgess. 'So whatever this means,' he said, 'if it means anything at all, it's nothing to do with us. All of this was over and done with a long time ago.'

'That's comforting to know,' said Banks.

'Why don't you tell me what happened?'

Banks told him, from the strange phone call to the arrival of the digital photograph in the middle of the night. Burgess puffed on his cigar as he listened, eyes narrowed to slits. When Banks had finished, he let the silence hang for a while. Someone scored a six and the cricket-watchers cheered.

'Could be a prank. Kids,' Burgess said finally.

'I've thought of that.'

'Could be someone trying to scare you off. I mean, if you're supposed to think it's your brother and he's been hurt in some way.'

'I've managed to work that out for myself, too.'

'You're not scared?'

'Of course I bloody am. But I want to know what's happened to Roy. What do you expect me to do? Give up and go home?'

Burgess laughed. 'You? I should cocoa. What about kidnapping? Have you considered that? A prelude to a ransom demand?'

'Yes,' said Banks, 'but I've received no demand so far.'

'So what are you going to do now?'

'I thought you might be able to help.'

'How?'

'The mobile,' Banks said. 'A forensic examination might give us all sorts to go on. It might even tell us where the image was sent from, maybe even where it was taken. I'm not exactly up on the technology but I know the computer experts can get a lot out of these things.'

'True enough,' said Burgess. 'What with DNA, computers, the Internet, mobiles and CCTV there's hardly any need for the humble detective any more. We're dinosaurs, Banksy, or fast going that way.'

'A sobering thought. Can you help?'

'Sorry,' said Burgess, 'but this is a lot different from looking up a name or accessing a database. My department doesn't actually have a great deal of contact with the technical-support people. We're closer to the intelligence services, information-gathering. It would look bloody odd if I suddenly turned up at the lab and dropped this on their desk without any explanation. They'd be all over me like a dirty shirt. Sorry, Banksy, but no can do. My advice is take it to the local cop shop. Let them deal with it.'

Banks stared at the phone. Burgess's response was what he had half expected, but even so he felt disappointed, lost. What the hell was he supposed to do now? He couldn't go to the local police. It wasn't only that he was worried Roy might be involved in something criminal, but there was no way he would be given any part in an official investigation into the disappearance of his own brother, and he didn't think he could bear standing on the sidelines with his hands in his pockets, whistling. 'OK,' he said. 'And you're sure you've got absolutely no idea why any of this is happening?'

'Swear on my mother's grave. Your brother fell off our map many years ago and we've had no reason to put him back on.'

'You've been watching him?'

'Not recently. We kept an eye on him for a while. Like I said, he's got some interesting contacts. But as for Roy himself, we soon lost interest. It's not guns or terrorism. Believe me, I'd know.'

'And you'd tell me if it was?'

Burgess smiled. 'Maybe.'

Banks took out the envelope he'd brought and slipped out one of the digital photos for Burgess to examine. 'Do you know who these people are?' he asked.

Burgess picked up the photo and examined it closely. 'Well, bugger me,' he said. 'It can't be. Where did you get this?'

Banks told him.

'When was it taken?'

'According to the computer details it was taken on Tuesday the 8th of June at 3.15 p.m.'

'But that's last Tuesday.'

'Who is it?'

'Gareth Lambert.'

'You said he was history.'

'That's what I thought. But look.' Burgess placed the photo in front of Banks and pointed to the grey-haired man. 'He's put on a bit of weight and his hair's turned grey, but it's him all right.'

'Is he bent?'

'Definitely.'

'What was his line?'

'Import–export. At least it used to be. Fancy word for smuggling, if you ask me. Knows the Balkan route like the back of his hand.'

'Smuggling what?'

'You name it.' Burgess ran his hand over his shaved head. 'Look, you might as well know. In his time, Gareth Lambert was a very nasty piece of work, indeed. I don't mean tough, but nasty, sly. Maybe he's mellowed with old age, though I doubt it.'

'What did he do?'

'It wasn't always so much what he did as who he knew. He rubbed shoulders with some of the nastiest bastards in Europe. Smuggled arms, drugs, people, anything. He had connections with the military down in the Balkans – Kosovo, Bosnia – knew all the generals. He smuggled medical supplies – morphine, antibiotics – sometimes diluted. Bit of a Harry Lime, when you come to think about it, and almost as elusive. Likes to keep on the move, one step ahead. He's a slippery bastard. If he's back, you can be certain he's up to his eyeballs in something dodgy, and if your brother Roy . . . well . . .'

That didn't make Banks feel any easier about the situation at all. 'Who's that with him?'

'I don't know. I don't recognize him. Lambert and his crew aren't really my brief any more. Can I hang on to this? I've still got a few contacts where it counts, and I'll make a few enquiries. There'll be quite a lot of old-timers around the Yard interested to know Gareth Lambert's back in business, if they don't know already.'

'Of course,' said Banks. 'I've got copies. And the mobile?'

'Hang on to it for the moment. You might need it. If that picture was intended for you, then more messages might follow.'

'I suppose you're right,' said Banks, pocketing the mobile. Maybe Annie would be able to hook him up with a computer expert to enhance the image. That way he wouldn't have to relinquish the phone.

'Right,' said Burgess, 'I'd better be off now.'

Banks wondered if he'd done the right thing in telling all and handing over the photo of the two men to Burgess. Now that he'd made Roy's disappearance semi-official there could be no turning back, whatever happened. He had already gone too far to avoid some sort of disciplinary proceedings by not reporting the first phone call and by living in Roy's house and accessing his computer data. He thought he could rely on Burgess's discretion, but there was a limit to everything.

At least this way he could continue his own investigation. He had already made a list of names and numbers, almost a hundred, and he still couldn't remember seeing any Gareth Lambert. He would have to check again, of course, but if Lambert was back in the picture, maybe there was a reason why neither he nor Roy wanted any records of their communications.

'Look,' he said to Burgess, 'I appreciate your help, but if Roy's in the clear and there's nothing really to link him with any serious criminal business . . .'

'You want me to keep your brother out of it?'

'If you can.'

'No guarantees,' said Burgess. 'Gareth Lambert turning up like this out of the blue changes everything. But I promise I'll do my best.'

'You'll keep me informed? I'd like to know where to find this Lambert, for a start.'

'Like I said, I'll do my best. I'll keep my ear to the ground. I'd ask you to bugger off back to Yorkshire and stay out of the way if I thought it would do any good, but at least try to avoid getting under my feet.'

'I'll think about it,' Banks said. He gave Burgess Roy's telephone numbers and glanced towards the window. 'It's almost stopped raining. I'd better go, too.'

Burgess gave him a stern look. 'Be careful, Banksy,' he said. 'Remember, I know you. And this conversation never took place.'

Banks walked out. His car was still parked near Corinne's flat, so he made his way to Liverpool Street, where he could take the District Line back to Earl's Court and pick up his car before meeting Julian Harwood.

While he was on the concourse of the mainline station, he wandered over to look at the Kindertransport Memorial. A sculpture to commemorate the rescue mission that helped over ten thousand children escape Nazi persecution in Europe during 1938 and 1939, it consisted of a glass case shaped like a large suitcase, which held a selection of objects the children had brought with them and, standing beside it, a bronze sculpture of a young girl.

Through the rain-beaded glass, amongst other things Banks could see school exercise books, pages filled with mannered German writing, letters, articles of clothing, dog-eared family photographs, a pair of old boots with clip-on ice skates, a hand-puppet of a kitten, a book of piano music, a battered suitcase and three coat-hangers. On one was written 'Für das Kind', on the second 'Fürs liebe Kind' and on the third 'Dem braven Kinde'. It made Banks think of Mahler's beautiful 'Kindertotenlieder', 'Songs for the Deaths of Children', though these children hadn't died: they had been saved. He wondered if Roy had the Mahler in his collection; he hadn't noticed it.

Looking at the children's personal belongings arrayed like this before him, Banks thought of all the mementoes he had lost for-ever when his cottage burned down: the family photographs and videos – wedding, holidays, kids growing up – letters, keepsakes, the poems he had written as a teenager, old diaries and notebooks, school report cards, the records of a life.

But he couldn't feel self-pity in the face of this memorial. He hadn't lost nearly as much as these children, who'd lost their homelands and, in many cases, their whole families. Perhaps they had gained something, too, though. They had at least escaped the concentration camps, been taken in by good, caring families, and had grown up to live their lives in relative freedom.

Banks looked at the bronze statue of the girl in her skirt and jacket. The raindrops looked like tears flowing down her face. He turned away and headed for the underground.

●

Annie was glad DI Brooke had suggested a quick lunch together in her hotel that afternoon. She had heard nothing from Roy Banks and she was beginning to wonder if the two brothers had made up their differences and run away together just to make her job difficult.

Brooke was in his Sunday best, red-faced, collar too tight around his neck, looking like a farmer just come from church. Annie, in jeans and a black V-neck jumper, felt underdressed. Neither felt terribly hungry, so they ordered coffee and cheese-and-pickle sandwiches, which came cut into quarters, neatly arranged in baskets.

'Well, Dave,' said Annie, 'I must say you cut a dashing figure.'

Brooke blushed. 'The suit? I've got a christening to go to this afternoon.' He sat down and pulled at his collar, finally undoing the button. 'There, that's better. Plenty of time to choke myself to death in church later.'

Annie laughed.

'I don't have a lot to report,' Brooke said, 'but I had a couple of lads ask around the victim's neighbourhood. I've also had a word with the uniform who walks the beat there, PC Latham.'

'What does he say?' Annie asked.

'Quiet sort of area. No trouble lately.'

'What about the enquiries your lads made?'

'A bit more interesting. A bloke down the street was looking for a parking spot about ten o'clock on Friday night. Seems he usually managed to park right outside his house, but this time he couldn't because someone was already there. Said it had happened before a couple of times that same week. He was a bit miffed, but there was nothing he could do. After all, it was a free spot. Anyway, he remembered there were two men in the car, one in the front and one in the back. He thought they might be leaving so he hung back for a couple of minutes but they ignored him.'

'What happened?'

'He found another spot nearby and that was that.'

'Does he remember anything else about the car?'

'Only that it was dark blue.'

'No number plate?'

'The car was parked. He couldn't see the front or back.'

'Of course. Anything else?'

'When he went out to walk the dog at eleven, it was gone.'

'Could he describe the men?'

'Not very well. Only that the one in the back had something around his neck, like a thick gold chain. He said they looked a bit thuggish. At least their appearance worried him enough that he didn't approach them and ask if they were going to move.'

'Interesting,' said Annie. 'I've just been on the phone with my SIO and one of our DCs has got a similar description from a man called Roger Cropley. Apparently, this Cropley saw Jennifer Clewes at the Watford Gap service station around half-past twelve on Friday night and a car like the one you just described, with one man in the front and one in the back, cut in front of him and went after her.'

'Then it sounds as if someone was waiting for her outside the flat.'

'It does, indeed,' said Annie. 'If it's the same car. I've thought there were two of them right from the start, one who could get out of the car quickly and do the shooting, the other a driver.' Annie consulted her notebook. 'Have you ever heard of a woman called Carmen Petri?'

Brooke frowned. 'Can't say as I have. Why?'

'It's just a name one of Jennifer Clewes's friends mentioned. One of the "late girls", she called her. Jennifer was worried about her, something she said.'

'Late girls?'

'Yes. Why? Do you know what that means?'

'Haven't a clue,' said Brooke. 'It just sounds odd, that's all.'

Given the context – a family planning centre – Annie had come up with a couple of possibilities: either 'late girls' were late with their periods, which was sort of self-evident when you were dealing with pregnancy, or they were 'late' in their pregnancies, beyond the time when terminations could be performed, which according to the law was the twenty-fourth week.

'I'll check our files for you, see if we've any record of this Carmen, but the name doesn't ring a bell.'

'No reason why it should. But thanks anyway. And, Dave? Check mispers and recent deaths, too, if you can.' If someone had been performing late terminations and something had gone wrong, Annie thought, then Jennifer Clewes might have stumbled across something very nasty indeed.

•

'I haven't seen Roy in over a month,' said Julian Harwood, 'so I don't see how I can help you.'

'You never know,' said Banks. 'It's good of you to spare me the time.'

'Nonsense. Roy's a good friend. Has been for years, even if we don't see enough of one another these days. Anything I can do, I'm only too willing.'

Harwood didn't seem out to impress, as far as Banks could tell. He didn't need to; he was a powerful, wealthy businessman, used to getting his own way. Corinne's impression had been different, but then perhaps Harwood behaved differently around women. Many men do. Also, she was Roy's girlfriend, an extremely attractive young woman, and he might have felt the need to compete, to impress her.

The sun was out again and they were sitting outside at Starbucks drinking grande lattes. Before meeting Harwood, Banks had shown a copy of the digital photo to Malcolm Farrow, Roy's neighbour across the street. Farrow had said that the bulky man with the grey curly hair might just have been the one Roy left with at nine-thirty on Friday, but he couldn't be absolutely certain.

Banks could smell Chinese food from somewhere nearby, but he couldn't see a Chinese restaurant. The street was crowded with shoppers, a mix of tourists and locals out for a drink and a stroll.

Two pretty young girls in shorts and tank tops were sitting at the next table talking French and smoking Gauloises.

Harwood was younger than Banks had expected, mid-forties most likely, about Roy's age, and completely bald apart from a couple of thick strips of black above his ears. He had a healthy tan and the lean physique of a regular tennis or squash player. His clothes were casual but expensive: a blue denim shirt, open at the collar, and khaki chinos with a razor crease. Only the Nike trainers looked a bit out of character, but they weren't cheap, either.

Banks lit a cigarette – one of the advantages of sitting outside – and said, 'I don't suppose you know where he is?'

'What do you mean?'

Banks explained about Roy's phone call and the unlocked house. Harwood's brow furrowed as he listened, and when Banks had finished, he said, 'Roy could be anywhere. He travels quite a bit, you know. Have you thought of that?'

'Yes,' said Banks. 'But his message was *urgent*, and it seems odd that he hasn't told anyone where he was going. No one I've spoken with so far has any idea where he might be. Is he usually that secretive about his movements?'

'Not usually,' said Harwood. 'It depends. I mean, if there's some sensitive overseas deal in the offing . . .'

'Is that likely?'

'I'm saying it's possible, that's all.'

'Anyway, you're a business associate. You might know if he had any trips scheduled.'

'He didn't as far as I know,' said Harwood. 'But I'm not his personal assistant. Roy has plenty of irons in the fire that have nothing to do with me.'

'Do you think he might have done a runner?'

Harwood thought for a moment. 'Possible, I suppose, if things got too much for him. Tax, debts, that sort of thing. But surely he'd lock his house and take his mobile?'

'Maybe he wanted it to look as if it had happened some other way. I wouldn't put it past him. I don't know,' said Banks. 'I'm just clutching at straws.'

Harwood cleared his throat. 'I know you're a policeman,' he said. 'Have you reported this?'

'No,' said Banks. 'I'm conducting my own investigation so far.'

Harwood nodded. 'Probably wise, given Roy's penchant for – how shall I put it? – sailing a little close to the wind.'

'How long have you known him?' Banks asked.

'Years. We met at university.'

'Have you been involved in business ventures together ever since then?'

'On and off.'

'What about arms deals?'

'What arms deals?'

'Roy was involved in one a few years back. I was wondering if you knew anything about it, as a close friend.'

'I'm afraid that's not my area of expertise,' Harwood said in a tight voice. 'Roy would have known better than to come to me about it, if indeed he was involved.'

'Oh, he was involved, all right. What about insider trading?'

'What about it?'

'It's something else my brother was involved in. I just wondered if you played a part.'

Harwood shrugged. 'There was a time . . . it wasn't uncommon.'

'So you did?'

'I'm not saying that.'

'But you knew Roy did?'

Harwood scraped his chair back and made to get up. 'Is this meant to be some sort of interrogation? Because if it is, I'm going right now.'

'I have questions to ask you,' said Banks. 'Does that constitute an interrogation?'

'Depends on what they are and how you go about it.'

'Then I'll be as gentle as I can if you'll be as frank as you can.'

Harwood moved his chair back to the table. 'Then I'm here to help,' he said. 'But let's leave arms deals and insider trading behind us, shall we? I'm not saying both of them don't still go on – you only have to read the papers to know that – but if Roy or I had any involvement, we left it behind us along with the nineties. You can take my word on that.'

'All right,' said Banks. 'From what I can gather, Roy has been investing in private healthcare recently, and you're a big player in that game.'

'It was me who brought him in. There are a lot of opportunities. I'm the managing director and CEO of a chain of private health centres and clinics offering various procedures and levels of care, all carried out by highly qualified doctors and nursing staff. Roy's one of our major shareholders.'

'What kind of procedures?'

'Pretty wide range, really, from hernia operations to terminal-cancer care.'

'Can you think of any reason why anyone would want to harm him?'

'Anyone connected with our business ventures, you mean?'

'Yes.'

'No,' said Harwood. 'It doesn't make sense. I can assure you that everything is completely in accordance with the law. Why do you ask?'

'Because I'm really stuck here, Mr Harwood, so I'm just casting around in the dark. As far as I can make out, Roy was last seen leaving his house and getting into a big light-coloured car, probably an expensive model, with another man. As far as I know there were no signs of coercion, but it's not out of the question, if the man was carrying a hidden gun or something. Later, possibly during the night, his computer was taken from his house, which was left unlocked. His mobile phone was lying on the kitchen table. There were no signs of a struggle. I've considered kid-napping, and it might still be a possibility, though there's been no ransom demand yet. Roy's a wealthy man.'

Harwood stroked his chin. 'Not *that* wealthy, I wouldn't have thought.'

'It's all relative,' said Banks. 'People have been kidnapped for less, I should imagine.'

'True enough. But wouldn't there have been some sort of communication by now? When did you say this happened?'

'Friday night. Yes, it's been nearly two days and I've heard nothing so far. Which leads me to think it's something else. It just doesn't look like a bunch of thugs, that's all. More like . . . I don't know.'

'Organized crime?'

'It's a possibility,' said Banks. 'But what connection could Roy possibly have to organized crime?'

'I've no idea,' said Harwood. 'Just an idea I was tossing out. I mean, I don't even know what those people do. It's not as if it's just the Mafia any more, is it? One reads about Russians and Yardies and Vietnamese gangs. People who'd cut your throat as soon as look at you. Who knows?'

Banks took a copy of one of Roy's digital photos out of his briefcase and set it on the table. 'Do you know either of these men?'

Harwood pointed to Lambert. 'Well, I know *him*. That's Gareth. But I can't say I know the other one.'

'You know Lambert?'

'Oh, yes. Roy and I have done a bit of business with him in our time. Not for a while, mind you. He sort of disappeared from the scene.'

'He's back.'

Harwood frowned. 'I didn't know that.'

'Interesting,' said Banks, putting the photo away. 'I mean that Roy would know, but not you.'

'Gareth Lambert and I had a disagreement some years ago,' said Harwood. 'We haven't communicated since.'

'What about?'

'A private business matter.'

'I see. Do you know how I can get in touch with him?'

'As far as I know, he moved to Spain.'

'Big country. You don't have his address?'

'No. As I said, we had a falling out. I no longer have any interest in where Mr Lambert is or what he does.'

Banks would have liked to know more about that falling out, but Harwood was a shrewd businessman, good at keeping secrets, at holding his cards close to his chest. 'Did Roy ever mention anything that led you to believe he was up to something dodgy?'

'No. Not that he would have told me. Sometimes, in the business world, ignorance is bliss.'

'Is it possible he stumbled across something? Maybe someone was stealing and he found out about it?'

'From one of the centres?'

'Wherever.'

'I have nothing to do with the day-to-day running of the health centres or clinics.'

'What about Roy?'

'Your brother's a hands-on sort of investor. He likes to know how the businesses operate, likes to put faces to names. I imagine he's been doing the rounds.'

'So it's likely he visited the centres?'

'I should think so. Some of them.'

'Could he have stumbled on some sort of fraud or something?'

'We keep a pretty close eye on the figures. I think we'd know if anyone was bleeding the company.'

'What about stuff going missing? Drugs, for example.'

'They're strictly controlled.' Harwood looked at his watch. 'Look,' he said, standing up to leave, leaning over the table with his palms spread on its surface, 'I have to go now. I don't know whether you consider me a suspect in whatever you think is going on, but I want you to know that Roy's a valued friend. If I can help you in any way, please don't hesitate to get in touch again.'

'Very well,' said Banks. 'Thank you for your time.'

Harwood walked off. Banks finished his cigarette then stubbed it out and set off along the Old Brompton Road. He turned through the narrow arch into the mews and reached for Roy's key. Just as he put it in the lock someone grabbed his arm and a familiar voice said, 'You're nicked.'

8

'**You look like** death warmed over.'

'Thanks. You know, you shouldn't go around creeping up on people like that doing your *Sweeney* impersonation. You might get hurt.'

'You do seem very jumpy.'

'Maybe I've got good reason to be.'

'Care to tell me about it?'

Banks gave her a look she'd seen before. It meant he'd get her to play out her hand first and then decide how much to share with her. So be it.

'All right,' Annie said. 'How about a drink?'

They were sitting in Roy's kitchen, afternoon sunlight pouring in through the open window. Banks picked a bottle of Château Kirwan from the wine rack and Annie watched him attack it with an expensive and complicated opener. A simple corkscrew would have taken less time, she thought. After Banks poured, they sat opposite one another in silence.

'Who's going first?' Annie asked.

'How did you find me?'

'That doesn't matter. The point is that I *have* found you.'

'No,' said Banks. 'The point is, why were you looking for me? Why come all the way down here when I'm sure you've got more important things to do?'

'You really don't know?'

'I've got no idea. As far as you're concerned, I'm on holiday. Do you know something I don't?'

'Lots of things, probably.'

'No need to be sarcastic.'

Annie flushed. She hadn't meant to be sarcastic, but he was driving her to it. She knew she used sarcasm to hide behind when she was feeling vulnerable or confused, the way others hide behind smoking or bad jokes. She realized it probably wasn't the right time, but she didn't think she could go on talking to Banks unless she cleared the air. He would have to meet her halfway. The last time she had tried to reach out to him and heal the rift he had dismissed her. She polished off her glass and held it out for a refill. Dutch courage. Banks narrowed his eyes and poured.

'I'm sorry,' Annie said. 'I don't mean to be sarcastic. After everything that's happened things just seem to come out wrong.'

Banks caught her eye for a moment, then gazed past her out of the window. There were flowering shrubs outside in the backyard and Annie could hear bees buzzing from one to another behind her. Impulsively, she reached across the table and put her hand on his arm. 'What is it, Alan? We can't go on like this. *You* can't go on like this.'

Banks didn't flinch when she touched him, but he didn't say anything at first, just kept staring over her shoulder, through the window. Finally, he turned his eyes back to her.

'You're right,' he said. 'I feel as if I've been a long, long way from everything that used to matter, but I'm getting closer again.'

'Light at the end of the tunnel?'

'And all the other clichés. Yes.'

'I'm glad,' Annie said, feeling herself choke up. There was so much more to say but she sensed that now was not the time. Besides, there were other things of more immediate concern that they needed to talk about. She took another sip of wine. Definitely not your everyday quaffing plonk. Banks lit a cigarette.

'I thought you'd stopped that,' Annie said.

'I had,' said Banks. 'It's only temporary.'

'I hope so.'

'So why do you want to see me?'

'Have you heard about the woman found dead in the car near Eastvale?'

'I've read about it in the paper,' Banks said, 'but they haven't really given out much information.'

'Her name is Jennifer Clewes. Do you know anyone by that name?'

'No,' said Banks.

'Guess what we found in the back pocket of her jeans?'

'I've no idea.'

'An address.'

'Whose address?'

'Yours.'

Banks's jaw dropped. 'What? I can't . . . What's her name again?'

'Jennifer Clewes.'

'I've never heard of her. What's it all about?'

'We don't know yet. She had your address and directions written on a slip of paper in her back pocket, in her own handwriting,' Annie went on. 'The directions were to the damaged cottage. It looks as if it has been broken into. You can imagine what a flap it created up there, finding your name and address on a victim's person. Superintendent Gristhorpe decided to sit on it until Monday.' Annie could see that Banks was thinking furiously, trying to make things connect. 'Come on, Alan, give. You know something. What is it?'

'I don't know anything. I'm telling the truth. I've never heard of the girl.'

'But you know *something*. I can tell.'

'It's complicated.'

'I've got time.' Annie was feeling a little tipsy from the wine, but what the hell, she thought, in for a penny in for a pound. 'Maybe you can start,' she went on, 'by telling me what you're doing here. Last I heard, you and your brother were hardly on the best of terms.'

'He's disappeared,' Banks said.

'What?'

Banks told her about Roy's phone call, and the empty, un-locked house.

'Have you reported this?'

Banks said nothing. His gaze shifted back to the window.

'You haven't, have you?'

'Why does everyone keep going on about it so?' said Banks, with a sudden flash of anger. 'You know as well as I do how much effort we put into looking for a missing adult when he's been gone less than forty-eight hours. I've probably done more myself than the locals would have.'

'Who are you trying to convince? Listen to yourself. There are suspicious circumstances and you know it. You told me he said it was a matter of life and death.'

'*Might* be a matter of life and death.'

'Fair enough, you want to split hairs. I'll say no more right now, but don't forget it might be your brother's life you're playing fast and loose with. For Christ's sake, Alan, you shouldn't even *be* here.'

'Thanks for reminding me.'

'Oh, sometimes I just wish you'd grow up. You might be able to see the light at the end of the tunnel but, quite frankly, you're still a mess. You've done nothing but paperwork for the past few months, you've barely spoken to a soul, you rarely bother to shave, you need a haircut, and you're half pissed most of the time. I was in your flat. I've seen how you live.' There was no point going on at him, Annie knew. She just had to let her frustration out from time to time.

'What put you in such a good mood?' Banks said.

Annie just shook her head. 'Look, I know you're concerned,' she went on in a softer tone. 'I know you're worried about your brother, but you've got to stop being so stubborn. For his sake as well as your own.'

'You're probably right,' Banks said, 'but look at it from my point of view. I'm worried they might find out a few things about

Roy our parents would rather not know, and I know there's no way they'll let me work on the case if it becomes official. Besides, how can I know the job's being done properly if I don't do it myself?'

'Sometimes I wonder how you made DCI,' Annie said. 'Such skills of delegation.'

Banks laughed. Annie was surprised, and it broke the tension.

'Are you sure you've never heard of Jennifer Clewes?' she went on. 'You've no idea why she should have your address in her pocket?'

'There's a Jenn in Roy's mobile call list.'

'That's what her friends called her.'

'Wait here a minute.' Banks disappeared upstairs. Annie sipped more wine and looked around the kitchen. Expensive, she thought, especially for a room that didn't get used much. Banks soon returned with a bulging folder under his arm, sat back down and started flipping through pages.

'Do you have her phone number?' he asked.

'Her mobile's missing, but I got the number from her flatmate.' Annie read out the number from her notebook. It was the same one Banks had on Roy's call list.

'My God,' said Annie. 'So there definitely *is* a connection between Jennifer Clewes and your brother Roy.'

'Corinne was right. He did have a new girlfriend.'

'Corinne?'

'Roy's fiancée. Ex-fiancée.'

'From now on this is official,' Annie said. 'I'm going to have a word with DI Brooke about your brother's disappearance. He won't be happy.'

'Suit yourself,' said Banks.

'Look,' Annie went on, trying to placate him. 'You know you're too personally involved to be assigned to the case – either case – but that doesn't mean you can't be of some use.'

'On whose terms?'

Annie managed a thin smile. 'Well, it's not as if anyone's going to be keeping tabs on you twenty-four hours a day, is it? As long as we stay on the same page.'

Banks nodded. 'I suppose that's the best I can hope for.'

'All I ask is that you share with me. Any sign of a Carmen Petri on that list, by the way?'

'Carmen? I don't remember one. It's an unusual name. Let me have a look.' Banks glanced through the list of names. 'No,' he said. 'Why? Who is she?'

'I don't know,' said Annie. 'The name just turned up in one of my interviews. So how do you think it all connects?'

'Let's review what we know.'

'The way it looks is that someone was watching Jennifer's house in Kennington on Friday evening,' said Annie. 'Maybe other evenings, too, that week. Waiting for her. We don't know why. One witness has already confirmed there was a dark blue car parked near her flat with two men inside around the time she set off, one in the front and one in the back, and he'd seen it there before. The same car – or at least we think it's the same car – was seen at the Watford Gap service station, where Jennifer stopped to eat and fill up with petrol. It cut off another driver pulling in right behind her when she left. The only half-decent description we have is of the man in the back – muscular, with a ponytail.'

'Is that the man who killed her?'

'We don't know, but it's the best lead we've got so far. Stefan's working overtime on the scene. Unfortunately the pursuing car wasn't scratched or anything so we've no paint chips to go on.'

'But why would Roy send this woman to see me? Why not come himself?'

'I don't know. Her flatmate said Jennifer received a phone call around a quarter to eleven that Friday and left right after. Said it shook her up a bit. Did your brother sound worried when he heard the doorbell?' Annie asked.

'No,' said Banks. 'I've thought a lot about that, and he sounded fine. I mean, if he'd been worried it was someone come to do him harm he wouldn't have answered it, would he? He'd probably have tried to scarper out of the back window. Besides, the bloke across the street said Roy just locked his door and got into the car with his visitor as if things were quite normal.'

'So what do you think happened?'

'I've been trying to piece together the events of that day,' Banks said. 'The way I see it is that Roy comes home just before half past nine, from where I don't know, but something has upset him. He puts his mobile on the kitchen table, or it's already there, pours himself a glass of wine and goes up to his office to check phone messages, e-mail, or whatever. He takes the wine with him. Maybe he sits and mulls things over for a minute or two, then he decides that whatever it is he's found out is worth calling his estranged policeman brother about. Maybe he even senses that he's in danger because of something he knows. Anyway, he phones me and tells me he needs my help. While he's on the phone the doorbell rings. He answers it and goes off in a car with whoever it is. Willingly, it appears. And he forgets his mobile, even though he's given me the number. I'd say that means he's more than a little distracted.'

'Maybe it was Roy who rang Jennifer later, then?' Annie suggested.

'And gave her directions to my cottage and told her to set off right there and then because he couldn't come himself? Maybe it was. But why? What happened between half past nine and a quarter to eleven?'

'That we don't know.' Annie paused. 'Poor lass,' she said. 'Everything I've found out about Jennifer tells me she was a decent, hard-working, caring person, perhaps a bit naive and idealistic.'

'So what got her killed?'

'I wish I knew.' Annie sipped her wine. The light changed and she could tell that clouds were gathering, the world darkening around them. 'What are you going to do next?'

'Carry on my own personal covert operation,' said Banks.

Annie smiled. 'What can I say?'

'Nothing. You?'

'I'll talk to Dave Brooke as soon as I can and I'm pretty sure he'll want to see you. I mean it, Alan. Our cases have crossed and I'm not leaving any loose ends. Besides, given what happened to Jennifer Clewes, Roy could be in danger. Have you thought about that?'

'I haven't thought about much else,' said Banks. 'Mostly I've been thinking that he's done a runner, with kidnapping a distant second. Your connecting him with the murdered girl puts a different complexion on things.'

'I'm glad you see it that way. If you'd bothered to keep in touch, we might have got to this point ages ago.'

'How was I to know you were looking for me?'

'You know what I mean. Anyway, I've still got a couple of things to do tomorrow. Jennifer was killed on our patch but her life was down here. It makes things awkward.'

'So what do you have to do?'

'Visit Jennifer's workplace, for a start. She worked at a family planning centre in Knightsbridge. It—'

'What's it called?' Banks asked.

'The Berger-Lennox Centre. Why?'

Banks opened the folder again and started turning over sheets of paper, some of them covered with his own spidery scrawl. Finally he pointed to a printed sheet. 'I thought I remembered the name,' he said. 'It's one of the centres Roy invested in. One of Julian Harwood's companies. Are you sure that's where Jennifer Clewes worked?'

'Yes.'

'Perhaps that's where they met, then. Harwood told me that Roy's a hands-on sort of investor, likes to check out his assets. And if Jennifer Clewes was a good-looking young woman . . .'

'Which she was,' said Annie.

'Bingo.'

'It doesn't necessarily mean anything.'

'Maybe not,' said Banks. 'But it's another connection. One person murdered, another disappeared. Her phone number is in his book, my address is in her back pocket, and they have this family planning centre in common. I don't know about you, but that's way too many coincidences for me. Maybe I'll go with you tomorrow. Find out for certain. Someone must remember if Roy's been there.'

Annie paused. She wanted to be diplomatic but didn't quite know how to do it. In the end, she threw caution to the wind. 'You can't,' she said. 'You know you can't. It's not your case. I've already made it clear I'm making your brother's disappearance official and I'm giving you a bit of room to manoeuvre, but you can't just come muscling in. You have no official standing in the Jennifer Clewes investigation whatsoever.'

'But what if there's a connection with what's happened to Roy?'

'Look, Alan, you've got no official standing there, either. I'm not taking you with me and that's that.'

'Fine,' said Banks. 'OK. I understand.'

'Don't sulk. It doesn't suit you.' Annie stood up. She felt a little wobbly, but it was nothing she couldn't handle. 'And stick around. DI Brooke will be wanting to take your statement.' Annie heard a light tapping sound on the leaves behind her. It quickly grew louder and faster. The rain had started again.

•

It was early evening and Banks was sitting in Roy's office reading through the files Corinne had printed out when he heard someone at the door. At first he thought it might be Roy, but why would he be knocking at his own door? Then he thought it might be DI Brooke come to interview him, and decided it would be best to get it over with. Even so, he looked for some sort of weapon, just in case. All he could find was a set of golf clubs in the landing cupboard, so he grasped one of the irons and answered the door.

The man who stood there was about Banks's age. He was wearing a dark suit, had a neat side parting in his greying black hair and a serious, intelligent look in his eyes. He could have been a policeman, Banks thought, except that he was wearing a clerical collar.

'Hello,' he said, reaching his hand out. 'Hunt's the name. Ian Hunt. Roy home?'

Banks shook his hand. It felt damp and cool. 'No,' he said. 'I'm his brother, Alan. What's it about?'

'He's mentioned you,' said Hunt. 'The policeman. But I didn't think . . . Never mind.'

Banks had a good idea what Ian Hunt didn't think, but he kept quiet. He needed all the information he could get, and a defensive attitude from the outset wouldn't help matters much. He wondered what the hell the vicar was doing calling around at Roy's house. 'Would you like to come in?'

'Yes. Yes, please, if it's all right.'

Banks propped the golf club by the front door and led the way to the kitchen at the back, where he had recently sat with Annie, and offered Hunt a chair. Hunt made no comment about the club. Banks didn't want to seem as if he was interrogating the man, but he realized he had practically forgotten the simple art of conversation after all his years in the force. His job affected the way he saw and dealt with everyone. He had even been brusque with Corinne. 'Why did you want to see Roy?' he asked.

'No real reason,' Hunt said. 'Only he didn't turn up at church this morning, and that's not like him.'

Banks nearly fell off his chair. 'Church?' Wonders never cease.

'Yes. Why? What's so strange about that?'

'Nothing,' said Banks, who hadn't set foot inside a church since his childhood, except for weddings and funerals. He and Roy hadn't been given a particularly religious upbringing, and neither of their parents had been regular churchgoers. At school, back in those days, there were prayers and a hymn every morning, of course, but apart from a few years of Sunday school and a brief stint in the Lifeboys and Boys' Brigade, that had been it as far as Banks was concerned. Now this.

'Normally, I wouldn't bother dropping by,' said Hunt, 'but there was a meeting of the restoration-fund committee after the service and Roy has always been a keen contributor. Not only financially, you understand, but also in terms of ideas. Very creative mind, Roy.'

'Cup of tea, Vicar?'

'Please. And call me Ian. Unless you want me to call you Chief Inspector?'

'Ian it is.' Banks put the kettle on. Tea with the vicar on a Sunday evening, he thought. How very genteel. This wasn't a world he would ever have suspected Roy of inhabiting. He found the teabags next to the coffee and put two in the flower-patterned teapot.

'If you don't mind me asking,' said Banks as the kettle was coming to a boil, 'when did Roy start going to church?'

'I don't mind at all,' said Hunt. 'He started attending services on the 16th of September 2001.'

'I didn't expect you to remember the exact date,' Banks said.

'But how could I forget? You'd be surprised how many people returned to the church, or first started attending, around that time.'

Banks had to think for a moment before he realized the significance of the date. It must have been the first Sunday after the attack on the World Trade Center. But why should that affect Roy so much? He poured boiling water into the pot. 'What drew him there?' he asked.

Hunt paused. 'You really don't know much about your brother, do you?'

'No,' said Banks. 'And the more I find out, the less I know.'

'That's the universal paradox of knowledge.'

'Maybe so,' said Banks, 'but at the moment I'm interested in more practical knowledge. I don't suppose you have any idea where Roy might be?'

Hunt blinked. 'I was the one who came here looking for him, remember?'

'Even so.'

Hunt looked at Banks with curiosity in his eyes. 'I can see you've been trained not to take anything at face value,' he said. 'No, I have no idea where he is.'

'Why did you come here?'

'I told you. The meeting. It's not like Roy not to even leave a message.'

'When did you last see him?'

'Last Sunday.'

'Did you talk to him?'

'We chatted briefly after the service.'

'How did he seem?'

'Fine. Quite normal.'

Banks got the milk from the fridge, giving it a quick sniff to see if it was still all right, poured the tea then sat down opposite Hunt. 'I don't mean to seem so abrupt,' he said, 'but I'm concerned. Roy left a rather disturbing message on my answerphone and when I came down here to see him he'd disappeared and the front door was unlocked.'

'I can see why you would be concerned,' said Hunt.

'So the two of you chatted often?'

'Yes,' said Hunt. 'We'd often spend an hour or two together, usually at the vicarage, sometimes over lunch.'

Lunching at the vicarage was an image Banks found very hard to visualize. 'Did Roy open up to you? I mean, did he . . .'

'I know what you mean.' Hunt shifted in his chair. 'Yes, I'd say he opened up about his feelings. At least to some extent.'

'Feelings about what?'

'Many things.'

'I'm afraid that's a bit vague for me,' said Banks. 'Do you think you could be more specific? It's not as if you took his confession or anything.' Banks realized that he hadn't ascertained what denomination Hunt represented. 'I mean, you're not Catholic, are you?'

'C. of E. But I don't know how much I can help you. Roy never went into great detail about anything he did.'

'I don't suppose he would,' said Banks. 'But did you get any sense of why he started attending church on the 16th of September 2001, other than some vague sense of unease about the way the world was going?'

'It wasn't that.' Hunt took a deep breath. 'It's my feeling that your brother had lost his moral compass, had become so engrossed in the making of money that how he made it no longer mattered to him.'

'He's not unusual in that,' said Banks.

'No. But it's my guess that what happened in New York and Washington on the 11th brought it home to him in no uncertain terms.'

'You're not saying he was somehow connected to the attacks, are you?'

'Oh, no,' said Hunt. 'No, you're missing the point entirely.'

'What, then?'

'Didn't he tell you? He was there.'

Banks had to pause a moment to take this in. 'Roy was in New York when the attacks took place?'

Ian Hunt nodded. 'According to what he told me, he had an appointment with a banker in the second tower. He was running late and his taxi got caught up in traffic. The next thing he knew, everyone was coming to a halt and getting out of their cars, some of them pointing up. Roy got out, too, and he couldn't believe what he was seeing. The smoke and flames. People jumping out of windows. It took him three days to get on a flight home.'

'Jesus Christ,' said Banks. 'Sorry. He never told me this.'

'But you're not close, are you?'

'No.'

'Anyway, it gave him pause for thought – the enormity of it all, fate, how everything was connected, what unimaginable consequences could arise from seemingly unimportant, unrelated actions. These were all things he wanted to talk about. I had no answers, but he seemed to find something of what he wanted in the church, in prayer, holy communion, and in our discussions.'

Banks remembered what Burgess had said about the arms deal. Roy had found out that a shipment he had brokered had found its way into the wrong hands. Had Roy really been so naive as to think that arms dealing was just a business like any other? He probably hadn't given it too much thought, Banks decided, lured by the money and the excitement. Warned off by Special Branch, he had backed away from that line of work immediately, but he had witnessed the attacks on the World Trade Center and he was stricken by conscience, by the fact that guns or missiles he had exported *could have* been used in something like this. Roy realized he had crossed a line and he didn't like what he saw on the other side.

Suicide bombers in distant desert places are one thing, but being there, in New York on September 11th 2001 and witnessing what happened must have been devastating. It certainly made it impossible for Roy to remain wilfully ignorant of the kind of things terrorists intended to do to the West, given the means and opportunity. And, unknowingly or not, Roy had once helped out with the means. Hence the guilt. Roy had turned to the Church for absolution.

This was a new perspective on his brother, and one that would take Banks a little time to get used to. It certainly didn't match the Roy he remembered from the last time he had seen him just eight months ago, but then that had been Roy-at-home, a careful image he projected for his parents. Had Roy even told their parents what he had seen? Banks doubted it. Despite his religion, though, Roy had continued to make money; he had hardly given it all to charity and taken a vow of poverty, or chastity, for that matter. Clearly guilt only went so far and cut so deep.

So what had happened to him? Had he lost his moral compass again? The making of money, perhaps even more than the money itself, was an addiction to some people, like gambling, heroin or cigarettes. Banks had given up smoking the previous summer when he found out that an old schoolfriend had died from lung cancer, but he had started again after a fire took his home, his possessions and, almost, his life. Where was the logic in that? But such is the nature of addiction.

'Has anything in your recent conversations given you any reason to think Roy might have got into some sort of dangerous grey area again?' Banks asked.

'No,' said Hunt. 'Nothing.'

'He didn't mention his business activities?'

'We didn't talk about business. Our conversations were mostly of a philosophical and spiritual nature. Look, I know Roy's not a natural man of religion, and I very much doubt that he's a saint, even after what happened, but he does have a conscience and sometimes it troubles him. He's still a hard-nosed business-man, the kind of person you'd expect to cut a corner or two and not always ask too many questions, but I'd say he's a lot more careful these days. He's drawn his own lines.' Hunt paused. 'He's always looked up to you, you know.'

'You could have fooled me.' Growing up, Banks had done everything wrong. He had stayed out too late, got caught shop-lifting and smoking, got into fights, neglected his schoolwork, and the final insult, he had turned away from business studies and chosen a career of which neither of his parents approved. Roy, on the other hand, from five years behind, had watched his brother's progress and learned what not to do.

'It's true,' said Ian Hunt. 'He did look up to you, especially when you were children. You just never paid him any attention. You ignored him. He felt neglected, rejected, as if he always let you down.'

'He was my little brother,' said Banks.

Hunt nodded. 'And always in the way.'

Banks remembered when he was going out with Kay Summerville, his first serious girlfriend. Roy was about twelve at the time, and whenever their parents went out for a night at the local pub and Banks invited Kay over to listen to records, among other things, he would always have to pay Roy to stay in his room. So maybe Roy was always in the way, Banks thought, but he found the means to profit from it.

'Anyway,' Banks said, 'I wasn't aware that he looked up to me in any way. He certainly never let it show.'

'I'm not saying Roy isn't competitive. You were good at sports, for example. He wasn't, so he worked hard at what he did best. He compensated.'

Good? Banks had been a tolerable fly-half then, fast and slippery. At cricket he hadn't been much of a batsman but had been a decent mid-pace bowler. Roy had been an overweight, bespectacled and unattractive child, not at all athletic, and at school the other kids teased him and called him a swot. Once the bullying got serious enough that Banks stepped in and put an end to it, so no one could say he never did anything for Roy. But he certainly hadn't done enough.

'Even now he looks up to you,' Hunt went on.

'That I find even harder to believe,' said Banks, wondering what there was to look up to: a failed marriage and a thankless job. Especially when Roy had it all: the flash car, women falling at his feet, the mews house. But they were all *things*, Banks realized, all material possessions. Even the women, to some extent, were status symbols. *Look at me with a beautiful young woman on my arm.* All for show. Roy's three marriages had ended in divorce, and not one of them had produced any children. He had even broken off his engagement to Corinne. Banks at least had Brian and Tracy.

He saw that Hunt was standing, ready to leave. 'Sorry,' said Banks. 'Just thinking about what you said.'

'That's all right,' said Hunt. 'I should go. I'm just sorry I couldn't be of more practical help. If there's anything you need, don't hesitate. It's St Jude's, just down the street.'

'Thanks. Oh, hang on a minute.' Banks fetched one of the

digital photos and showed it to Hunt. 'Do you recognize either of those men?'

Hunt shook his head.

'You've never seen Roy with either of them?'

'No, never.'

They shook hands again and Ian Hunt left.

Maybe the mistake Banks had made in trying to figure Roy out was to dismiss his spiritual and emotional sides. Now he had discovered that Roy had become a regular churchgoer, it changed things, added a dimension he hadn't suspected. Did it help him figure out what had happened to Roy? Perhaps not, but it might affect the way in which he conducted his investigation. Previously, he'd been looking for something dodgy that Roy had been connected to, something he had perhaps run away from; now, though, the field was wide open. Possibly Roy had stumbled over something he shouldn't have done, or perhaps he had become a threat to people he had once worked closely with, and instead of turning a blind eye he had planned on blowing the whistle? But on what, on who?

•

Gaps in the cloud let through bright lances of light and the western sky turned vermilion and violet. The crowds queuing for the sunset ride on the London Eye shifted restlessly in the downpour and people on Westminster Bridge watched on from under their umbrellas and rain hoods.

Eight-year-old Michaela Toth had been excited all day about the promised ride. It was to be the highlight of her first ever weekend in London – even better than Madame Tussaud's and the zoo – and her mum and dad were letting her stay up late especially. Even the rain didn't dampen her spirits as she stood in the queue hopping from foot to foot, clutching her yellow plastic handbag with the pink flower on it. It seemed as if they would never get there, edging forward at a snail's pace like this. Michaela could hardly believe that the Eye was so much bigger than she had imagined, or that it never stopped turning, even when you got on and off. The thought made her just a little bit scared, but nicely so.

Slowly, inch by inch, they moved forward. As soon as the cars emptied, they filled up again. A squat red tugboat chugged down the river leaving its arrowhead wake in the darkening water. It was still light enough to see the men standing on the deck and Michaela noticed one of them point in her direction. At first she thought he was just pointing at the Eye, but more men joined him and the tug changed direction, heading for the bank.

Michaela pulled on her father's hand and asked him to take her to the wall to see what the men were pointing at. At first she thought he wasn't going to, but then she could tell he got curious too because he asked her mother to keep their place in the queue and said they'd be back in just a moment.

The tug was getting closer to the embankment as they got to the railings beside the Eye. The people on Westminster Bridge were pointing their way now, too, and Michaela wondered if they'd seen a dolphin, or even a whale, though she didn't really believe there were any whales or dolphins living in the River Thames. Maybe one had escaped from an aquarium. Or maybe someone had fallen in the river and the men on the tugboat were going to rescue him.

Holding her father's hand, Michaela strained to see over the embankment wall. She was just tall enough to manage it. The tide was very low and a shingle bank stuck out of the water like a whale's back just below the wall. Lying on the shingles was the dark shape of a man. A sprawled figure, he was lying on his stomach and his arms were stretched out in front of him, his lower half in the water. Michaela's father pulled her away quickly.

'What is it, Daddy?' she asked, frightened. 'What's that man doing there?'

Her father didn't answer; he simply led her away. When they rejoined her mother in the queue, her father spoke and Michaela heard the words 'dead body'. Soon, others started drifting towards the wall. One woman screamed. Michaela worried she might not get her ride after all. If there was a dead body down there, perhaps the London Eye would even stop turning.

•

After the Reverend Ian Hunt had left, Banks put away the golf club, feeling rather foolish, locked up the house and went upstairs with the remains of his wine. He rang Julian Harwood, who confirmed that he was managing director of the Berger-Lennox Centre but said he had never actually been to the place and had never heard of Jennifer Clewes. Banks had no reason to disbelieve him.

Banks felt a sudden urge to listen to some music. He found a CD he had never heard before: Lorraine Hunt Lieberson singing two Bach cantatas. Roy's top-of-the-line stereo system brought out the rich timbre of the strings, and when he closed his eyes Banks could imagine himself in a room surrounded by the small ensemble. And the voice was sublime, almost enough to make you believe in God. He thought of Penny Cartwright singing 'Strange Affair'. Different, but another wonderful voice.

Banks sipped wine, feeling a pleasant buzz, let the music roll over him and thought about Annie, Roy, Jennifer Clewes and the Berger-Lennox Centre. He would like to have been invited to go along with Annie in the morning, but she was right – it wasn't his case, and he was a bit of a mess. When he examined his feelings, it was curious how little her comments really hurt. At the time, they had stung, but they had quickly sunk in, and he knew they were true. He had let things go. If he wasn't as bad as the hapless fellow in one of his favourite Nick Lowe songs, he had been getting there.

Perhaps a few months ago, before the Phil Keane business, Annie would have welcomed his company, but now she didn't quite seem to trust him. And she was right not to do so. The last thing he had on his mind was going back up to Yorkshire.

The CD finished and Banks looked for something else to put

on. Roy didn't have the Mahler songs, but he did have Strauss's 'Four Last Songs', one of Banks's favourite pieces of music, so he put that on. As it turned out, he didn't get far into the second song before he heard the phone ring in Roy's office. Putting his glass down, he hurried across the landing to answer it.

•

The London Eye towered over the scene, a huge dark semicircle against the moonlit clouds. It was closed for the night now, but still turning slowly, always turning. Nearby, on the stone steps that led down to the hump of shingle bared by the ebbing tide, the SOCOs came and went like ghosts in their protective clothing. It was a ballet in which every dancer knew his steps. Despite the occasional shout and chatter or static over police radios, there was an odd hush about the scene, and no sense of hurry, as if the mighty heart of the city were lying still. Arc lamps lit rough slimy stone, shingle and greasy water alike, and a video camera recorded everything. The rain had stopped, and from Westminster Bridge a few curious onlookers watched over it all, silhouettes against the light dying in the west.

When Banks arrived at the taped-off area, Burgess was already waiting for him, a grim look on his face. He had explained to Banks over the telephone that when he saw on the news that the body of a white male about Roy's age had washed up by the London Eye, his alarm bells had automatically gone off. They had found no identification on the body, so there was no evidence yet that it *was* Roy, and indeed he hoped it wasn't, but it might be worth Banks's coming along and having a look.

Banks hadn't needed asking twice.

Burgess took him by the arm and led him over to a thickset man with a red moon-shaped face. 'DI Brooke, Lambeth North,' said Burgess. 'Meet DCI Banks, North Yorkshire Major Crimes.'

The two men nodded at one another. 'DI Brooke?' said Banks. 'You'll be the chap Annie Cabbot's working with on the Jennifer Clewes case?'

'Annie and I go back a long way.'

Banks gestured towards the river. 'Is he still down there?'

'The police surgeon's pronounced death, but the SOCOs haven't finished yet. They'll have to move fast, though, because the tide's coming in.' Brooke paused and looked down at his feet. 'Look, Superintendent Burgess here told me he thinks there's a possibility it might be your brother down there?'

'I hope to God it's not,' said Banks, 'but it's a possibility, yes. He's missing.'

'Sorry to have to put you through this.'

'Better than not knowing,' said Banks. 'Can we go down?'

'There's some extra overalls in the SOCOs' van. And mind your step, those old stone stairs are worn and slippery.'

Kitted out in protective clothing, Banks and Burgess showed their identification to the officer guarding the scene, ducked under the tape and approached the steps. The landing at the bottom didn't quite reach as far as the exposed shingle, so the SOCOs had already set up a makeshift bridge made of planks. It wobbled a little as Banks and Burgess crossed. Once, Banks almost lost his footing and he became suddenly aware of how much he had had to drink that day. Water lapped gently against the stone wall.

Banks felt a tightness in his chest as he approached the shingle and breathing became an effort. Burgess gave a nod and one of the SOCOs gently turned the top half so that the face was visible. Banks squatted, feeling his knees crack, and looked into Roy's dead eyes. There was a little hole in his left temple, close to the childhood scar Banks had accidentally inflicted with a toy sword. Banks felt himself sway on his haunches and stood up so fast it made him dizzy. Burgess grabbed his elbow.

'I'm all right,' said Banks, disengaging himself.

'Well, is it him?'

'It's him,' Banks said, and the only thing he could think as he tried to rein in his surging emotions was, *What the hell am I going to say to my parents?*

'Let's get back up on shore,' Burgess said.

Banks followed him back over the planks and up the steps. DI Brooke and his DS were waiting for confirmation. The sooner you identified the body, Banks knew, the sooner you put the machinery of a major investigation in motion. He nodded to Brooke.

'I'm sorry,' Brooke said.

'Look,' said Banks, 'do you think you could keep it under wraps? His identity, that is. I'd like to be the one who tells our parents, in person, but not tonight. It's too late.'

Brooke looked at the crowd on the bridge and the reporters and camera operators behind the crime-scene tape. 'We can tell them we're still awaiting official identification of the body,' he said. 'That should hold them off for a while.'

'First thing tomorrow,' said Banks. Just not tonight, he prayed. He couldn't stand the idea of going over to Peterborough right now and waking his parents up and spending the night comforting them in their grief, knowing they would probably prefer it was him rather than Roy. Daylight would make it easier, he thought. Let them have just one more night of peace; there would soon be enough dreadful nights to come. 'Can you tell Annie for me, please?' he asked.

'Of course. In the morning.'

'Thanks.'

Brooke paused. 'I'm sure you know I was intending to visit you, anyway,' he said. 'In fact, DI Cabbot and I had a little word about you earlier this evening.'

'I thought you might,' said Banks.

'This changes everything, of course, but I've still got a few questions for you,' Brooke went on. 'When you're up to it, that is.'

'I'm up to it now,' said Banks.

'Right. Superintendent Burgess tells me you've been staying at your brother's house. How about we go there?'

'Fine,' said Banks, fumbling in his jacket pocket for his cigarettes. 'Let's go.'

9

The Berger-Lennox Centre opened at nine o'clock on Monday morning and Annie was there on the dot. The centre took up the first two floors of a four-storey Georgian crescent house in Knightsbridge, which looked like something out of *Upstairs, Downstairs*. Still, when you paid through the nose for the service, Annie reflected, you didn't expect some bog-standard NHS prefab concrete-and-glass block.

As soon as she got through the front door, the impression of elegant age gave way to one of muted modernity. The walls were painted in pastel hues of blue and green, and there was the kind of hissing hush about the place that made her ears feel stuffed-up, as if she were in an aeroplane. It took her a moment to notice the music playing softly in the background: something classical and soothing, something Banks would probably recognize.

The scent of sandalwood in the air materialized into a sudden vision of Annie's mother leaning over her, smiling. The image shocked her, as her mother had died when she was six and she didn't remember much about her. But now she could almost feel the long soft hair tickling her face. Jane had been something of a hippie, and Annie remembered that sandalwood incense had often been burning in the artists' commune where she had grown up. The memory also made her realize how far she had moved away over the past few years from so many of the ideals of her youth, and she resolved to spend more time on yoga and meditation; she hadn't practised at all since the business with Phil Keane.

The blonde behind the polished-wood reception desk looked up from her computer monitor and smiled as Annie approached.

A brass plate said her name was Carol Prescott. Behind her, in the open-plan office space, a young woman stood at an open filing cabinet.

Annie showed her warrant card and explained she was investigating Jennifer Clewes' murder. Carol's public smile dropped and was replaced by sadness. Her eyes moistened slightly.

'Poor Jennifer,' she said. 'It was in the papers this morning. She was really sweet. I can't imagine why anyone would want to do something like that to her. I don't know what the world's coming to.'

'Did you know her well?'

'She was my boss. We didn't socialize outside the centre or anything, but she was always ready with a hello and a smile.'

'How was her state of mind recently?'

'Fine,' said Carol. 'Though come to think of it she did seem a bit scatter-brained last week.'

'Any idea why?'

'No. She just seemed sort of on edge.'

'Was she happy working here?'

'She always seemed to be, but I didn't know her well enough for her to confide in me. Anyway, how can you tell if someone is *really* happy? I mean you read in the papers about people killing themselves when their friends think they've got everything to live for, don't you?'

'Sometimes,' Annie said. 'But Jennifer didn't kill herself.'

'No. I know that. I'm sorry.'

'No need to be. Look, I want to speak to a few people here, people who knew her, but maybe you can give me a bit of background on the place first.'

The phone rang and Carol excused herself. She adopted her professional voice and made a consultation appointment for a new patient.

'Sorry,' she said when she'd hung up. 'Of course, I'll fill you in on what I can.'

'How many people work here?'

'Seven,' said Carol. 'That's including Jennifer. She was administrative director of the centre. Then there's her assistant Lucy behind me there in the office. Andy and Georgina are our two consultation advisers, counsellors, then there's Dr Alex Lukas, the medical director, and Nurse Louise Griffiths.'

'What's Julian Harwood's role?'

'Mr Harwood? He's managing director of the whole group. But we never see him. I mean, he doesn't really have anything to do with the day-to-day running of the centre, or with the clinics.'

'Clinics?'

'Yes. We don't carry out terminations here. If a client decides that's the route she wants to go, we make an appointment at whichever of our clinics is most convenient for her.'

'I see,' said Annie. 'So this centre would hardly be a magnet for anti-abortion activists?'

'Hardly,' said Carol. 'We've had one or two small demonstrations, you know, when there's something in the news, but nothing violent. We offer advice on all aspects of family planning, not just abortion.'

'How does the system work?'

Carol sat back in her chair. 'Well,' she said, 'first they come to me, or phone, and I explain what our services and charges are and give them some pamphlets to read then send them to Lucy, who handles all the basic paperwork. Usually at that point Louise runs a proper pregnancy test, just to make sure. We usually tell them to bring a urine sample with them, but there are facilities here if they forget. Anyway, then they'll go to the waiting room where they can read through the brochures until Andrea or Georgina is ready to see them.'

'Then what?'

'It's up to them, really. Our counsellors will ask a few personal questions, and they'll also answer any questions the client has at that point. You'd be surprised how many are confused by their pregnancies, poor things.'

No, I wouldn't, thought Annie. She had become pregnant after a rape and while there was no doubt that she was going to have an abortion, she could remember the inner turmoil and the guilt she felt. And Annie thought of herself as a modern, forward-thinking woman. Very few women, if any, approached termination lightly.

'After that they'll discuss the choices available,' Carol went on, 'give guidance and advice if necessary. They're specially trained. Then the client sees Dr Lukas, who asks them about their medical history and examines them to confirm the gestation of the pregnancy, then Nurse Griffiths takes a blood sample. There's more paperwork – consent forms and so on – and the doctor will discuss the different methods available and help them decide on the type of procedure most suitable.'

'What if the client decides against abortion?'

'Then Andrea or Georgina will give her information about adoption agencies and so on. She'll still see the doctor, though, to determine her general health and so on.'

'Do you offer antenatal care?'

'No. Not here, at any rate. We usually refer.'

'You say Jennifer was administrative director. What exactly was she responsible for?'

'Everything to do with the running of the place except the medical side. That's an awful lot of work,' said Carol. 'Sometimes she had to work late just to keep up.'

'That reminds me,' said Annie. 'Have you ever heard the term "late girls"?'

Carol frowned. '"Late girls"? No. Why, what does it mean?'

'That's what I'm trying to find out.'

'I'm sorry, but it's not familiar to me.'

'Do you remember ever having a client here called Carmen Petri, or Peters?'

'No.'

'You're sure.'

'You can ask Lucy to check the records, but I think I would remember a name like that.'

'Probably,' said Annie. 'Lucy and Jennifer were close, were they?'

'They worked together. Jennifer was Lucy's boss, too, so that always puts a bit of wedge between you, doesn't it? Not that Jennifer was one to play the high and mighty.'

'Who was closest to her?'

Carol thought for a moment, then said, 'Georgina, I'd say. They'd talk about the centre, some of the clients, and I think they even went out for a drink a couple of times after work if Jennifer didn't have to stay late.'

'Thanks,' said Annie. 'Is Georgina in this morning?'

'Yes, she's in her office.' Carol picked up her phone. 'I don't think there's anyone with her right now. Would you like me to let her know you want to see her?'

'That's all right,' said Annie, who preferred the element of surprise. 'You can just show me where her office is.'

Carol's hand faltered. Clearly this went against standard procedure. 'OK,' she said, putting the phone back. 'It's up the stairs, second door on the right. It's got her name on it: Georgina Roberts.'

'Did you ever have any trouble with a man called Victor Parsons?' Annie asked. 'He's an ex-boyfriend of Jennifer's.'

'Oh, *him*. I remember him all right. Had to get security to throw him out.'

'What was he doing?'

'Making a fuss. Upsetting our clients.'

'About what?'

'He demanded to see Jennifer, but she'd given me instructions not to let him in.'

'What happened?'

'He went away in the end.'

'Did this happen more than once?'

'The first time he went without too much fuss. It was the second time I had to get security.'

Twice, then. 'Did he make any threats?'

'Not that I heard. He just said he'd be back.'

'When was this?'

'Couple of weeks ago.'

That recently, Annie thought. Yet Jennifer and Victor had split up over a year ago. Anyone who could maintain a fixation for that long was definitely worth looking at.

'One more thing,' said Annie. 'Have you ever seen anyone by the name of Roy Banks here at the centre. Or Gareth Lambert?'

Carol's face brightened, then reddened a little. 'Mr Banks? Yes, of course. He and Jennifer were . . . you know, an item. I know she's a bit young for him but he really is quite tasty. I don't blame her at all.' Her face fell. 'Oh. Poor Mr Banks. He'll be just devastated. Does he know?'

'Not yet,' said Annie. 'So he came here quite often?'

'Quite. He'd pick Jennifer up after work sometimes and we'd chat if he had to wait.'

'What about?'

'Oh, nothing in particular. Films, the weather, just small talk. And Arsenal. We're both big Arsenal fans.'

'Was he ever here at the same time as Victor Parsons?'

'No.'

'You know he was an investor in the centres?'

'Yes, he mentioned it once. But he didn't have any airs or graces.'

'Is that why he came here the first time, when he met Jennifer?'

'Oh, no,' said Carol. 'No, he was here as a client. *Accompanying* a client, I should say.'

Now it was Annie's turn to feel surprised. 'Accompanying a client?'

'Yes,' said Carol. 'His daughter. She was pregnant.'

•

Long before Annie paid her visit to the Berger-Lennox Centre, Banks was ploughing his way through the Monday morning rush-hour traffic on his way to Peterborough. He felt curiously numb after grappling with the demons of fear and loss most of the night, but he also felt apprehensive about what was to come. His parents doted on Roy; something like this could push his father's heart over the edge. But he had to tell them himself: he couldn't let the news come from some anonymous copper knocking on the door.

Brooke had gone out of his way to protect the identity of the victim from the media. As soon as Banks had told his parents, he had to ring Brooke and tell him it was done; the rest would follow. He remembered he had also promised to keep Corinne and Roy's neighbour, Malcolm Farrow, up to date, but they would have to wait their turns.

After some relatively gentle questioning by DI Brooke – *very* gentle, given the circumstances – Banks had handed over Roy's mobile, the USB drive and the CD to Brooke and tried to get some sleep. The effects of the wine were fast wearing off, leaving him with a throbbing head, and sleep had refused to come. Luckily, there wasn't much of the night left by then, and the dawn came early in June. At six o'clock, Banks was in the shower, then it was time to go and pick up his car from where he had left it the night before, near Waterloo Station, grab a coffee for the road, and head for home.

Progress was slower than he remembered, or expected, and a journey that should have taken under two hours took almost three. Every time the news came on the radio, no matter what station he tuned into, there was the story about the mystery body fished out of the River Thames just below the London Eye last night. In the end, Banks turned it off.

When he finally pulled up outside his parents' house on the Hazels estate in Peterborough, it was close to ten o'clock. Back in London, the murder investigation would be following its natural course: the technical-support-unit experts would be going over Roy's mobile and the SOCOs would be tracking every piece of evidence retrieved from the crime scene. DCs would be out on the streets asking questions and DI Brooke would be sifting through it all, looking for that promising line of enquiry.

The front door was painted green, Banks noticed, which was surely different from his last visit. The tiny lawn looked a little overgrown and some of the flowers in the bed didn't look in peak condition. That wasn't like his mother. He knocked and waited. His mother answered and was, naturally, surprised to see him. She had lost weight, and looked tired and drawn, with dark crescents under her eyes. God only knew what the news of Roy's murder would do to her.

He could tell she knew something was wrong by her ceaseless nervous chatter as she led him into the living room, where his father sat in his usual armchair, newspaper on his lap.

'Look who it is, Arthur. It's our Alan come to call.'

Maybe it was Banks's imagination, but he thought he sensed just the slightest air of neglect about the place; a patina of dust on the TV screen, a picture frame out of alignment, a teacup and saucer on the floor beside the settee, a slight bunching of the rug in front of the fire.

'Hello, son,' said Arthur Banks. 'Just happened to be passing, did you?'

'Not exactly,' said Banks, perching on the edge of the sofa. His mother fussed about, heading for the kitchen to put on the kettle for that great English cure-all, tea. Banks called her back. There would be time and need enough later for copious quantities of tea. On his way he had rehearsed over and over what he was going to say, how he was going to handle it, but now the time had come he couldn't remember what he had decided would be best.

'It's about Roy,' he began.

'Did you find him?' Ida Banks asked.

'In a way.' Banks leaned forward and took his mother's hand. This was even harder than he had imagined it might be; the words seemed stuck deep inside him and when he spoke he felt them come out as little more than a whisper. 'He wasn't at home and I looked for him all weekend. I did my best, Mum, honestly I did, but I was too late.' He felt the tears brim in his eyes and let them course down his cheeks.

'Too late? What do you mean, too late? Where's he gone?'

'Roy's dead, Mum.' There, he'd said it. 'I'm afraid he's gone.'

'Are you sure?' Ida Banks asked. 'Maybe he's only joking.'

Banks thought he'd misheard. 'What?' he asked, wiping his face with the back of his hand.

Ida Banks laughed and touched her hair. 'Don't you understand?' she said. 'It's a joke. Our Roy's a great practical joker, isn't he, Arthur? He's playing a joke on us.'

Arthur Banks said nothing. Banks noticed he had turned pale and seemed to be clutching the newspaper tightly by its edges. It was already ripped. 'Dad, can I get you anything? Do you need a pill or something?'

'No,' Arthur Banks managed. 'Nothing. I'm all right. Go on.'

'There's not much more to say,' Banks went on, turning to his mother again. 'They found him last night in the river.'

'Swimming in the river?' Ida Banks said. 'But surely the water's too dirty to swim in? I always told him he had to be careful. You can get terrible diseases from dirty water, you know.'

'He wasn't swimming, Mother,' said Banks. 'He was dead.'

His mother took a sharp breath. 'Don't say that,' she said. 'You shouldn't say things like that. Tell him, Arthur. You're only trying to upset me. You never did like Roy. If this is supposed to be some sort of joke then it isn't very funny.'

'It's not a joke.'

Arthur Banks stood up with some difficulty and shuffled over to his wife. 'I think we'd better have that tea now, love,' he said, 'then our Alan can explain it all over a nice cuppa.'

Ida Banks nodded, happy to have a purpose in life. 'Yes, she said, 'that'll be best. I'll make some tea.'

When she had gone to the kitchen, Arthur Banks turned to his son. 'There's no mistake, then?'

'Sorry, Dad.'

His father grunted and glanced towards the kitchen. 'She's not been well. She's got to go in for tests and stuff. We didn't want to worry you. Doctors haven't figured out what's wrong with her yet, but she's not been well. She's not eating properly. She gets confused.' Arthur Banks pointed to his newspaper. 'It's that story in the paper, isn't it? The body pulled out of the Thames. It's on the front page. That's our Roy, isn't it?'

'Yes,' said Banks. 'We've managed to keep his identity from the media so far, but it'll have to come out. It's going to get worse, Dad. Our Roy was shot. We don't know why yet. But it's a big story. Reporters will be around.'

'Don't you worry, son, I'll soon send that lot packing.'

'It might not be as easy as you think. I'll get in touch with the local police, if you like.' Banks knew his father's attitude to the police, had suffered it all his life, but the need to protect his parents was stronger even than his respect for the old man's opinion.

Arthur Banks shook his head in resignation. 'Whatever you think best. I just don't know. I can't seem to think straight. Our Roy . . . dead. It's a terrible thing when your children die before you do. Shot? No. I can hardly believe it.'

Banks felt a sudden chill, a premonition of what he would feel like if anything happened to Tracy or Brian, and it gave him a stronger sense of empathy with what his parents were suffering. For him it was the loss of a brother, perhaps one he never particularly liked and never really knew, but family nonetheless, and it hurt. For his parents, it was the loss of their favourite son.

'I know, Dad,' he said. 'And I'm sorry to be the one to have to tell you, but I just didn't want you to find out any other way.'

'I appreciate that,' said Arthur Banks, looking at his son. 'It can't have been easy. Will we have to identify the body?'

'It's been done.'

'What about the funeral?'

'I'll deal with all that, Dad, don't worry yourself.'

'What was he . . . I mean, would it have been quick?'

'Yes,' said Banks. 'He wouldn't have felt a thing.' Except the fear, the anticipation, he thought, but didn't say.

'The paper said he was in the river.'

'Yes. He was spotted on a shingle bank just below the London Eye.'

'You don't know where he went in?'

'Not yet. The tides and currents are pretty strong, especially with the rain we've been having. It's for the experts to figure out.'

'Do you know anything about why? Was he in trouble?'

'I think he was,' said Banks.

'Roy always sailed a bit close to the wind.'

'Yes, he did,' Banks agreed. 'But somehow this time I don't think that's what it was.'

'Why's that?'

'Just a feeling. There's been another murder, a young woman. They might be connected.'

Arthur Banks rubbed his face. 'Not that girl he brought around last year, Corinne?'

'No, Dad. Corinne's fine. It's someone else. Her name's Jennifer Clewes. Did Roy ever mention her to you?'

'No.'

'Look, I'll help around here all I can,' said Banks, 'but I might be more use back in London trying to find out what happened. That's what I do, after all. Right now, though, I'm just worried about you and Mum. Is there someone you'd like me to call? Uncle Frank, perhaps?'

'Bloody hell, no. He'd be more a hindrance than a help, would Frank. No, you leave it to me. I'll handle your mother. Maybe if she wants, I'll ask Mrs Green to pop over later.'

'That's a good idea. I'm sure—'

At that moment Banks and his father heard a cup break on the kitchen floor, followed by a long wail of anguish that froze their blood.

•

Annie mulled over the information she'd got from Carol Prescott as she made her way upstairs to Georgina's office after a quick word with Lucy, who had nothing much to say except that Jennifer was a good boss and a 'nice' person. Annie certainly hadn't known that Roy Banks had a daughter. It had been in April, Carol said, and the girl, eleven weeks pregnant, had opted for an abortion, which had cost Roy Banks about £500 in all. Roy had met Jennifer then. Carol remembered them chatting while the daughter went through her meetings with the counsellor and doctor. Since then, he had been by a number of times to meet her after work or take her for lunch.

The name Carol gave Annie rang a bell: Corinne. Banks had mentioned that Roy had a girlfriend called Corinne, so either he had passed her off as his daughter for reasons of his, or her, own, or the people at the centre had simply assumed she was his daughter because of the age difference. But wouldn't they have seen her name on the forms? Still, for all they knew, she could have been divorced, yet kept her married name, Annie supposed. Perhaps this was a different Corinne? When Annie asked Carol if Roy had specifically mentioned the girl being his daughter, she couldn't recall, and she said she didn't really pay attention to the girl's name.

Well, Annie told herself, it probably meant nothing. She already knew that Roy Banks and Jennifer Clewes were seeing one another, no matter how they first met. It didn't show Roy Banks in a particularly good light, Annie thought, chatting up his next girlfriend while bringing in last year's model for an abortion, but worse things happened. He probably got a discount for being a shareholder, too. And what had Jennifer thought about it? By all accounts she was a 'nice' girl, decent, caring, hard-working. She had never mentioned the 'daughter' at work. Roy Banks must have a hell of a smooth tongue on him, Annie thought, to explain that one away.

Annie knocked on Georgina's office door.

'Come in,' called a voice from inside.

Annie entered and found a pleasantly plump woman with dark curly hair and the hint of a double chin sitting behind a desk. She looked as if her normal expression was a smile. Today, though, it was banished in favour of a frown. Annie introduced herself and the frown lines deepened.

'I understand the two of you were quite close?' she said.

'Yes,' Georgina agreed. 'I'd like to think we were friends. I'm simply devastated by what's happened. I know that sounds like a cliché, but I just can't articulate my feelings any more clearly.'

'I'm very sorry,' said Annie.

'Would you like me to get us some coffee?' Georgina suggested. 'It's really not that bad.'

'No, thanks. I've had my ration for today.'

Georgina stood up. 'Would you mind if I . . . It's not far. I won't be a minute. Sit down. Make yourself at home.'

'Go ahead.' Left alone, Annie first walked over to the open window, which looked out on the hustle and bustle of the street below. Delivery vans came and went. Taxis stopped to pick up or drop off fares. Men and women in business suits dashed across the roads before the lights changed.

Annie sat down. The room was painted a soothing shade of blue, and it reminded her immediately of Bank's old living room at the cottage. Various framed certificates hung on the walls, along with a Monet *Waterlilies* print. There were no family photographs on Georgina's desk. The room was sparsely decorated – no filing cabinets, bookcases or computer – and Annie guessed its primary purpose was to put people at ease. Georgina no doubt had her files and books stored elsewhere.

Moments later Georgina reappeared with a mug of milky coffee.

'I've asked Carol to hold all the calls, so we're not disturbed,' she said. 'Though I don't see how I can help you.'

'That's what everybody thinks,' said Annie, 'but you'd be surprised. First of all, how long did you know Jennifer?'

'About two years. I was here when she started.'

'What was she like?'

'In what way?'

'Whatever comes to mind.'

'She was good at her job. It was important to her, that's why I mention it. She was considerate, cared about people. Maybe a bit too much.'

'What do you mean?'

'Well, as a counsellor you come into touch with a lot of grief, a lot of people with problems. You learn to sort of separate it out of your normal life, distance yourself a little bit. I don't think Jenn could have done that so easily. That's probably why she was in administration.'

'Did she get friendly with the clients here?'

'I wouldn't say "friendly", but she did take an interest. We run a very open office here, as you might have noticed. Everybody pitches in. You know, one day some poor girl would have a crying jag and Jenn would be the first one over to comfort her with tissues and a few kind words. That sort of thing.'

'But she didn't socialize with clients?'

'Not that I know of. Oh, I suppose you mean that girl she shares the flat with, Kate? But that was different. Kate wasn't pregnant. She just had a pregnancy test and that was that.'

'What about Roy Banks?' said Annie. 'She met him here, didn't she, when he was bringing his daughter in.'

'I wouldn't know about that.'

'She never mentioned how they met?'

'No. Jenn didn't like to discuss her private life, not in any detail.'

'Didn't you counsel Corinne?'

'Is that her name? No, it must have been Andrea. I'm afraid she's on holiday at the moment.'

'Never mind,' said Annie, making a note to ask Banks about how things were between Roy and Corinne. 'How had Jennifer been behaving during the past week or so? Did she seem worried, upset, depressed?'

'She certainly had something on her mind last week.'

'But she didn't tell you what it was?'

'No. I didn't see much of her. I was worked off my feet, so we didn't get to have our little chats.'

'She didn't confide in you about anything that was bothering her?'

'No.'

'What about Victor Parsons?'

'That waste of space. What about him?'

'I heard he caused a bit of trouble here at the centre.'

'Yes, but he's all bluster. I mean, he's obnoxious enough, but I can't imagine him doing . . . you know.'

'What happened between them?'

'Search me. I think Jenn wanted to settle down, have a family, but he wasn't interested. To be quite honest, from what I could gather he's a bit of a layabout, a sponger. She was well shut of him.'

'Do you know if he ever hit her?'

'I don't think so. At least she never said, and I never saw any evidence of it. The break-up hit her hard, though. She didn't say much, but you could tell she was under a lot of stress, poor thing. She lost weight, let herself go, as you do.'

'But this was before Roy Banks?'

'Oh, yes. She'd bounced back by then. Even tried one or two dates. They didn't lead anywhere.'

'But Victor Parsons turned up again, as recently as two weeks ago, I understand?'

'Yes, made a terrible scene. I was down in reception at the time.'

'What did he say?'

'He begged her to go back with him. Said he couldn't live without her.' Georgina's lip curled in distaste. 'Pathetic little shit.'

'Did he and Roy Banks ever bump into one another?'

'Not that I know of.'

'But you think that's what might have been upsetting Jennifer this last week? Victor? Or Roy?'

'Maybe they'd had a row or something. Bear in mind, though, I'm only guessing. It could have been something else entirely.'

'You said she had a tendency for getting involved, trying to help people.'

'Yes.'

'Did she have any particular causes lately?'

'I don't think so. None that she mentioned to me, anyway.'

'Did she ever mention someone called Carmen Petri?'

'No, not to my knowledge.'

'What about the "late girls"? Do you know what that means?'

'I'm afraid I don't. What was the context?'

'It was just something Jennifer said to a friend, to describe this Carmen person. "One of the late girls." It still doesn't ring a bell?'

'No, not at all. I mean, it could be someone late with her period, or late in her pregnancy. As you know the law only allows abortions up to the twenty-fourth week.'

'Yes,' said Annie, 'I'd thought of that. Apart from Roy Banks and this Victor, did Jennifer have any other visitors here, or any other friends you know about?'

'Not that I know of.'

'Do you know anyone who drives a dark Mondeo, either black or navy blue?'

'My father does, but I doubt it's him you're interested in.'

Annie smiled. 'I doubt it. No one else?'

'No. Sorry.'

'Do you think Jennifer would have confided in you if there was anything seriously wrong?'

'Wrong?'

'Say at the centre. Something going on.'

'I can't imagine what you mean, but she might have done. The thing is, though, if there was anything untoward going on here, Jenn would have been in the best position to know about it as she practically ran the place single-handed. She and Alex Lukas, at any rate.'

'Dr Lukas?'

'Alex doesn't stand on ceremony.'

'Is he in today?'

'She. It's Alexandra. You might have noticed that the centre prefers to employ women. It's not some sort of positive-discrimination thing. It's just that we've noticed that the kind of clients we get here respond better to dealing with another woman.'

Annie understood. She had felt the same when she went for her NHS abortion. She certainly wouldn't have wanted a man asking her questions or poking about inside her.

'Look,' Georgina went on, leaning forward so her ample bosom rested on the desk, 'I can't imagine who would want to kill Jennifer, or why, but I think you're barking up the wrong tree if you think it was anything to do with this place. She had no enemies here.'

'I'm just trying to cover all the angles. That's all a lot of police work is, Ms Roberts, covering the angles so you don't look stupid for missing something obvious.'

'A bit like counselling.'

'How?'

'Well, it seems a bit of a cliché asking people how they get on with their parents, how they feel about their father, but if it turned out there was an incestuous relationship you'd look pretty damn silly for not even probing the area, wouldn't you?'

'I see what you mean. Can you think of anything else that might help me?'

'I'm sorry, no.' Georgina paused. 'Look, Jenn wasn't raped or anything, was she?'

'No.'

'Because I thought that might be something the police were holding back, like they do.'

'Sometimes it's important to keep key pieces of information from the public, but not that. Jennifer was shot in the head, pure and simple.' Annie noticed Georgina flinch at the brutality of the remark.

'But what I can't understand,' Georgina said, 'is why on earth someone would want to kill her like that. Don't get me wrong, I'm glad for her it was quick. It's just that I might be able to get my head around some pervert raping her and killing her to gratify his own filthy lust, but this . . . ? It doesn't make sense. It's almost as if someone actually had a *reason* for killing her.'

'We'll do our best to make sense of it,' said Annie, standing up to leave. 'In the meantime, if you can think of anything else at all – and I do mean anything, something Jennifer might have said, done, not done, whatever – then please get in touch with me. Here's my card.'

'Thank you.' Georgina took the card and looked at it.

On her way to Dr Lukas's office, Annie's mobile rang. She went into the stairwell, took it out of her pocket and put it to her ear.

'Hello?'

'Annie, it's Dave here. Dave Brooke.'

'What is it, Dave? Have you got something for me?'

'In a way,' Brooke said. 'Brace yourself. It's not good news.'

'Go on.'

'We found Roy Banks's body last night. Pulled him out of the Thames near the Eye.'

'My God. That story in the paper this morning? That was Roy Banks?'

'Yes. Shot. A .22 by the looks of it.'

'Alan . . . ?'

'He identified the body. Asked us to sit on the identity until he told his parents. He was pretty shaken up.'

'I can imagine. Poor Alan,' said Annie. 'Is there anything I can do?'

'Not right now. He's gone off to Peterborough. I just heard from him. He's going to stay with his parents for a while. I just thought you should know.'

'Yes. Thanks, Dave. Bloody hell, what's going on?'

'I wish I knew.'

10

The Banks family had been seeing Dr Grenville down at the local health centre for more than twenty years, since back when he had his own practice, and he was only too willing to pay a house call when Banks rang him and told him what had happened. A fussily neat man near retirement age, with salt-and-pepper hair and a matching moustache, he tut-tutted over Ida Banks before giving her a sedative and issuing a prescription for more, which Banks rushed down to the chemist's to fill. He felt like taking one or two himself on his way back but resisted the temptation. He'd need a clear head over the next few days.

Ida lay on the sofa, a small, lost figure covered with a blanket. She was mumbling, but she wasn't making much sense, and after a while she drifted off. Banks offered a pill to his father, who gave him a look of distaste and declined. It had always been his way to face life's harshness head on, without a mask, and he wasn't going to change.

'What do we do now?' he asked. 'I mean, aren't there forms to fill in and such like?'

'Don't worry, Dad. I'll take care of it all down in London. Do you know if Roy left a will?'

'Will? Don't know. He never said.'

'I'll talk to his solicitor. He's in Roy's phone book. Can I just make a couple of calls right now? It's important.'

'Go ahead. Make as many as you want.'

First Banks rang Tracy's mobile. The last thing he wanted was his children finding out about their uncle's murder from the television or newspapers.

'Dad, what's up?'

'How are things going?'

'Fine. What's wrong?'

'Does something have to be wrong for me to ring my own daughter?'

'You just sound funny, that's all.'

'Well, you're right this time. It is bad news, I'm afraid,' said Banks.

'What's happened? Are you all right?'

'I'm fine,' said Banks. 'It's your Uncle Roy.'

'What about him? Is he in jail?'

'Tracy!'

'Well, you always seemed to think he'd end up there.'

'I'm sorry to have to be the one to tell you, but he's dead.'

There was a moment's silence at the other end, then Tracy's voice came back on again, shaking a little. 'Uncle Roy? Dead? Are you serious? An accident?'

'No. I'm sorry, love, but he was killed. I don't know how to put it any better.'

'Killed how?'

There was no point trying to save her from the knowledge, Banks realized. She would soon find out from the newspapers. 'He was shot. Murdered.'

'My God,' said Tracy. 'Uncle Roy. Murdered.'

'It'll be in the papers and on the TV,' Banks said. 'I just wanted you to know first.'

'Is there anything I can do?'

'It's under control. Just don't talk to any reporters, if they track you down.'

'Do Grandma and Granddad want me to come and stay with them?'

'You get on with your studying. I'll take care of them and I'll try to come and see you soon. You can do me a small favour, though.'

'What?'

'Will you tell your mother?'

'Dad!'

'Please. Look, normally, I wouldn't bother. They weren't close or anything and she has her own life now. But it'll be high-profile. Maybe the reporters will trace her, too. I don't want it to come as too much of a shock to her.'

'Oh, all right. But this is silly. You've got to talk . . . Oh, never mind. I'm really sorry about Uncle Roy. I know . . . I mean, I know we didn't see him often but he always sent really cool presents.'

'Yes,' said Banks. 'I've got to go now. Keep in touch.'

'I will. I love you, Dad.'

Next Banks rang Brian, who didn't answer. Banks left a message for him to ring as soon as he could, then phoned DI Brooke to thank him for his patience and give him the go-ahead to release Roy's identity. Finally he rang Corinne. She sounded devastated after her initial stunned silence, and he wished he could be there for her, but all he could do was murmur useless words of comfort over the telephone as she cried. He promised to drop by next time he was in London, which he said would probably be soon.

He didn't have Malcolm Farrow's phone number, so that call would have to wait until he went back to Roy's house. Then he realized he probably couldn't go back there, as the whole place would be sealed off by the police investigating Roy's murder. He hesitated, then he called Annie Cabbot on her mobile. She was on the line. DI Brooke would have already told her about Roy, so Banks just left a message asking her to give him a ring at Peterborough as soon as she could, then he went back to his mother and father.

'Would you close the upstairs curtains, son?' Arthur Banks asked. 'Your mother would want it that way.'

'Of course.' Banks remembered how, when he was younger, if someone in the family died his mother would always close the upstairs curtains.

Up in his old room again, Banks looked out over the backyards and the deserted alley to find that the housing estate the builders had been working on during his last visit was now almost finished. Most of the houses were as yet unoccupied, and some were still without windows, but rows of them, all the same, filled the stretch of wasteground where he used to play football and cricket as a child, where he had his first kiss and first furtive feel of a girl's breast as a teenager. He tried to remember whether Roy, too, had had such formative experiences there, but he didn't know. Most likely, if he had, it had all happened after Banks had left home, when they hardly communicated.

He did remember one incident. When he was about thirteen and Roy eight, he saw an older, bigger boy of about ten or eleven bullying Roy out in the field. Poor Roy was in tears as the bigger boy punched him repeatedly in the stomach and jeered at him for being a weakling. Banks rushed over to stop it, and even though he knew that he was now the bully, he couldn't hold himself back from giving the bastard a bloody nose and a split lip.

It came back to haunt him, too, when the boy's parents called at his house that night. Only because Roy corroborated his story in every detail did Banks get off with a mere admonishment to pick on people his own age in future. It could have been much worse. So he had stood up for Roy, and Roy had stood up for him. What had happened then? What had come between them?

As he usually did on his infrequent visits home, Banks looked in the wardrobe where the boxes of his adolescence were stored. The last couple of times he had been back he had discovered a treasure trove of old records, comics, diaries, books and toys. There were even more boxes he hadn't got around to yet, and he found himself wondering if any of them were Roy's.

The toy box with the lock was long gone, but he did eventually manage to dig out a small cardboard box full of things that definitely weren't his: Corgi toys – better than Dinkys, he remembered Roy arguing, because they had plastic windows and more realistic detail – a stamp album full of bright but worthless stamps, a portable chess set that folded into a box, a Scalextric set that he was never allowed to play with, and several of those tiny submarines that came out of a cornflakes box, the kind you stuffed with baking soda to make them submerge and surface. There were no diaries or old school reports, nothing to flesh out the vague sense of Roy that the toys implied, but down at the bottom was a Junior Driver, a toy steering wheel. Banks remembered Roy used to stick it on the dashboard on the passenger side of their father's Morris Traveller whenever they went anywhere and pretend he was driving. Even back then Roy had been car mad.

Banks held the plastic steering wheel in his hands for a moment, then he put it back, returned the box to the wardrobe and closed the curtains.

•

By mid-morning the whole of Western Area Headquarters in Eastvale knew about the murder of Banks's brother. Gristhorpe went into conference with ACC McLaughlin, and a hush fell over the Major Crimes squad room. Even the telephone conversations seemed to take place in whispers. If it wasn't exactly one of their own who had fallen in the line of duty, it was too damn close for comfort.

'Did you ever meet him?' Winsome asked Jim Hatchley, who had known Banks the longest of all of them.

'No,' said Hatchley. 'I got the idea he was a bit of a black sheep. Alan didn't have much to do with him.'

'Still,' said Winsome. 'It's family.' She thought of her own younger brother Wayne, a school teacher in Birmingham, and how rarely she saw him. She would ring him tonight, she resolved.

'Aye, it is that, lass,' said Hatchley.

Winsome chewed on her lower lip and got back to the telephone. She had had a bit of luck tracking down the Mondeo, first through the DVLA Wimbledon office and then through the Police National Computer database of stolen cars. A car matching the description, with a '51' registration number plate, had been stolen from a cheap long-stay parking facility near Heathrow Airport shortly before Jennifer Clewes's murder. When the car's owner, who had been on a business trip to Rome since Thursday, arrived back on Sunday evening and found his car missing, he had immediately informed the local police. Winsome had rung Heathrow, who would be the first to hear if the car turned up, and asked them to let her know as soon as possible.

If all the leads in this case led to London, as they seemed to be doing so far, it could be a while before DI Cabbot got back to Yorkshire. Winsome envied her. A nice little shopping trip down Oxford Street or Regent Street wouldn't go amiss right now. Not that Winsome was a clothes junkie, but she liked to look fashionable and she liked to look good, even if it meant creeps like Kev Templeton ogling her. She did it for herself, not for anyone else.

Winsome was just about ready to head down to the canteen for lunch when her phone rang.

'DC Jackman?' the unfamiliar voice enquired.

'That's me.'

'PC Owen here, Heathrow.'

'Yes.'

'We just got a report in about a stolen vehicle, a dark-blue Mondeo. I understand you were enquiring about it?'

'That's right,' said Winsome, pencil in her hand. 'Any news?'

'It's not good, I'm afraid.'

'Go ahead.'

'The long version or the short one?'

'The short first.'

'It turned up in the early hours of Sunday morning on the A13 just outside of Basildon.'

'Where's that?'

'Essex.'

'Excellent,' said Winsome. 'Can we get a SOCO team over there?'

'Hold on a minute,' said Owen. 'I haven't finished yet. I said it had turned up, but what I didn't get a chance to tell you was it was involved in an accident.'

'Accident?'

'Yes, the driver lost control and wrapped it around a telegraph pole. By all accounts he was going way too fast.'

'Do you have him in custody?'

'He's in the mortuary.'

'Damn,' said Winsome. 'Any identification on him?'

'Oh, we know who he was all right. His name's Wesley Hughes. The bugger of it is he was only fifteen.'

'Jesus Christ,' whispered Winsome. 'Just a kid. But what happened to our two men? The descriptions we have put them at way over fifteen.'

'I'm afraid I don't know anything about that. We did get one lucky break, mind you: there was a passenger, and he was uninjured. Well, he got a few cuts and bruises, but the doc's checked him out and he's basically OK. A little shaken, though, as you can imagine.'

'How old is he?'

'Sixteen.'

'Have the local police questioned him?'

'I don't know. It's out of my hands now. If I were you I'd give them a ring. I've got the number. Sergeant Singh is handling it. Traffic.' He gave Winsome the number. She thanked him and hung up.

Next she rang Sergeant Singh of the Essex Police at Basildon Divisional Headquarters. He answered immediately.

'Ah, yes, I've been expecting your call,' he said. 'Just hold on a minute.' Winsome heard some muffled words, then Singh came back on the line. 'Sorry about that. It gets a bit noisy in here.'

'That's all right. What have you got?'

'A real mess is what.'

'Are we sure it's the right Mondeo?' Singh gave her the number. It matched what she'd got from the DVLA and the police computer. 'PC Owen gave me the basics,' Winsome said. 'Have you talked to the surviving boy yet?'

'Just. It took forever to track down his parents, and even when we found them they seemed more interested in opening another bottle of cheap wine than coming down to the station. No wonder the kids run wild. Anyway, he's a cocky young bastard, name of Daryl Gooch, but the crash took some of the wind out of his sails and DI Sefton took the rest.'

'What's his story?'

'According to him, he and his mate Wesley Hughes saw the car in Tower Hamlets, off Mile End Road, when they were coming home from a party at about half-past three on Sunday morning.'

'Tower Hamlets?'

'Yeah, the East End.'

'I know where it is. I'm just surprised and confused, that's all. I thought the car had been stolen from Heathrow on Friday by two men in their early forties who drove it up to Yorkshire to commit a murder in the early hours of Saturday morning. Now I find it was stolen from Tower Hamlets in the early hours of Sunday morning by two teenage joyriders. None of this makes any sense.'

'Well,' Singh went on, 'I wouldn't know about that, but this is how Daryl Gooch says it happened. Young Daryl said the driver's door was open, the key was in the ignition and there was no one around, so him and his mate thought they'd have a little ride in the country. Pity his friend wasn't a better driver. Witnesses say he was doing close to a hundred when he lost control. As far as I can gather from Daryl they were still pissed and stoned from the party.'

'Do you believe him?'

'I don't know,' said Singh, 'but there's not much advantage to him lying at this point, is there?'

'With some kids it's habitual,' said Winsome.

'I suppose so. Anyway, both kids are from Tower Hamlets, so they'd have had no reason to be out at Heathrow. They're not exactly your jet-setting types. Any idea exactly when the car was stolen from the car park there?'

'Not really,' said Winsome. 'Sometime between Thursday and Friday evening, I suppose.'

'Sorry I can't be any more help,' said Singh. 'Ring me if you have any more questions.'

'Thanks,' said Winsome. 'I will.'

She hung up and nibbled on the end of her pencil as she thought things out. Assuming it *was* the same Mondeo that had been spotted near Jennifer Clewes's flat on Friday night and the one Roger Cropley had seen at Watford Gap, then after killing Jennifer and breaking into Banks's cottage, the two men had probably driven back to London through the night, kept the car out of sight for a day then dumped it in a decidedly dodgy neighbourhood where it was likely to go AWOL very quickly indeed, and hoofed it back home, wherever that might be. It didn't tell her much, but it did tell her one thing about them: they weren't scared of visiting dangerous neighbourhoods at night.

It was a good move to steal a car from a long-stay because the odds were good it wouldn't be reported stolen for a while. If it was, there was always a chance that it might be picked up by a camera on the Automatic Number Plate Recognition system that reads them against the database of stolen vehicles. But that hadn't happened; the car's owner didn't report it stolen until Sunday evening, by which time it was wrapped around a telegraph pole outside Basildon.

Well, Winsome thought, even if there wasn't much chance of finding trace evidence in the Mondeo now, at least they could check the tyres, and there was always a chance that someone in Tower Hamlets had seen the men who dumped the car there. Time to get on the phone again.

•

Dr Lukas's office boasted the same non-threatening decor as the rest of the Berger-Lennox Centre. The seats were padded and comfortable, colourful still-lifes hung on the aquamarine walls and there were no surgical instruments in sight, not even a hypodermic. Still, Annie realized, Dr Lukas didn't perform abortions, at least not here, so there was hardly any need for such things. There was, however, an examination room, and Annie imagined that behind the door would be the table, the instruments, the stirrups.

'It's tragic about Jennifer,' said Dr Lukas, before Annie could start with her questions. 'She was so young and vital.' The doctor had a slight accent, which Annie couldn't place. Eastern European, at any rate.

'Yes,' Annie agreed. 'Were the two of you very close?'

'Not really. We worked together, that's all. Our jobs are very different, of course, but we obviously had to meet regularly to ensure the smooth running of the centre.'

'But you didn't know her socially?'

Dr Lukas managed a weak smile. 'I don't have much of a social life,' she said. 'But, no, we didn't meet socially, only at work.'

Annie looked around the room. 'It's a nice place,' she said. 'Nice centre altogether. It can't be cheap to maintain. I suppose it must be doing rather well?'

'As far as I know,' said Dr Lukas. 'The finances were Jennifer's domain. I stick to what I know best.'

'Everyone tells me that Jennifer wasn't her usual self the week before her murder. They say she was anxious, edgy, worried. Did you notice this?'

'We had one of our regular meetings last Wednesday,' Dr Lukas said, 'and come to think of it, she did seem a little on edge.'

'But you've no idea why?'

'I assumed it was man trouble, but as I said, I know nothing about her private life.'

'Why did you assume man trouble, then?'

The doctor smiled. She was a slight, thin figure, around forty, short dark hair sprinkled with grey, hollow cheeks and a tired look about her eyes. Her body language seemed tense, too tightly strung. 'I shouldn't jump to conclusions, I know,' she said, 'but I have seen her leave here with a man on a number of occasions.'

That would be Roy, Banks's brother. 'Yes, we know about him,' Annie said. 'But we don't think that's what was bothering her.'

The doctor spread her hands on the table, palms up. 'Then I can't help you,' she said.

'What about her previous boyfriend, Victor Parsons? Have you ever met him?'

'Not that I know of.'

'Apparently he's turned up at the centre and created a fuss once or twice.'

'I'm a bit isolated up here,' Dr Lukas said. 'I probably wouldn't have noticed.'

'When Jennifer met her present boyfriend here, he was accompanying a young woman everyone assumed to be his daughter. Her name is Corinne and I don't believe she is his daughter. Did you examine her?'

'When would this be?'

'About two months ago. April.'

Dr Lukas turned to the laptop on her desk and pressed a few keys. 'Corinne Welland?'

'I assume that's the one,' Annie said. 'I don't know her surname.'

'It's the only Corinne I had.'

'Then it must be her.'

'Then yes, I did,' said Dr Lukas. 'And I had no idea whether she was this man's daughter or not. I never met him and she never said anything about him. It was just a straightforward consultation.'

'What happened to her?'

'She had her termination, and I assume she got on with her life.'

'Have you ever heard of Carmen Petri?'

'No,' said Dr Lukas, just a little too quickly for Annie's liking.

'Do you know what "late girls" are?'

'Girls who are late with their periods? Girls who are dead? I have no idea.'

Annie hadn't thought of that one, and she knew that she should have done. Dead. Was Carmen dead? Is that why she was one of the late girls? If so, how many others were there?

'What about girls who are pregnant and too late to have an abortion?'

'Then there would be no abortion. For one thing, it's illegal and for another, it's dangerous.'

'Except if the mother or the foetus is at risk?'

'Exactly. In that case surgery may be performed. But it is not, strictly speaking, an abortion; it is a surgical procedure performed in order to save a life, or lives. Emergency surgery.'

'Yes, I understand the distinction,' said Annie. 'Has the centre ever been involved in such surgery?'

'Not to my knowledge.'

'And you, as medical director, should know?'

'Well, you could check with the individual clinics where the terminations are actually carried out, but I very much doubt it. We're essentially a family planning centre, though we offer a broader range of services than many other such organizations. Anyone requiring a termination after twenty-four weeks would automatically be referred to a hospital. It becomes a medical problem, not a matter of individual choice.'

'I see,' said Annie. She wasn't going to get much further with this. If the centre was a party to illegal abortions, Dr Lukas certainly wasn't going to admit it, but Annie wasn't entirely convinced by her saying that she had never heard of Carmen, or by her evasion of the 'late girls' issue. Perhaps she would come back to Dr Lukas again later, she thought, as she stood up and made her polite farewell. After she'd seen Victor Parsons, at any rate. But the next time she would make sure they didn't meet in the sterile domain of the Berger-Lennox Centre, where Dr Lukas was clearly used to being in control.

•

DC Kev Templeton soon got fed up sitting around talking on the telephone. He was a man of action; he liked to rattle a few doors and feel a few collars. Now it was Monday and the world was on the move again, he was in his element. With Gristhorpe's approval, he had set up a meeting with a DS Susan Browne, who was still working the Claire Potter case. They had agreed on a late lunch at a pub just off the motorway about halfway between Eastvale and Derby, and Templeton pulled into the car park at half-past two thinking if this Susan Browne was a bit of all right he might even get his end away before the day was done.

He walked through the dim, cavernous bar, where a few regulars sat quietly smoking and watching cricket on the TV, and went out of the back door into the garden. Templeton didn't know if he looked like a detective or not in his jeans, T-shirt and trainers, Ray-Bans covering his eyes.

He scanned the tables for a likely looking woman. There was only one, and when he approached her and she stood up to shake hands, Templeton's heart sank. She was short and a bit thick around the middle, not his type at all. He liked the Keira Knightley type, coltish girls, long-legged and limber. Still, she had nice eyes, he thought, and her manner seemed pleasant enough. She also had a thin gold ring on the third finger of her left hand. A glass of fizzy water sat on the white table in front of her beside the menu, one of those colourful laminated types you usually find in chain pubs, which were the only sort of pubs where you were likely to get lunch at half-past two on a Monday afternoon.

'Let's get the ordering out of the way first, shall we?' she said, sliding the menu over to him. 'I've already decided.'

Templeton scanned the colourful images of burgers, curries and fish and chips and decided that all he felt like was a prawn sandwich. Susan said she wanted a cheeseburger and chips. He almost warned her against it, given her waistline, but decided that probably wasn't the most diplomatic way of starting off the meeting.

He ordered at the bar, bought himself a Coke and went back to the garden. Their table was in the shade of a large copper beech, and a light breeze came and went, ruffling Susan's tight blonde curls and susurrating through the leaves. At the other end of the garden a few children played on the swings and roundabout while their parents sat at nearby tables enjoying the sunshine. Templeton put his Ray-Bans on the table and gave Susan the full benefit of his heart-melting brown eyes.

'You're from Western Area Headquarters, then?' she asked.

'Yeah,' said Templeton.

'Eastvale?'

'You know it?'

'Used to work there. How's DCI Banks? Still around, I suppose?'

Templeton grinned. 'We haven't got rid of all the dinosaurs yet.'

'As I remember, he got results, and he was a pretty good boss.'

'Yeah, well . . . When were you there?'

'A few years back. I left just after I passed my sergeant's boards. Did a year in uniform in Avon and Somerset, then transferred to CID in Derby. How is Alan doing? I heard about the fire. Sent him a card and all.'

'All right, I suppose,' said Templeton, realizing he had to be a bit more circumspect about what he said now that Susan had shown her true colours. 'Actually, he's probably not doing so well right at the moment. They just pulled his brother Roy's body out of the Thames last night.'

'Jesus,' said Susan. 'That's terrible. Look, give him my condolences when you see him, will you?'

'Sure.'

'What happened?'

'Looks as if he was killed. Shot. Did you know him?'

'No. But that's still terrible news. Poor Alan. Do tell him I'm sorry. My name was Susan Gay back then. He'll remember. Browne's my married name.'

There was something in her tone that stopped Templeton from making the obvious comment. Imagine going through life with a name like Gay, he thought. No wonder she changed it when she got married.

'And give my regards to Superintendent Gristhorpe and Jim Hatchley, if they're still around.'

'Oh, they're still around.'

'Right.' DS Browne waved a fly away from the rim of her glass. 'Down to business, then.'

'Claire Potter,' said Templeton. 'Like anyone for it?'

'We've got no suspects at all. Except . . .'

'Yes?'

'Well, can you imagine how many times he must have done practice runs, how many times he must have followed someone, only for her to get home before he could strike? For something like this to work out you need so many things to go right. A woman turning off on to a dark country road, nobody around, an unlocked driver's door. Anyway, we checked around and it seems that a couple of months earlier, the 20th of February to be exact, a woman turning off the M1 north of Sheffield was attacked in a similar way, only she had her doors locked. Paula Chandler.'

'What happened?'

'She managed to start up and drive off. He didn't pursue her.'

'Description?'

'Nothing useful. It was dark and she was scared. She didn't really get a look at his face because she was desperately trying to get the car started again while he was tugging at her door. He was wearing a dark suit, she said, and he had a wedding ring on. She saw his hand go to the door handle.'

'No gloves?'

'No. She said she could see the ring clearly.'

'Prints?'

'Nothing but blurs.'

'Make of car?'

'She couldn't say. Only that it was dark in colour, blue or green. And compact. Maybe Japanese.'

Roger Cropley drove a dark green Honda, Templeton remembered, with a little shiver of excitement. And he wore a wedding ring. 'Not a lot of use, is it?' he said.

'Very frustrating. And there are others, equally vague. One girl thought a car was following her, another reported someone giving her a funny look at a service station. That sort of thing. We followed them all up but got nowhere.'

'But you still think it's the same man?'

'Yes. Like I said, he'd have to practise, and he'd need to get lucky. And Paula Chandler had stopped at Newport Pagnell services.'

'You think that's where he trawls for his victims, the motorway cafes?'

'Yes. It makes sense. Find a woman alone, follow her and see if she turns off on a quiet stretch of road late at night. Both attacks we know about happened late on a Friday, and both happened after the victim had stopped at a service station.'

'Tell me about Claire Potter.'

'Her car was found in a ditch and the SOCOs found evidence that she'd been driven off the road.'

'Tyre tracks?'

'Nothing we could use.'

'Where did the assault take place?'

'There was a wooded area nearby.'

'And nobody reported seeing the cars?'

'No. Either nobody passed them or someone just didn't want to get involved. It wasn't till the next morning when a chap driving a local delivery van got curious and reported the car in the ditch. When our blokes did a quick search of the area they found her.' She paused and sipped some water. 'I was there. It was bad. One of the worst.'

'What did he do to her?'

Templeton noticed that Susan didn't look him in the eye as she talked. 'Everything. Clothes ripped off. Rape, both vaginal and anal. He also used some sort of sharp object for penetration. We found a bloody stick nearby. Then he stabbed her and she bled to death. Fifteen stab wounds. Breast, abdomen, pubic area. I've never seen such anger.'

'DNA?'

'No. Either he used a condom or he didn't ejaculate.'

'Did the lab find any traces of lubricant?'

'No.'

'I take it they examined the earth around her.'

'Of course. No seminal fluid. No DNA. He'd also subdued her with chloroform so she couldn't struggle or scratch.'

'No hair or skin, then?'

'No. He was very careful, this one, and it looks as if he cleaned up after himself.'

'They usually miss *something*.'

'Not this time. There was a stream nearby. He even washed the body and laid it out properly. Her torn clothes were found beside her. He'd covered her face with her own underwear.'

'For Christ's sake. The knife?'

'Ordinary sheath knife. The kind you can buy just about any-where.'

'Claire was last seen at Trowell services, right?'

'Right. She stopped for a coffee and a Penguin biscuit. The woman behind the counter at the cafe remembered her.'

'But nobody was taking any undue interest?'

'That's the way it seems. And she didn't need petrol, the tank was more than half full, so she didn't stop at the pumps.'

'Any marks on the car? Paint scrapings, broken headlights, that sort of thing?'

'No. It was untouched. Whoever did it must have just pulled in front of her and she swerved into the ditch to avoid a collision.'

Their meals arrived and the day's warmth had made them both thirsty, so Templeton went and got another fizzy water for Susan and another Coke for himself. 'This case you're working on,' Susan said when he got back, already halfway through her cheese-burger. 'Do you seriously think there's any connection?'

'I don't know. It's a strange one. Look, this might seem like an odd question, but do you think there's any chance that there were two of them killed Claire Potter?'

'It wasn't a scenario we considered seriously. I mean, usually these things, the degree of rage, the location of the wounds, it all indicates a sexual predator, and they usually act alone.'

'What about Fred and Rose West?'

'I said usually. We've considered other possibilities but we're pretty sure it was just one man. It must have happened quickly, like yours did, only Claire wasn't shot. She suffered much more and for much longer.' She sipped her water. 'It's hard to say whether the differences outnumber the similarities. Probably, if you look at it realistically, they do. I mean, even if you can account for the difference between weapons, our killer went for overkill, showed a remarkable degree of anger. Your killer just coldly shot the victim and drove away. It sounds more like an execution than a botched sex crime to me.'

'You're probably right,' said Templeton, 'but we had to follow up on it. Don't these sorts of killers usually strike more than once, though?'

'Sexual predators? Yes, sometimes. I mean, you can't really predict, but it's doubtful he'll be satisfied for long. We've had the profilers in and run some pretty sharp computer programs and they all seem to indicate a strong likelihood of his striking again. After all, it's been nearly two months since Claire Potter.' She paused. 'There's something that never made it to the papers.'

'What's that?'

'He took a souvenir.'

'What?'

'A nipple. The left one, to be precise.'

'Jesus Christ,' said Templeton. He looked at his prawn sandwich and felt sick. He sipped some Coke.

'Sorry,' said Susan. 'Just thought we should get it all out in the open. I don't suppose that happened with Jennifer Clewes, did it?'

'No,' said Templeton.

Susan had finished her meal. She pushed her plate aside. 'Is there anything else you want to tell me?'

Templeton thought of Sunday's interview. 'We did have a bloke looked likely. For Jennifer Clewes, that is.'

'Oh?'

'Yes. Chap by the name of Cropley. Roger Cropley. Apparently he was paying her quite a bit of attention in the motorway cafe and at the petrol pumps, and he followed her back onto the motorway. Trouble is, he's got an alibi.'

'Does it hold up?'

'Watertight. He was on the hard shoulder with a broken fan belt. Called the AA. They confirm the time. He couldn't possibly have killed Jennifer Clewes.'

'Pity.'

'But it doesn't mean he didn't want to, does it? Thing is,' Templeton went on, 'he's a funny sort of chap. Thought it was all a bit of a game, then got really stroppy. Seems he works in London and commutes every week. Every Friday, as a matter of fact. And he usually stops for a break. Probably wears a dark suit. Drives a dark green Honda. Married. Wears a ring. Like I said, he's on the M1 most Fridays. Not always that late, he told us, but sometimes. I was just thinking . . . you know.'

'Well, it wouldn't do any harm to have another little chat with him, would it?' DS Browne said. 'And if your suspicions continue, perhaps I could come up and have a word, too? I trust your SIO would OK it?'

'I should think so. It's not a lot to go on, I admit,' said Templeton, 'but there was something about him.'

'A hunch?'

'Call it that if you like. I happen to believe that hunches are made up of hundreds of little observations we're not directly aware of. Body language. Tone of voice. Little things. They all add up to a hunch.'

'Maybe you're right,' said Susan, smiling. 'In my case they usually call it women's intuition.' She looked at her watch. Nice gold band, Templeton noticed. Her husband must have a bob or two. Probably not a policeman, then. 'I'd better be off,' she said. 'Thanks for the tip. You'll keep me posted about Cropley?'

'Absolutely,' said Templeton.

'And do give my best to everyone at the station, and my condolences to Alan Banks.'

'Of course.'

Templeton watched her walk away. Her legs weren't bad at all. If only she could trim down that waistline a bit she might be worth a crack, husband or no. He swatted a wasp away from his prawn sandwich and it buzzed him a few times before zigzagging off into the trees. Time to head back to Eastvale, he thought, and see if anything new had turned up.

11

Late on Monday afternoon, the rain came down again, out of nowhere, splashing against the windscreen of Dave Brooke's Citroën as he drove Annie through the rush-hour traffic to Tower Hamlets, not exactly the kind of place you'd find in a tourist's guide to London. They were in Bow, and the house they wanted stood in a row of run-down terraced houses that had survived both bombing and slum clearance. Across the street lay a couple of acres of tarmacked waste ground with weeds growing through the cracks, surrounded by a six-foot wire-mesh fence with barbed wire on the top. Who was protecting it, and from what, Annie had no idea. She guessed it was earmarked for development. Beyond the waste ground, through the slanting rain, stood more grimy terraced houses, slate roofs dark, and beyond them tower blocks rose bleak as monoliths against an iron-grey sky.

'Pretty, isn't it?' said Brooke, as if reading her mind.

Annie laughed. 'If you like that sort of thing.'

'It's a piece of history. Enjoy it while you can. In a year or so it'll probably be all new tower blocks or an entertainment complex.'

'You sound as if you'd be sorry to see it go.'

'Maybe I would. Here we are.' He pulled up at the kerb and they looked at number forty-six. The front door, Annie thought, could definitely use another coat of paint to cover the cracks and gouges time and, perhaps, would-be burglars had inflicted.

Alf Seaton, a retired ship's carpenter, had not only seen Wesley Hughes and Daryl Gooch drive away in the Mondeo, but he had also seen it arrive in the early hours of Sunday morning, and this was what interested Annie and Brooke. Annie was beginning to wonder if she would ever get home again, the way things were going. She had hoped to be off that afternoon after her visit to the Berger-Lennox Centre, but Brooke called. All roads seemed to lead to London.

Alf Seaton was expecting them, and Annie noticed the edge of the lace curtain twitch just a little when their car pulled up. Before they reached the door, it opened, and a plump, grey-haired man with a broken nose beckoned them in out of the rain.

'Miserable day, isn't it?' he said, in an unmistakable cockney accent. Well, Annie thought, he was in the right area, probably even within the sound of Bow Bells, come to think of it. 'Make yourselves comfy. I'll put the kettle on. Got some chocolate diges-tives, too, if you're interested.'

Annie looked around the small living room while Alf Seaton busied himself in the kitchen. There was an old-fashioned look and feel to the place, she thought, visible in the ornate pipe rack, the dark wood bureau and the low bookcase under the window, filled mostly with nautical tales, she noticed: Alexander Kent, Douglas Reeman, Patrick O'Brian, some old Hornblower editions. On the wall above the fireplace was a romantic seascape depicting Lord Nelson's fleet engaging the French in rough waters, cannons blazing. The armchairs were old but still firm, and there wasn't a speck of dust in sight. When Seaton came back in with the tea and biscuits, Annie complimented him on the house.

'I do my best,' he said. 'Just because you're poor doesn't mean you have to be slovenly, does it? That's what my mother always used to say.'

'Are you married?'

'Fran died a couple of years ago. Cancer.'

'I'm sorry.'

'No reason for you to be, love. Life goes on.' He looked around the room. 'We had nearly fifty happy years, me and Fran. Moved here in 1954, our first home. Only one as it turned out. Course, I was just a young lad then, still wet behind the ears. And things have changed a lot. Not all for the best, either.'

'I'm sure not,' said Annie.

'Still you won't be wanting to hear an old man's reminiscences, will you?' he said, winking at Annie. 'You'll be wanting to know what it was I saw.'

'That's why we're here, Mr Seaton,' said Brooke.

'Alf, please.'

Alf was a name you didn't hear much these days, Annie thought, and if you did you could guarantee it belonged to someone of Mr Seaton's generation.

'Alf, then.'

'I'm not sure I can tell you anything I didn't already tell the uniformed bloke.'

'Let's start with what you were doing.'

'Doing? I was sitting here in this very armchair reading. I don't sleep very well, so I've taken to getting up, making myself a cup of tea and settling down for a good read. Beats lying there thinking about all your problems the way you do at that time of night.'

'Yes, it does,' said Annie. 'So what was it that happened first? Did you see or hear the car?'

'Heard it first. I mean, we do get a bit of traffic down here throughout the night, but not that much. It's not a main road, or even the quickest way to one. And as you can see, it doesn't have a great deal of natural charm. Anyway, at three on a Sunday morning it does tend to be quiet apart from the odd group of kids stumbling home from a party.'

'Do you remember the exact time?' Annie asked.

Alf Seaton glanced at the solid, ancient clock on the mantelpiece. 'Ten past three,' he said. 'I remember looking, wondering if it was later. Anyway, first I heard it, then I saw the lights. It parked just across the street there, by the wasteground. Then another car pulled up behind it.'

'And you saw the driver?'

'Yes. Quite clearly. There's a street light and my eyesight's still pretty good for distances.'

'What can you tell us about him?' Annie asked, glancing at Brooke, who nodded, indicating that she should carry on asking the questions. Alf seemed comfortable talking to her.

'I was a bit nervous, I suppose. I mean, there's been quite a lot of crime in the neighbourhood and when you're old and frail in your health like I am, you do worry a bit, don't you. Twenty years ago I'd have given anyone a good run for his money, armed or no, but these days . . .'

'I understand,' said Annie. 'But you did get a look, didn't you?'

'I wasn't *that* scared. I like to know what's going on in my street. Anyway, I didn't want to draw attention to myself, so I turned the light off. I'm glad I did because I saw him look over at the house for a moment and pause, as if he was trying to decide whether there was anyone watching him. He seemed to look right at me, but he must have decided there wasn't.'

'What did he look like?'

'He was a big fellow, hard-looking, as if he lifted weights. He was wearing a dark-coloured tracksuit, the sort with a white stripe down the arm and the outside leg. His hair was a bit long, tied in a ponytail at the back like a right poofter. Black, it was, and shiny, as if he sloshed axle grease on it. And he had a heavy gold chain around his neck.'

It sounded like a better description of the man who Roger Cropley had seen in the back of the Mondeo at Watford Gap, and who the neighbour had noticed on Jennifer's street around the time she set off for Banks's cottage. 'What happened next?' Annie asked.

'That's when I saw him get in the other car.'

'Can you remember anything more about the second car?'

'No, except it was lighter than the first one, maybe cream or silver, something like that. There wasn't really enough light to show up the colour properly, everything was a sort of monochrome, but it was a bit more . . . I don't really know cars . . . but it looked maybe more expensive, more flashy.'

'Did you notice any logos, ornaments, that sort of thing?'

'Sorry, no.'

'It's OK. You're doing fine. I don't suppose you got the number, did you?'

'No.'

'Did you get a good look at the driver?'

'Just a glimpse when the door opened and the inside light came on for a second. It was further back, out of the range of the street lamp.'

'Can you describe him?'

'All I could really see was that he had short fair hair. Really short. Cropped. Then the door shut, the light went off and they drove away.'

'What direction?'

'South. Towards the river. Not long after that I heard the kids talking and the car door slam. I just caught a glimpse of them, then they were gone. I know I should have called the police right there and then. Maybe then that poor boy wouldn't have died. But I didn't know what was going on and it doesn't pay to get too involved unless you really have to.'

'It's not your fault,' said Annie.

'Even so, I feel bad.'

'Mr Seaton. Alf,' Brooke cut in, 'do you think you would be able to work with a police artist on a sketch of the man you got a good look at?'

'I think so,' said Seaton. 'I mean, I've got a fairly clear picture of him in my mind. It's just a matter of getting it down.'

'That's what the artist's for. With a bit of luck, we might be able to get him here by tomorrow morning. Would that be all right?'

'I'm not going anywhere.'

'Good. I'll make the arrangements. Is there anything else you can tell us?'

Seaton thought for a moment, then said, 'No, I don't think so. It all happened very quickly, and as I said, I didn't know what was going on. Why would a man abandon a nice car like that and leave it unlocked in a neighbourhood like this unless he *wanted* it to be stolen?'

'Exactly,' said Annie.

•

Banks fetched fish and chips from the Chinese chippie over the road for lunch, but his father just picked at them. He didn't even complain the way he usually did that they tasted of chop suey, his only notion of Chinese food. After a cup of tea Banks was seriously thinking of heading back to London, but he sensed that he should stay. Not that his father asked him, or ever would, but it seemed the thing to do. The family should be together, at least for now.

He felt restless, though, cooped up, so he drove into town and wandered around Cathedral Square and the Queensgate Centre. While he was there he remembered that he had left his mobile back in Gratly and he had given Roy's to Brooke. If he was planning on heading back to London, which he was, he might need one. He went into the first electronics shop he saw and bought a cheap pay-as-you-go mobile and a £10 card. Once he'd got the battery charged back at his parents' house it would be ready to use, but he bought an in-car charger as well.

It was a cloudy afternoon, holding the threat of rain. A group of buskers were playing jigs and reels in the square, a small crowd gathered around them. A steady stream of tourists entered the Cathedral precincts.

When Banks found himself wandering by the Rivergate Centre flats he thought of Michelle Hart, who used to live there, on Viersen Platz. On the opposite side of the river was Charters Bar, an old iron barge moored near Town Bridge, and Banks remembered the blues music he'd heard issuing from it on weekends he had stayed with her.

Banks stared into the murky water and wondered if he should have tried harder with Michelle. He had let her slip away far too easily. But what could he do? Her career was important to her, and when the opportunity in Bristol came up he could hardly plead with her not to go. Besides, there had been problems with the relationship well before the move, so many that he had often thought the new job was at least partly an attempt to put more distance between them.

He walked back to his car and just sat there for a while with the windows open, smoking. How bloody ironic it was, he thought, that he had only come to know his brother after his disappearance. If Roy had died two, three years ago, Banks would have grieved, of course, but he wouldn't have felt the loss in such a personal way. Now, though, it actually hurt, squeezed at his heart. Now there was someone to miss, not just a distant memory.

It wasn't so much that he had revised his opinion of Roy as that he had put it in a larger context. Roy was a rogue, no doubt about it; he had about as much sense of business ethics as a flea and he was a bastard to women. That he'd made a fortune, driven a Porsche and had women falling over him was only a testament to one of those grim truths of life, that the bastards thrive. Maybe they get their just deserts in the afterlife, maybe they come back as cockroaches, but in this life, they thrive.

Roy's crisis of conscience after witnessing the horror of 9/11, his turning to the Church, had probably sharpened what moral instinct he had to some degree. Had he stumbled across something in that last week that offended his sense of right and wrong? Had he gone through a struggle of conscience before ringing his policeman brother? Or had it been business much as usual? Throughout his life Roy had probably stolen, cheated and lied without giving a damn for the consequences, or a moment to worry over those he had hurt. Had he changed that much? Banks wouldn't find out in Peterborough, he knew that, so tomorrow he would have to head back to London and start digging again.

Banks thought it might be a good idea to let a few people, especially his children, know he had a new mobile number, so he turned on the engine, plugged the phone in the car-charger and rang to leave messages. To his great surprise, Brian actually answered in person.

'Dad. Nice to hear from you. We're on a break. Sorry I didn't get back to you sooner but we were in the studio. I was going to ring tonight.'

'It's OK,' said Banks. 'I've been out a lot. Look, it's a long story, but I've got a new mobile. Want the number?'

Brian sounded puzzled. 'Sure, if you like.'

Banks gave it to him. 'How's it going?'

'Well. Slowly, but well.'

'And how's Dublin?'

'Great.'

'Tried the Guinness yet?'

'A pint or two. Look, what is it, Dad? Why did you want to talk to me? Nothing's wrong, is it?'

'I'm afraid it is,' said Banks, thinking, 'Here we go again,' then taking a deep breath and plunging in. 'Your Uncle Roy's been killed. It'll be all over the news in a while, so I wanted you to know.'

'Uncle Roy? No. I mean, I never really knew him, but . . . he always sent cards and stuff. I can't believe it. Why? What happened? Did he have some sort of accident?'

'I'm trying to find out what happened,' said Banks. 'But, no, it wasn't an accident. He was shot.'

'Jesus Christ!'

'Look, I'm sorry, Brian, really. I can't think of an easier way to break the news. Anyway, there's nothing you can do. I've told Tracy, and she's going to tell your mother. Just get on with your recording.'

'You sure?'

'Yes. And be prepared for reporters.'

'When's the funeral?'

'We don't know yet.'

'You'll let me know how it goes? Keep me informed?'

'I'll let you know,' said Banks. 'I'll be back in London in a day or so, probably staying at Roy's house if the police have finished with it. Do you want the address and phone number there?'

'Sure. Might as well. Shot . . . Jesus.'

Banks gave him Roy's address.

'Thanks, Dad,' Brian said. 'And I'm really sorry.'

'Take care,' said Banks, then he broke the connection.

He sat there for a moment longer, thinking he'd probably gone and ruined his son's big recording session, then he stubbed out his cigarette and set off back to the Hazels estate.

•

Victor Parsons shared a flat with two other young men in Chalk Farm. When Annie called around teatime he was sitting in the living room reading a film magazine. Annie's first impression was of a nice-enough-looking bloke with a bland and unassuming personality, quite a contrast to the chic, successful and dynamic Roy Banks.

Parsons clearly hadn't shaved for a couple of days, and it looked as if he'd been wearing the same T-shirt and jeans for much longer. There was a snail-like lethargy about him that hinted at lack of ambition. Yet, Annie had to remind herself, he had turned up at Jennifer Clewes's place of work and caused a scene. Quite frankly, he didn't look as if he had it in him.

Annie didn't like to make snap judgements, but all she had seen and heard of Jennifer, admittedly only after her death, indicated that she outclassed Victor by far. Had she had such low self-esteem, then, had she been so insecure that she had really seen something of value in him? Still, she thought, there was no accounting for taste and no explanation for many of the strange couplings in life.

The room itself seemed clean and tidy enough, which pleased and surprised Annie. Knowing she had been about to visit a bachelor pad, she had mentally girded herself for dirty laundry over chair backs and posters of Kelly Brook and Jordan in lacy black lingerie plastered to the walls. As it turned out, the only poster in view was for *Kill Bill I*.

'I suppose it's about Jenn?' Victor said, without offering Annie a seat, let alone a cup of tea or coffee. As he was slouching on the sofa, she took an armchair and sat. 'I suppose that bitch Melanie Scott's been talking?'

'Among others,' said Annie. 'You're not exactly popular among Jennifer's friends and acquaintances.'

'I don't care what people think about me. They don't really know me, anyway. They're just a bunch of superficial losers.'

'Oh, it's like that is, it? Poor, hard-done-by misunderstood genius takes on the world.'

He gave her a look of scorn. 'What do you know? You wouldn't understand.'

'You're right,' said Annie, 'so why don't I ask the questions and you answer them? I find this sort of thing works best that way.'

'Whatever.'

'Good. I'm glad we've got that sorted. Now let's get down to business. Where were you last Friday night?'

'Here.'

'Doing what?'

'Watching TV.'

'What were you watching?'

'*Coronation Street*, *EastEnders*, Lenny Henry, *Have I Got News For You*, then Jools Holland and a late film. It was a horror film called *Session 9*.'

'Any good?'

'It had its moments.'

'That's pretty impressive, Victor, remembering all that.'

'I've just got a good memory, that's all, and it's pretty much the same every Friday. Different film, of course.'

'Anyone else with you?'

'Gavin was out till about one o'clock, but Ravi was here most of the time. You can ask him.'

'Thanks. I will.'

'Look, I'm gutted, you know. By what's happened. I loved her.'

'So I hear. Can be a nasty thing, unrequited love.'

'She loved me, too. She just didn't realize it. She would've, if . . .'

'If?'

'Given time.'

Annie sighed. 'Victor, it sounds to me as if somewhere along the line you lost touch with reality. Jennifer wasn't in love with you. She'd moved on, found someone else.'

'You don't know her.'

'What do you do?'

'Do? What do you mean?'

'Your job. Work.'

'I'm an actor.'

'Resting?'

'At the moment, yes. It's true, though. I've had roles. I've even done TV. Only adverts, and one non-speaking part, but it's a start.'

'Earn much money?'

'Not a lot, no.'

If Annie had held out any hopes that it was Victor who hired someone to kill Jennifer, they were soon dashed. He obviously couldn't afford it.

'Why did you pester her?' she asked. 'You went to her place of work and caused a scene. Why did you do that if you loved her?'

'I'm not proud of that. I was pissed. I'd been drinking with Ravi at lunchtime and I'm not used to it. The booze went to my head, that's all, and I got overexcited. I was sorry about it afterwards. I even rang her to apologize but she wouldn't talk to me.'

'Did you talk at all after you split up?'

'No. I couldn't get near her at work and she always hung up the phone if I tried her at home. Or the other girl did.'

'Kate Nesbit?'

'Is that her name? I don't know.'

'But you knew where she lived, where she'd moved to?'

'Yes. I made it my business to find out.'

'Have you any idea if anything, or anyone, was bothering her over the past while?'

'No. Like I said, she shut me out of her life completely.'

'Did you ever hang around outside her house?'

'I walked by once in a while, yes. I was hoping I might see her in the street.'

'Once in a while?'

'Well, not every day, but regular, like.'

'And did you see her?'

'No. Never.'

'When were you last there?'

'Couple of weeks ago.'

'Did you notice anyone else hanging around?'

'No.'

Of course he didn't, Annie thought. He wouldn't even notice if Godzilla stamped on the house next door. All he had eyes for was Jennifer. 'What about her place of work?'

'She worked late sometimes. I used to wait across the street. Just to see her.'

'Did you ever approach her when she left?'

'No. I didn't have the bottle. I'd just watch her. I told you, it was only because I was pissed that I made a scene.'

'When was the last time?'

'Last week. Monday.'

'And did you see her leave?'

'Yeah, but she was with someone.'

'Who?'

'It wasn't anyone I knew, just some girl, by the looks of her.'

'A young girl?'

'Yeah. Probably one of the rich pregnant teenagers they deal with there. Only this one didn't look particularly rich.'

'What time was this?'

'About eight o'clock.'

'Wasn't the centre closed by then?'

'Yeah. They close at five. I think everyone else had gone home, but Jenn worked late a lot.'

'Can you describe the girl?'

'Long dark hair. Bit skinny, but a nice figure, apart from the bump. She was just wearing ordinary clothes. You know, a flowery dress, sandals. I didn't get a really good look at her face.'

'I take it by the "bump" you mean her pregnancy was showing?'

'Yes.'

'Where did they go?'

'Nowhere.'

'Why not?'

'A bloke got out of a car parked in front, had a word in her ear, and she got in the car with him.'

'Who, Jennifer or the girl?'

'The girl.'

'What did Jennifer do?'

'Walked towards the tube station.'

'Did you follow her?'

'No. I just went for a drink.'

'What did the man look like?'

'Like he lifted weights. You know, big, broad shoulders, no neck. And he had a ponytail.'

'And the car?'

'Didn't notice.'

'Dark or light?'

'Light, I think. Maybe silver.'

'Was there anyone else in it?'

'I didn't see.'

'Did he force the girl into the car?'

Parsons frowned. 'No. But it was like he was in charge and he was saying that's enough, time to go.'

'She didn't resist?'

'No.'

'OK,' said Annie. 'Were you outside Jennifer's house or place of work last Friday?'

'No. I already told you, I stayed in. I do most nights.'

Did Victor Parsons kill Jennifer or have anything to do with her death? Annie doubted it. Stalkers could turn violent, true, but more often than not they didn't. Most of the time they were sad, pathetic pillocks like Victor, or like peeping Toms, irritating and upsetting, but ultimately harmless.

'Tell me something,' she asked, 'just out of interest. Why did you split up with Jennifer?'

'It was all a misunderstanding. That's it, you see. I thought we wanted different things. You know, Jenn wanted marriage, family, all that, and I wanted to pursue my acting career. But I was wrong.'

'So you chucked her?'

'No. It wasn't like that. All I said was that we should give one another a bit more space and get clear about what we wanted, that's all. And I did. I decided I wanted her, no matter what, that I'd even give up my career, she meant that much to me.'

'Generous of you.' No doubt, Annie guessed, as soon as Jennifer had got over the immediate shock of the break-up and got pissed with Melanie Scott a few times in Sicily, she had probably realized just how lucky she was to get out of the relationship.

There was nothing more to be gained talking to Victor Parsons, Annie decided; she would get someone else to check his alibi with his flatmate and cross him off her list. It was only early evening, but it had been a long day, and Annie felt tired, felt like simply going back to her hotel, ordering room service and vegging out in front of the TV. She had rung Peterborough earlier in the afternoon, but Banks was out. Maybe she would try ringing again later.

'What am I going to do now?' Victor asked as Annie opened the door. 'What am I going to do?'

'Maybe you should get out of the house a bit more often and try to get an audition?' Annie suggested, and left.

•

'How is she?' Banks asked when he got back from town.

'No different,' said his father. 'I told you, she wasn't well even before all this. It's only made her worse. Anyway, she's still in bed. Doesn't seem to want to get up.'

'I'll go up and see her in a while. I've decided to stay tonight.'

'You've no need to,' said his father. 'Not for our sake. We can manage.'

'I'd like to.' One thing Banks knew that his father might not have thought of was that Roy's identity would now be public knowledge and there was a good chance that the phone would be ringing off the hook. He wanted to be there to field the calls for them.

'Suit yourself. Your room's always here, you know that.'

'I know,' said Banks.

'I still can't believe our Roy's dead. Murdered.'

'Me neither. I wish there was something I could do.'

'You can't bring him back.'

'No. Any signs of reporters while I was out?'

'No.'

'Thank the Lord for small mercies, then. Look, Dad, I don't suppose Roy ever talked to you about his business interests, did he? What he was up to, that sort of thing?'

'Me? You must be joking. He knew I'd about as much understanding of business as I have about rocket science.'

'And that you might not approve of how he made his money?'

'I'm not a bloody communist. All I've ever asked for is a fair share for the working man. What's so wrong about that?'

'Nothing,' said Banks, who didn't want to get into that old argument again. Not here, not now. Besides, he agreed. His father had been given a raw deal, made redundant from his job as a sheet-metal worker during the Thatcher years. He had seen the riot police taunting the striking coal miners, and as a result he had come to see the police as the right hand of the oppressor. Banks knew that could happen, had done in some countries, and there was a certain feeling, not entirely unjustified, that it had happened during the Thatcher years. But most of Banks's attempts to explain to his father that he simply put in a long day's work trying to catch criminals fell on deaf ears.

'Anyway,' said his father, 'Roy was always generous to us.'

The implied barb wasn't lost on Banks, but he managed to bite his tongue before asking his father whether it mattered where the money came from. 'So he never mentioned any names?'

'Not as I remember.'

'The Berger-Lennox Centre, Gareth Lambert, Julian Harwood?'

'Never heard of them.'

'What about his girlfriends?'

'Only that young lass he brought over last year, for the anniversary.'

'Corinne. Yes, I've talked to her. He never mentioned anyone called Jennifer Clewes?'

'That girl that got shot up in Yorkshire? You mentioned her earlier. No, I'm certain he never mentioned her to us.'

Arthur Banks sagged back in his favourite armchair. The television was turned off, which was unusual, and there was no sign of a newspaper. Even in the short while Banks had been absent, he noticed more signs of neglect. And his father was clearly as much in the dark about Roy's activities as he was. He picked up two empty cups from the floor beside the armchair. 'Fancy a cup of tea?'

'If you like,' said his father.

'What about dinner?'

'Doesn't matter as long as it's not from that place over the road.'

Banks put the kettle on and found the tea bags. Never an easy task, as his mother kept moving them around like a shell game. This time they were in a jar in the pantry marked cocoa. While the kettle boiled, he washed the few dishes that had been used and stacked them in the rack to dry. He found some bread, tomatoes, cheese and boiled ham and made some sandwiches. They would have to do for dinner.

'Any more idea when the funeral will be?' his father asked when Banks brought in the tea and sandwiches.

'I can't say,' said Banks. 'It depends when they release the body.'

'What do they want to hang on to it for?'

'Sometimes, if someone's arrested and charged, they can ask for a second, independent post-mortem. I don't think that's likely in this case, but it's not my decision. Believe me, Dad, I'll stay on top of it. I don't want you and Mum worrying about the details.'

'Don't we have to register the death?'

'You can't do that until the coroner's released the body. I'll take care of it all when the time comes.'

'What else are we going to do except sit around and mope?'

'Just try to get through it day by day. It'll take time.'

His father sat forward. 'But that's just it. We haven't got time.'

Banks felt a shiver at the back of his neck.

'What do you mean? Has your heart been giving you more problems?'

'My heart's fine. A touch of angina, that's all. It's not me. It's your mother.'

'What about her?' Banks remembered his mother's tired and listless appearance when he first arrived, before he had even told her about Roy, and again he took in the air of neglect about the house. 'Is it something to do with these tests she's been having?'

'They think she's got cancer. That's why they want her in hospital to do some more tests.'

'When?'

'They say they can't fit her in until next week.'

Banks felt the need for a cigarette, but he didn't give in to it, not there and then. He wished he could afford private cover for his parents, then they wouldn't have to wait. 'Christ,' he said. 'It never rains but it pours.'

'You can say that again.'

'What does the doctor think?'

'You know doctors. Won't commit themselves without the test results. Anyway, it's her colon they're worried about. I can tell you what I think, though. The life's slowly going out of her. I've been watching it drain away for weeks.'

'But even if it is cancer, there are treatments. Especially colon cancer. As far as I know the cure rate's pretty good.'

'Depends how far it's spread, doesn't it, how soon they catch it?'

'Look, Dad,' said Banks, 'there's no point being pessimistic. You've got enough on your plate with our Roy. See her through this. That has to be your priority right now. We'll deal with the other thing when we know more about it.'

'You're right, but . . . it's just so bloody hard, all the time think-ing I might lose her. Now Roy.'

Banks could see that his father was close to tears, and he remembered that he had never seen him cry. His mother, yes, but not his father. He wanted to spare him the embarrassment, know-ing he was a proud man, so he went upstairs to see his mother. She was lying in bed with the sheets pulled up to her neck, but her eyes were open.

'Roy?' she said when he first entered the room. 'Is it really you?'

'No, Mum,' said Banks. 'It's me, Alan.'

He could swear he saw the disappointment register in her face. 'Oh,' she said. 'Where's our Roy?'

Banks sat at the edge of the bed and grasped her hand. It felt dry and thin. 'He's gone, Mum. Our Roy's gone.'

'Oh, yes,' she said. 'I remember now. In the water.' She closed her eyes and seemed to drift off.

Banks leaned forward and kissed her quickly on the cheek, then said goodnight and went back downstairs.

'She's in and out,' he told his father.

Arthur Banks had pulled himself together. 'Yes,' he said. 'It's probably those tablets the doctor gave her.' He looked at Banks. 'You said before you wished there was something you could do, and there is, you know. I've been thinking while you were up with your mother.'

'What's that, Dad?'

'You're supposed to be a detective, aren't you? You can do your job and go back to London and catch the bastard that killed our Roy.'

Banks sat down, picked up his mug of tea and reached for a sandwich. 'Yes,' he said. 'You're right. And that's exactly what I intend to do first thing tomorrow.'

12

Late on Tuesday morning, after breakfast and a brief meeting with Brooke to review their progress so far, Annie went back to her room, packed her meagre belongings and checked out. She was looking forward to getting home, digging out some clean clothes and sleeping in her own bed again, if only for one night. She knew she would have to come back, especially as she planned on visiting Dr Lukas at home in the near future. For the meantime, though, Brooke was leading the Roy Banks investigation, and Annie needed to show her face to the troops back up in Eastvale, talk to Stefan Nowak and Gristhorpe, see how Winsome and Kev Templeton were getting on.

She wondered what Banks was up to as she waited for a taxi. She hadn't tried to ring him again the previous evening, deciding it was probably best to leave him and his parents in peace. From what she could remember Banks telling her, they had doted on Roy. And even though he and Roy hadn't been close, she knew he must be distraught. Though she wasn't unduly worried about him, he had been depressed lately, and something like this could push him over the edge. She would like to talk to him, anyway, to see him, if only to reassure herself and offer her condolences. A taxi pulled up and Annie got in.

'King's Cross, please,' she told the driver.

They had hardly got over Lambeth Bridge when her mobile rang.

'Annie, it's Dave Brooke here.'

'Dave. What is it?'

'Thought you might be interested. I've just got the patholo-gist's report on Roy Banks. Can you talk?'

'It's OK,' said Annie, 'I'm in a taxi on my way to the station.' The driver was listening to an interview on BBC London, and there was a Plexiglas window between the front and the back.

'Fair enough. Bottom line is, the shot to the head killed him outright. It's a .22 calibre bullet, just like the one that killed Jennifer Clewes.'

'Anything on time of death?'

'He'd been in the water about forty hours. Had to have been to get in the state he was and fetch up on that patch of shingle, so the tide experts tell me.'

'So it can't have been the same killers.'

'No. They couldn't possibly have got back from Yorkshire in time.' Brooke paused. 'DCI Banks isn't going to like hearing this, but it also appears that his brother was tortured before he was shot.'

'Tortured?'

'Yes. There's evidence of serious bruising to the body and cigarette burns on the arms and soles of the feet. Some of the fingernails have been pulled out, too.'

'Jesus,' said Annie. 'Someone wanted something from him?'

'Or wanted to know how much he knew, or had given away.'

'Either way, you're right. Alan won't like that at all. The press—'

'They're not going to find out.'

'Are you sure?'

'Not from us. We're keeping this to ourselves. All the press will be told is that he was shot. That will be enough for them. I can see the gun-crime editorials right now.'

'True enough,' said Annie. 'They're already having a field day with the Jennifer Clewes shooting. Anything else?'

'Just a couple of things,' said Brooke. 'Remember the digital photo that came through on Roy Banks's mobile?'

'Yes. Alan mentioned it to me.'

'As we suspected, it came from a stolen phone. Technical support didn't have much trouble enhancing the image. They've got all sorts of fancy software that can filter and stretch and make predictions based on pixel statistics. The upshot is, though, that it doesn't tell us a hell of a lot. We still can't be absolutely certain whether the man in the chair is Roy Banks. They did manage to get something from the wall in the background.'

'What?'

'It looks as if there were two rows of letters, or words, stencilled on the rough brick. The first ends in NGS and the second in IFE. We've no idea how long the lines were or how many words. We're getting a list of all abandoned factories in the Greater London area, and the experts are working on identifying some of the rusted machines. It might help figure out what sort of a factory it was. If the tide experts can come up with a general idea of where Roy Banks might have been dropped in the river, we should be able to put it all together and pinpoint where the murder took place.'

'That sounds promising,' said Annie. 'Any leads on who might have wanted Roy Banks dead?'

'We've turned up a couple of iffy names from his business correspondence. Oliver Drummond and William Gilmore. Ever heard of them?'

'No,' said Annie.

'Well, they're definitely in our bad books. The first one's been involved in a couple of frauds and we think the second's been running a chop shop. High end. Mostly Jags and Beemers for rich Russians and Arabs. Never managed to track it down, though, and Gilmore always seems to turn out squeaky clean. We've managed to get him on a few minor charges, which is why he's on our books, but nothing big.'

'What about the men in the photograph DCI Banks gave you?'

Brooke paused. 'Gareth Lambert,' he said. 'He's got no form. The other one we don't know.'

'Doesn't it seem important, though? Roy Banks did think it necessary to take and then hide the photo. Maybe blackmail was involved?'

'Give us time, Annie,' Brooke snapped. 'You know damn well how it is with manpower and budgets. And half the bloody team's on holiday right now. We'll get there, eventually.'

'OK, Dave. Hold your horses. I was only trying to be helpful.'

'I'm sorry. I know, Only we're stretched to the limit.'

'I understand. Best of luck, then, and thanks for bringing me up to date. I'll see what's happening up north and probably be back in a day or so. Keep in touch?'

'Absolutely. Oh, by the way, our artist's finished with Seaton now. The impression doesn't look bad. Want a copy?'

'Thanks. It might be useful.'

'I'll get it faxed to you.'

The traffic slowed to a crawl as the taxi got closer to the chaotic and seemingly endless construction of the Channel Tunnel Rail Link around King's Cross. Annie didn't have a lot of time and worried she might miss her train, but the driver found a gap in the traffic and pulled up at the side with fifteen minutes to spare. Annie paid him, picked up a couple of magazines for the journey at W.H. Smith's then checked the platform number on the board and headed out to the train. The station was bustling with people and it smelled of warm engines, diesel oil and smoke. Annie found her coach and seat, popped her small bag on the rack and sat down to make herself comfortable.

About three minutes before the train was due to set off, a decidedly nervous announcement came over the PA system: 'Would all passengers calmly leave the train and exit the station.'

Everyone sat there for a moment, stunned, wondering if they'd heard correctly. Then it came again, not sounding calm at all: 'Would all passengers calmly leave the train and exit the station.'

That was enough. Everyone grabbed their bags, dashed for the door and ran down the platform to the street.

•

Banks had hoped to be back in London by late morning, early afternoon at the latest, but it wasn't to be. For a start, he slept in. Lying there in his old bed, he hadn't been able to get to sleep for thinking about Roy and worrying about his parents, and only after the light started to grow and the birds started singing did he finally doze off until 9.30. Even then, he was the first one up.

If that had been the only problem, he could probably still have made fairly good time, but after he had made a pot of tea, checked his new mobile was fully charged and walked across the road for a copy of the *Independent*, his mother was up and fussing. Whether the fact of Roy's death had really sunk in yet, he couldn't tell, but she seemed unnaturally calm, alert and in command.

'Your father's having a lie-in,' she said. 'He's tired.'

'That's OK,' said Banks. 'You could have rested a while longer yourself.'

'I rested quite enough yesterday, thank you. Now . . .'

And then she launched into the most extraordinary litany of 'things to do', the upshot of which was that Banks spent a good part of the day driving her around the various relatives who lived close enough to visit, the ones in Ely, Stamford and Huntingdon, at any rate. Many had already phoned the previous evening after hearing about Roy on the news, but Banks had taken care of the telephone – including the reporters – and made sure neither his mother nor his father were disturbed.

Now Ida Banks told each one, calmly, that Roy had died and she didn't know when the funeral would be, but they should be on the lookout for a notice in the paper. Banks's father was up when they got back from the first visit, just sitting in his armchair staring into space. He said he was OK, but Banks worried about him; he seemed to have no energy, no will.

Banks had already seen a piece about the murder in the *Independent*, which referred to Roy as the 'wealthy entrepreneur brother of North Yorkshire policeman Alan Banks, who almost lost his life in a fire earlier this year.' Uncle Frank told him it had been on the television, too, and there had been a picture of Banks and some old footage of his cottage after the fire. Banks was glad he hadn't seen it. God only knew what stories the tabloids were telling. Were they implying a link between the fire and Roy's murder?

By the time he saw his mother settled back at home and fed her another of Dr Grenville's pills, it was mid-afternoon. Mrs Green, a neighbour, came over to sit with them for a while and Banks was finally able to say his goodbyes and set off back to London. Before he left, he rang Burgess, gave him his new mobile number, and arranged to meet in a pub in Soho around five o'clock. It was time to pick up the threads of the investigation again.

Lacking CDs, the best he could do was turn on the car radio. Classic FM was playing Beethoven's 'Moonlight' sonata and Radio Three had Tippett's 'Concerto for Double String Orchestra'. Banks chose the Tippett because he didn't know it as well as he did the Beethoven.

On the A1(M) somewhere around Stevenage, Banks noticed that a red Vectra had been following him for some time. He slowed down; the Vectra slowed. He speeded up; the Vectra kept pace. It was the middle of a warm summer afternoon on a busy road, but still Banks felt the chill of fear. He played cat and mouse with the Vectra for a while longer, then it shot past him. He couldn't get a really good look, but he could tell there were two people in the car, one in the front and one in the back. The one in the back had a ponytail, and when the car was passing Banks's Renault, he turned sideways and smiled, miming a shooting gun with his left hand, thumb signifying the hammer, then he tilted his hand up and blew over the tops of his first two fingers, smiling. It was a split-second vignette, then they were streaking ahead.

Banks tried to keep up with them, but it was no good. The driver was skilful and managed to weave in and out of the lanes of traffic until they had left Banks far behind. Not before he had memorized the number, though.

As he approached Welwyn Garden City, where it started to rain again, Banks wondered what the hell all that had been about. Then he realized with a sudden chill that they must have followed him from Peterborough. *They were letting him know that they knew where his parents lived.*

•

'You again,' said Roger Cropley, when Kev Templeton turned up at his front door again. 'You've got a bloody nerve. What the hell do you want?'

'Just a few more questions,' said Templeton. 'I'm by myself this time. As a matter of fact, I'm very surprised to see you here. I thought you'd be down in London. It was your wife I was planning on talking to.'

'I'm off sick,' said Cropley. 'Summer cold. What do you want to talk to Eileen about?'

'Oh, this and that. But now that you're here, too, let's have a party, shall we?' Templeton edged his way into the hall. Eileen Cropley was standing at the bottom of the stairs. 'Ah, Mrs Cropley. Good afternoon. I don't believe we had a proper chance to get acquainted on my last visit.'

'That's because you were so rude, if I remember correctly. Roger, what does this man want? What have you been up to?'

'I haven't been up to anything. It's all right, dear.' Cropley sighed. 'You'd better come through,' he said.

'Don't mind if I do.'

The living room still smelled of lavender, but the flowers had wilted and shed a few petals. 'I might have been a little hasty last time,' said Templeton, when both Mr and Mrs Cropley had sat down. They sat on the sofa, Templeton noticed, one at each end, like bookends. Mrs Cropley was definitely frosty. Cropley himself seemed resigned. 'I hadn't got all my ducks in a row.'

'You can say that again,' said Cropley.

'But that's water under the bridge, isn't it? No hard feelings?'

Cropley regarded him suspiciously.

'Anyway,' Templeton went on, 'I'm glad I found both of you in.

Gives me a chance to make up for bad first impressions. We've talked to the AA, Mr Cropley, and they verify that you were indeed at the time in question stuck on the hard shoulder of the M1 just south of the Derby turn-off.'

'As I told you.'

'Indeed. And I apologize for any . . . disbelief . . . I might have shown at the time. We tend to get quite wrapped up in our search for justice, and sometimes we trample on people's finer feelings.'

'So what do you want this time?'

'Well, we've got a bit more information than we had before, and it looks as if these two men you saw in the dark Mondeo followed Jennifer Clewes – that was the victim's name – off the A1 on the road to Eastvale, where they ran her into a drystone wall and shot her. They then returned to wherever they came from and the following night they dumped the Mondeo in the East End of London, where it was immediately stolen and became involved in a serious accident. Now, we've got some tyre tracks the car made in a private lane in Gratly and some fingerprints that might possibly belong to one of the men. Our forensic scientists are checking the Mondeo for fingerprints to compare, but as you can imagine, after a crash like that, well . . .'

'This is all very interesting,' said Cropley, 'but I still don't see how my wife or I can help.'

'Hear the man out, Roger,' said Mrs Cropley, who seemed interested despite herself.

'Thank you, Mrs Cropley. Anyway, we got a description of the man who dropped off the car in London and a colleague down there faxed me an artist's impression. I was wondering if you'd have a look at it and see if you can identify him.'

'I told you,' said Cropley, 'I didn't get a good look. I'm not very good at describing people.'

'Most of us aren't,' said Templeton. 'That's why looking at a picture helps.' He lifted his briefcase. 'May I?'

'Of course,' said Cropley.

Templeton showed him the sketch.

Cropley stared at it for a while, then he said, 'It could be him.'

'Only could be?'

'As I said, I didn't get a good look.'

'But he did turn to look at you when the driver pulled right in front, didn't he? You told me that.'

'Yes, but it was dark.'

'The petrol station was well lit.'

'I'm still not certain. I mean, I wouldn't want to swear to it in court. Is that what you want?'

'Not yet. We just want to find him.'

'Well, it definitely looks like him. The hair, the general shape of the head, but it was too dark to make out his features.'

'I understand that. Was he well built?'

'He did have rather broad shoulders, now I come to think of it, and not much of a neck. And he seemed tall, high in the seat.'

'Fine,' said Templeton, putting the drawing away. 'Many thanks.'

'You're welcome,' said Cropley. 'But you said you came to talk to my wife. She wouldn't have been able to identify this man as she wasn't with me.'

'Just seizing the opportunity, Mr Cropley. Saved me a trip to London, this has.' Templeton took out his notebook.

'So what did you want to ask *me*?' Mrs Cropley said.

Templeton scratched the side of his nose. 'That's another matter entirely, Mrs Cropley. At least we think it is. On 23rd of April this year, a young woman named Claire Potter was raped and stabbed just off the M1 north of Chesterfield. She was last seen at the Trowell services a short time earlier.'

'You mentioned this the last time you were here,' said Cropley. 'It meant nothing to me then and it means nothing now.'

Templeton ignored him and faced Mrs Cropley. 'We've now got quite a bit more information about that crime,' he said, 'and believe me, whoever did it must have picked up quite a bit of blood. I was just wondering if you had ever noticed anything about your husband's clothing around that time – you know, unusual stains, that sort of thing. Devilishly hard to get rid of, blood. You do the washing around here, don't you?'

'I can't believe you're asking me this,' said Mrs Cropley. 'The sheer nerve of it.'

'Well, I've never been faulted for my lack of nerve,' said Templeton. 'Nothing ventured, nothing gained. That's my motto. So if there's anything you'd like to get off your chest . . .'

'I saw nothing out of the ordinary.'

'Well, the clothes might have been beyond salvation, I suppose,' said Templeton. 'Have any of your husband's clothes gone missing over the past few months?'

'No.'

'Still,' Templeton mused aloud, 'the killer washed the victim's body, so the odds are he managed to deal with his own clothes. Very fastidious, he was. Are you a fastidious man, Mr Cropley?'

'I like to think so,' said Cropley, 'but it doesn't make me a killer, and I resent these accusations.'

'Of course you do. It's only natural. But I have to ask. I'd be a pretty useless detective if I didn't, wouldn't I?'

'Quite frankly I don't care what kind of bloody detective you are,' said Cropley. 'One thing I do know is that you're a very offensive person and I'd appreciate it if you'd leave my house immediately.'

'Just one more question, please, then I'll be out of your hair.'

Eileen Cropley glared at him.

'How often has your husband been unusually late home from work on a Friday? Say after midnight.'

'I don't know.'

'Surely you ought to be able to remember something like that? Don't you wait up for him?'

'No. I usually take a sleeping pill at eleven o'clock and go to bed. I'm fast asleep before midnight.'

'So he usually gets back after eleven then, can we say?'

She looked at her husband. 'I suppose so.'

Templeton turned to Roger Cropley. 'Nearly done now, sir. I remember the last time I was here with DC Jackman that you distinctly told me you usually tried to get away by mid-afternoon to beat the rush-hour traffic.'

'If I could. I didn't always succeed.'

'How often?'

'I don't know. I don't keep track.'

'I think I'd remember,' said Templeton.

'I'm not you.'

'No, you're right about that.' Templeton put his notebook back in his inside pocket. 'Well, I'll be off now. Thanks for your time. No need to see me out. I know the way.'

Templeton walked towards the door, but just before he opened it, he turned to face Cropley again. 'One more thing.' He took out his notebook again, frowned and consulted it. 'The 20th of February. Were you on your way home late that Friday, do you remember? Did you stop at Newport Pagnell?'

'I don't remember.'

'Only a young girl called Paula Chandler was driven off the road and an attempt was made at assaulting her. It failed. Her car doors were locked. There's a chance she might be able to identify her assailant.'

'Am I under arrest?' Cropley said.

'Of course not,' said Templeton, 'I'm only—'

'Then I want you to leave now or I'm calling my solicitor,' said Cropley, getting to his feet. 'Go on, get out!'

For a moment, Templeton thought Cropley was going to hit him, but he merely grabbed his shoulder and steered him towards the front door. Templeton didn't resist. When the door slammed behind him, he stood for a few moments enjoying the fresh, wet smell of the late afternoon air. It had stopped raining but the sky was still overcast and the streets were glistening. To the west, the low hills were faint grey outlines against a darker grey background. He could hear the sound of flowing water nearby, probably a beck, and a bird was singing in one of the trees. All in all, he thought, it had been a much more successful interview than the previous one.

As he got in his car, Templeton noticed a few flakes of Cropley's dandruff on the sleeve of his jacket and moved to brush it off. Then he had a better idea. If Roger Cropley was their man, he thought, he was damned if DS Susan Browne was going to get *all* the glory.

•

Annie stood in the rain among the massed crowds held back by barricades at the far side of Euston Road. The entire area had been blocked to traffic and all the station exits sealed, the underground shut down. People had swarmed out of the nearby offices, shops and cafes to stand at a safe distance and see what was going on, and their presence only served to swell the crowds. Annie began to feel uncomfortably penned in. Across the road, police in protective clothing moved about like shadows inside the station itself. Obviously the words that were on most people's lips were terrorists, bomb-threat, a fact of life in London. Annie had asked one of the officers on crowd control how long it would be before the trains started running, but he didn't know. Could be a couple of hours, could be longer, was all he would say. Annie saw her trip home quickly slipping away. There was no point going if she didn't get back until evening.

She made her way through the crowds, narrowly avoiding a poke in the eye from one of the many umbrellas raised. She didn't care where she was walking as long as she was getting away from the people. Eventually, when she got off Euston Road and took her bearings, she found herself winding her way via the back streets towards Bloomsbury.

When she got to Russell Square, she remembered the small hotel she and Banks had stayed at a few years ago, when their relationship had been just beginning and seemed full of possibility. She couldn't stay there by herself. It would be far too depressing. She would go back to her faceless, modern, efficient chain hotel; they would be sure to have a room available, perhaps even the same one she had just vacated, though they all looked so much the same that it didn't matter.

If she found herself stuck in London for another night, so be it. She took out her mobile and rang Brooke. He had already faxed the artist's impression up to Eastvale, but said he'd be more than happy to fax it to her hotel right away. Annie then rang the hotel, made a reservation and told them she was expecting a fax. They said they would take care of everything.

In the evening she would go and visit Dr Lukas at her home, but before that, Annie knew she couldn't spend another day and night in London without some new clothes, so she headed for Oxford Street. A bit of retail therapy would help dispel the gloom that seemed to have descended on her with the rain.

●

The pub was on Frith Street and at five o'clock it was already crowded. Burgess was there ahead of Banks, sitting on a wooden stool at a small table in the far corner, and he gestured to Banks, holding up an empty pint glass. Banks bought himself an orange juice and Burgess a pint of lager.

'Not drinking?' Burgess said, when Banks made his way back from the bar.

'Not right at the moment. Tell me,' said Banks, 'why do you always want to meet me in pubs? I don't believe I've ever seen your office. I'm not even entirely convinced that you have one.'

'They'd never let you in. Besides, if they did, they'd probably have to kill you. Best this way. Easier all round.'

'Are you ashamed of me or something?'

Burgess laughed, then turned serious. 'How are you doing?'

'Not bad. It's . . . I don't know. Roy and I weren't close or anything, but it still feels like a piece of me's died.'

'It's family.'

'I suppose so. That's what everyone says. I feel as if I've only just started getting to know him and he's been snatched from me.'

'I had a sister die a few years back,' Burgess said. 'She lived in South Africa. Durban. Hadn't seen her in years, not since we were kids. She was murdered during a robbery. Shot. I felt the same way, though, and I just couldn't stop thinking about her for ages, what it must have been like when she knew she was going to die. Still, it was quick.'

'Roy, too.'

'Nothing like a bullet for that. So what are you up to?'

Banks told him about the men who followed him on the A1(M), the shooting gesture through the window.

'What have you done about it?'

'I almost turned back, but that's probably what they wanted me to do. I called the locals in Peterborough and asked them to keep an eye open. They said they'd post surveillance on the estate.'

'Anything I can do?'

'Can you still run down a number plate?'

'Nothing could be easier.'

Banks gave him the Vectra's number.

'You realize it's probably stolen, don't you?' Burgess said.

'Attention to detail,' said Banks. 'Sometimes they make little mistakes.'

'True enough.'

'Ever heard of the Berger-Lennox Centre?'

'What's that when it's at home?'

'A private family planning centre. They deal with the whole lot. Abortions, adoption, whatever you want.'

'No,' said Burgess, 'I can't say I've heard of them, but then I wouldn't have any need for such a place, would I?'

'I suppose not. But Roy was an investor and Jennifer Clewes worked there, in administration.'

'Sounds interesting, but I still don't know anything about it. What are you going to do next?'

'I want to find out who killed Roy and why.'

'Why doesn't that surprise me? The caped crusader rides again.'

'Aren't you mixing your metaphors?'

'Probably. I don't suppose it's any use telling you to leave it to the locals?'

'No.'

'Thought not. What is it you want from me?'

'You've already told me a bit about Roy's chequered past.'

'The arms thing?'

'Yes.'

'That was years ago. I told you, as far as we know your brother's been clean for the past while. Forget about it.'

'So why is he dead?'

'Some of the nicest people end up dead.' Burgess lit a Tom Thumb cigar and added to the general fug.

'Any idea who the bloke in the photo sitting at a cafe with Lambert is yet?'

'Nope. I'm working on it, though. It's still doing the rounds. Believe me, I want to know as much as you do. Trouble is, this time of year, a lot of blokes are on holiday. And quite a few have retired since back then. Anyway, be patient. Remember it's not the local nick you're dealing with here. I promise you'll be among the first to know.'

'Tell me more about Gareth Lambert.'

'I told you. He was a business associate of your brother's and an all-round nasty piece of work. Charming enough on the surface. Like I said, Harry Lime. I take it you have seen *The Third Man*?'

'It's one of my favourite films. Look, according to Julian Harwood, Lambert's been living in Spain.'

'My, my, you have been a busy boy, haven't you?'

'Why come back?'

'I suppose he got bored with paella. He also got married to some beautiful Spanish actress. Centrefold material. England's quite sexy these days, or didn't you know? Madonna, Gwyneth

Paltrow, Liv Tyler and all the rest. They all want to live here. Anyway, he's back, and apparently he's in the travel business.'

'Legit?'

'I didn't say that. But there's no evidence to the contrary. Like I said, Lambert's elusive. He's got no form, never once been arrested. Not in this country, at any rate. Not yet. Always manages to keep one step ahead. Sure you won't have a real drink?'

'No, thanks. I need to keep my head clear.'

'For what?'

'For Roy.'

'OK.' Burgess went up to the bar and bought himself another pint. Banks noticed that the pub was filling up even more with the after-work crowd. There had been a blackboard outside advertising hand-pulled 'real' ale, so perhaps that was what brought them in. Most of the newcomers had to stand and the crush at the bar was getting to be three deep. Some people took advantage of the break in the rain and stood outside drinking, but from what Banks could see through the open door, the sky was darkening again and they'd all be dashing back inside soon.

Burgess came back and squeezed through the bodies to his stool without spilling a drop. 'Are there any other leads on Roy's murder?' he asked.

'I don't know,' said Banks. 'I'll have a word with Annie Cabbot later and see if I find out what's going on with DI Brooke's investigation.'

'Still shagging the lovely DI Cabbot, are you, or have you moved on to pastures new?'

Banks ignored him. Burgess was always looking for buttons to push. Usually he succeeded, but not this time. 'Tell me,' Banks said, 'honestly, do you think Roy could have got involved in something crooked with Lambert again?'

'Anything's possible. But what I'm telling you is that I, we, have no knowledge of it. If they were into something together, it's a smooth operation. You're dealing with pros here. At least, Lambert's a pro.'

'And you'd know if there was something?'

'Maybe. If it was big enough and nasty enough. We spend a lot of time just watching and thinking, but we're not omniscient. We don't know everything, just most things. Besides, it's not my brief any more. And Lambert hasn't been back here very long. Only a couple of months if my sources are right, which they usually are. So if there is anything, it's either new or it's something international and he was working it from Spain, too. Let me ask around. I've still got a few contacts. There's a bloke from Interpol, Dieter Ganz, I know is interested, if I can get in touch with him. I'll see what I can do.'

'I want to know where Lambert lives.'

'I was wondering when you'd get around to asking me that.'

'I'd have got around to it a lot sooner if I hadn't had my parents to cope with. Are you going to tell me?'

'Can't see why not.' Burgess gave him an address in Chelsea. 'You'd only find out some other way. He's got a place out in the country somewhere, too, where he keeps 'her indoors', but this flat's his pied-à-terre when he's in town. He still travels a fair bit. And he runs his business out of an office above a dry-cleaning shop on the Edgware Road, the Marble Arch end. But watch him, Banks. He's slippery. Remember Harry Lime.'

Banks finished his orange juice. 'Tell me something,' he said. 'You always put up a show of resistance, but in the end you usually tell me what I want to know. Why?'

'Entertainment value,' said Burgess. 'Besides, I like you. I like to watch you work. It interests me. I see you getting more and more like I used to be. You want something, you go after it, and bugger the consequences. Bugger the law, if necessary.'

'Used to be?'

Burgess sipped some beer. 'I've mellowed, Banksy. Grown up.'

'Bollocks.'

'It's true. Anyway, let's just say that DI Brooke's interests and mine don't always coincide. Brooke's a plodder. I know the type.

No imagination. No breadth of vision. He's only interested in short-term results, another tick on his report card for his next promotion.'

'And you?'

'I'm more interested in the big picture, the long-term view. And I like to know what's going on. Information's my stock in trade these days, after all. I don't get out on the street much.'

'Miss it?'

Burgess looked away. 'Sometimes.' He laughed and raised his glass. 'Now bugger off. And good luck with Lambert.'

It had started raining again and Banks had to fight against the influx of people trying to get back inside. He found a sheltered doorway and dialled Annie's number on his mobile. She answered on the fourth ring.

'Annie, it's me, Alan.'

'Where are you? I've been wanting to speak to you ever since I heard. I'm really sorry about what happened to your brother.'

'Thanks, I appreciate it. I'm back in London. Where are you?'

'As a matter of fact,' Annie said, 'I'm in Liberty's at the moment, in one of the changing rooms. You might not have heard, but they've closed King's Cross. Bomb threat. Anyway, it means I'm stuck here for another night. I need something to wear. I'm just about to head back to the hotel. Look, Alan, we have to talk again.'

'I know, but it'll have to wait. Couple of quick questions. Have Brooke's blokes talked to Gareth Lambert yet?'

'I don't think so,' said Annie. 'Last time I talked to him Dave didn't seem all that interested. They're concentrating on a couple of local low-lifes called Oliver Drummond and William Gilmore. Their names came up in your brother's business correspondence and phone records.' Banks remembered the names, but they didn't mean anything to him.

Then Annie told him about her visit to Alf Seaton's that morning, the description of the man with the pony tail and what had become of the Mondeo. Banks knew immediately that it was one of the men who had followed him from Peterborough, the one who had made the gesture.

'Another thing you might as well know,' Annie said. 'It looks as if your brother's girlfriend had an abortion, arranged through the Berger-Lennox Centre. That's when he met Jennifer Clewes.'

'Jesus,' said Banks. 'That'll be Corinne you're talking about?'

'Are there any others?'

'Probably,' said Banks, 'but I think she was the most recent model, the one before Jennifer. Thanks for telling me.'

'Can we meet up? We really should talk about all this.'

'Maybe tomorrow,' said Banks. 'Breakfast? I've still got a couple of people to talk to tonight. How about I give you a bell when I'm finished?' He rang off before she could protest.

The rain was really pelting down now and all Banks had for protection was his light raincoat. He stood in the doorway looking at the people drifting back and forth between the curtains of rain then stepped out and headed as fast as he could for Tottenham Court Road tube station.

13

'**How did you** get my address?' Dr Alex Lukas asked Annie as she stood under her umbrella on the front step of the Belsize Park house shortly after seven o'clock that evening. 'I'm not in the telephone directory.'

'We have our sources,' said Annie, who had taken a peek at the personnel records when she made a quick, and otherwise fruitless, search of Jennifer Clewes's office at the Berger-Lennox. 'Can I come in?'

'What do you want? It's not a police state yet, is it?'

'Not the last time I checked,' said Annie with a smile. 'But it is raining fast.'

Dr Lukas took the chain off the door and stepped back. Annie folded up her umbrella, took off her raincoat and hung it on the coat stand. She followed Dr Lukas down the thick carpet into a cosy and comfortable living room. The curtains were still open and rain streaked the windowpanes. The radio was playing quietly, an orchestral concert of some sort. Dr Lukas excused herself for a moment and went upstairs. While she waited, Annie looked around the room.

What looked to her like original works of art hung on the wall, mostly abstract expressionist and cubist pieces, and various knick-knacks and framed photographs stood on most available surfaces. The crowded dark-wood bookcase boasted a colourful array of spines, none of them medical. There were novels, mostly Tolstoy and Dostoevsky, poetry by Mandelstam, Akhnatova, Yevtushenko, Tsvetayeva, and a few biographies, Shostakovich, Gorbachev, Pasternak. Annie could see by the lettering that some of the books were in Russian. Taking into account the matryoshka doll on the mantelpiece, and remembering the hint of an accent, it didn't take much to surmise that Dr Lukas hailed from Russia, or somewhere in the former Soviet republics.

Beside the doll stood a black-and-white photograph of a family group in a wooded area: parents and three children. Annie walked over to have a closer look at it. They were all wearing overcoats and no one was smiling; they had that hard, pinched look you get when there isn't enough food on the table or coal on the fire. Beside it stood another photo of what Annie took to be the parents, more recent and in colour. This time they were smiling into the camera, standing beside a large lake in the sunshine.

'On holiday,' said Dr Lukas, behind her.

'I'm sorry, I didn't mean to be nosy,' said Annie. 'Is that your parents?'

'Yes. It was taken two years ago.'

'So you come from Russia?'

'Ukraine. A city called L'viv, in the west, not far from the Polish border. Do you know it?'

'Sorry,' said Annie, whose geography was terrible.

'It doesn't matter.'

'Do they still live there?'

Dr Lukas paused before answering with a tentative 'Yes.'

'How long have you been here?'

'Thirteen years. I was twenty-five when the Soviet Union broke up. I was lucky. I got into medical school in Edinburgh. I'd had some training in L'viv, of course, but this country didn't recognize my qualifications. Do you know how many foreign-trained doctors there are over here driving minicabs and working in restaurants and hotels?'

'No,' said Annie.

'It's a shame, a terrible waste,' said Dr Lukas, with a hint of tragic fatalism in her voice.

'You don't have a very strong accent,' Annie said.

'I worked hard to get rid of it. Foreign accents don't work in your favour here. But all this is beside the point. What have you come to see me about?'

Dr Lukas was perching uncomfortably at the edge of an armchair, Annie noticed, body hunched forward and tense, hands clasped in her lap. She was wearing faded jeans and a man's white casual shirt, no make-up. She looked tired and drawn, as she had in her office.

'You're right,' said Annie. 'It's not a social call.' She paused and searched for the right way to begin. 'Look, in a murder investigation, people sometimes hide things, mask the truth. Not because they're guilty, but because they've maybe committed some minor crime and they're afraid we'll uncover it and prosecute them. Do you understand?'

'I'm listening.'

'When that happens, it makes a difficult job even harder. We don't know what's important and what isn't, so how can we know where to focus our line of enquiry?'

'All jobs have their difficulties,' said Dr Lukas. 'Mine included. I don't see what point there is in you telling me how hard yours is.'

'I thought if you understood, then you'd see reason and tell me the truth.'

'Pardon?'

'I think you heard me.'

'But I'm not sure I heard you correctly. Are you suggesting I lied?'

'I'm saying that you might be hiding something because you think it reflects badly on you. I don't think you're lying so much as you're obscuring the truth. Now it may or may not be important, or it may not seem important to you, but I'd like to know what it is, and I think you'd like to tell me.'

'What makes you think that?'

'You get to know people in this job. I think you're a decent person and I think you're under a tremendous amount of pressure.

Now that could simply be a matter of your work, or it could be due to personal problems which are nothing at all to do with this investigation. But the feeling I get is that there's something else, and that it is connected.'

'I see.' Dr Lukas stood up and walked to the cocktail cabinet. 'I think I need a drink,' she said, and took out a tumbler and a bottle of Southern Comfort. 'What about you?'

'Nothing, thanks,' said Annie.

'As you wish.' She poured herself a large measure and sat down again. This time she seemed to relax a little more into the armchair and the strain that etched the lines on her forehead and around her eyes and mouth seemed to ease. The concert ended and Annie heard the radio audience applaud before the announcer's voice cut in. Dr Lukas switched it off, took a sip of Southern Comfort and regarded Annie closely with her serious brown eyes. Annie got the sense that she was trying to come to some sort of decision and realized that she might well end up with a partial truth, if anything, as was so often the case.

The clock ticked and rain tapped against the window. Still Dr Lukas thought and sipped. Finally, when Annie could almost bear it no longer, she said, 'You're right.'

'About what?'

'About people withholding the truth. Do you think it doesn't happen in my profession, too? People lie to me all the time. How much they drink. Whether they smoke. What drugs they take. How often they exercise. As if by lying they'd make themselves healthy. But I haven't done anything wrong.'

'Sometimes people use a different standard to measure them-selves by,' said Annie. 'You might not think you have done any-thing morally or ethically wrong, but you might have broken the law. Or vice versa.'

Dr Lukas managed a flicker of a smile. 'A fine distinction.'

'I'm not after getting you struck off.'

'I'm happy to hear it.'

'But I do want the truth. What are late girls?'

Dr Lukas sipped some more Southern Comfort before answering, then she ran a finger around the rim of her glass. 'It's really very simple,' she said. 'They are girls who come late to the centre.'

'In what sense? Late in their pregnancies?'

'No. There you are quite wrong.'

'Well, I've hardly been steered in the right direction. This isn't supposed to be a guessing game.'

'Now I am telling you. There have been no surgical procedures performed on girls beyond the twenty-four-week legal limit.'

'OK,' said Annie, 'so what *is* it all about?'

'Girls who come late to the centre, after regular hours. In the evening.'

'When you're working late?'

'I have a lot of paperwork. You wouldn't believe it, even a doctor . . . but I do.'

'So why do these girls come after hours?'

'Why do you think?'

'They want to bypass the system for some reason, and you help them to do it?'

'These girls are prostitutes, for the most part, and many of them are illegal immigrants or asylum-seekers. They can't go through the National Health and they can't afford our fees.'

'Pro bono work, then?'

'You could say that.'

'What exactly do you do for them?'

'I handle the forms, the papers necessary to secure an abortion, if that's what they want. If another doctor's signature is needed I get that too from someone at one of the clinics. They don't ask me too many questions. It's very easy and it harms no one.'

'Do you perform the abortions?'

'No, they are done elsewhere, at one of the clinics.'

'What do you do, then?'

'I examine them, make sure they are in good general health. There are sexually transmitted infections to worry about. And

Aids, of course. Some girls have drug and alcohol problems. Many of the foetuses would be born with severe handicaps, if they lived.'

'Do you supply drugs?'

Dr Lukas looked directly at Annie. 'No,' she said. 'I understand why they might want to take drugs, the life they are living, but I won't supply them. They seem to have no problem getting drugs elsewhere, though.'

'So if we were to check the drugs at the centre against records, they would match?'

'If they don't, it's not me who's been taking them. But, yes, I think they would. Besides, we have no need for the kind of drugs you're talking about at the centre.'

'How often does this happen?'

'Not very often. Maybe once, sometimes twice a month.'

'Why do these girls come to you? How do they know about you?'

'Many of them are from Eastern Europe,' Dr Lukas said, with a shrug. 'I'm known in the community.'

That sounded a bit vague, Annie thought – Eastern Europe covered a large area – but she let it go. Now Dr Lukas was on a roll it was better to get as much as possible out of her than labour one point. 'What about Jennifer Clewes? Did she know about this?'

'Yes.'

'When did she find out?'

'She's known for a month or two. I didn't realize she worked late sometimes, too. I thought I was alone there. You've seen how isolated my office is. The girls usually buzz the front door and I let them in myself. This time Jennifer got there first. She didn't say anything but later she asked me what was going on.'

'What did you tell her?'

'What I'm telling you.'

'And what was her reaction?'

'She became interested.' Dr Lukas swirled the remains of her drink in her glass. 'Jennifer was a truly decent human being,' she said. 'When I explained to her about the girls and the situation they were in, nowhere to turn to for help, she understood.'

'It didn't disturb her, upset her?'

'No. She was a bit uncomfortable about it at first, but . . .'

'But what?'

'Well, she was the administrator. She helped to protect me. Paperwork got lost, that sort of thing. I told her it would be best if she didn't tell anyone, that not everyone would understand.'

'We think she must have told her boyfriend.'

Dr Lukas shrugged. 'That was for her judgement alone.'

'So Jennifer became involved in it with you?'

'We were both trying to help unfortunate girls. It's not that this happened often, you understand. It wasn't a regular thing. These girls would not have been able to come if they'd had to pay. And remember, they couldn't just walk into the nearest NHS clinic. What do you think would happen to them? Do you think there are no longer back-street abortionists using rusty coat hangers?'

'So what went wrong?'

'Nothing went wrong.'

'Jennifer Clewes is dead.'

'I know nothing about that. I've told you what I was keeping from you, who the late girls are and how and why I helped them. I've told you Jennifer's part in all this. There is nothing more. Once in a while a girl who needed help would come to me and I provided it. That's all there is to it.'

'Did anyone else know? Georgina, for example?'

'No. At first it was only me, then Jennifer. She was the only other person who ever stayed late.'

Somehow it didn't all add up, Annie thought. There were too many pieces missing and the ones she had didn't fit together properly. 'What about Carmen Petri? Was she one of the late girls? What was so special about her?'

Dr Lukas seemed to tense up again, the lines on her forehead deepening, her posture stiffening. 'I don't know the name.'

'She was one of the late girls, wasn't she? What happened to her?'

'I told you I've never heard of her.'

'Did something go wrong? Is that it?'

'I've told you, I don't know anyone called Carmen.'

Annie took out the sketch that Brooke's police artist had coaxed from Alf Seaton. 'Do you recognize this man?' she asked.

'No,' said Dr Lukas. Annie couldn't be certain that she was telling the truth.

'About a week ago, Jennifer was seen leaving this building with a young girl. The person who saw them said that the girl looked pregnant. They were talking, then a man who looked very much like this one came over and the girl went away with him in a car. Do you know what that was about?'

Annie could have sworn that Dr Lukas turned a shade paler. 'No,' she said. 'I told you, Jennifer sometimes worked late, too, saw the girls. Sometimes she talked to them. She was a very caring person and it's a tragedy what happened to her.'

'It is,' said Annie, standing up to leave. 'And I'm going to find out what was behind it, with or without your help.'

'Please, you don't know . . .'

'Don't know what?'

Dr Lukas paused, rubbing her hands together. 'Please. I'm telling you the truth.'

'I think you're telling me part of the truth,' Annie said, 'and I'm going to leave you to think over your position. When you've made your mind up you can call me at this number.' Annie scribbled her mobile number on the back of her card and left it on the coffee table. 'I'll show myself out.'

•

Well, you can't win them all, Banks thought, after a wasted trip to Chelsea. One of the problems with paying surprise visits was that sometimes the object of your visit wasn't at home, and such was the case with Gareth Lambert that wet Tuesday evening, though

Banks had even hung around in a shop doorway over the street for about an hour, waiting. Burgess had said that Lambert was elusive.

The humidity and damp clothing made the crowded underground carriage smell like a wet dog, and Banks was glad to get off at Green Park for the Piccadilly Line. The second carriage was half empty and he passed the short trip reading the adverts and trying to work out the language of the newspaper that the person opposite him was reading. The letters were Roman, but it definitely wasn't anything he recognized. Sometimes the depths of his own ignorance appalled him.

When he got to Corinne's flat he was soaked and she gave him a towel for his hair and made him take off his raincoat and his jacket and hung them up in the bathroom under an electric fire to dry them out. His trousers were stuck to his thighs and shins and he thought of asking her to dry those, too, but she might get the wrong idea. Besides, what would he wear? It would be rather undignified carrying out an interview, albeit a friendly one, sitting around in his underpants.

'Warm drink?'

'Tea, if you've got any. No milk or sugar for me.'

'I think I can manage that.'

Despite, or perhaps because of, the rain, it was a close, muggy evening. Sweat filmed Corinne's upper lip and forehead, and she looked as if she hadn't been sleeping well. Her hair was tangled and her eyes had dark circles under them. So Roy had the power to make a woman feel this way, no matter what he'd done to her. What the hell was it about him? Sandra wouldn't give Banks the time of day, and even Annie couldn't get away quick enough if he talked about anything other than the case at hand. He thought of Penny Cartwright again and her revulsion at the idea of dinner with him. She would probably have jumped at the chance if Roy had asked her.

'I'm sorry I haven't been able to get here before,' Banks said, when he had a cup of tea in his hand. 'You can guess what it's been like.'

'Have you seen your parents? How are they? Your mother was very nice to me. Not that your father wasn't . . . but you know what I mean.'

Banks remembered that last October, much to his surprise, his mother had taken Corinne into the kitchen to help her prepare the anniversary spread and in no time they had been chatting away to one another like old friends.

Thinking of his parents, he also remembered the message that the thug in the red Vectra had given him. *We know where your parents live.* How did they know? From Roy? When it came right down to it, though, it wasn't that difficult to find out such things. Most likely they had followed Banks to Peterborough the day before and he hadn't spotted them. He would ring his father before it got too late and make sure everything was all right there. He would also ring the Peterborough police again to make sure they had someone watching the house at all times. If this man with the ponytail had killed Jennifer Clewes, as Annie seemed to think he had, then he and his friends didn't make idle threats. Banks wished he could arrange for his parents to go away for a while, but they would never agree to it. Not at a time like this.

'They're coping,' he said finally. 'My mother took it rather hard, as you can imagine. Dad's trying to be a rock but the strain's beginning to show.'

'I hope they get through it. Do you think I should give them a ring?'

'It wouldn't do any harm,' Banks said. 'Maybe in a couple of days.' He sipped his tea – a pleasant, scented Earl Grey – then leaned forward and set the cup and saucer down on the low table. 'Look, Corinne, this probably isn't anything to do with what happened to Roy but in a murder investigation you have to follow up all the loose ends.'

'I understand.'

'A couple of months ago, you went with Roy to the Berger–Lennox Centre.'

Corinne looked away. 'That's right. It was a private matter.'

'I'm not here to judge you, either of you. Whose idea was it?'

'Was what?'

'To go to the Berger-Lennox.'

'Oh, Roy's. He'd invested in it. He'd also visited the centre before, checked it out. He said it was a good place.'

So Roy had probably already met, or at least seen, Jennifer Clewes. 'And was it?'

'They treated me well enough.'

'The woman on reception thought you were Roy's daughter.'

'Well, I used my own name. I wasn't trying to pretend or anything.'

'There's plenty of reasons these days for a girl having a different name from her father.'

'I suppose so.'

'So you went through with the procedure?'

Now she looked directly at him. 'Yes. I had an abortion. OK?'

'I assume you're sure it was Roy's baby?'

'Yes, of course. What do you think I am?'

'Why didn't you want to keep it?'

'I . . . I didn't feel ready.'

'What about Roy?'

'He'd already made it clear he wasn't interested. He wasn't much interested in me, either. He thinks I didn't see him chatting up that redhead in the reception area, but I did.'

'Jennifer Clewes?'

Corinne put her hand to her mouth. 'Oh, my God. Is that who it was? The girl who got shot? I've read about her in the papers. What happened?'

'That's where he met her, perhaps even before the visit with you. Perhaps you can see now why I'm asking all these questions. There too many connections and similarities here, but I'm missing something.'

'I don't think I can help you. I mean, I saw him talking to her, but he's always like that, flirting with girls. And I knew there was someone. I just didn't put two and two together. Story of my life.'

'No reason why you should, or could. So you and Roy were splitting up when you found out you were pregnant?'

'It happened at the worst possible time.' She gave a harsh laugh. 'Like these things always do.'

'And you discussed it and both agreed abortion was the way to go?'

'Yes. Look, it's nothing to do with what happened. It can't be. It was a private matter. You're not trying to say I killed him because I had an abortion and he found a new girlfriend, are you?'

'Of course not,' said Banks, though the thought had crossed his mind. Rejection and jealousy, coupled with the emotional trauma of abortion, could be a lethal mix. She hadn't done it herself, Banks knew, but maybe she had enough money to hire someone, and maybe she even knew how to find someone to hire. After all, she was an accountant to the entertainment world, and that was full of villains, or celebrities who liked to rub shoulders with them. But Banks had dismissed the idea as quickly as it had come into his head. Wronged lovers usually go for a more direct method, as any cop who has responded to a domestic will tell you.

'Roy was chatting up his new girlfriend while you were in the doctor's office,' Banks said. 'How does that make you feel?'

Tears brimmed in her eyes. 'How do you think it makes me feel?' she said. 'He always was a bastard. I knew that. But I loved him.'

And this time there was no stopping her. The dam burst and the flood was unloosed. Banks went over and sat beside her on the sofa, putting his arms around her. She didn't resist. She just melted against him, buried her head in his already wet shoulder and let it all pour out. Banks held her and stroked her hair. After a few minutes the tears subsided and she gently extricated herself. Banks went back to the armchair and picked up his tea. It was lukewarm now but it was something to hide behind in the awkward moments that follow an emotional outburst. The cup rattled against the saucer as he picked it up.

Corinne went and fetched some tissues. 'I'm sorry about that,' she said. 'It's the first time . . . I was just bottling it all up. It feels better.'

'I'm glad,' said Banks, 'and I'm sorry if I sounded abrupt or rude.'

'It must be very frustrating for you,' Corinne said. 'And I know you and Roy weren't very close, but you must . . . I mean, he was your brother, after all.'

'This might sound an odd question,' said Banks, 'but did Roy ever tell you he'd witnessed the attacks on the World Trade Center?'

'Yes,' said Corinne. 'I didn't know him back then, of course, but he told me it devastated him. He had nightmares for months. I could only imagine what it must have been like.'

'Did he ever talk to you about religion, about spiritual matters?'

'Not really, no. I mean, I knew he went to church on Sundays, and he said he liked his local vicar, but it didn't really interfere with our life.'

'You're not interested in spiritual matters yourself?'

'Spiritual matters, as far as I can understand them, yes. But not in organized religion. Look at the misery and bloodshed it's caused throughout history. Still causes.'

'Did the two of you ever argue about this?'

'Yes, but we always reached an impasse, the way you do when you talk about such things. He said that was just an excuse and that it was mankind who caused the bloodshed and misery, and I said his must be a pretty rotten God if he was so all-powerful and he let it all happen anyway. We learned to stay away from the subject in the end. I mean, where do you go from there?'

Where, indeed? wondered Banks, who had been involved in one or two similar arguments himself over the years.

'He didn't push religion on me, or on anyone else for that

matter, if that's what you're getting at. And he obviously didn't use it to try to talk me out of having an abortion.'

'I just wondered how big a role it played in his life, that's all.'

'Like I said, he went to church on Sunday and had a philosophical chat with the vicar every now and then.'

'OK. Fair enough. Did he ever mention someone called Gareth Lambert, an old friend?'

'Yes, I remember him mentioning the name.'

'Did you ever meet him?'

She pulled out a tissue and blew her nose. It looked raw when she'd finished. 'No,' she said. 'But I heard his name.'

'Do you remember the context?'

'Roy was just talking about an old friend of his who was back in the country. They hadn't seen each other in a long time.'

'When was this?'

'A couple of months ago. Around the time of the abortion. He said he was going to meet him for a drink at some club or other they belonged to on the Strand, talk about old times and see if there were any business opportunities. He was always on the lookout for a new angle. I'm afraid I suspected something else. I asked him who he was going out with and that's what he told me. I didn't believe him, though.'

'Did Roy go for that drink?'

'Yes.'

'Do you remember the name of the club?'

'Sorry, no.'

'Well, if it's any consolation, he was probably telling the truth. Did he say anything about it afterwards?'

'No, not really. He was vague, as usual, and a little tipsy. He just said that he'd had an interesting time. He seemed excited about more business possibilities.'

'Did he say what?'

'No, he was very vague.'

Something dodgy, then, Banks thought. Not arms, in all likelihood, but something crooked if Lambert was involved. He had nothing more to ask Corinne but thought he would stay for a while, anyway, just to keep her company, talk about Roy. It was after nine o'clock; it had been a long day and he was feeling pleasantly tired. He could ring Annie and ask her to meet him in the morning, if that was OK with her.

As if she was reading his mind, Corinne said, 'Look, I've got a nice bottle of white wine in the fridge. I've got red, if you want it, too. I don't want to drink by myself. I don't want to be alone just now. Would you care to keep me company for a while longer? I mean, if there isn't anywhere you have to go. Where are you staying?'

Banks realized that he had completely forgotten about finding somewhere to stay. He had driven to London without making any arrangements and the incident on the motorway had pushed all such practical thoughts from his mind. There was always Roy's – he still had a key – but there was a chance the police weren't finished there yet.

'Don't know,' he said. 'I thought I'd just check into a hotel.'

She looked away and reddened a little. 'You can stay here if you like. I mean, there's a spare room, all made up and everything.'

The idea made Banks nervous. He knew the offer was entirely innocent. The poor girl was alone and devastated by the murder of her lover, and Banks would no more think of letting anything sexual happen than he would with his own sister, if he had one. Then again, she was a very attractive young woman and he was just a man, after all. What if she cried out in the night? What if Banks went to comfort her and she was naked under the sheet? What would they do then?

What really made up his mind, though, was that right at the moment he was so weary he could hardly lift himself out of the armchair, let alone hit the wet streets looking for a cheap hotel, so he said, 'Thanks, that's very good of you. That'll be great. And I prefer red, if that's OK?'

14

Annie woke early on Wednesday morning, and when she opened her curtains she was happy to see that the sun was shining again and the sky was robin's egg blue. She managed twenty minutes of meditation and a short yoga session – ten salutes to the sun, cobra, locust and peacock – then she dressed in her new white cotton slacks, red short-sleeved top and light denim jacket and went down to the restaurant for breakfast with Banks, her wavy brown hair still damp from the shower.

The meditation and yoga hadn't made her feel as calm as she had hoped, and she felt anxious and tense about meeting Banks again, especially after the way he had phoned and so casually put her off late the previous evening. Their last meeting had gone well enough, but nothing had been resolved and Annie still felt as if she was bursting with questions and insecurities.

The stories in the morning paper upset her, too, brought back too many bad memories. Because the reporter was trying to link Banks's fire with his brother's murder, they had also raked up all the stuff about Phil Keane and his hapless policewoman girlfriend. Where they had got it all from in the first place, she didn't know, but there's always a leak somewhere.

Banks didn't look in too bad shape, she thought, when she saw him already sitting at a cloth-covered table drinking coffee. In fact, he looked a lot more like his old self than he had in ages. All he really needed now was a decent haircut and a few more good nights' sleep to get rid of the bags under his eyes. And maybe some fresh clothes. The pallor had all but gone, and there was a certain edginess back in his body language instead of that infuriating languor. There was also a brightness in his dark-blue eyes that she hadn't seen in a long time. Perhaps, she thought, his brother's death had made him realize how lucky *he* was. Or more likely it had just given him something he cared about, a sense of purpose. For there was no denying that he was on the case, officially or not.

She sat down opposite him and noticed that he smelled just a little of original Old Spice. It was a smell she liked, something she remembered from their intimate time together. It had taken her a while to throw out the deodorant stick he had left in her bathroom cabinet, but she had done so eventually, along with the razor, shaving cream and toothbrush.

'So what were you up to last night that you couldn't meet up with me then?' Annie asked.

'Social duties,' said Banks.

'Pull the other one.'

'I went to see Corinne,' he said.

'How is she?'

'She's suffering plenty,' said Banks. 'I don't know about you,' he went on, 'but whenever I'm having breakfast in a hotel, it has to be the bacon and eggs. Don't know why. I'd never have that at home.'

'It's because you don't have to cook it yourself and wash the dishes after,' said Annie.

'And because I never have time to sit around and eat it.'

'How are things going?'

'Not so bad, considering,' said Banks. 'My dad's just worn down by the whole thing but my mother's acting strange.'

'Strange how?'

'As if it's just another family event, like the anniversary party. She's already talking about sandwiches for the funeral tea.'

'Might not be a bad idea,' said Annie. 'The post-mortem's over. Given cause of death I shouldn't imagine they'll be holding on to the body for too long. I'm really sorry about your brother, Alan. I know Dave Brooke will do his best. He's a good copper.'

A waitress came over. Banks ordered the full English, and Annie decided on a cheese and mushroom omelette. She felt a twinge of guilt – her first morning she'd had only a Continental, and the next day muesli – but if you didn't treat yourself once in a while what was the point?

'Anyway,' Banks asked, 'how are things progressing up north?'

Annie ran her hand over her hair. 'I've only been in touch over the phone but they seem to be moving along nicely. Mostly it's forensics on the tyre tracks and fingerprints we found at your cottage and on the door of Jennifer's car. We've also got people asking around, you know, did anyone see anything, that sort of thing. But we don't expect much to come from that. It was late and in a remote place. Anyway, Winsome's on the case, and I know I can trust her.'

'What about Templeton and Rickerd?'

'They're on it, too. You know as well as I do Rickerd's a born office manager. And Kev might be a bit of an arsehole, but he's got good instincts. He's off on a tangent, but it's not a bad idea to give him some space. Anyway, it's in good hands. I'm hoping to get back up there today, if only for a flying visit to bring everything up to speed. The telephone has its limitations.'

'Indeed it does.'

'What about you?' Annie asked. 'What have you been up to?'

'Me? Apart from keeping my parents company, and Corinne, nothing much, really,' said Banks. 'I doubt that I've discovered anything you'd be interested in hearing.'

'Try me. What is it you usually say to witnesses or suspects? "Let me be the judge of that"?'

'Touché,' said Banks. 'OK. I've found out that Gareth Lambert is back from self-imposed exile in Spain and that one evening a few weeks ago he had drinks with Roy. That mean anything to you?'

'No.'

'They're old pals, known one another for years. No doubt they were mixed up in all sorts of criminal enterprises before the arms deal put the wind up them. Up Roy, at least. Lambert we're not so sure about. Anyway, it's a bit too much of a coincidence for my liking, the two reunited and one of them dead.'

'I suppose you got all this from Burgess, didn't you? That man's a walking disaster area.'

'Dirty Dick has his good points, but I don't know why you should think I got any of it from him.'

'I can't imagine where else, that's all.'

The waitress delivered their breakfasts. Banks asked for more coffee, Annie for tea.

'Anyway,' Banks said, when the waitress had gone, 'DI Brooke's got everything I found: the mobile, the CD and USB drive, even the digital photos I'd printed from the CD. Everything.'

Annie's eyes narrowed. 'But you kept copies.'

'It's not illegal. I didn't withhold or tamper with anything.'

'Damn it, Alan, you broke into a murder victim's house, you went through his stuff, you used his mobile phone, you found and copied personal information. Don't tell me you haven't tampered.'

Banks rested his knife and fork at the sides of his plate. 'In the first place, I didn't know he was a murder victim at the time. He was simply missing and had been gone for less than twenty-four hours. What would we have done if a call like that had come in? If he'd been a child or a teenager, then perhaps we might just have set the wheels in motion. But a healthy man in his late forties? Come on, Annie, you know as well as I do what would happen. Nothing. And he was my brother. Family. I think that gave me a right to enter his home. What is it that really upsets you?'

'It's that you keep going off all on your own like some kind of maverick,' Annie said. 'You don't tell anyone what's going on. You think you're the only one who can work it all out. You think you can handle everything by yourself. But you don't know everything. You can't do it all yourself. For God's sake, Alan, you nearly got yourself killed.'

When one of the nearby diners looked over, Annie realized she'd let her voice get too loud. The thing was, it had come out spontaneously. She hadn't known what she was going to say when Banks asked her what her problem was because she hadn't really known. Perhaps the stories in the newspaper had stirred it all up, but now she did know. It went back to Phil Keane and the way Banks had suspected him but said nothing, gone and tried to build his own case against Phil on the quiet.

When she thought about it, though, she realized that it went even further back than the Phil Keane case. Banks had been just the same when he went off looking for Chief Constable Riddle's wayward daughter, Emily, and he'd held back so much information from Annie during that case that her hands had been tied. At one point she had even suspected him of being sexually involved with the girl's mother, if not the girl herself. That was what happened when you held things back; the truth got warped and twisted in people's minds. Lacking the facts, they made up stories based on fancy, like stories in the tabloids.

Now she'd said it, though, she felt embarrassed, and she sneaked a look at Banks as she took a bite of her omelette. He seemed to be eating his breakfast again quite placidly. The waitress came with more coffee and tea. Annie thanked her.

'Listen to us,' said Banks, 'bickering over breakfast like an old married couple.'

'We're not bickering,' said Annie. 'It takes two to bicker. Aren't you going to respond?'

'What can I say? I'm glad you got it off your chest.'

'Simple as that, is it?'

Banks looked at her directly, his eyes clear and bright. 'It's a start. If we're going to go on working together, we have to get one or two things sorted.'

'On whose terms?'

'That's not the point. I'm not going to change my ways. Nor are you.'

'Then maybe we *shouldn't* go on working together.'

'Up to you.'

'Not entirely. What do *you* want?'

'I want to carry on working with you. Believe it or not, I like you, and I think you're damn good at your job.'

Annie felt absurdly pleased at the compliment, but she hoped it didn't show in her face. 'But you're still going to leave me in the dark half the time?'

'I don't deliberately hide things from you. If I had told you all my suspicions about Phil Keane as soon as I had them – and God knows I tried to hint – you'd have thrown me out on my ear, accused me of being jealous – which you did anyway – and never talked to me again. All I had to go on was a feeling, at first, some sense that all wasn't what it seemed with him.'

'But I might not have had to run into a burning house and drag you out.'

'So it's that, is it?'

'No, it's not even that, when you come right down to it . . . If you really want to know, it's the way you treated me afterwards.'

'What do you mean?'

'Nothing.' But Annie had gone too far now to hold back. She put her knife and fork down.

'Come on, Annie,' said Banks. 'We've got this far. Let's clear the air. See if we can't come up with a chance of working this out.'

'That's a change of tune.' This was more difficult than Annie thought it would be, especially given the context, the hotel restaurant with its trees and potted plants, waitresses carrying trays, the businessmen in their pinstriped suits planning their days, some of them already on their mobiles and PDAs. 'It's just that you seemed to brush me off,' she said, 'push me aside as if my feelings didn't matter. God knows, I felt bad enough about making the mistake I did over Phil. I mean, can you imagine, sharing your bed with a fucking serial killer?' She shook her head. 'But you. I'd have expected . . . I don't know . . . support . . . comfort, maybe. You went to Corinne last night, didn't you, but you weren't there for me. I know we have our history and it hasn't always been easy, but you should have been there for me and you weren't. I was hurting as much as you, if not more.'

There, she'd said it, said more than enough. Christ, he was staying silent an awfully long time. *Say something. Say something.*

At last Banks spoke. 'You're right,' he said. 'And if it means anything, I'm sorry.'

'Why did you do it? Why did you abandon me? Was it her?'

'Who?'

'Michelle, or whatever her name is.'

Banks looked surprised. 'No, it wasn't Michelle. It's just that Michelle didn't have anything to do with what happened, seeing her didn't make me think about it. She took me away from it, distracted me. It was thinking about it that was doing my head in. I couldn't remember a thing between answering the door and waking up in hospital. Still can't. All I know is what you've told me, and the smell of whisky still gives me panic attacks. Christ, for a while, for weeks, I didn't even want to get out of bed in the morning, let alone have a serious heart-to-heart about what happened. What's the point? It's like these interminable daytime chat programmes, people talking on and on about their bloody feelings and problems and it gets them nowhere. It's just talk, talk, talk, blather, blather, blather.'

'Some people think that might be better than keeping it bottled up inside.'

Banks ran his hand over his hair. 'Look, Annie, I feel like I'm crawling out of a deep trough. By all rights, Roy's murder should have pushed me back in, but it hasn't. Cut me a little slack here.'

'Maybe you're fuelled by anger?'

'Maybe I am, but at least I'm fuelled.'

Annie looked at him for a while over her tea and let his words sink in. Maybe he was right. Maybe it was time to put it all behind them and move on, and maybe part of doing that was allowing Banks some leeway in the investigation of his brother's murder. After all, it wasn't as if she could stop him.

'OK, let's imagine you were investigating the case,' she said. 'Hypothetically, of course. What would your next move be?'

'What's the official line of enquiry?'

'Basically, they're working their way through Roy's mobile phone book and his business contacts listed on that USB drive you handed over. Oliver Drummond and William Gilmore, the names I mentioned last night, are DI Brooke's priorities because their names are on his computer. Chop shop and fraud. Do they sound like enterprises your brother might have been interested in?'

'Probably,' said Banks. 'Though I'd say fraud was the more likely of the two. I can't see Roy in the stolen-car racket. Has Brooke got anywhere with either of them so far?'

'I don't know,' said Annie. 'I haven't talked to him yet this morning.'

'He should be going after Lambert,' Banks said. 'He knows as much as I do, that Roy had taken a photo of Lambert and an unidentified man and hidden it away shortly before he disappeared. That ought to set off a few alarm bells, don't you think?'

'I'm sure Dave has his reasons. Does Lambert have a record?'

'No.'

'And is his name in the mobile call list or address book?'

'No.'

'There you are, then. Drummond and Gilmore both have form and they appear in the call list.'

'Even so . . .' said Banks. 'What have you been up to?'

'I've been pursuing leads of my own in the Jennifer Clewes murder.'

'They're linked. Roy and Jennifer were lovers.'

'I know that. But they can't both have been killed by the man with the ponytail. The timing's way off. Which is why Dave thinks it's worth looking elsewhere for Roy's killer. And like I said, both Drummond and Gilmore have criminal records. Brooke also has a man trying to find anyone who knows about Roy's movements on the day he disappeared. Apparently the mobile isn't much use there as he only used it once that day. To call his hairdresser.'

'I know that,' said Banks.

'Of course you do. You got to the mobile first. They've also enhanced the photo you received. Brooke's not convinced yet that the man is Roy, but I'd say it seems likely. Anyway, they think it might lead them to the spot where it happened.'

Banks nodded.

'Any idea who Roy went off with yet?' Annie asked.

'I'm not sure, but I think it might have been Gareth Lambert. Roy's known him for years. I'd still like to know who that other man in the photo is.'

'Any leads?'

'Nothing yet, but I'm working on it.' He smiled. 'Obviously, I don't have the manpower to follow up every name in Roy's life, the way you and DI Brooke do, so I plan to go straight to Lambert, when I can find the slippery bastard. It still surprises me that Brooke hasn't been there already.'

'I've told you why,' Annie said. 'And his team's overstretched, anyway.' She paused. 'Look, I shouldn't be telling you this, but there was something going on at the Berger-Lennox Centre. Dr Lukas told me she was helping young Eastern European prostitutes who got pregnant – mostly illegal immigrants, she said – to get free abortions on the quiet. She called them "late girls". Jennifer Clewes found out about it, but instead of blowing the whistle she helped bury some of the paperwork. I don't think that's everything Dr Lukas knows, but it's a start. And don't even think of going to see her. She's on the edge and a visit from a stranger would alienate her completely.'

'Don't worry,' said Banks. 'I'm not altogether stupid. I'll leave her to you. You don't believe her story?'

'Most of it,' Annie said. 'I think she might be willing to tell me more, but she'll only do it in her own time, on her own terms.'

'How long has this been going on?'

'About a year.'

'How much money is involved?'

'The centre charges between four hundred and a thousand pounds for consultation, termination and post-operative care, depending on how advanced the pregnancy is.'

'So it could add up to quite a tidy sum over time?'

'Yes. But not worth killing over.'

'I suppose not,' said Banks. 'Did Roy know about it?'

'Jennifer knew, and I'll bet she told Roy. The problem is that Dr Lukas says Jennifer had known about it for a couple of months, but it was only in the last few days that people noticed any difference in her behaviour.'

'So perhaps she found out something else?' Banks suggested. 'Something we don't know. How did the girls find Dr Lukas?'

'That's what seems a bit vague about it all. She's from Ukraine. She said she's known in the community. It's possible, I suppose. Some of these communities are very close-knit. Word gets around.'

'But you don't think so?'

'I think she's holding something back. And I think she's scared.'

'I'm not surprised,' said Banks. 'Two people have been murdered.'

'I think there might be three.'

'Oh?'

'Jennifer mentioned a girl called Carmen Petri – one of the late girls – to her close friend Melanie Scott shortly before she was killed. Her ex-boyfriend Victor Parsons was sort of stalking Jennifer. Ironically enough, it's the first time a stalker's actually been any practical use to us. He saw Jennifer come out of the centre last Monday evening with a young girl who looked pregnant. A man immediately came out of the shadows and the girl went off with him in a car.'

'And you think that girl was this Carmen?'

'Yes. And I think she's dead, too. The man she went off with was a muscle-bound lump with a ponytail, the one I told you about before, and he sounds remarkably like the man we think shot Jennifer Clewes and broke into your cottage.'

'And followed me back here from Peterborough,' said Banks.

Annie's eyes widened. 'What?'

Banks told her what happened on the A1(M) the previous day and what measures he had taken to protect his parents.

'Did you get the number?' Annie asked.

'What do you take me for?'

'Give it to me. I'll trace it.'

'It's already being done.'

'Burgess?'

Banks said nothing.

Annie sighed. 'Give it to me anyway.'

Banks did as she asked.

'I take it you haven't told Dave Brooke about this yet?'

'I told you. I rang the Peterborough police. It's their manor. I checked with them again this morning and nothing out of the ordinary happened during the night.'

'Fine,' said Annie. 'I'll tell him myself.'

'Ponytail might well have killed Jennifer and tried to scare me off, but we know he can't have killed Roy.'

'So there's someone else involved.'

'Well, if ponytail is the muscle and prostitution is the business, I'd say there's a pimp somewhere at the top of it all, wouldn't you?'

'Possibly,' Annie agreed. 'Lambert?'

'Maybe.' Banks stood up. 'Anyway, we won't find out the answer by sitting around here, however pleasant it is. Thanks for breakfast, Annie, and for clearing the air.'

'Where are you going?'

Banks smiled. 'Well, if I told you that, you'd really be in trouble, wouldn't you?'

Annie put her hand on Banks's arm. 'I know I can't stop you,' she said, 'but promise me a few things?'

'Go on.'

'Keep in touch, let me know what you find out.'

'OK. You, too.'

'Stay away from Dr Lukas. She'll come around in her own time You'll only scare her away.'

'No problem.'

'And be careful, Alan. This isn't a game.'

'Believe me, I know that.' Banks bent forward, kissed her lightly on the cheek, and left. Annie watched him go, then she hurried back up to her room to pack. This morning, after checking in with Brooke, she was going back to Eastvale come hell or high water.

•

'You wouldn't believe it. It was like a bloody three-ring circus here the last couple of days,' said Malcolm Farrow as he settled in his armchair with a stiff gin and tonic in his hand. Banks had declined the offer of gin as it was only ten o'clock in the morning, but he accepted the tonic water gratefully. Farrow had looked puzzled but poured it anyway. 'As you can see, things have settled down a bit now.'

Banks looked out of Farrow's window at Roy's house. The detectives must have finished their search and removed everything they thought pertinent to their investigation, because the place was unguarded.

They would have gone through Roy's stuff for any evidence related to the crime and also for information about his lifestyle, his habits and his associates that might give them a lead to follow. Banks knew what they would find because he had already made a thorough search himself and handed over everything to Brooke. Now the formalities were done with, the house would be turned over to Roy's next of kin – their parents, Banks assumed.

'I can imagine what it was like,' said Banks. 'Look, I'm sorry I didn't ring you straight away, but I had to go and take care of my parents and I didn't have your number handy.'

'That's all right. I was really shocked to hear the news. It's been all over the papers, and the television. We've had reporters around. They've gone now the police seem to have moved on.'

'There's nothing left for them here,' said Banks.

'Anyway, it's nice of you to remember me and drop by.'

'No problem. Did the police want to talk to you?'

'The police? Oh, yes. They were all over the street.'

'What did you tell them?'

'Just what I told you. It's all I know.'

'What about the reporters?'

His face reddened. 'Sent them packing. Bunch of scavengers.'

'Have you thought any more about that photo I showed you?' asked Banks, slipping the envelope out of his briefcase.

Farrow looked at it again through his reading glasses, which were wedged tightly to his bulbous, purple-veined nose. 'Look, I'm not going to have to say anything in court, am I?'

'This is just between you and me,' said Banks. As Farrow squinted at the photos, Banks sipped some tonic water. The fizziness made him burp and he could still taste the bacon and eggs he'd eaten for breakfast.

'Well,' said Farrow, 'it certainly could be him. The more I look, the more I see the resemblance. As I said, my eyesight's not so good on detail, but there are street lights and the man's size and the grey hair look about right.' He passed the photo back to Banks. 'A bit vague, I know, but it's the best I can do.'

'I appreciate that.'

'Who is he, anyway? He's surely not the one who . . . ?'

'I don't think so,' said Banks. 'If it really is him, he's an old business partner of Roy's.' Someone Roy would probably open the door to and accompany for a drink or whatever, which was the way it seemed to have happened. Someone he trusted.

Banks thanked Farrow for his help, made his excuses and left.

There were no signs of activity around Roy's house on Wednesday morning, not even a police seal across the door. Banks used his key and walked inside. The only sound he could hear was the humming of the refrigerator. There was a deep silence at the core of the house, the silence of Roy's absence, and it felt heavier now than it had when Banks first arrived.

First he checked the kitchen. The laptop he had left on the table there was missing, and he assumed the police had taken it. There was nothing he could do about that right now, but he would have to let Brooke know that he wanted it back when they had finished with it.

Next he went upstairs to look at Roy's office. Whoever had searched the room had made a neat and tidy job of it. Nothing looked out of place

Banks went into the entertainment room and flopped on the sofa. He thought about the CD he had found. Roy must have known that he was involved in something dodgy by Wednesday, when he buried the photos of Lambert and friend among the pornographic images. And perhaps he knew that the something dodgy – whether it was prostitution or illegal immigrants or something else – was fast reaching critical mass. Did he know that his life was in danger? Banks doubted it. If Roy was used to skirting the edges of the law and mixing with bad company, as he seemed to be, then he was probably cocky enough to think there was nothing he couldn't handle. But something had changed all that, and it had happened between Wednesday and Friday evening – or even a couple of days earlier, if Jennifer Clewes's behaviour was anything to go by.

What had Roy's movements been during those crucial days? Where had he been? Who had he talked to? If Banks could get the answer to those questions, he thought, then he might be able to answer the riddle of Roy's death. And Jennifer's.

He thought about what Annie had told him over breakfast, the doctor helping out prostitutes. Had Jennifer Clewes told Roy? Most likely she had. What had his reaction been? Was it anything to do with their deaths? But Banks failed to see how helping out a few unfortunate illegal immigrants could lead to murder. Unless, of course, the people who brought them in were involved and were beginning to feel threatened by something.

Banks also hadn't forgotten that Burgess had told him Gareth Lambert was a smuggler with a large network of underworld connections. Burgess had also said that Lambert knew the Balkan route like the back of his hand, and now Annie was telling Banks about Eastern European prostitutes using the Berger-Lennox

Centre. At least a vague picture was beginning to form in his mind, but he still didn't know Roy's place in it, or why he had been killed.

Banks thought back to his chat with Corinne the previous evening. He had found out a lot about his brother through talking to her. Roy loved *The Goon Show* and *Monty Python*; he did a hilarious Ministry of Silly Walks impression and quite a decent version of the Four Yorkshiremen sketch; New York was still his favourite city, Italy his favourite country; he had recently taken up digital photography and all the photos on his walls were his; he played golf and tennis regularly; he supported Arsenal (typical, Banks thought, who lumped Arsenal in the same category as Manchester United, the best teams money could buy); his favourite colour was purple; his favourite food was wild-mushroom risotto, his favourite wine Amarone; he loved opera and often took Corinne to Covent Garden (though she admitted that she never quite *got* opera); and they both enjoyed going to see Hollywood musicals and old foreign films with subtitles – Bergman, Visconti, Renoir, Fellini.

Roy gave money to beggars in the street but complained when he thought he was being overcharged in shops and restaurants. He could be moody, and Corinne had to confess that she never quite knew what was going on in his mind. But she loved him, as she told Banks when her tears flowed for the second time, after the third glass of wine, no matter that she hadn't known where she stood with him for weeks, no matter that he had left her largely alone to deal with the trauma of her abortion. She had still hoped, somehow, that he would tire of his new conquest and come back to her.

There was only one family photograph in Roy's entertainment room. It was taken on the prom at Blackpool, Banks remembered, in August 1965, and you could see the Tower in the background.

There they stood, all four of them, parents on the inside and Roy, freckled then, his hair a lot fairer than it was when he got older, and Banks at fourteen looking moody and what he had supposed passed for cool back then, in his black drainpipe trousers and polo-neck Beatles jumper. He hadn't really looked at the photo closely before, but now he did he realized that it must have been taken by Graham Marshall, who had accompanied the Banks family on that holiday only a week or so before he disappeared during his Sunday morning paper round.

This was the holiday when Banks had fallen for the beautiful Linda, who worked behind the counter at the local coffee bar. She was far too old for him, but he had fallen nonetheless. Then he and Graham had picked up a couple of girls at the Pleasure Beach, Tina and Sharon, and taken them under the pier for a bit of hanky-panky. He didn't remember having the photograph taken, but that was no surprise. He hardly remembered Roy being on that holiday, either. What fourteen-year-old would waste his time hanging around with his nine-year-old brother?

Graham Marshall was dead, another murder victim, and now Roy. Banks looked at his father in an old grey V-necked pullover, shirt sleeves rolled up, cigarette dangling from the corner of his mouth, hair swept back with Brylcreem. Then he looked at his mother, hardly a dolly bird, but surprisingly young and pretty, with a full-bodied perm and a summer dress showing off her trim waist, smiling into the camera. What would they find when they explored her insides next week, Banks wondered. Would she survive? And his father, after all this trauma? Banks was beginning to feel as if everyone he came into contact with was cursed, that all his companions became hostage to death, like the wraiths that haunted 'Strange Affair'.

Then he told himself to stop being so maudlin. He had solved Graham Marshall's murder more than thirty-five years after it had been committed, his mother would suffer the inconvenience of a small operation at worst, and his father's heart would go on beating for a long time yet. Roy was dead and Banks would find out who killed him. And that was that.

As Banks headed out to try Gareth Lambert again, his mobile rang.

'Alan, it's Annie.'

'Thought you were on your way home.'

'So did I, but something's come up.'

Banks gripped the phone tighter. 'What?'

'Technical support have worked out where the digital photo on your brother's mobile was taken.'

'How on earth did they manage that?'

'From the list of abandoned factories,' Annie said. 'There were some letters visible on a wall in the background: NGS and IFE. One of the factories listed was Midgeley's Castings, and one of the older detectives on the team remembered he used to pass by the place on his way to school and they had a sign that read MIDGELEY'S CASTINGS: CAST FOR LIFE. The place shut down in 1989 and nobody's done anything with it since.'

'Where is it?'

'By the river, down Battersea way. I'm sorry to be so brutal, Alan, but the tide experts also agree that it's very likely the area where your brother's body was dumped in the river, so it's looking more and more as if it was Roy in the foreground of the picture. We're heading out there now. Want to come?'

'You know I do. What does Brooke have to say?'

'He's OK with it. Meet us there?'

'Fine.'

Annie gave him an address and directions and Banks hurried out to his car.

•

'DS Browne?'

'Speaking.'

'This is DC Templeton from Eastvale. How are things down your way?'

'Fine, thanks. Anything new?'

'Maybe,' said Templeton, fingering the plastic bag on the desk in front of him. 'I went to talk to Roger Cropley's wife and found him at home. Says he's got a summer cold but I didn't notice any sniffles. Anyway, I think I rattled him a bit more. He seemed nervous when I told him the surviving woman thought she might be able to recognize her attacker.'

'But that's not true,' Susan said.

'Cropley doesn't know that. And I think his wife might know a lot more than she's letting on, too. Anyway, I've got an idea. Did your SOCOs do a thorough trace-evidence search of the victim's car?'

'I'm sure they did,' said Susan. 'But there was no evidence that he was ever in the car. He clearly dragged her out and into the bushes.'

'But he'd have to lean in to apply the chloroform.'

'True. What are you getting at?'

'You've still got all the collected samples, I assume? Hair? Skin?'

'Of course.'

'And the car?'

'That, too. Look, what's going on? What are you getting at?'

'Can you check if they found any dandruff on the seat back?'

'Dandruff?'

'Yes.'

'I'll check. What do you have in mind?'

'I've been on the Web, and it all sounds a bit complicated, but as far as I can gather you can get DNA from dandruff. I mean it is just skin, isn't it?'

'It won't do us much good,' said Susan, 'unless we have a sample for comparison.'

'Er . . . well, as a matter of fact, we might have.'

'What do you mean?'

'I've got a sample of Cropley's dandruff. Can I send it down to you?'

'I trust you didn't ask Mr Cropley for this?'

Templeton laughed. 'No. Believe me, he gave it quite freely, though.'

'That's not the point,' Susan said. 'I'm sure you know as well as I do that you have to get the suspect's written permission even for a non-intimate sample, unless you've detained him for a serious offence and the super gives permission to take one.'

'I know my PACE regulations,' said Templeton. 'What I'm saying is that this could confirm my suspicions. If you knew it was him, if *we* knew it was him, then it would make a difference and we could start to build a real case. He wouldn't even have to know about the previous sample. Nobody does except you and me. Right now we've got no real grounds to arrest him and demand a sample, but if the sample I took matches any of the dandruff found in the car, then we'd know where to look and you can be damn sure we'd come up with something to arrest him for. After that . . . well, then we'd get an official sample, of course.'

'What if it's not him?'

'Then he's off the hook.'

'But there'd be records, paperwork relating to the first test. These things are expensive.'

'I know that, but so what? It needn't come out. Surely you must know *someone* at the lab with a bit of discretion? How is anybody going to know?'

'A good defence lawyer would use it as ammunition against our case.'

'Only if they found out. Besides, it wouldn't matter. By that point we'd have *officially* matching DNA which we'd have no trouble getting admitted, all by the book. You can't argue with that. Christ, I'll even pay for the test myself if that's your problem.'

'That's not the problem. And I doubt you could afford it, anyway. The point is that if it does turn out to be Cropley, the real evidence could be thrown out because of what you're asking. It's iffy. No, I don't like this at all.'

Templeton sighed. He hadn't realized what a stickler DS Browne was. 'Look,' he said, 'do you want this guy or not? Maybe it'll rule him out. I don't know. But we should at least keep an eye on him. If I'm right – and the DNA would prove that one way or another – he's done it before and he'll do it again. What do you think? Wouldn't you like to *know*?'

Templeton felt himself tense during the silence that followed.

Finally, Susan Browne said, 'Send it down. I'll talk to my SIO, see what I can do. I'm not promising anything, though.'

'Great,' said Templeton. 'It's already on the way.'

•

Banks felt more trepidation than he could ever have imagined as he walked with Brooke and Annie over the weeds and stony ground towards the dirty brick factory, its ugly facade covered in graffiti. Was he now going to see the exact spot where his brother had been shot and killed? Little Roy, whom he'd saved from a bully and scarred with a toy sword. He gritted his teeth and felt his neck and arm muscles tense up.

The doors looked forbidding, but they were easily opened, and the three were soon crossing the vast shop floor, footsteps echoing. There was something about abandoned factories, with the gaping holes in their roofs, rusted old machines, drums, pallets and weeds growing through cracks in the walls and floor, that always disturbed Banks. He thought it had something to do with a dream that had scared him when he was young, but he couldn't remember the details. He also thought it had something to do with the ball-bearing factory across the road from where he grew up, though it had been in operation during his time there and he had no unpleasant experiences associated with it. There had always been derelict houses, workshops and factories, though, and he had explored most of them with his friends, tracking down imaginary monsters. Whatever the reason, places like that still gave him the shivers, and this one was no exception.

'You do take me to the nicest places, Dave,' said Annie. 'This is almost as cheerful as that street in Bow.'

'At least it's not raining today,' Brooke said.

A rat scuttled out from under a rusted sheet of metal and practically ran over Annie's feet on its way out. She pulled a face but made no sound. Sunlight lanced through missing sections of roof, illuminating the dust motes the three of them kicked up as they walked. The large windows behind their protective grilles were all broken, and shattered glass was strewn all over the floor, sparkling in the rays of light. Here and there were oily puddles and damp patches from the previous night's rain.

At the centre of the shop floor, almost hidden by rusty machines, Banks saw a wooden chair. On the floor beside it lay snake-like lengths of cord.

'Better stand back,' said Brooke as they approached it. 'The SOCOs will be here soon and they won't appreciate it if we trample all over their scene.'

Banks stood and looked. He thought he could see spots of blood on the cord and splatters on the ground near the chair. For a moment, he pictured Roy tied there, felt his terror as he knew he was going to die in this filthy place, then his policeman's instinct kicked in and he tried to interpret what he was seeing.

'Roy was shot in the head with a .22, like Jennifer Clewes, right?' he said.

'That's right,' said Brooke.

'And there was no exit wound?'

'No.'

'So where did all the blood come from?'

Banks noticed Brooke exchange a glance with Annie.

'Come on,' said Banks. 'I'm not a fool.'

'The pathologist found some evidence that he was beaten,' Brooke admitted.

'So they tortured him, the bastards.'

Brooke stared down at his shoes. 'It looks that way. But we don't know for certain that your brother was even here yet. You can't really tell who it is from the photograph.'

'And just who else do you think it would be?' Banks said. 'Anyway, now you've got all the blood samples you could possibly need to make a match.'

'I suppose we have,' said Brooke.

'But why torture him?' Banks asked.

'We don't know,' Annie said. 'Obviously to make him tell them something. Or to find out how much he knew about something or how much he'd already told.'

'I don't think it would have taken long to get Roy to talk,' Banks said. The image of the boy bullying Roy flashed though his mind, Roy crying and holding his stomach in pain. Banks's intervention. But this time he hadn't come to the rescue. He hadn't been there for him. And this time Roy had been killed. Banks could only hope that his parents never found out about the torture. He didn't blame Annie and Brooke for trying to keep it from him – he'd probably have done the same if it was one of their relatives – but now he had the job of protecting his own mother and father from the truth.

'They didn't bother tidying up after themselves,' said Annie, pointing to a single shell casing on the floor close to the chair.

'Probably thought no one would ever find the place,' said Brooke.

'Some kids would have found it eventually,' Banks said. 'Kids love places like this.'

Pigeons flew in and out through the holes in the roof and walls, perching on the rafters and ruffling their feathers. Their white droppings speckled sections of floor, and even the chair itself. Despite its partial openness to the elements, the factory smelled of dead animals and stale grease.

'I'll see if I can get some uniforms to canvass the neighbourhood,' Brooke said. 'Who knows? Someone might have noticed unusual activity around the place.'

The wind made a mournful sound as it blew through the broken windows, harmonizing strangely with the cooing pigeons. Banks gave a little shiver, despite the warmth of the day. He'd seen all he wanted, the godforsaken place where Roy had spent his last few hours being tortured, then shot. No matter how long he lived, he knew he would never get the image out of his mind. For now, though, he had other things to do. He told Brooke and Annie he was leaving, and neither asked him where he was going. As he was getting in his car, the technical-support van turned into the factory yard. They would scrutinize the place where Roy had died, scrape blood, search for fingerprints, fibres, hair, skin, any traces that the murderers left behind. With any luck, they would turn up enough to secure a conviction, should the police ever find a viable suspect. Banks left them to it.

15

After dropping his car off outside Roy's – he didn't fancy spending the day driving in London traffic, trying to find parking spots, and the tube was much faster – Banks tried Lambert's travel operation on the Edgware Road first but was told that Mr Lambert was unavailable. Next he went back to the Chelsea flat and found to his surprise that Gareth Lambert was just on his way out of the front door.

'Going somewhere, Gareth?' he said.

'Who the fuck are you?' Lambert tried to push past him.

Banks stood his ground. 'My name's Banks. Detective Chief Inspector Alan Banks.'

'You're Roy's brother.' Lambert stood back and eyed Banks up and down. 'Well, fuck a duck. The old killjoy himself.'

'Can we go back inside?'

'I'm busy. I've got to get to the office.'

'It won't take long.' Banks stared Lambert down. Finally Lambert shrugged and led Banks upstairs to a first-floor flat. The interior was functional enough but lacked the personal touch, as if Lambert's real life lay elsewhere. The man himself looked just the same as he did in Roy's photo: bearish, a bit overweight, with a red complexion – part sun and part hypertension, Banks guessed – and a thick head of curly grey hair. He was dressed in ice-blue jeans and an oversized, baggy white shirt. Burgess had made a comparison with Harry Lime, but as far as Banks could remember, Lime was suave and charming on the surface, more like Phil Keane. Lambert was rougher around the edges and clearly didn't seem to rely on charm to get by. They sat down opposite one another like a pair of chess players, and Lambert regarded Banks with a vaguely amused look in his eyes.

'So you're Roy's big brother, the detective.'

'That's right. I understand the two of you go back a long way?'

'Indeed we do. I met Roy just after he'd graduated from university. We were a bit wet behind the ears back then. 1978. As I remember it, all the kids were wearing torn T-shirts and safety pins in their ears, listening to the Sex Pistols and The Clash, and there we were in our business suits sitting in some square hotel bar planning our next venture. Which was probably marketing torn jeans and safety pins to the kids.' He laughed. 'They were good days. I was very sorry to hear about what happened to Roy, by the way.'

'Were you?'

'Of course. Look, I really am a busy man. If you're just going to sit there and—'

'Because you really don't seem to be grieving very deeply for someone you'd known for so long.'

'How do you know how much I'm grieving?'

'Fair enough. Did your ventures together involve arms dealing?'

Lambert's eyes narrowed. 'Why bring that up?' he said. 'It's ancient history. Yes, we were involved in what we thought was a perfectly legitimate weapons sale, but we were hoodwinked and the shipment was misdirected. Well, that was enough for me. What do they say? Once bitten, twice shy.'

'So you stuck with less risky ventures after that?'

'I wouldn't say any of our ventures were without risk, but let's just say the risk was of a more monetary kind, not the sort of risk where you could end up in jail if you weren't careful.'

'Or dead.'

'Quite.'

'Insider trading can carry a hefty penalty.'

'Hah! Everybody was doing it. Still are. Have you never had a hot tip from the horse's mouth and made a few bob on it?'

'No,' said Banks.

'So if I said right now such and such a company is making an important merger next week and their share prices will double, you can honestly say you wouldn't run right out and buy as many shares as you could get your hands on?'

Banks had to think about that one. It sounded easy, and perhaps just a little bit naughty, put that way. Hardly criminal. But he didn't understand the stock market, and that was why he didn't play it. Besides, he never felt that he had the money to spare for such gambles. 'I might splurge on a couple,' he said in the end.

Lambert clapped his hands. 'There you are!' he said. 'I thought so.' It sounded as if he was welcoming Banks to a club he had no desire to join.

'I've also heard rumours that you have been involved in smuggling,' Banks said.

'That's interesting. Where did you hear them?'

'Are they true?'

'Of course not. The word has such negative connotations, don't you think? *Smuggling*. It's so emotive. I regard what I've done more as a matter of practical geography. I move things from one place to another. With great efficiency, I might add.'

'I'm glad you've got no time for false modesty. What things?'

'Just things.'

'Arms? Drugs? People? I hear you know the Balkan route.'

Lambert raised an eyebrow. 'You do have your ears to the ground, don't you? Roy never told me how sharp you were. The Balkan route? Well, I might have known it once, but these days . . . those borders change faster than you can draw them. And you'd better stop accusing me of breaking the law right now or I'll have my solicitor on you, Roy's brother or no. I've never been convicted of anything in my life.'

'So you've been lucky. Still lots of opportunities for entrepreneurs in the Balkans, though. Or the ex-Soviet republics.'

'Much too dangerous. I'm afraid I'm too old for all that. I'm semi-retired. I have a wife I happen to love very much and a travel agency to run.'

'When did you last see Roy?'

'Friday night.'

Banks tried not to let his excitement show. 'What time?'

'About half-past twelve or one o'clock in the morning. Why?'

'Are you sure it was Friday night?'

'Of course I am.'

Lambert was playing with him, Banks sensed. He could see it in the man's restless, teasing eyes. Lambert knew that the neighbour had seen him getting into his car with Roy, and that Banks had no doubt talked to the neighbour and got his description. But that was at half-past nine. What were they doing until half-past twelve or one o'clock?

Lambert picked up a box of cigars from the table and offered one to Banks. 'Cuban?'

'No, thanks.'

'Suit yourself.' Lambert fiddled with a cutter and matches and finally got the thing lit. He looked at Banks through the smoke. 'You seem surprised that I said I saw Roy on Friday evening. Why's that?'

'I think you know why,' said Banks.

'Indulge me.'

'Because that's when he went missing. He hasn't been seen alive since half-past nine on Friday.'

'I can most sincerely assure you that he has. By me and countless other members of the Albion Club.'

'The Albion Club?'

'On the Strand. It's a rather exclusive club. Membership by invitation only.'

Banks remembered that Corinne had told him Roy went to a club on the Strand with Lambert a few weeks ago. 'What goes on there?'

Lambert laughed. 'Nothing illegal, if that's what you're thinking. The club has a gaming licence. It also has a top-class restaurant and an exceedingly comfortable bar. Roy and I are both members. Have been for years. Even when I was living abroad I'd drop by if I happened to be in town.' He puffed on his cigar, eyes narrowed to calculating slits, as if daring Banks to challenge him.

'Let's backtrack, then,' said Banks.

'Of course.'

'What time did you first see Roy on Friday night?'

'About half-past nine,' said Lambert. 'I dropped by his place and picked him up.'

'Was this a regular arrangement?'

'I wouldn't say regular, but we'd done it before, yes. Roy prefers to leave the car when he goes out drinking, and I hardly touch the stuff these days, so I don't mind driving. It's not far out of my way.'

'And you'd arranged to pick him up and take him to the Albion Club on Friday?'

'Yes.' The cigar had gone out. Lambert lit it again. Banks got the impression that it was more of a prop than anything else.

'What happened when you got there?'

Lambert shrugged. 'The usual. We went into the bar and got a couple of stiff brandies and chatted for a while. No, I tell a lie. I had a brandy – my only drink of the night – and Roy had wine. The club does a decent house claret.'

'Who did you talk to?'

'A few of the other members.'

'Names?'

'Look, these are important people. Influential people. They won't take too kindly to being harassed by the police, nor to knowing it was me who set you on them.'

'Maybe you haven't quite grasped the seriousness of this,' Banks said. 'A man has been murdered. My brother. Your friend. You were one of the last people to see him alive. We need to trace his movements and activities on the evening he disappeared.'

'This puts me in a difficult position.'

'I don't bloody care what position it puts you in. I want names.'

Banks locked eyes with him. Eventually Lambert reeled off a string of names and Banks wrote them down. He didn't recognize any of them.

'How did Roy seem?' Banks asked. 'Was he depressed, worried, on edge?'

'He seemed fine to me.'

'Did he confide in you about any problems or anything?'

'No.'

'What did he talk about?'

'Business, golf, cricket, wine, women. You know, the usual man talk.'

'Did he mention me?'

Lambert gave a tight little smile. 'I'm afraid he didn't, no.'

Banks found that hard to believe, given that Roy had just phoned him out of the blue with an urgent problem, a 'matter of life and death', but he let it go for the time being. 'Did Roy ever mention a girl called Carmen Petri?'

It was over in a second, but it was definitely there, the shock, the slight hesitation before answering, a refusal to look Banks in the eye. 'No,' Lambert said.

'Have you ever heard the name before?'

'There's an actress, Carmen Electra, but I doubt that it's her you're thinking of.'

'No,' said Banks. 'There's also an opera called *Carmen* but it's not her, either.' Casually, he slipped a copy of the photograph he had printed from Roy's CD out of his briefcase and set it on the low table. 'Who's the other man sitting with you in this photo?' he asked.

Lambert peered closely at the photograph then looked at Banks sideways. 'Where did you get this?' He gestured at the photo with his cigar.

'Roy took it.'

Lambert sat back in his chair. 'How strange. He never told me.'

'I assume you do know who the man you're sitting with is?'

'Of course I do. It's Max. Max Broda. He's a business colleague. I can't imagine why Roy would want to take a photo of us together.'

'What business would that be?'

'Travel. Max puts tours together, recruits guides, works out itineraries, hotels, suggests destinations of interest.'

'Where?'

'Mostly around the Adriatic and Mediterranean.'

'Including the Balkan countries?'

'Some, yes. If and when they're safe to visit.'

'I'd like to talk to him,' said Banks.

Lambert scrutinized the end of his cigar and took another puff before answering. 'I'm afraid that will be rather difficult,' he said. 'He's gone home.'

'Where's that?'

'Prague.'

'Do you have an address?'

'Are you thinking of going there? It's a beautiful city. I know someone who can fix you up with the best guided tour.'

'Maybe,' said Banks. 'I would like his address, though.'

'I might have it somewhere.' Lambert scrolled through the files on his PDA and finally spelled out an address for Banks, who copied it down. 'What time did you leave the club?' he asked.

'Roy left sometime between half-past twelve and one o'clock.'

'You weren't still together at that time?'

'No. We weren't joined at the hip, you know. Roy likes to play the roulette tables. I prefer poker, myself.'

'Did he leave alone?'

'As far as I know.'

'Where did he go?'

'I've no idea.'

'What time did you leave?'

'About three. I was knackered by then. Not to mention broke.'

'Where did you go?'

'Back here.'

'Not home to your wife?'

Lambert leaned forward, face thrust forward, and stabbed the air with his cigar. 'You leave her out of this.'

'Very understanding, is she?'

'I told you. Leave her out of it.' Lambert relit his cigar and his tone softened. 'Look,' he said, running his free hand through his curly grey hair, 'I was tired, I came back here. I don't know what you suspect me of, but Roy was a good friend and a colleague of many years' standing. I didn't kill him. Why would I? What possible motive could I have?'

'Are you sure he didn't say where he was going?'

'No. I assumed he was going home.'

'Was he drunk?'

Lambert tipped his head to one side and thought for a moment. 'He'd had a few,' he said. 'Mostly wine. But he wasn't staggering or slurring his speech. Not fit to drive, I'd say, but fit enough to get a taxi.'

'Is that what he did?'

'I've no idea what happened once he got outside.'

'And you didn't see him again?'

'No.'

'OK,' said Banks, standing to leave. 'I suppose we could always ask around the taxi drivers.'

'One thing,' said Lambert, as he walked Banks to the door. 'You already know about the arms deal years back. You mentioned it earlier.'

'Yes?'

'I think he wanted to get involved in that sort of thing again. At least, it might be a direction worth looking in. I mean, Roy had been making a few noises, you know, sounding me out, asking about old contacts and such.'

'On Friday?'

'Yes. In the club.'

'And?'

'I told him I'd lost touch. Which is true. The world has

changed, Mr Banks, in case you haven't noticed. And I warned him off.'

'How did he respond?'

Lambert clapped a hand on Banks's shoulder as they stood near the door. 'You know Roy,' he said. 'Or maybe you don't. Anyway, once he's on the trail of something, he's not easily deterred. He persisted, got a bit pissed off with me, as a matter of fact, thought I was holding out on him, depriving him of a business opportunity.'

'So you ended the evening on a sour note?'

'He'd have got over it.'

'If he hadn't been killed?'

'Yes.'

'Why did you fall out with Julian Harwood, by the way?'

Lambert looked surprised. 'You know about that?'

'Yes.'

'It was years ago. Storm in a teacup. Harwood insisted I'd cheated him out of some money in a land sale, that I knew the new motorway was going to run right by it.'

'And did you?'

Lambert did his best to look innocent and outraged but it came out like a poor parody. 'Me? Of course not. I wouldn't do a thing like that.'

'Of course not,' Banks echoed. 'Is there anything more you can tell me?'

'I'm afraid not. Except . . .'

'What?'

Lambert stood by the door and scratched his temple. 'Don't take this amiss,' he said. 'Just a piece of friendly advice. Roy's dead. I can't change that. I don't know anything about it, and I certainly don't know who did it, but don't you think you should think twice, take heed of what you're getting into, and perhaps be a bit more careful lest you disturb a nest of vipers?'

'Is that a warning, Mr Lambert?'

'Take it as you will.' Lambert looked at his watch. 'Now I'm afraid I really must head for the office. I've got business to take care of.'

•

Annie hardly had time to call at her cottage in Harkside and water the wilting potted plants before heading to Eastvale for the three o'clock team meeting. It was another beautiful Dales day, a little cooler than it had been, with one or two fluffy white clouds scudding across the pale blue sky, but she didn't have time to pause and enjoy any of it. Sometimes she wondered what the point of living in the country was, given her job and the hours she put in.

They were all waiting in the boardroom: Gristhorpe, Hatchley, Winsome, Rickerd, Templeton and Stefan Nowak, crime-scene coordinator. The long table was so highly polished you could see your reflection in it, and a whiteboard hung on the wall at one end of the room surrounded by cork boards where Stefan had pinned the crime-scene photographs. They made quite a contrast to the paintings of the wool barons on the other walls.

After Annie had brought everyone up to speed on the Berger-Lennox Centre, Roy Banks, Carmen Petri and their possible connection with Jennifer Clewes's murder, Gristhorpe handed the floor over to Stefan Nowak.

Stefan stood by the boards and the photographs and cleared his throat. Not for the first time Annie wondered what sort of life Stefan led outside of work. He was one of the most charming and elegant men she had ever known, and his life was a complete mystery to her.

'First of all,' said Stefan, 'we have fingerprints from DCI Banks's door that don't match the builders', we have tyre tracks from his drive and . . .' Here he paused dramatically and lifted up a plastic bag. 'We also have a cigarette end found near the beck on DCI Banks's property, fortunately before the rain came. From this we have been able to get the saliva necessary for DNA.'

'What about the tyre tracks?' Annie asked.

'They're Michelins, of a type consistent with tyres often used on a Mondeo,' said Stefan. 'I've sent the necessary information to Essex for comparison with what's left of the Mondeo that crashed outside Basildon. I'm still awaiting results.'

'So,' Gristhorpe said, 'you've got prints, tyre tracks and DNA from the scene of DCI Banks's cottage, and if and when we find a suspect, these will tie him to the murders of Jennifer Clewes and Roy Banks?'

'Well,' said Stefan, 'they'll tie him to DCI Banks's cottage.'

'Exactly,' said Gristhorpe. 'And no crime was committed there.'

'That's not strictly true, sir,' said Annie. 'Someone definitely broke in.'

Gristhorpe gave her a withering look and shook his head. 'Not enough.'

'We've got Jennifer Clewes's mobile records from the network,' Winsome said. 'Not that they tell us a great deal. As far as I can gather the calls are all to and from friends and family.'

'What about the last call?' Annie asked. 'The one Kate Nesbit remembered on Friday evening.'

'Yes, I was coming to that,' said Winsome. 'Jennifer received a phone call at 10.43 p.m. on Friday the 11th of June, duration three minutes. The problem is that it's an "unknown" number. I've got the mobile company working on it, but they're not offering a lot of hope.'

'Thanks for trying,' said Annie.

Gristhorpe looked at his watch. 'I've got to go,' he said. 'I've got ACC McLaughlin and the press breathing down my neck. I appreciate your progress so far, but it's not enough. We need results, and we need them fast. Annie, you'd better get back down to London tomorrow and keep pushing the Berger-Lennox connection. The rest of you keep at it up here. Winsome, get back to the mobile company and see if they can come up with a number for us. Get them to cross-check with Jennifer's outgoing calls. That's it for now.'

When he left the room, everyone breathed a sigh of relief.

'He's in a bit of a grumpy mood this morning, isn't he?' said Stefan to Annie as they all filed out a few moments later.

'I think he's had the chief constable as well as ACC McLaughlin on his case,' said Annie. 'And it's my guess that however enlightened he thinks he is, he still doesn't like being given a bollocking by a woman.'

Stefan smiled. 'Ouch,' he said.

'Ma'am, can I have a word?'

It was DC Templeton. 'Of course, Kev,' said Annie, waving goodbye to Stefan. 'Let's grab a coffee in the canteen.'

Templeton pulled a face. 'With all due respect, ma'am . . .'

'I know,' said Annie. 'It tastes like cat's piss. You're right. We'll go to the Golden Grill.'

They threaded their way through the crowd of tourists on Market Street and were lucky to find a free table. The poor waitress was rushed off her feet but she managed to bring them each a cup of filter coffee quickly enough. 'What is it, Kev?' Annie asked.

'It's this Roger Cropley business,' Templeton said. 'I haven't bothered you with it much so far because, well, you've been down south and you've had lots of other things on your plate. I mean, it might be a bit tangential, but I really think we're onto something here.'

'What?'

'The Claire Potter murder.'

'I don't know,' said Annie. 'Seems like a bit of a coincidence, doesn't it?'

'That's what I thought at first,' said Templeton, warming to the subject, 'but if you really think about it, if Cropley has been preying on young women alone on the motorway on Friday nights, then the only coincidence is that he was at the Watford Gap services at the same time as Jennifer Clewes, and that's exactly the kind of coincidence he'd always be hoping for. He trolls those places: Watford Gap, Leicester Forest, Newport Pagnell, Trowell. Claire Potter and Jennifer Clewes were exactly what he was looking for.'

'I see your point,' said Annie. 'But I mean a coincidence that this time he picked on a girl who was already singled out by someone else to die.'

'OK, but strange things happen sometimes. It still doesn't mean Cropley's harmless.'

'You don't need to tell *me* that, Kev,' said Annie.

'There was another woman, too: Paula Chandler. Someone drove her off the road late on a Friday night in February and tried to open her car door, only it was locked and she managed to get away.'

'Did she get a good look at him?'

'Just his hand.'

Annie thought for a moment. 'It still doesn't mean Cropley's the killer.'

'Maybe there's a way we can find out.'

'Go on.'

Templeton leaned forward, the excitement clear in his eyes. 'I met DS Browne from Derby,' he went on, 'and she agrees it's worth a shot. I've talked with Cropley and his wife again since then and I'm still convinced there's something there. Anyway . . .' He went on to tell Annie about the dandruff.

'I must say,' Annie commented when he'd finished, 'that's very clever of you, Kev. I didn't know they could get DNA from dandruff.'

'They can,' said Templeton. 'I checked with Stefan and DS Browne confirmed it when she phoned to tell me she put a rush on it. They can also process DNA pretty quickly these days when they've a mind to.'

'Leaving aside the problem of its being inadmissible,' Annie went on, 'what do you expect to happen next?'

'It doesn't need to be admissible,' Templeton explained, as he had done to DS Browne. 'We just need some concrete evidence that we've got the right guy, then we can pull out all the stops and nail him the right way. We get legitimate DNA samples. We interview him again. We get him to account for every minute of every Friday night he's ever spent on the motorway. We get his colleagues and his employers to tell us what they know about him and his movements. We interview people at all the motorway garages and cafes again. All the late-night lorry drivers. *Someone* has to have seen *something*.'

Templeton was looking at her with such keenness that she felt it would be churlish to disappoint him, despite her misgivings. And if Derby CID was involved, too, at least he couldn't go too far off the rails. Templeton was beginning to show all the signs of becoming a bit like Banks, Annie thought, and two of them she didn't need. But he had at least talked to her, told her about his thoughts, which was more than Banks did most of the time.

'OK,' she said finally. 'But I want you to work directly with Derby CID on this. If you talk to Cropley, I want this DS Browne or someone else from Derby with you. I don't want you going off on your own with this, Kev. Understood?'

Templeton nodded, still looking like the dog who'd got the bone. 'Yes, ma'am. Don't worry. It'll be a solid case, by the book.'

Annie smiled. 'Don't make promises you can't keep,' she said. 'But when it comes to it, I do expect a case that the CPS will be willing to take to court.'

'That's a tall order.'

Annie laughed. The Crown Prosecution Service were notoriously reluctant to take on anything they didn't feel gave them 100 per cent chance of getting a conviction. 'Do your best,' she said. 'Let's get back to the office.'

They finished their coffees, paid and set off back across Market Street. Annie had no sooner got inside the station doorway than her mobile rang. She gestured for Templeton to go on ahead of her.

'Detective Inspector Cabbot?' a familiar voice asked.

'Yes, Dr Lukas.'

'I'd like to talk to you.'

'Go ahead.'

'Not on the telephone. Can we meet?'

Well, thought Annie, there went her evening at home relaxing in the tub with a good book. It had better be worth it. 'I'm up north,' she said, glancing at her watch. 'It's twenty to four now. Depending on the trains I should be able to get down there by about eight.'

'That will be fine.'

'At the house, then?'

'No.' Dr Lukas named a French restaurant in Covent Garden. 'I will wait for you there,' she said, and hung up.

●

After his talk with Gareth Lambert, Banks took the tube to Charing Cross and headed for the Albion Club. It didn't open until late evening and the doors were locked. He tried knocking a few times, then he rattled them, but no one answered. A few passers-by gave him disapproving glances, as if he was an alcoholic desperate for a drink. In the end he gave the door a hard kick, then walked to Trafalgar Square and wandered among the hordes of tourists for a while, trying to rid himself of the sense of frustration and anxiety that had been building up in him ever since he had seen Roy's body laid out on the shingle.

It was mid-afternoon, and he felt hungry despite the full English breakfast at Annie's hotel that morning. He found an American-style burger joint near the top of Old Compton Street, just across from a body-piercing studio, and ordered a cheese-burger and a Coke.

As he sat eating and watching the world go by outside, he thought about his talk with Gareth Lambert: the theatrics with the cigar, the joke about Carmen Electra, the reference to Roy's being interested in arms deals again, the garbled warning as he was leaving – none of these things had been necessary, but Lambert hadn't been able to resist. Innocence? Arrogance? It wasn't always easy to tell them apart.

But there was something else that left him feeling very unsatisfied indeed. Banks, perhaps more than anybody, felt that

Roy might have been less than legal in his business dealings over the years, and as Corinne had pointed out, Banks had always been ready to think the worst of his brother. It wasn't something he was proud of, but he thought he was right.

After the talk with Ian Hunt, though, not to mention after looking a bit deeper into Roy's life, he had come to believe that Roy really had learned a lesson from the foolhardy arms deal he had been involved in once. What he had seen in New York on September 11th 2001 had shaken him to the core and brought home to him the stark reality of terrorism. It was no longer a bus full of strangers in Basra or Tel Aviv, but people just like him going about their daily routine, some of whom he knew, dying right in front of his eyes.

Banks was starting to think that perhaps Gareth Lambert had overplayed his hand. He didn't believe that Roy wanted to get into arms dealing again and had been asking Lambert about old con-tacts. Unless he intended to seek retribution, which was unlikely at this late stage in the game. If Roy had any old scores he wanted to settle he would have done so years ago in the white heat of his rage after 9/11. But he hadn't. Which made Banks think that Lambert was lying. And there was only one clear explanation of that – to put Banks off the scent, divert him from the real business. More and more he was beginning to believe that that had something to do with the goings on at the Berger-Lennox Centre, with Jennifer Clewes and Roy, with Dr Lukas, with the mysterious Carmen Petri and the late girls. But how Lambert him-self fitted in, Banks still didn't know. So what was the missing piece?

He doubted that Lambert would give it up. He was far too shrewd for that. He had enjoyed toying with Banks, telling him he had seen Roy on Friday when he no doubt already knew that was the day Roy disappeared. But he had done that because he knew Banks had got a description from Malcolm Farrow and because he thought there was nothing in his actions that night to incriminate him. No doubt it was true that Roy had left the Albion Club between half-past twelve and one o'clock, and that Lambert hadn't left till three. Banks would go back to the club and check later that evening.

He finished his burger and took the tube back to South Kensington with a view to nosing around Roy's files again to see if there was anything there relating to the Albion Club or any of the members' names Lambert had given him. Perhaps he could phone some of them and see if they would verify Lambert's story. He also wanted to get in touch with his parents and the Peterborough police again and make sure everything was all right on the Hazels estate.

All was still quiet inside Roy's house. Banks locked the door behind him, slipped the keys in his pocket and headed for the kitchen. When he got there, he was surprised to see a man sitting at the kitchen table. He was even more surprised when the man turned and pointed a gun at him.

16

'Sit down slowly,' the man said, 'and keep your hands in sight.'

Banks did as he was told.

'Who are you?' the man asked.

'I might well ask the same.'

'I asked first. And I've got the gun.'

'My name's Alan Banks.'

'Do you have any identification?'

Banks put his hand slowly in his inside pocket and brought out his warrant card. He shoved it across the table to the man, who examined it carefully then pushed it back and slipped his gun inside a shoulder holster hidden by his jacket.

'What the fuck was all that about?' said Banks, feeling a rush of anger as the adrenalin surged back.

'I had to be sure,' said the man. 'Dieter Ganz, Interpol.' He offered his own card, which Banks studied, then stuck out his hand. Banks didn't feel like shaking it; he felt more like thumping him. Ganz shrugged. 'I'm sorry,' he went on. 'Detective Superintendent Burgess told me you might be here, but I had to make certain.' He didn't have much of an accent, but it was there, if you listened, in his speech patterns and careful diction.

'How did you get in?'

'It wasn't difficult,' said Ganz, glancing towards the back window. Banks saw that a circle of glass about the size of a man's fist had been cut out of it just below the catch.

'Well, I don't know about you,' said Banks, 'but after that little scare I could do with a drink.'

'No, thank you,' said Ganz. 'Nothing for me.'

'Suit yourself.' Banks opened a bottle of Roy's Côte de Nuits and poured himself a generous glass. His hand was still shaking. 'So Burgess sent you, did he?'

Ganz nodded. 'He told me where you would be. I'm sorry it took so long but he had a little difficulty finding me. I've been out of the country. It seems that we have interests in common.'

'First of all, you'd better tell me what yours are.'

'At the moment, my interest is in people-smuggling, more specifically the smuggling of young women for the purposes of sexual exploitation.'

Ganz looked undercover, Banks thought. He was young, early thirties at most. His blonde hair was a bit too long and greasy, and he clearly hadn't shaved for four or five days. The linen jacket he wore over his shirt was creased and stained, and his jeans needed a wash.

'And what interests do we have in common?' Banks asked.

Ganz took a piece of paper from his side pocket and unfolded it on the table. It was the photo Banks had given to Burgess. 'You've been asking questions about who this man with Gareth Lambert is,' he said.

'Lambert told me his name is Max Broda.'

'That is correct,' said Ganz. 'Max Broda. He's an Albanian travelling on an Israeli passport.'

'Why would he do that?'

Ganz smiled, showing a missing front tooth. 'No troublesome visas to worry about.'

'What's his business?' Gareth Lambert had told Banks that Max worked in the travel business, organizing tours and cruises, but somehow or other Banks didn't think Ganz would be here if that were the case.

'Broda's a trader,' said Ganz. 'Do you know what that is?'

'A trader in what?'

'Have you ever heard of the Arizona Market?'

'No.'

'It's in Bosnia, between Sarajevo and Zagreb. It's like those old markets you see in movies, you know, the Kasbah, so romantic with its stalls of colourful goods and its narrow winding streets. During the day many people go there to buy pirated CDs and DVDs and knock-off Rolexes and Chanel perfume. But at night it becomes a market of a different kind. At night you can buy stolen cars, guns, drugs. And young women. They are sold there like sheep and cattle are sold at your country shows. Sometimes they are auctioned off, made to parade naked holding numbers while the traders touch them and caress them before they make their bids, look in their mouths like you would if you were buying a horse. When they've been bought, many of them end up working in clubs and brothels in Bosnia, servicing the international peace-keeping forces, but many are also smuggled into other countries to work in peep-shows and massage parlours.'

'I suppose that's where Lambert comes in?' Banks said. 'The Balkan route.'

'That's one way,' Ganz agreed. 'Serbia, Croatia, Albania, Macedonia, Bosnia-Herzegovina, Montenegro and Kosovo. But there are others, and they are always changing. They cross wherever the border is unguarded. Many women from Russia, Ukraine and Romania are smuggled through the eastern route, through Poland to Germany, or through Hungary. From Serbia to Italy many smugglers prefer to use Albanian seaports and ship the women over on rubber dinghies. But however they get here, once they are inside the EU, they can be moved around more freely.'

'So Lambert and Broda are in business together?'

'Yes. But not just England. That's why it is difficult to pin them down. We are trying to build up dossiers on similar operations in Paris, Berlin and Rome. It's a widespread problem.' He paused. 'I have seen these women, Mr Banks, talked to them. To call them "women" is not strictly accurate in the first place. They are no more than girls, some as young as fourteen or fifteen. They are lured from their homes by promises of jobs overseas as nannies and models, maids and waitresses. Sometimes they are smuggled out and sold straight away, sometimes they are taken to breaking-houses in Belgrade. There they are forced to live in filthy conditions. They are humiliated, beaten, starved, denied even the most basic human decencies, raped repeatedly, drugged, made to be compliant. When their spirits are broken, they are taken to the markets and sold to the highest bidder. After that, even if they are smuggled to Rome, Tel Aviv, Paris or London, they are forced to live in terrible conditions and service ten, twenty, even thirty men a night. If they don't play the game and pretend they are enjoying what is done to them, they are beaten and threatened. They are told that if they try to escape they will be hunted down and killed along with their families back home.'

'I've heard something of this,' said Banks shaken by the images Ganz was offering up, 'but not . . . the extent.' He shook his head.

'Most people do not know,' Ganz said. 'Many prefer not to know. People like to think that girls who end up as prostitutes deserve no less, that they *chose* what they do, but many didn't. You can buy a young girl for as little as a thousand pounds and make over a hundred thousand pounds a year from her. Once she is worn out, you buy a new one. It makes good business sense, does it not?'

'I can't believe my brother was involved in this.'

'He wasn't, as far as I know,' said Ganz. 'From what Superintendent Burgess has told me, it is my guess that your brother and his girlfriend found out what was going on.'

'Through the Berger-Lennox Centre?'

'And through Dr Lukas, yes.'

'What's her part in all this?'

'She is trying to help the girls who get pregnant. That is all. She asks no questions. They are lucky they have someone like her, otherwise . . .'

'But what's her connection?'

'That we do not know for sure. This investigation here is very new. Most of the work we have been doing has been in Bosnia, Romania and Serbia.'

'Was Carmen one of the girls she was trying to help? Carmen Petri?'

Ganz frowned. 'I'm sorry, I do not know the name.'

'Are you certain?'

'Yes. Petri, you say?'

'Something like that.'

'It sounds Romanian.'

'But you haven't heard of her?'

'No.'

'OK,' said Banks. 'Go on.'

'Anyway,' Ganz went on. 'No matter what Dr Lukas does or does not know, there's a pimp involved somewhere, and Lambert and Broda supply him with girls smuggled from Eastern Europe. He probably keeps them in more than one house, depending on how many girls he owns. Perhaps there is even more than one pimp. I do not know. We have been waiting for Broda or Lambert to lead us there.'

'But they haven't?'

'Not yet. We were worried they might be onto us. Lambert's moving between the flat and the travel office, and he spends most weekends playing the local squire in his country manor.'

'Where's that?' Banks asked.

'A village called Quainton, near Buckingham. That's where he leads his exemplary life. Anyway, where there are pimps and smugglers you will usually find organized crime, too, and that is always dangerous.'

'The Russian Mafia?'

'Most likely.'

Banks told him what he had heard from Annie about the two men suspected of killing Jennifer and, perhaps, Roy.

Ganz nodded slowly. 'Sounds like their style.'

'So what next?'

'We think these recent murders might bring things to a boil. Someone might make a mistake.'

'Are you here to warn me off?'

Ganz laughed. 'Warn you off? Superintendent Burgess told me you would probably say something like that.'

'Oh? What else did he tell you?'

'That it would do no good. Some people we can warn off easily, but not you. He said you're nobody's man.'

'He's right.'

Ganz waved his hand in a dismissive gesture. 'No, I don't want to warn you off. I want to use you in a way I can't use the police who are investigating the case. I want you to keep on doing right what you're doing. I just want you to know that you're involved in stirring up a wasps' nest.'

'Go on.'

'I'm not saying that you're not in danger – they might have killed you if you had been at the address your brother gave his girlfriend – but I think with all the trouble caused by the two murders they have already committed, they would think twice right now about killing a policeman. When you came down here they no doubt kept an eye on you, just for form's sake, but they had other things to occupy them, and they knew your brother hadn't had time to tell you anything, or you wouldn't have been floundering around in the dark the way you were. They also tortured him before they killed him and he told them you knew nothing. He also told them where you lived, and they rang the men in the car. Fortunately, your brother gave them the wrong address. They sent the digital image on the mobile, too. Perhaps they didn't know you had it, but they knew your brother didn't. That's just their style, a sick joke. Max Broda himself, most likely. If you hadn't got it, whoever had the phone at the time would have. Even the police. It didn't matter to them. It couldn't be traced. It was stolen and they threw it away as soon as they had used it. After that, they let you know that they know where your parents live. That is also very much their style. And don't worry, your parents are safe. It wasn't something we could leave for the locals to deal with alone.'

'You have men there, too?'

'One. Armed. Anyway, now that you have actually been to see

Gareth Lambert, and probably got him worried, things might be a bit different, I'm not sure.'

'You know I've seen Lambert?'

'Superintendent Burgess said he'd told you where to find him. I didn't think you would just sit around and not act on that information. What did you think?'

'I didn't believe him, didn't trust him.'

'In that, you were right. From now on, we'll try to watch your back as best we can, but for obvious reasons I can hardly show my hand. It is a shame you English police are unarmed.'

'I'm not too sure about that,' said Banks, thinking that there weren't many times in his career when he had felt the need for a gun, though now might be one of them. 'And by the way, do you have a licence for that one you're carrying?'

Ganz laughed. 'I have your government's permission, if that's what you mean. Do you want one? I'm sure I can get one for you.'

'I'd probably shoot myself in the foot,' said Banks. 'But thanks for the offer.'

'I almost forgot,' Ganz said. 'Mr Burgess told me to tell you he checked the number and the red Vectra was stolen from a multi-storey car park in Putney. Does that mean anything to you?'

'Yes, thank you,' said Banks. It meant the car that had followed him from his parents' house was stolen, as he had expected.

'What are you going to do now?'

Banks looked at his watch. 'I'm going to have another glass of wine and think over what you've said.' Later, when it was open, he planned to visit the Albion Club on the Strand and see if he could find out more about Roy's final hours, but he didn't see any reason for telling Dieter Ganz that. If Interpol were keeping an eye on him, they'd find out soon enough, anyway.

●

DS Browne arrived in Eastvale from Derby at four o'clock, just after Annie had left for the station, bearing the positive fruits of the very discreet DNA comparison, and more.

She told Templeton on their way to Roger Cropley's house that DI Gifford had made enquiries at Cropley's software firm in London and found that he regularly left late on Fridays and that he had left late on Friday 23 April as there had been an office party that evening to celebrate a lucrative new contract.

Cropley was clearly not thrilled to see the two detectives on his doorstep late that afternoon. He tried to shut the door, but Templeton got a foot in. 'It's better if you let us in,' he said. 'Otherwise I'll stay here while DS Browne goes for a warrant.'

Cropley relaxed the pressure on the door and they entered, following him into the living room. 'I don't know why you won't leave me alone,' he said. 'I've told you time after time I know nothing about any murders.'

'You mean you've lied time after time,' said Templeton. 'By the way, this is DS Browne. She's come all the way from Derby just to talk to you. Say hello.'

Cropley said nothing, just stared at Susan Browne. She sat down and smoothed her skirt. 'Mr Cropley,' she said, 'I'll come right to the point. When DC Templeton here first came to me with his suspicions I was sceptical. Now I've had time to think about it and make a few enquiries, I'm not too certain.'

'What enquiries?'

Susan slipped a folder out of her briefcase and opened it. 'According to my information, you left your office in Holborn at about eight o'clock on Friday the 23rd of April this year.'

'How do you know that?'

'Is it true?'

'I don't remember. How can you expect me to remember that far back?'

'It's true according to our evidence. That would put you at Trowell services around the same time as Claire Potter.'

'Look, this is absurd. It's nothing but circumstantial.'

'On two other occasions you left late,' Susan went on reading, 'two other women were either followed or assaulted shortly after leaving the M1.'

'I haven't assaulted anyone.'

'What we're going to do, Mr Cropley,' Susan went on, 'is take you down to the police station for further questioning. There you will be fingerprinted and photographed and a sample of your DNA will be taken. Once we have—'

The door opened and Mrs Cropley walked in. 'What's going on, Roger?' she demanded.

'They're harassing me again,' Cropley said.

His wife looked at Susan and Templeton, then back at her husband, an expression of scorn on her face. 'Maybe you deserve it,' she said.

'Do you know something, Mrs Cropley?' Templeton asked.

'He's my husband,' Mrs Cropley said.

'A woman has been murdered,' Susan said. 'Raped and stabbed.'

Mrs Cropley folded her arms.

Susan and Templeton looked at one another and Susan turned back to Cropley, who was now ashen. 'Once we have the photographs we'll be showing them to every worker in every cafe and petrol station on the motorway. Once we have your DNA we'll be comparing it with traces found at the scene of Claire Potter's murder. You might have thought you were thorough, Mr Cropley, but there's always something. In your case it's dandruff.'

'Dandruff?'

'Yes. Didn't you know we can get DNA from dandruff? If you even left one flake at the scene, we'll have it in the evidence room and we'll be testing it.'

Cropley looked stunned.

'Anything to say?' Susan went on.

Cropley just shook his head.

'Right.' Susan stood up. 'Roger Cropley, you're under arrest for suspicion of the murder of Claire Potter. You do not have to say anything, but it may harm your defence if you do not mention when questioned something which you later rely on in court. Anything you do say may be given in evidence.'

When Cropley left between Susan and Templeton, head hung, his wife turned her back and stood in the centre of the room rigid as a statue, arms still folded.

•

Annie was half an hour late as she made her way through the crowded pavements of Covent Garden to the restaurant Dr Lukas had mentioned on Tavistock Street. She had just missed the 4.25 and as the 5.05 was a slow train she had to catch the 5.25, which arrived on time at 8.13. On the train, she rang Dr Lukas at the centre, but was told the doctor wasn't there that day. She left a message, which she couldn't be sure Dr Lukas had received, and then she had phoned the restaurant to leave a message there, too. She also rang her usual hotel to book a room for the night. The desk clerk recognized her name and voice and got so chatty it was embarrassing.

Well, Annie thought as she dashed into the crowded restaurant, Dr Lukas had said she would be waiting, and there were worse places to wait. She spotted the doctor at a corner table and made her way over. It was a small restaurant with intimate lighting and white linen tablecloths. A blackboard on the wall listed specials and wine suggestions. There was music playing, but it was so faint Annie couldn't make out what it was. It sounded French, though.

'Did you get my message?' she asked, sitting down and catching her breath.

Dr Lukas nodded. 'It's all right,' she said, tapping the paperback she was reading. 'I have my book. I was prepared to wait. They know me here. They are very understanding.'

Annie browsed the menu, which was decidedly traditional, and decided on coq au vin. Dr Lukas had already settled on bouillabaisse. Once they'd got their orders in, the doctor poured Annie a glass of Chablis and topped up her own.

'I'm sorry I made you come all this way,' she said, 'but I couldn't possibly tell you over the telephone.'

'It's all right,' said Annie. 'I had to come back anyway. You're going to tell me everything?'

'Everything I know.'

'Why not tell me before?'

'Because the situation has changed. And things have gone too far.'

The waiter appeared with a basket of bread and Annie broke off a chunk and buttered it. She hadn't eaten on the train and realized she was starving. 'I'm listening.'

'It's very difficult for me,' Dr Lukas began. 'It's not something I'm proud of.'

'Helping the girls?'

'Not that so much. If I hadn't done, who would?'

'Is it about Carmen Petri?'

'Only partly. To understand what I have to say, you have to know where I come from. L'viv is a very old city, a very beautiful city in many ways, with many fine ancient buildings and churches. My mother was a seamstress until arthritis made her fingers no more use. My father was a mining engineer. My parents remember when Jews were rounded up and killed by the Germans in the war. You hear about the massacre at Babi Yar, near Kiev, but there were many smaller massacres elsewhere, including L'viv. My parents were lucky. They were children then and they hid and were not found. When I lived there, Ukraine was still part of the Soviet Union. I grew up in a modern part of the city, ugly Stalinist blocks. We were poor and ill-fed, but there was a strong sense of community, and sometimes you could even believe in the ideals behind the reality of Soviet life. When Ukraine became an independent state in August 1991, things were chaotic for a while. Nobody knew what was going to happen. That was when I left.'

Annie listened, interested in Dr Lukas's story but curious as to where it was leading. Before long, their food was served and Dr Lukas poured more wine. As if reading Annie's mind, she smiled and said, 'You might be wondering where all this is going, but please indulge me.' She talked more about her childhood, the state school, unsanitary living conditions, her ambition to become a doctor. 'And here I am,' she said. 'Ambition fulfilled.'

'You must be very proud.'

Dr Lukas frowned. 'Proud? Yes. Most days. About a year ago a man came to see me at my home. I remembered him from school, from the building in L'viv where his family lived, close to mine. He said he had heard I was here through his parents, who had read an article about me in the local newspaper. It's true. Many people left Ukraine but their stories continue to be of interest to those who have not experienced the world outside.'

'What did he want?'

'When he was at school he was a bully. When he got older he and his gang terrorized the building we lived in, extorting money, burgling units, selling black-market goods. Nobody was safe from him. Then suddenly he was gone. You can imagine how relieved we all were.'

'But he turned up here, in London?'

'Yes, he told me he travelled all around Europe, learning the ways of the free world, the free economy, and his training in L'viv served him well.'

'He's the man who sends the late girls to you, isn't he?'

Dr Lukas said nothing for a moment. She had turned pale as she was talking, Annie noticed, and her bouillabaisse sat mostly uneaten in front of her. Finally, she whispered, 'Yes. That's what he is now. A pimp. When he first came to see me it was because one of his girls had problems with her periods that made her unreliable. Then he realized what a good idea it would be for me to be their unofficial doctor, so to speak. And that was the start of it all.'

'And this has been going on for a year?'

'Yes.'

'And how many girls have you seen during that time?'

'Maybe fifteen, sixteen.'

'All pregnant?'

'Most. Some had sexually transmitted infections. One had a

bad rash in her pubic area. One girl was bleeding from her anus. Whatever it was, he brought them to me at the centre after it was closed for the day. I would get a phone call telling me to stay late.'

'Why did you help him?' Annie thought she knew the answer to the question as she was asking it, but she needed to hear it from Dr Lukas. A noisy party across the room broke into gales of laughter.

Dr Lukas looked over at them, then turned to face Annie, her expression sombre. 'He told me he would kill my parents back in L'viv if I didn't do as he said or if I told anyone. I know he can do it. He still has contacts there.'

'What's changed?'

'My parents are no longer in L'viv. They have left for America to live with my brother in San Francisco. I was waiting to hear confirmation. They telephoned me today.'

'What about you?'

'I don't care about me,' said Dr Lukas. 'Besides, he's not going to hurt me. I'm far too useful to him alive.'

'If it's any consolation,' Annie said, 'he'll be in jail.'

Dr Lukas laughed. 'Yes,' she said. 'Running his empire from a cell. And on the outside someone will replace him. Another monster. The world has no shortage of monsters.' She shook her head. 'But it's gone far enough. Poor Jennifer . . . that man . . .'

'Roy Banks was his name. What about Carmen Petri?'

Dr Lukas gave Annie a curious look. 'That was the beginning of the end, really. Carmen.'

'What do you mean?'

'Until Carmen, I could turn a blind eye, could even believe that what I was doing was good and that the girls had better lives as prostitutes here than they would in their war-torn villages and towns back home. I didn't know the truth. Like everyone, I thought they chose what they did, that there must be something wrong with them to start with, something bad about them. I was naive.'

'How did Carmen change this?'

'The girls wouldn't talk. I asked them about their lives but they refused to tell me anything. They were too scared. Carmen . . . she was a bit more confident, more intelligent . . . I don't know. Perhaps it was even Jennifer, the way she was kind to her. What-ever the reason, Carmen did let something slip.'

'What was that?'

'She told me that one of the new girls had been locked in a small room and beaten because she refused to perform some vile sex act. She also told me that the girl had been on her way home from school in a small village in Bosnia when two men abducted her at knifepoint and forced her into prostitution. She was fifteen. That was the first time I realized that these girls didn't start out one step from prostitution, that there was nothing "bad" about them. They were normal girls, like you and me, and they were forced to do what they do. Like me, they fear for their families back home. Those who have families. These poor girls . . . He has them smuggled from Bosnia, Moldavia, Romania and Kosovo. Many are orphans because of the wars. When they have to leave the orphanages at sixteen they often have no money and nowhere to go. His men are waiting for them on the doorstep. The girls are terrified of him. They won't talk about what happens, but I've seen bruises, cuts sometimes. I didn't ask questions, and I am not proud of that, but I saw. Then Carmen . . . she spoke out.'

'When was this?'

'A week last Monday.'

'What happened to her?'

'Nothing, as far as I know.'

'She's not dead?'

'I don't think so. I can't see why she would be.'

'But if they thought she told you and Jennifer what was really going on . . . ?'

'I don't think they knew what she told us, and she's too valuable to them.'

'But they must have found out something,' Annie said.

'Jennifer and Roy Banks are dead. When Jennifer told Roy, he must have started digging, asking questions. He had contact with people who . . . well, let's just say he knew criminals.'

'Perhaps I am wrong, then. I don't know. All I know about Carmen is what she told me. She got pregnant, so he sent her to me. I suppose the only unusual thing is that Carmen has decided to have the baby. She's a devout Catholic and she refused to have a termination.'

'That's permitted?'

'In some circumstances,' said Dr Lukas. 'It would depend on the loss of income. Carmen is one of the special girls, blessed with good looks and a fine figure. She is also a very intelligent girl and she speaks English very well. She was never a street prostitute, more what you would term a call girl.'

'So how is he going to make up for his loss of income?'

'I can only guess,' said Dr Lukas. 'There are some men who like to have sex with pregnant women and are willing to pay extra for it. That way she would have fewer customers but make as much, or more, money.'

Annie's stomach turned. She could understand why Dr Lukas wasn't eating. She'd lost her appetite as well. 'And the baby?'

'Adoption. She spoke about the way they were taking care of her and feeding her well for a Mr Garrett, who I assume is paying good money for Carmen's baby.'

'Will you tell me the pimp's name?'

'His real name is Hadeon Mazuryk. He calls himself Harry. His nickname is "Happy Harry" because he looks eternally sad. He is not, of course, it's just a freak of physiognomy.'

'Do you know where he keeps the girls?'

Dr Lukas nodded. 'There's a house near King's Cross. I went there once. An emergency. You must be careful, though.'

'Why?'

'He has a gun. I've seen it.'

•

Banks had raided Roy's wardrobe again for suitable attire. He didn't think he would get far in the Albion Club wearing jeans and a casual shirt. Trousers were a problem. Roy's didn't fit him and he had only brought one pair with him, which didn't match any of Roy's jackets. In the end he just had to hope the place was poorly lit so that black and navy blue didn't look too bad together.

The man on the door, looking rather like a cross between a butler and a bouncer, asked him for his membership. Banks flashed his warrant card.

'Police? I hope there's no trouble, sir?' he said.

'None at all,' said Banks. 'Just a few questions and I'll be out of your hair.'

'Questions?'

'Yes. Were you on duty here last Friday?'

'Yes, sir.'

'Do you remember Roy Banks arriving with Gareth Lambert?'

'Such a tragedy about Mr Banks. The perfect gentleman. Who could do such a thing?'

'Who indeed? But did you see them arrive?'

'Yes. It would have been about a quarter, maybe twenty, past ten.'

'And were you here when they left?'

'They didn't leave together, sir. Mr Banks left first, at about twelve thirty, and Mr Lambert stayed much later. Perhaps three o'clock, something like that.'

So Lambert was telling the truth about that much, at least. 'Did they leave alone?'

'Yes, sir.'

'Do you know where Mr Banks went after he left?'

'Mr Banks didn't say. He just bade me goodnight as usual.'

'You didn't call a minicab for him?'

'There are always plenty of taxis on the Strand, and there's a taxi-rank at Charing Cross.'

'Right,' said Banks. 'OK to go inside?'

'Please try not to upset the members.'

'I only want to talk to the staff.'

'Very well.'

Banks was surprised when he got inside the club. The door opened into a spacious, low-ceilinged bar, and where he had been expecting dark wainscoting, chandeliers and waiters in burgundy bum-freezers, he found tubular fittings, muted pastel lighting and waitresses in pinstripe suits, with trousers rather than skirts. Fan-shaped splashes of colour from well-hidden lights decorated the walls in shades of blue, pink, green, red and orange. The chrome tables were high, with matching leather-topped stools. This definitely wasn't one of those old gentlemen's clubs where the right sort of people stay over when they are down in the city for the weekend; it was primarily an upmarket casino with bar and restaurants facilities, the sort of place you might have found James Bond in fifty years ago. Now it played host to a hipper, younger crowd of stockbrokers, investment bankers and the occasional old smuggler like Gareth Lambert.

As it turned out, the dress code was also a lot more relaxed than Banks had expected – he had never been to a club before and he still thought in terms of Lord Peter Wimsey and Bertie Wooster – and he was surprised to see that not everyone was wearing a tie or a suit. Business casual was in. The place wasn't very busy, but a few people sat around drinking and chatting, and a group of Japanese businessmen had the one large table by the far wall, where they were entertaining some expensive-looking women. Most of the people in the place seemed to be in their thirties, which made Roy and Lambert slightly older than the average member. Still, from what Banks had learned, Roy was certainly young at heart. Nobody paid Banks any undue attention. There was no music.

Banks took one of the stools at the bar and ordered a bottle of Stella. The price was every bit as outrageous as he had expected. The bartender was a woman in her late twenties, by the look of her, about the same age as Corinne and Jennifer. She had very fine short hair dyed pink and blonde. She smiled at Banks when she took his order. She had a nice smile, dimples too.

Banks showed her his card. 'Do you work here every night?' he asked.

'Most nights,' she said, scrutinizing the card more closely than the doorman had. 'Yorkshire? What brings you down here?'

'Cases can take you all over the place,' Banks said. 'People move around a lot more than they used to.'

'You can say that again.'

'Actually, I'm making a few enquiries about Roy Banks. I understand he was a member.'

'Poor Mr Banks,' she said. 'He was a real sweetheart.'

'You knew him?'

'Not really "knew". I mean, not outside of work. But we talked from time to time. You tend to do that, in this job. He always had time for the bar staff, not like some of our more stuck-up members.'

'Did he sit at the bar and tell you his troubles?'

She laughed. 'Oh, no. That only happens in films.'

'What's your name, by the way?'

'Maria.'

'Pleased to meet you, Maria.'

'What relation are you?'

'What do you mean?'

'Your name's Banks, too. I saw it on that card. Are you his brother?'

'Yes,' Banks said.

'You must be gutted.'

'I am. But I'm also trying to find out what happened. Did you talk to him last Friday?'

'Yes. He and Mr Lambert were sitting at that table just over there.' She pointed to a discreet corner table. 'Mr Banks always made a point of coming over and saying hello and asking me how I was doing. And he always made sure he left a decent tip.'

'Did he have anything to say that night?'

A waitress appeared asking for drinks. Maria excused herself for a moment and filled the order with graceful efficiency. 'What was it you wanted to know?' she asked when she came back.

'Just if Roy had said anything out of the ordinary to you.'

'No. Nothing. Not that that I remember.'

'Did he seem worried?'

'Not at first. A bit preoccupied, maybe.'

'Later?'

'After he'd been talking to Mr Lambert for a while he seemed to be getting uncomfortable, if you know what I mean. I don't know how to describe it, but you could sort of feel the tension, even from over here.'

'Others noticed?'

'I wouldn't say that. I've always been very sensitive to the vibes people give off.'

'And these were bad?'

'Yes, I think so.'

'Were they arguing?'

'No. They never raised their voices or anything like that. It was just a sort of tense negotiation.'

Lambert had told Banks that Roy had been pressing him for contacts in the arms business, but he didn't believe that. 'What happened next?'

'After he used the telephone, Mr Banks went through to the casino and I didn't see him again.'

'Mr Lambert?'

'He sat by himself for a while, then he went into the casino, too.'

'You say Roy used the telephone?'

'Yes.'

'Where is it?'

'There's a public telephone in the corridor by the toilets,' she said. 'Down there.' She pointed directly across the room. Banks turned and saw the phone on the wall. From where Lambert had been sitting, he couldn't possibly have seen Roy make the call.

'Not a lot of people use it because everyone's got a mobile these days, haven't they, but he must have forgotten his or the battery was dead or something.'

Banks thought of the mobile sitting on Roy's kitchen table. 'Was it a long phone call?'

'No. Just two or three minutes.'

'How long had he been here when he made it?'

'Not long. Maybe half an hour or so, a bit longer.'

That must have been the call he made to Jennifer, Banks thought, sending her up to Yorkshire, and to her death. 'And how did he seem after that?'

'Like I said, he went into the casino. He didn't say goodbye, though, and that's not like him.'

'Did Mr Lambert make any phone calls?'

'Not that I saw.'

'Could he have done?'

'Oh, yes. I mean, he went to the toilet. He could have used his mobile there, if he had one with him. But I didn't see him make any calls, that's all I meant.'

'Thanks very much, Maria,' said Banks. 'You've been a great help.'

'I have?'

Banks made sure to leave her a decent tip and wandered out onto the Strand. He glanced about him to see if there was anyone watching for him, but if there was, he didn't notice. According to the doorman and Maria, Roy had left the club around half-past twelve. There were plenty of taxis passing by, Banks could see. So what had Roy done? Got in a taxi? Or had someone offered him a lift? It couldn't have been Lambert, because he was still in the casino. So who?

17

The sun was up by the time the operation had been approved by the brass in SO19, the Metropolitan Police Force Firearms Unit at Scotland Yard, and the team had been assembled and briefed. Annie and Brooke gathered with the specialist firearms officers outside the house near King's Cross station, in the narrow streets around Wharfdale Road. The house was part of a terrace, and the SO19 team leader had acquired a set of plans. There were eight officers, all wearing protective headgear and body armour and carrying Glock handguns and Heckler and Koch MP5 carbines. Each man had been told what section he was to secure. Three more men watched the back of the house.

It was an eerie sight, Annie thought, and there was something slightly unreal about it. One or two onlookers had gathered at the street corners, held back by uniformed officers stationed there. It was a humid morning and a light mist hung in the air. There was little traffic in the immediate area but Annie could hear horns and engines in the distance. Another day in the big city was beginning.

In a way, Annie wished that Banks had been granted permission to attend; she would have liked him by her side. But these operations were strictly regulated and there was no way they were letting Roy Banks's brother be a part of it. She had talked to him on the phone late the previous evening, and he had told her about his visit to the Albion Club. In exchange, she had told him what Dr Lukas told her about the late girls and Carmen Petri.

On the prearranged signal, the SO19 team battered down the front door and stormed into the house. Annie and Brooke, unarmed, had instructions to wait outside until the place was secured, then they would be allowed in to question any witnesses or suspects. Brooke was unusually quiet. Annie felt herself tense up as she heard sounds from inside the house, shouts, commands, a woman's scream, something thudding on the floor.

But there were no shots, and she took that as a good sign.

She had no idea how long it took, but eventually the team leader emerged and told them the house was secured. There had been one guard armed with a baseball bat and three other men, none of them armed. The rest of the occupants were young women. They had best take a look for themselves, he told them, shaking his head in disbelief.

Annie and Brooke went inside. It was a shabby place, in poor repair, with old wallpaper stained and peeling off in places, no stair carpet and only dirty linoleum on the ground floor. The smells of stale sex and cigarette smoke permeated the air. Little light got in through the windows, so the officers had turned on all the lights they could find, mostly bare bulbs, and they hardly flattered the scene, just gave it an extra harsh edge.

The seven girls were all in a small room upstairs. Probably more lived there, Annie guessed, but they would be out working the streets around King's Cross. No matter what the time of day, business never stopped. The area had had a bad reputation for years, and Annie remembered how the girls were once called Maggie's Children because they came down on the trains from the north when all the jobs disappeared up there. These days they might be known as Putin's Children, Iliescu's or Terzic's.

The SO19 officers wandered around as Annie and Brooke went over to the girls. The sparsely furnished room smelled of sweat and cheap perfume and the girls were all dressed in skimpy cloth-ing, tight hot pants, micro skirts, thigh-highs, see-through tops, and their faces were garish with lipstick and eye make-up. Some of them looked high; none looked much older than fifteen. Beyond the fear in their expressions Annie could see only resignation and despair. This was truly the generation of lost girls Dr Lukas had described, she thought. Christ, she wanted to take them home and scrub the make-up off and feed them a decent meal. Most of them were skinny, and some had sores on their lips. Several of them were smoking and that added to the cloying atmosphere of the room.

Other rooms in the house were equipped with beds and wash-basins for the girls to entertain clients, but this seemed to be a general sitting room. The four men the SO19 team had found had all been handcuffed and bundled out into the van. The girls had been checked for weapons as a matter of routine, then left alone, a guard on the door.

'Ma'am?' One of the team stood at the door and beckoned Annie. 'I think you should see this.'

He led Annie to a room no bigger than a cupboard. Inside was a young girl, naked but for the thin sheet another officer was wrapping around her. She was painfully thin and blood crusted the cleft between her nose and upper lip. She was alive, but her eyes looked dead. The only other thing in the room was a bucket, its stench abominable.

'Get an ambulance,' Annie said. She helped the girl to her feet, keeping the sheet wrapped around her and slowly took her back to the others. One of the girls ran forward and took the new-comer in her arms, mumbling endearments, and helped her sit in an armchair, perching on the arm beside her.

'Can you speak English?'

The girl nodded. 'A little.'

'What happened to her?'

'She's new,' the girl told her, in heavily accented English, still stroking her friend's hair. 'She would not do what they tell her so they lock her up and beat her. She has not eaten for three days.'

Brooke was trying to talk to the other girls but it didn't appear they spoke English. Whatever the reason, they all seemed afraid of him and no one would say a word. Most of them wouldn't even look at him. Annie thought she understood why. She took him aside.

'Look, Dave,' she said, seeing his crestfallen expression. 'It's not your fault, but they don't know you're a decent man. They don't know any decent men. It might be best if you went down and questioned the men.'

Brooke nodded. 'You'll be OK?'

'I'll manage,' said Annie. She touched him gently on the shoulder and he left.

'What will happen to us?' asked the girl on the chair arm, who seemed to have taken charge. She had dark hair down to her shoulders, thin arms and a pale complexion.

It was a good question and Annie wasn't sure she knew the answer. The object of the raid had been to take Happy Harry Mazuryk and, with any luck, find Carmen Petri. Annie didn't know if Harry had been one of the men arrested, though from what she had seen in passing, none of them matched his description.

'You'll all be taken care of,' she said. 'What's your name?'

'Veronika.'

'Right, Veronika. I'd like to ask you a few questions.'

'I can't tell you anything. He will kill me.'

'No, he won't,' said Annie. 'We'll put him in jail.'

'You don't understand. *He* wasn't here, only his stupid guard. Those men are here for . . .' She made an obscene gesture with her hips.

'Where is Hadeon Mazuryk?'

She flinched at the sound of his name. 'I don't know.'

'OK,' said Annie. 'What about Carmen? Do you know Carmen Petri?' She looked around at the frightened girls. 'Is she here?'

They all shook their heads. One started crying. Annie turned back to Veronika. 'Do you know Carmen?'

Veronika nodded.

'Where is she?'

'She is not here. Carmen is one of the special girls.'

'What do you mean?'

'She is very beautiful. She speaks very good English. She does not have to go out to the street. Men come to her. Pay more.'

This was what Annie had heard from Dr Lukas. Still she

wondered whether Carmen had been killed. 'Do you know where she is, Veronika? I really need to talk to her.'

Veronika turned to the girl in the sheet and stroked her hair again, then she looked back at Annie, her face stern. 'There is another house,' she said. 'I have talked to Carmen. She has told me. She is there.'

•

Banks didn't regret too much being barred from the King's Cross raid. He had been on such operations before and generally found the paramilitary elements quite tedious. He did, however, want to know the results, which was why he was sitting anxiously at the kitchen table early with his morning coffee and newspaper, mobile beside him at the ready.

He was still puzzling over what had happened between Roy and Lambert at the Albion Club that Friday, and the best he could come up with was that Lambert had proposed something Roy didn't approve of and became worried he'd give the game away. Their friendship went back to university days and they had got up to all sorts of things together. They had been out of touch for a long time, though, and Lambert probably didn't know that Roy had redrawn his moral lines.

If Lambert wanted him to come in on importing abducted teenage girls for the sex trade, as Annie suggested was happening, then Roy would probably have balked at that, Banks thought. If he had been ignorant of the true way in which the girls were forced into prostitution, as Dr Lukas had told Annie she was, then he would have found out via Jennifer, who had talked with Carmen Petri and learned something of the truth on the Monday of the week she died. The timing was important here. Roy might have been on the verge of getting involved when he found out the truth after Carmen told Jennifer, and Lambert spent the next few days trying to convince him it was OK. Then something else must have tipped the balance, something Roy found out the day he disappeared.

Banks guessed that when Roy left the bar for the casino, Lambert went into the toilet and phoned someone – maybe Max Broda – and told him the situation was critical. After that, Broda took control and had a car ready to pick Roy up outside the club and take him to the abandoned factory in Battersea. Ponytail and his crony must also have been working for Broda, and they had been assigned to watch Jennifer and keep an eye on her movements. Banks could imagine the mobile conversations back and forth between the Mondeo, following Jennifer, and the factory, where Roy had been taken, culminating in the order to kill her. Perhaps Roy had also intended to head up to Banks's cottage when he realized things had gone too far, but he hadn't had the chance. They'd got to him first.

As Banks thought about it all, a number of things came together in his mind, the way it sometimes happened when he felt most lost. Annie had told him that Dr Lukas had said the baby was being adopted by a 'Mr Garrett'. He remembered Dieter Ganz saying 'Gareth' with his slight accent yesterday, and imagined that the men Carmen Petri had heard saying it also had accents, as she no doubt did herself. In Ganz's case, it had come out sounding like 'Garrett' and that was exactly what Dr Lukas had said, that the men were taking good care of Carmen and her baby for 'Mr Garrett'.

Was that it, then, the new thing that Roy had discovered? Was Lambert himself adopting Carmen's baby, buying it, and was that why it was so important for him to stop Roy blowing the whistle? There was one way to find out, one person he could ask.

Banks went up to Roy's office, where he thought he had seen an atlas. He pulled it down and found that Quainton was in Buckinghamshire, not too far from Aylesbury. It was a nice day for a drive in the country, he thought, and it would be interesting to meet the elusive Mrs Lambert. He grabbed his jacket and his mobile and set off for the car.

•

The second house was about a mile away, in Islington, but light years away in comfort. It was a detached house with a small garden, the curtains all shut tight against the morning light. If the SO19 team leader hadn't verified that it belonged to Mr Hadeon Mazuryk, Annie would have thought it the home of a perfectly normal family with a couple of kids, a dog, and a people carrier.

The team had had to move fast, before Mazuryk found out about the King's Cross raid, and the SO19 team had reassembled in the van for a quick briefing. The layout of the house was similar to many others in the area, including the house one of the men lived in, and between them, the officers were able to sketch out a likely floor plan. Then they quietly evacuated the houses on either side and sealed off the street at both ends.

Annie sat across the street in the car with DI Brooke, who had got nowhere talking to the men at King's Cross, and watched. She could hear faint music from one of the downstairs rooms, a bass line of some pop song she didn't recognize. Then she heard a man cough and someone laugh.

'You're very quiet, Dave,' she said, turning to Brooke, who was staring down the street.

'I was warned off,' he said, without looking at her.

'What?'

'I was warned off, Annie.' Now he looked her in the eye and she could see his self-disgust. 'Orders from the top. Gareth Lambert's part of an international investigation. If the police swarmed over him, all the major players would disappear into the woodwork for years. That's what I was told. If I valued my promotion . . . well, I think you can fill in the rest. Oliver Drummond and William Gilmore seemed likely leads.'

'I'm sorry, Dave,' Annie said, feeling embarrassed for him. 'You were only following orders.'

He gave her an ironic glance. 'Isn't that what the Germans said?'

'This is different. What else could you do?'

Brooke shrugged. 'I don't know. I just don't like the feeling, that's all. I doubt they'd warn off your pal Banks so easily.'

Annie smiled. 'DCI Banks is a law unto himself,' she said. 'Partly because he doesn't feel he has anything to lose. It's not necessarily a position to envy.' She gestured to the SO19 officers in the street. 'Anyway, for better or for worse we're getting some action now.'

Brooke nodded. 'It's gone too far. Even the brass couldn't justify leaving vulnerable underage girls in captivity like that for one night longer than they had to. Besides, we still don't know if or how Lambert is connected. Maybe it's something completely different.'

'Whatever it is, we'll find out soon,' said Annie. 'They're going in.'

Half the men went around the back and the rest prepared to enter through the front door. Annie held her breath as one of them slammed the battering ram and the wood splintered, then they were in. She heard similar sounds from the back.

This time, in addition to the shouting and screaming, Annie heard shots. So did the neighbours further down the street, who soon appeared at windows and in doorways, only to be kept at bay by the uniformed officers deployed on crowd duties. After an agonizing period of silence, the team leader stepped out and waved Annie and Brooke inside.

'Everybody all right?' Annie asked.

'We are,' he said. 'Eddie took one on the chest but the body armour worked fine. He's feeling a bit sore, that's all. Look, we're waiting for the ambulance and for the brass to get here. You know what it's like whenever shots are fired. Forms in triplicate. Questions. You feel more like a criminal than a copper.'

Annie and Brooke followed the grumbling team leader into the front room. Four men had been sitting around playing cards at a folding table. Two of them were handcuffed and two of them were slumped against the wall with holes in their chests, covered in dark bibs of blood. Blood had also sprayed on the walls and carpeting. Annie felt a bit sick. She hadn't seen many gunshot victims before and hadn't been prepared for the smell of the exploded ammunition mingled with fresh blood in the room.

One of the dead men resembled the description she had heard of Hadeon 'Happy Harry' Mazuryk, and the other one had a body builder's physique, with long greasy hair tied back in a ponytail and a thick gold chain around his neck. One of the bullets must have severed the chain because it snaked in one long piece down his bloody chest.

Annie didn't recognize the other two men. Both were looking sullen, handcuffed and guarded by SO19 officers with their Heckler and Kochs at the ready. One of the men might have been the driver of the Mondeo, but all the descriptions she had of him were vague. The more she looked at the other one, the more he seemed familiar: spiky hair, goatee. Then she remembered: the photograph Banks had showed her, the one his brother apparently took just days before he died. This was the man who had been sitting with Gareth Lambert at an outdoor cafe. Now there was a connection, whatever it meant.

An ambulance arrived and men filled the room. Annie and Brooke followed one of the officers upstairs. There were three bedrooms, all of them occupied by beautiful young girls, who were all more than a little unnerved by the shooting. SO19 officers dealt with the other two and Brooke hung back as Annie entered the room and walked over to the only pregnant girl, who was lying on the bed looking frightened.

'Carmen?' she said. 'Carmen Petri?'

The girl nodded, seeming surprised that Annie knew her name. She looked a little older than the girls in the King's Cross house, perhaps as old as nineteen or twenty, and she wore much less make-up. It was difficult to tell what her figure had been like because she was about six months pregnant, but she had a beautiful face: full lips with a Bardot pout, a perfectly proportioned nose, flawless complexion – apart from a beauty spot by the side of her mouth – and deep dark-blue eyes damp with tears.

Annie couldn't read her expression and guessed that Carmen was a girl who had become adept at hiding her feelings and thoughts for the purposes of self-preservation.

'What happened?' Carmen asked.

'I'll explain it all later,' Annie said. 'I'm happy to meet you at last. I'm Annie Cabbot. Will you answer some questions?'

'Where's Hadeon?'

'Dead.'

'Good. And Artyom?'

'Who's he?'

'Big man. Ponytail.'

'He's dead, too.'

'That is good, too,' she said, shifting on the bed slightly. Annie could see an expression of discomfort cross her features as she moved. Probably the baby kicking.

'What happened to you?' Annie asked. 'How did you get here?'

'Is a long story,' she said. 'And a long time ago. I was taken from the street when I was a young girl.'

'How young?'

'Sixteen.'

'By who?'

She shrugged. 'A man.'

'Where.'

'A village near Craiova, in Romania. You will not have heard of it.'

'You went to see Dr Lukas at the Berger-Lennox Centre?'

'Yes. She was good to me.' Carmen reached for a cigarette. 'She wanted me to stop smoking, but I tell her a girl must have one vice. I don't drink and I don't take drugs.' Her English was remarkably good, Annie thought, and she could see what Veronika meant about her being beautiful. There was a sophistication about her beyond her years, and Carmen had the kind of class you don't usually associate with people in her profession.

Annie wondered how on earth she could stand the life without some form of escape, but what did she know? And what could she presume to know about someone who had been through what Carmen had been through?

'Do you remember Jennifer Clewes?'

'Yes. She works with Dr Lukas.'

'She's dead, too, Carmen. Someone killed her.'

Carmen looked alarmed. 'Why?'

'We don't know. We think it might have to do with something you told her. Jennifer and her boyfriend seemed to know something about what was going on here. Did you say anything to her when you were talking last week?'

Carmen looked down at her swollen belly. 'The doctor think we do this because we want to,' she said. 'I tell her she does not know how bad things are, that none of us are here because we want. I tell Jennifer, too. Some stories of what happen to girls. I should not have said that. But I think I was feeling brave because they were treating me well, different from the others.'

'When did you tell her this?'

'Last time I go to clinic. Not long. Monday, I think.'

'Did Artyom know you'd been talking?'

'He took me back in the car and told Hadeon. They could not hurt me to make me tell them anything. I knew that. But . . .'

'I think I know,' said Annie. 'They threatened to harm your parents back home, didn't they?'

'Yes,' Carmen whispered.

'So you told them.'

'Yes.'

Annie nodded. 'That house in King's Cross,' she said. 'We've just come from there. Those girls were treated terribly. I've never seen anything like it.'

'I have been there. Hadeon always tells me I have been very lucky. For me men pay hundreds of pounds a night, for those girls they must have many men to make such money. Hadeon makes his girls work very hard. He tells me if I am not good he will send me there, too. I am happy he is dead.'

'Do you think he would have people killed who found out what he was doing?'

Carmen nodded. 'Harry once killed a girl with his bare hands for refusing to have sex with him.'

'Did Artyom work for him?'

'Yes. And Boris.'

'With the cropped blonde hair?'

'That is Boris.'

The driver, Annie thought. 'There was another man down-stairs.' Annie described him. 'Do you know who he is?'

'All I know is that his name is Max and that he brings new girls for Harry. He is not always here. I have never talked to him.'

Annie imagined that when Mazuryk knew Carmen had talked, he or Max had brought Lambert in to handle damage control, and that was what had been going on all week. Mazuryk had also set Artyom and the driver to keep an eye on Jennifer, watch where she went. Perhaps Lambert had talked to Roy and managed to assure Mazuryk that no one would be ringing the police, but negotiations were tense, then something else happened, some-thing that changed it all.

'Do you know a man called Lambert?' Annie asked.

'Lambert? No,' said Carmen.

Annie gestured towards her stomach. 'What's going to happen to you?'

'I'm going to have my baby. It makes them take good care of me. I get food and they leave me alone. I get bored sometimes. The only times I can go out is to see Dr Lukas, and then Artyom usually takes me. But it is much better than before.'

'Do you know who the father is?'

Carmen gave her a scornful look.

'And what about the baby? Dr Lukas told me it was going to be adopted.'

'Yes. They want to sell the baby to a rich man. She will go to a good family and have a good life. That is why they treat me well, to keep the baby healthy. Harry always jokes when he sees me, how he must keep me healthy for Mr Garrett.' A sudden anxiety came into her voice. 'But Harry is dead. What is going to happen to me now?'

'I don't know,' said Annie. 'I really don't know.'

•

Banks remembered something on his way out and opened the door to Roy's garage. The Porsche still stood there, gleaming and immaculate. He opened the driver's door and sat down, reaching into the side pocket for the AA road atlas. It was still open to the same page, and this time Banks spotted Quainton somewhere towards the top right. Well, he thought, it was hardly conclusive, but a bit of a coincidence nonetheless. Perhaps Quainton had been Roy's port of call before he got home, rang Banks and went off to the Albion Club with Lambert. What had he found out there that disturbed him so?

Banks took the AA atlas, locked up the car, garage and house behind him and headed for the M41 and Quainton. As far as he could gather, after a number of diversionary manoeuvres, there was no one on his tail. He had his mobile on the seat beside him and just beyond Berkhamsted Annie rang and told him about the raids, the deaths of Hadeon Mazuryk and Artyom, and about her interview with Carmen Petri. It put a few things in perspective and persuaded him that he was certainly heading in the right direction.

An hour and a half after leaving London, he was there.

Quainton stood at the bottom of a hill, a straggling sort of place scattered around a village green. Banks parked there, near the George and Dragon. He paused a moment and glanced at the brick windmill at the top of the hill, then went into the pub. He hadn't got an address from Ganz, just the village name, but he guessed the place was small enough that they would probably know Lambert and his Spanish wife at the local.

It looked like a good place to eat. Blackboards offered steak and Stilton pie, French country chicken and Thai red curry. Maybe he'd call back after talking to Lambert and his wife. The barman knew the Lamberts and told him they lived in a big house on the Denham Road, and he couldn't miss it. Banks thanked him and set off.

He found the house easily enough on the outskirts of the village. It looked the sort of place that had had a few additions over the years – gables, an extra wing, a garage – so it was hard to tell in what period the original building had been erected. Banks pulled into the drive, parked at the front and went to ring the doorbell.

In no time at all a young woman answered, smiled at him and asked what he wanted. Banks didn't want to alarm her, so he showed her his warrant card but told her that he was Roy Banks's brother.

The woman made a sympathetic face. 'Poor Mr Banks,' she said. 'Please come in. Gareth is still in London at the moment but you are welcome to a cup of tea. I know you English love your tea. I am Mercedes Lambert.' She held out her hand and Banks shook it lightly.

Her accent matched her sultry Mediterranean looks and Banks could indeed believe that she had been a Spanish actress and pin-up. She still had a fine figure, shown to advantage in the shorts and sleeveless top she was wearing, and her olive skin stretched taut over exquisite bone structure and her long chestnut hair fell in waves over her shoulders.

When they got inside she led Banks to a large living room, big enough to hold a grand piano along with a damask three-piece suite. Every inch the English country lady, she called the maid and asked her to bring tea. Banks should have known she wouldn't be taking care of a place as big as this by herself. He wondered if she was bored stuck out in the country and whether she often stayed at the St John's Wood flat with her husband. She looked a good few years younger than Lambert, but not as young as Corinne or Jennifer. Banks pegged her at mid- to late thirties.

'I understand you were an actress in Spain?' he said, sitting in a chair with carved wooden arms.

She blushed. 'Not very good. I was in . . . what do you call them, films where monsters come after me and I scream a lot?'

'Horror films?'

'Yes. Horror films.' She shrugged. 'I do not miss it.'

I'll bet you don't, thought Banks, glancing around the room. French windows opened on a patio beyond the piano, and Banks could see sunlight shimmering on the blue surface of a swimming pool like a Hockney painting. 'Did you know Roy well?' he asked.

'No,' she said. 'I met him only once, last week, when he came here, but Gareth told me what happened. It is terrible.'

She pronounced the name 'Garrett', too.

'When did you meet him?' Banks asked.

'I think it was last Friday.' She smiled. 'But sometimes the days all seem the same here.'

'What did he want?'

At that moment, the maid came in with the tea and set the tray down on the table between Banks and Mercedes Lambert. After she had added milk and poured, she left as soundlessly as she had entered. Banks didn't usually take milk, but it didn't bother him.

Mercedes frowned. 'I don't really know why he came,' she said. 'He wanted to talk to me about a girl called Carmen, but I said I didn't know her. Carmen sounds very Spanish, I know, but you also find it in other countries.'

'What did he say next?'

'He told me this Carmen was pregnant and that she was selling her baby to me for adoption.' Mercedes frowned. 'He said Gareth told him this was so.'

'*Are* you adopting Carmen Petri's baby, Mrs Lambert?'

'No, of course not. That's what your brother asked me. I didn't understand why he would think such a thing.'

'Are you sure?'

'Yes, as I told your brother. Then a very strange thing happened.'

'What?'

'Little Nina cried, and I showed her to him and told him all about her, and Mr Banks said he was sorry he'd made a mistake, and he left very quickly.'

'I'm sorry,' said Banks. 'I don't understand. Who's little Nina?'

And then he heard it himself. A baby crying upstairs. Mercedes Lambert smiled. A few moments later, a nanny brought the baby down. She couldn't have been more than a few months old, and Mercedes held the tiny bundle, tears in her eyes.

'She is sick,' she explained to Banks. 'This is what I told your brother. There is a problem with her heart. It is, what do you say? Con . . . con . . .'

'Congenital?'

'Yes. Congenital. And if she does not get a new one very soon she will die.' Then her expression brightened. 'But Gareth says we are high on the list. He has arranged with a clinic in Switzerland – the best in the world, he says – to be ready at a moment's notice. So maybe my Nina will be lucky, yes?'

'Are you sure you have no intention of adopting another baby?' Banks asked, feeling his blood start to turn cold.

Mercedes smiled. 'No. Of course not. Nina will have her new heart and she will become strong. I know it. Do you not think so?'

Banks looked at Mercedes Lambert, saw the desperate hope in her face, and he looked at the pale face buried in the blankets and said, 'Yes. Yes, maybe you will.'

•

The train ride did Annie good and when she got back to Eastvale around lunchtime she didn't feel quite so depressed as she had after the raids. Before leaving, she had tried to console Brooke over what he perceived to be a lack of backbone in giving in to 'orders from above', but in the long run she knew it was something he would have to live with and get over by himself. For reasons of their own, the powers that be, maybe through Burgess, had hampered the official police investigation and encouraged Banks to go stirring things up by himself, no doubt in the hope of luring more players out into the open rather than causing them to disappear. And no one had given a damn whether Banks got killed in the process.

When Annie got to the station, Gristhorpe, Stefan, Winsome and Rickerd were all in the squad room and there was an air of celebration around the place. It seemed appropriate. After all, Jennifer Clewes's killer was dead, along with his boss, and the accomplices were in custody. Case solved.

'I hear you've been in the wars,' Gristhorpe said, looking up as she entered.

Annie sat at her desk and automatically turned on the computer. 'More like doing battlefield triage,' she said. 'Anyway, DI Brooke and the SO19 guys have got it all under control now. My job's done down there.'

'Congratulations,' said Gristhorpe.

'Anything new, Stefan?' Annie asked.

'I was just telling the superintendent here that we got a quick match on the fingerprints found on DCI Banks's door: Artyom Charkov. He doesn't have a record but the prints match the body in the mortuary in London, the one who was shot this morning in the second raid. And they also match the partial we found on the door of Jennifer Clewes's car. London say they found a gun on Charkov, too, a .22. It's being checked out.'

'That's what got him shot,' said Annie. 'Opening fire on an armed police officer.'

'Well, I'd have used something with a bit more stopping power than a .22.'

'Just as well for the officer concerned he didn't. Anyway, it's all a bit academic now he's dead, isn't it?' said Annie.

Stefan looked disappointed.

'Oh, Stefan, I'm sorry. I didn't mean to belittle your efforts. There's always the other one, Boris, the driver.'

'Essex technical support got his print from the Mondeo,' said Stefan, suppressing a smile. 'From inside the glovebox.'

'Excellent. Things have been happening, then.'

'How's Alan?' asked Gristhorpe.

'He's doing OK, as far as I know, sir,' said Annie. 'I think he'll be heading back to Peterborough later today to spend more time with his parents. At least he'll be able to tell them some sort of justice has been done.'

The door opened behind Annie and she saw Gristhorpe get to his feet, a big grin on his face. 'Well, if it isn't Susan Gay,' he said, advancing towards the slightly stocky woman with the tight blonde curls who stood in the doorway, Kev Templeton beaming beside her. 'Come on in, lass. Join the party.'

'We've got him,' Susan said. 'Cropley. He's down in the custody suite. All by the book. We've taken a DNA swab and it's on its way to Derby. We're also getting three DCs to do the motorway service stations with his photo. But the DNA itself will be enough.'

Templeton was beaming, too, Annie noticed. 'Congratulations, Kev,' she said. 'Good one.'

Templeton grinned. 'Thank you, ma'am.'

'Right, then,' said Gristhorpe. 'Seeing as we've got two reasons to celebrate, who's going for the beer?'

•

Banks worked most of it out on his drive back from Quainton, but he still needed some answers. He tracked Gareth Lambert down at the travel agency on the Edgware Road, leaving his Renault parked outside. Lambert seemed surprised and more than a bit put out at being practically manhandled into the street as his staff looked on open-mouthed, but he went without putting up a struggle.

Banks opened the passenger door and shoved him in. 'Buckle up.'

'Where are we going?'

'I've got something to show you.' Banks made his way through the traffic down the side of Hyde Park to Chelsea Bridge, then across the river and along to the old Midgeley's casting factory. If Lambert realized where they were going or recognized the place when they arrived, he didn't show it.

Banks pulled up on the weed-cracked concrete in front of the door and got out. He opened Lambert's door and almost dragged him out. Lambert was heavier, but he was in poor shape, and Banks's wiry strength was enough to push him towards the factory door.

'What the hell's going on?' Lambert protested. 'There's no need to rough-handle me this way. Roy's brother or no, I'll bloody report you.'

Banks pushed Lambert through the door and into the factory. Birds took off through the holes in the roof. The police had finished with the scene, and the chair and ropes were gone, but there were still bloodstains visible on the floor. Roy's. The lab had confirmed it. Banks stopped and shoved Lambert down onto a heap of broken pallets and rusty, twisted scrap metal. Lambert groaned as something sharp stuck into his back.

'I'll have your fucking job for this,' he yelled, red-faced, struggling to get up.

Banks put a foot on his chest and pushed him back. 'Stay there,' he said. 'And listen. This is where they brought Roy. You can still see his bloodstains here.' He pointed. 'Look at that, Gareth, that's my brother's blood.'

'That's nothing to do with me,' said Lambert, sitting up now and rubbing his back. 'I've never seen this place before. You don't know what you're talking about. You're rambling.'

'That's a good one,' said Banks. 'Let me be perfectly clear about it, Gareth. After you and Roy had your little talk in the Albion Club, you rang Hadeon Mazuryk or Max Broda on your mobile from the club's toilet and asked for help. I'm sure your mobile records will bear this out. You needed to get Roy out of the way. Mazuryk came himself or sent someone else, and they got him in a car outside the club and brought him here. They tortured him, you know, Gareth, to find out how much he knew, what my address was and what I knew. Maybe they even got our parents' address out of him, because they've made threats in that direction, too. He was tied up on a chair just over there, bleeding, knowing he was probably going to die at the end of it all.' Banks felt close to tears of rage as he talked and it was all he could do to hold himself back from thrashing Lambert. He found an iron bar on the floor, picked it up and slapped it against his palm.

Lambert cringed. 'I told you,' he said. 'It's nothing to do with me. Why would I do that? The girl and your brother were a danger to Mazuryk, not to me.'

'But you're connected with Mazuryk. You arranged to get the girls to him after Max Broda bought them at markets in the Balkans.'

'You'll never find any evidence of anything like that.'

'It doesn't matter,' said Banks, 'because that wasn't what it was really all about. At first I thought it was about the girls you and Max Broda conspired to smuggle in for Mazuryk. Girls who had been lured by false job offers or abducted from the street. You wanted Roy in it with you, didn't you, just like old times, and you'd been talking about it for a while, a couple of months. Roy didn't know the whole story at first, and he might even have shown a flicker of interest if there was enough money in it for him. Lord knows, Church or no, my brother was no saint.

'Then Carmen Petri let slip to Roy's girlfriend that these girls were not willing participants. Jennifer told Roy and that changed things for him. I'd guess at that point he wanted nothing to do with it. I imagine he gave you a chance, though, for old times' sake. I think on the Tuesday, the day after Carmen told Jennifer, Roy had lunch with you and Max Broda and you both tried to convince him everything was above board. But he wasn't convinced. That's when he took the photograph of the two of you. He left the cafe first, didn't he?'

Lambert said nothing.

'Maybe he wouldn't have turned you in to the police,' Banks went on, 'no matter how much what you were doing sickened him. I doubt that my brother had a very healthy regard for the boys in blue, given his track record. But there was his girlfriend to consider, too, wasn't there? And she was even more outraged, being a woman. Roy must have told you at lunch on Tuesday that he'd persuaded her to keep quiet for the time being, not to contact the police, and that you needn't harm her. But Mazuryk set Artyom and Boris to watch her just in case, to see where she went and who came to see her. If she had rung the police, they wouldn't be content with just some anonymous voice over the phone; they'd want to visit her, or have her visit their station. That's what Artyom and Boris were looking out for. Then, when things came to a head that Friday night in the Albion Club and Roy told Jennifer to drive up to see me, they followed her and killed her on a quiet country road.'

'This is ridiculous,' said Lambert, a condescending smirk on his face. 'If only you could hear yourself. You can't prove any of this. When I get out of here I'm going to—'

Banks kicked him hard in the stomach. Lambert groaned and rolled over, clutching his mid-section and retching. 'Bastard,' he hissed.

Banks swung the iron bar and hit him on the shoulder. Lambert screamed. 'But it wasn't even about the girls, was it?' Banks went on. 'That was just the start of it. Oh, I'm sure you tried to convince Roy how they had a better life here, away from their war-torn countries, away from the poverty and disease and death. Maybe he even wanted to believe it. Then, in a final bid to enlist his sympathy, you told him that you were adopting Carmen Petri's baby yourself. You probably gave him some sob story about how your wife couldn't bear children and desperately wanted a family. You told him you'd give the child a much better life than it could have hoped for in Romania, or as the child of a prostitute in London. That was supposed to be the clincher. How benevolent of you. He'd hardly stand in the way of his old mate adopting a child privately, would he? It might not be strictly legal, but people do it all the time, don't they? How can it be that much of a crime, to give a child hope? And even Roy had to see that any child you adopted had far more advantages than most. Financial advantages, that is.'

'So what?' Lambert argued. 'So what if I was adopting her child. It's true. The kid *would* have a much better life with us. Any fool can see that.'

'Maybe so,' said Banks. 'But that wasn't the real intention, was it?'

'What do you mean?'

'I know why Roy had to die,' said Banks.

'What are you talking about?' Lambert's voice was scarcely more than a whisper.

'Because of where he went earlier that day, before you came to call on him. He found out the truth.'

'I don't understand.'

'It's where I've just been. Quainton.'

Lambert said nothing. He seemed to shrink into himself.

'Roy went to see your wife to ask her about the adoption,' Banks went on. 'They'd never met before. If it was true, he would probably have agreed to keep quiet about it all and keep Jennifer quiet, too. But Roy found out what I found out. That you and your wife have a baby girl called Nina and she needs a new heart. And the only heart that can help a baby in need of a transplant is the heart of another baby. You know what the chances are of getting your hands on one by normal routes, so when you found out one of Mazuryk's girls was pregnant – not just any girl, mind you, but Carmen, intelligent, healthy and clean – you struck a deal. You'd pay Mazuryk for the privilege of adopting Carmen's baby. That way he wouldn't be out of pocket when she couldn't work during her pregnancy. But you weren't adopting the baby, were you? You were buying the baby's heart. I don't know if Mazuryk was in on it with you, but one way or another, as soon as that baby was born, it was going to be on its way to Switzerland. Were you going to kill it yourself or have you paid a crooked doctor to do that for you?'

'Don't be absurd. This is pure fantasy.'

'Is it? My guess is that you had someone lined up, a crooked doctor from your Balkan days, probably. You wouldn't have the stomach to do it yourself. And then there's the Swiss clinic, all ready to go at a moment's notice, no questions asked. Got it all organized, haven't you?'

Lambert squirmed like a toad on his bed of broken wood and twisted metal. At some point he had cut his lip and the blood welled up as he spoke. 'Look, you're obviously off your rocker, Banks. Let me go and we'll say no more about this.'

He made to get up again but Banks kicked him down and swung the bar dangerously close to his head.

'Stay where you are. Don't you realize, it's over? Do you think that even your wife will want to know you after what you had planned?'

'She doesn't know,' said Lambert. 'If you've—'

'I haven't. Not yet. Tell me the truth, Gareth. How could you be sure you had a match? Who did the tests?'

'What tests?' Lambert paused and rubbed his shoulder.

'Come on, Gareth. Humour me. Tell me all about it.' Banks swung the bar again and caught it with a smack in his palm.

Lambert was quiet for several moments, then he spoke. 'The blood groups matched,' he said. 'That's the best you can hope for with babies, and even the blood group doesn't matter if they're newborn. Do you think I haven't researched it? The heart only survives six hours outside the body, so you do the transplant first and ask questions later. A chance. It was all I asked for.'

Though Banks had pieced it all together after seeing Mercedes and Nina, he could still hardly believe it, now that he was actually hearing it, that this man had cold-bloodedly bought a baby and planned to use its heart to save his daughter's life.

'Do you have even the slightest idea what you're saying?' he said.

'Look,' said Lambert. 'What chance did it have with a mother like that? Huh? Tell me? Look at her. A common prostitute. A slut. This way at least the baby could serve some *purpose* in being born. These people give birth in fields and think nothing of it. You haven't seen them, Banks. You haven't been there. I have. I know them. I've lived with them. They're animals. Their filthy children wander the streets and beg and steal and grow up to be criminals and prostitutes, just like their parents. The orphanages are full of abandoned children and none of them have a chance. My child *will* have a chance. She can make a difference in life. Achieve something. Contribute something.'

Banks shook his head in disgust. 'I wondered where Roy drew the line,' he said, 'and now I know. He'd turn a blind eye to most things for the sake of money and an old friendship. To the girls. To the illegal adoption. But not to this, not to the murder of an innocent baby for its heart. What did you do on Friday at the Albion Club? Offer him money to keep quiet or try to convince him you were morally right?'

'We'd been talking all week about the girls, the adoption. Seeing Mercedes and finding out . . . well, that was the last straw for him.'

'Why not tell the police straight away? Why did he bother to meet with you?'

'He wasn't going to tell the police. He was going to tell you.'

'What? But I am the police,' said Banks.

Lambert shook his head. 'You don't understand. You're his big brother. He expected you to handle it.'

Banks felt stunned. He hadn't realized Roy had been calling on him as much, if not more, as a brother than as a policeman: the brother who defended him from bullies. It made a difference. Roy always shied away from the police and he would expect Banks to sort the situation without letting it become official. Banks didn't know if he could have done that even if they hadn't killed Roy and Jennifer, even if he'd wanted to. Things had probably gone too far already.

'So what happened at the club?' Banks asked.

'He said he'd give me an hour to think about it, for friendship's sake. He'd be in the casino if I wanted to talk. He also told me that he already had someone on her way to see you, but he could ring her mobile and bring her back if I agreed to drop my plans.'

'What did you say after the hour was up?'

'Nothing.'

'You could have lied, told him you'd drop the plans.'

'He would still have known. Do you think he'd have let it go, not kept checking?'

'I suppose not,' said Banks. 'So you sent him to his death?'

'I had to. What else could I do? I couldn't abandon Nina and Mercedes. He was going to ruin everything. Mazuryk's business, my Nina's life. Mercedes's life. Everything. Don't you understand? I *couldn't* give in to him. Without a new heart my daughter will die.'

Blood dribbled over Lambert's lower lip and bubbled as he spoke. Banks felt like hitting him again but he knew if he started he might never stop.

'So you had Roy killed.'

'Not me. Mazuryk.'

'Did Mazuryk know what you planned to do with Carmen's baby?'

'Are you crazy? Nobody knew except me and the doctor I was paying. And the doctor owed me. I helped him out of a jam once. You can't prove anything, you know. I'll deny it all. I'll tell them you beat me up and made me admit to things I haven't done. Look at me, I'm all bruised and bleeding.'

'Not nearly enough,' said Banks. 'You made a call to Mazuryk from the Albion Club about Roy being a loose cannon, and Mazuryk came himself, or sent Broda to pick up Roy outside and bring him here.'

'I told him Roy was threatening to tell everything. All Mazuryk cared about was the girls, the profits they made for him.'

'So Mazuryk protected his interests, and you protected yours?'

'What else could I do? What would you do if it was your daughter?'

Banks didn't want to think about that one. 'Why did they go

back and take Roy's computer? Who did that? There couldn't be anything on it about the baby because he'd only just got back from seeing Mercedes when you arrived.'

'Mazuryk's men. Not Artyom and Boris. Others. Not very bright. We thought he might have information on it. About me. About Mazuryk's operation, the girls. We had talked a lot that week. I really thought he was interested at one time. I told him things. Roy used his computer a lot.'

And they hadn't taken the mobile because they hadn't been in the kitchen, hadn't even known it was there, Banks guessed. Not that it mattered. Roy and Lambert had been careful not to use mobiles in their communications. They knew how wide open and incriminating such phone use could be. That was why most criminals used stolen ones. And Banks doubted that Roy had ever been in direct telephone contact with Mazuryk or Broda. Later, of course, Broda had used the mobile to send his calling card, his sick joke.

'What changed things in the first place?'

'If that stupid whore hadn't told Roy's girlfriend that some girls had been abducted and badly treated, I don't think any of this would have happened,' said Lambert, 'and your brother and me would have been partners. I spent that week trying to convince Roy it was still the right thing to do but he didn't like the idea that the girls were working against their will. That's when I told him about the adoption. I thought he would see what a good thing it was.'

'And did he?'

'He wasn't convinced. Obviously. But it softened him a bit. Until he went to see Mercedes.'

Roy a pimp, or procurer? Banks found it hard to imagine. He would probably have described himself as an investor in an escort agency, or perhaps as a travel consultant. At least his spiritual and moral conversion hadn't cut into his desire to make a profit from just about anything, short of illegal body parts. 'And to threaten my parents? Whose idea was that?'

'Mazuryk's. When the digital photo they sent didn't scare you off, they had to try stronger measures. They could have killed you, but I told them the last thing they needed right then was a dead policeman hot on the heels of his brother. I told them that, Banks. I saved your life. These people are not always reasonable, but I have spent time with them. I can talk to them. They followed you home and back and showed themselves on the road, to frighten you off.'

'I don't frighten that easily. And Jennifer Clewes?'

'They were already worried about her. At first she was happy enough to help Dr Lukas take care of the girls, but she got too friendly and Mazuryk was worried someone might actually let something slip about how they really came to be there. They thought Carmen was getting too cocky because she didn't have to turn tricks any more and when Artyom saw them talking together, Carmen and Jennifer Clewes, he got suspicious and told Mazuryk. They made Carmen tell them what she had said. Without hurting her physically, you understand. They couldn't risk harming the baby.'

'Don't tell me. They threatened to harm *her* parents back home.'

'Possibly. But Artyom and Boris had been keeping an eye on Roy's girl for a few days, then when she took off like that at the same time I told Mazuryk that Roy was out of control . . . Look, I wasn't there . . . I don't know for sure how it happened. But it wasn't me.'

'But you know *what* happened. You set it in motion.'

'Max told me after it was done. They found out where she was going. Roy told Mazuryk when they were beating him and he phoned Artyom in the car. As soon as she got to a quiet spot on the road they killed her. Artyom was going to kill you, too, just in case, but you weren't there. He's not very bright.'

'It's a pity he didn't,' said Banks, 'because now Mazuryk is dead, Artyom is dead and the rest are going to jail. And you . . .'

'What about me?'

'I can't decide whether to kill you or turn you in.'

And it was true. Banks had never in his life felt like killing someone as much as he felt like killing Gareth Lambert at that moment. If he'd had a gun, he might have done it. He hefted the iron bar, heavy in his hand, and smacked it against his palm. That would do it. One swift blow. Crush his skull like an eggshell. Lambert was looking at him, fear in his eyes.

'No!' he said, holding his hands out to protect his face. 'Don't. Don't kill me.'

It wasn't just revenge for Roy, but also because he had never come across anyone so loathsome he'd even contemplate doing what Lambert was doing, let alone defend it and justify it. He could not have imagined such a thing if he hadn't gone to see Mercedes Lambert, as Roy had, and heard poor Nina cry. Mercedes Lambert obviously knew nothing about her husband's unholy scheme. The disgust Banks felt churned the bile in his stomach and he could bear to look at Lambert no longer.

'What are you going to do? Are you going to hurt me?' Lambert whined.

Banks hurled the iron bar. It clanged into the tangled metal about two inches above Lambert's head. Then Banks walked away, bent over and vomited on the floor. When he had finished, he took a few deep breaths, hands on his knees, wiped his mouth with the back of his hand and took out his mobile.

•

A few days later, Banks crossed the old packhorse bridge at the western end of Helmthorpe High Street and turned right on the riverside path. It was a walk he had often enjoyed before. Flat and easy, between the trees and water, no hills to climb, and he'd end up back in Helmthorpe, where there were three pubs to choose from.

As he walked he thought about the events of the past month, how it had all started that night he saw Penny Cartwright in the

Dog and Gun singing 'Strange Affair'. He thought about Roy, Jennifer Clewes, Carmen Petri, Dieter Ganz and the rest.

And Gareth Lambert.

Now it was just about over. Artyom and Mazuryk were dead. Gareth Lambert was in custody, along with Boris and Max Broda, and the odds were good that they would get very long sentences. Banks's actions had forced his hand, but Dieter Ganz seemed to think his team had enough evidence to convict them on charges of trafficking in underage girls across international borders for the purposes of prostitution. Unfortunately, raids on similar houses in Paris, Berlin and Rome had netted only minor players, as word of what happened in London had spread fast. In the Balkans, guides, drivers, kidnappers and traders had scattered. They would be back, though, Dieter had told Banks, and he would be waiting for them.

Whether Lambert would be tied to the conspiracy to kill Roy Banks and Jennifer Clewes was another matter. Lambert's more sinister intentions couldn't be proved. And as he had said, only he and the doctor knew what they intended to do with Carmen's baby, and neither was talking. Banks had received a reprimand for his treatment of Lambert at the abandoned factory, which would also tend to discredit anything he claimed Lambert had told him. Still, there was a good chance that Max Broda would implicate him in the conspiracy rather than take the fall alone. And Lambert's mobile phone records for that Friday, 11th June, at the Albion Club, showed a call to Mazuryk's number at about eleven o'clock.

As for the rest, Banks wasn't quite sure how things would turn out. Mazuryk's girls would eventually be processed and sent home, but who was going to repair their lives, heal their broken spirits? Perhaps some would recover in time and move on, but others would drift back into the only life they knew. Carmen Petri, Annie had told Banks, was to be reunited with her parents in Romania, where contrary to what Gareth Lambert thought, there was a good chance that her baby might end up with a decent crack at life. Carmen had been abducted from the street three years ago and in all that time her parents hadn't given up hoping she was still alive.

Of all of them, perhaps Mercedes Lambert had come out of it worst of all, and Banks felt deeply for her. Not only was her husband probably going to jail for a long time, but in all likelihood, short of a miracle, her baby Nina was going to die soon. The police were investigating Banks's accusation and had questioned her about it, so now she also had to live with the knowledge of what her husband had been about to do. Banks could only imagine how knowledge like that might tear a mother apart and haunt her dreams forever. What might have been. The nameless, faceless issue of a Romanian prostitute she had never met measured against the life of her daughter.

His mind turned to other thoughts. He had just got back from Roy's funeral in Peterborough. Needless to say, it had been a sad and tearful affair, but at least he had spent some time with Brian and Tracy, who had come in for the occasion, and it had given his parents some sense of that closure they valued so much. Banks never really got it. For him there was no closure.

The good news was that his mother had managed to get speedy results on the medical tests. Her colon cancer was operable and her chances of making a full recovery were excellent. She also seemed to be coping a bit better with the loss of her son, though Banks knew she would never fully recover from it, never be her old self again.

Brilliant green dragonflies hovered above the water's surface and clouds of gnats and midges gathered above the path. The sun had almost set and the water was dark blue, the sky streaked with blood orange. Banks could hear the calls of night birds from the trees and the sounds of small animals scuttling through the undergrowth. Across the river he could see the backs of the shops and houses on Helmthorpe High Street. People were sitting outside in the beer garden of the Dog and Gun and he could hear muffled conversations and music from the jukebox. It should have been

Delius's 'Summer Night on the River', he thought, breathing in the perfumed air, but it wasn't even 'Strange Affair', it was Elvis Costello's 'Watching the Detectives'.

Banks paused to light a cigarette and saw a figure walking towards him from the other direction. He couldn't make out any more than a dark shape but when it got closer he saw it was Penny Cartwright. He stood aside to let her pass. The overhanging leaves brushed the back of his neck and made him shiver. It felt like a spider had slipped under his collar and was making its way down his back.

As she passed, Banks nodded politely and said hello, making to hurry along, but her voice came from behind him. 'Wait a minute.'

Banks turned. 'Yes?'

'Got a light?'

As Banks flicked his lighter she leaned in towards him, cigarette in her mouth, and her eyes were on his as she inhaled. 'Thanks,' she said. 'Fancy meeting you here.'

'Yes. Fancy. Good night, then.'

'Don't go. I mean, wait a sec. OK?'

She sounded nervous and edgy. Banks wondered what was wrong. They stood and faced one another on the narrow path. An owl hooted deep in the woods. Elvis continued to watch the detectives. It was almost dark now, only a few streaks of purple and crimson in the sky like some great god's robes.

'I was sorry to read about your brother,' she said.

'Thank you.'

Penny pointed to the beer garden. 'Do you remember that night?' she said. 'All those years ago?'

Banks remembered. He had sat in the garden with his wife Sandra, Penny and her boyfriend Jack Barker, explaining the Harry Steadman murder. It had been a warm summer evening, just like tonight.

'How's Jack?' he asked.

Penny smiled. She wasn't a woman who smiled easily, and it

355

was worthwhile when she did. 'I'm sure Jack's doing fine,' she said. 'I haven't seen him in ages. He went off to live in Los Angeles. Does a bit of TV writing. You even see his name on the screen sometimes.'

'I thought you two were . . . ?'

'We were. But it was a long time ago. Things change. You ought to know that.'

'I suppose so,' said Banks.

'Kath behind the bar told me about the fire, about what happened to your cottage, after she saw us talking. I'm really sorry.'

'Water under the bridge,' said Banks. 'Besides, I'm having it restored.'

'Still . . . Anyway,' she went on, not looking at him. 'I was rude that night, and I'm sorry. There, I've said it.'

'Why did you react the way you did?'

'It wasn't deliberate, if that's what you mean.'

'What, then?'

Penny paused and stared into the river. 'You really don't know, do you? All those years ago,' she said finally, 'the way I felt. It was like some sort of violation. I know you saved my life and I should thank you for that, but you treated me like a criminal. You actually believed that I killed my best friend.'

At one point, that was probably true, Banks thought. It was just a part of his job, and he had never stopped to think how it might have made Penny feel. Everyone gets tainted by a murder investigation. Roy had wanted his big brother, Banks remembered, not a policeman. But where did the one end and the other begin?

'And there you were,' she went on, 'asking me out to dinner, casual as anything, as if none of it had ever happened.'

'People aren't always what they seem,' he said. 'When the police come around asking questions, people lie. Everyone's got something to hide.'

'So you suspect everyone?'

'More or less. Anyone who might have motive, means and opportunity.'

'Like me?'

'Like you.'

'But I cared about Harry Steadman. He was my best friend.'

'That's what you told us.'

'I could have been lying?'

'As I remember it, that case was full of lies.'

Penny took one last drag on her cigarette and flicked the stub into the river. 'Oops,' she said. 'I shouldn't have done that. The river police will be after me.'

'Don't worry,' said Banks. 'I'll put in a good word for you.'

She favoured him with another flicker of a smile. 'I'd better be going,' she said, edging away. 'It's getting late.'

'All right.'

She started along the path, paused and half turned to face him. 'Good night, then, Mr Policeman. And I'm sorry I reacted so badly. I just wanted to tell you why.'

'Good night,' said Banks. He felt a tightness in his chest, but it was now or never. 'Look,' he went on, calling after her, 'maybe I'm being insensitive again, and I'm sorry I got off on the wrong foot, but is it at all within the bounds of possibility, you know, what I asked you about the other night, maybe the possibility of us, of you and me, you know . . . having dinner some time?'

She turned briefly. 'I don't think so,' she said, shaking her head slowly. 'You still don't get it, do you?' And she walked off into the shadows.

Acknowledgements

I **would like** to thank the following people for the time and care they have put into helping this book into its final shape: Sarah Turner, Maria Rejt and Nicholas Blake at Pan Macmillan; Dan Conaway and Jill Schwarzman at William Morrow; and Dinah Forbes at McClelland & Stewart. I would also like to thank Michael Morrison, Lisa Gallagher, Sharyn Rosenblum, Angela Tedesco, Dominick Abel, David Grossman, David North, Katie James, Ellen Seligman and Parmjit Parmar for all their ongoing hard work and support.

I also want to thank Commander Philip Gormley, head of SO19, the Metropolitan Force Firearms Unit, and Detective Inspector Claire Stevens of the Thames Valley Police. As usual, any mistakes are my own and are made entirely in the interests of the story.

I also owe a debt of thanks to the music of Richard Thompson and to Victor Malarek for his book, *The Natashas*.